THE CAROUSEL KEEPS TURNING

THE CAROUSEL KEEPS TURNING

Pamela Evans

HEADLINE

First published in 1998
by HEADLINE BOOK PUBLISHING

10 9 8 7 6 5 4 3 2 1

British Library Cataloguing in Publication Data

Evans, Pamela
 The carousel keeps turning
 1. Fairs - Fiction 2. Wife abuse - Fiction
 I. Title
 823.9'14 [F]

ISBN 0-7472-2179-0

Typeset by
CBS, Felixstowe, Suffolk

Printed and bound in Great Britain by
Mackays of Chatham PLC, Chatham, Kent

HEADLINE BOOK PUBLISHING
A division of Hodder Headline PLC
338 Euston Road
London NW1 3BH

Chapter One

Nothing was more damaging to the commercial aspirations of the Fenner family than rain, especially when it came down in buckets on a Bank Holiday Monday.

When they awoke to find this happening on Whit Monday of 1960 they cursed the weather and braced themselves for a washout. But the changeable nature of the British climate worked in their favour on this occasion, and by early afternoon both the sun and the crowds were out in force at Fenner's Fun Park, an enclave of pleasure and excitement nestling among the trees beside the Thames near Richmond.

The younger of the proprietor's two sons, Sam Fenner, headed purposefully through the exuberant masses towards the fairground's main attraction, the Scenic Railway which soared above the treetops and was said to be one of the most thrilling roller-coasters in England.

A strong man with tanned skin and windblown brown hair, Sam's rugged appearance didn't reflect his true personality, for he had a kind and gentle nature. His job demanded a certain authority but he wasn't aggressive about it. Casually dressed in jeans and an open-necked shirt, his tawny eyes shone with pleasure as he passed such favourites as the Carousel Horses, the steel frame of the Big Wheel glinting against the blue sky, the Chairoplanes spinning high on their metal chains.

Feeling the warm sunshine on his face, he thought how good it was after the dismal start to the day, a few lingering puddles reminding him of the rain.

Like most showmen, Sam had never considered any other occupation. The fair was not just a job but a way of life into which he was proud to have been born. Work and leisure were virtually the same thing to him, an attitude scathingly denounced by his wife Tania. The business was in Sam's blood and it warmed his heart to see so many people flocking here to sample the fun and thrills that had been provided at this amusement park by the Fenner family for several generations.

His childhood enchantment with the fair was just a memory now, of course, but the special essence of the business in full flow still set Sam's adrenalin pumping. Even the sickly smell of hot dogs, candy

1

floss and toffee apples mixed with pungent drifts of engine oil from the machinery was all part of the magic to him, as was the repetitive beat of pop music thumping from the loudspeakers and competing with the traditional waltzes of the Carousel organ. Brashness was an essential ingredient and there was a loud joyful vitality here that could be found nowhere else but a working fairground.

Above the noise of the vociferous crowds, piercing shrieks from the plunging carriages could be heard as he approached the Scenic Railway where the queue was snaking out of sight.

'You got a problem?' Sam asked his brother Josh who was in charge of this ride and currently working in the paybox, having sent one of his assistants to the office with a message.

'Yeah, I'm short-handed.'

'Oh? I thought this ride was fully staffed.'

'It was. But I've had a couple o' people go off sick and I urgently need a brake man,' explained the stunningly handsome Josh, referring to the worker who actually operated the train. 'I've one train out of action until I get a replacement. I'm also a man short on the platform.'

'Eric's free to give you a hand on the platform,' said Sam, referring to their cousin who wasn't as bright as he might have been.

'Don't lumber me with him, for Gawd's sake,' groaned Josh.

'Eric's all right.'

'Don't make me laugh . . .'

'He isn't as simple as people make him out to be.' Sam was adamant. 'He can certainly be trusted to work on the platform, making sure all the passengers are seated safely.'

'I'll admit that he knows every nut and bolt on the fairground,' said Josh because, although Eric's IQ was lower than average for a man in his late-twenties, he was brilliant with the machinery that made the rides work. 'But he's too slow when it comes to dealing with people. He'll just be a liability.'

'Give him a chance.'

'Do me a favour, mate,' protested Josh who wasn't over blessed with the milk of human kindness. 'I know Eric's our cousin and he can't help having a few marbles short of a set but there are places for people like him. And the working side of a fairground on a busy Bank Holiday Monday isn't one of 'em.'

'You're not being fair,' said Sam. 'Eric's quite capable if you take the trouble to explain things to him properly.'

'I need help, not hindrance,' said Josh, his voice gruff with temper. 'I haven't time to play nursemaid.'

'No one's asking you to,' said Sam. 'Admittedly Eric's a bit slow but he isn't stupid. He *has* worked on the fair all his life, remember.'

'*I am not having Eric working with me on this ride and that's definite!*'

'Okay, okay,' said Sam, raising his hands defensively and mentally

2

running through the workforce. 'I'll have to juggle the staff around and try to get you the help you need.'

'You do that.'

'It won't be easy finding someone to work on the platform as well as a brake man, though, if you won't make do with Eric.'

'It's your job to solve the problem and I don't care how you do it. But get me another two pairs of hands for the evening shift,' demanded Josh, dark eyes gleaming against his smoothly tanned skin, black hair worn in a quiff and sideburns. He was thirty, two years older than Sam. 'And I don't mean Eric.'

'We're fully stretched . . . this *is* Whit Monday, remember. One of the busiest days of the season.' Sam looked worried.

'Exactly. And this is our most popular ride.' Josh wasn't prepared to put himself out. He didn't go along with the prevailing attitude in fairground communities of everyone pulling together. It was too much like hard work.

Josh frowned at the queue of people waiting to pay, his gaze moving on to those already on the wooden platform ready to get on to the ride; eager but orderly. The crowd might not be so patient this evening. Bank Holidays always produced a fair proportion of stroppy yobbos who thought courtesy was a sign of weakness.

'You can see how I'm fixed here, and things will be even more frantic tonight when the lads come out on the prowl, showing off to impress the local crumpet.'

'Yeah, I know.' It was important to Sam that the fair should run smoothly, and a little co-operation from his brother would have been much appreciated. But he knew he wouldn't get it because it wasn't in Josh's nature to make an effort for the good of the firm.

'Janice is busy on the Hoopla, I suppose,' he remarked.

Sam nodded. Their sister had been running the Hoopla Stall ever since she was old enough to work in the business.

'What about Mum?' suggested Josh. 'If she could take over from me in the paybox, I'd be free to work on the platform.'

'She's helping out in the restaurant doing afternoon teas at the moment and she'll be busy with suppers tonight,' explained Sam. 'The weather's brought the punters out in droves and it's packed to the doors in there.'

'Well, if you can't find anyone else, you'll have to help me yourself.'

'I don't mind what job I do on the fair, mate, you know that,' said Sam. 'But I'm on call around the ground. Dad's orders.'

Josh stopped what he was doing and gave his brother a hard look. 'I'm not asking for anything to which I'm not entitled,' he said. 'This is our main attraction – it needs to be fully staffed.'

'I've told you, I'll do what I can.'

'The old man doesn't do anything much in the beer garden of an evening except ponce about chatting to the customers,' Josh pointed out, turning back to his work. '*He* could come over and give me a hand.'

'You must be joking,' said Sam lightly and without malice. 'He wouldn't leave his precious beer garden on a Bank Holiday Monday.'

'The jammy devil! Putting himself in charge of that particular attraction was a sly move on his part. It's just one big party to him,' said Josh, critical of their devil-may-care father. 'Strutting about talking to the customers while the staff do all the work.'

'He's officially the guv'nor – even though Mum makes all the rules – so I suppose he thinks that gives him the right,' remarked Sam. 'Anyway, he's a natural for the job with his outgoing personality. The customers love him.'

'He does have a way with him, I suppose,' Josh reluctantly admitted.

'No doubt about that,' said Sam. 'People drink in our beer garden instead of the pub across the road if they know he'll be around to give 'em all the old chat.'

Josh paused, counting the change from a ten-shilling note into a customer's hand. 'I expect the old bugger will be off to some drinking club after we've closed the fair tonight.'

'Probably,' agreed Sam without censure. 'He seems to need to go somewhere to relax after a busy day during the season, doesn't he? Has done ever since I can remember.'

'You'd think he'd be content to stay at home with Mum, wouldn't you?' said Josh disapprovingly. 'A man of his age.'

'It's just his way. He'll never change. And it doesn't seem to bother her, which is the only thing that really matters.'

'She lets him do just as he likes.'

'Because she trusts him,' said Sam. 'Anyway, I don't think he gets up to any mischief – he just has a few drinks with his cronies.'

'The chance of mischief would be a fine thing at his age,' snorted Josh.

Their conversation was halted by a sudden flurry of activity around them. Carriages clanked to a halt and people clambered out; the queue moved forward. Josh continued to relieve sweaty fingers of sticky coins while giving his brother final instructions.

'You make sure you get me some help for tonight,' he said with an air of such authority he might have been Sam's employer. 'Or there'll be hell to pay.'

'Yeah, yeah, I'll do what I can,' said Sam and strode off into the crowds, mentally reorganising the staff to accommodate Josh's needs.

Sam's obliging nature and love of the job was the main reason he was a glorified dogsbody while his brother did whatever he chose to on the fair. Josh made no secret of the fact that he didn't share Sam's dedication to the family business. Their mother doted on her eldest child and tended to indulge him for fear he would leave if he

4

wasn't given a job he found congenial. This was why he was in charge of the fair's most prestigious ride while Sam spent most of his time rushing about the park solving staff problems, arranging cover while attendants went for meal breaks, controlling the crowds, keeping queues moving, and generally making sure the fair was efficiently run.

But Sam wasn't bothered. He was a natural showman and enjoyed being at the heart of the business that had been started by his great-grandfather. Sam knew he was popular with the staff, and found that people responded more readily to a firm but friendly approach rather than the authoritative attitude Josh preferred to adopt.

Because funfairs didn't make good neighbours their site was especially valuable, screened by trees and not too close to the pretty town of Richmond, considered by many to be London's most beautiful suburb. Although the Fenners lived within a closed community, they maintained a good relationship with the other local residents by conducting their business within reasonable hours and discouraging the presence of drunks and trouble makers who were 'escorted' from the ground by the men of the fair at the first sign of a disturbance. Some of the men were related to the Fenner family, others were just employees. This being a family business, only a few pitches were rented out to independent traders running their own rides.

The two brothers weren't close. Sam would have liked a more matey relationship but Josh kept his distance, especially outside business hours. He was a bachelor and it was common knowledge that he played the field with women. Sam had seen him drinking with some very dodgy-looking blokes too – criminals if Sam was any judge.

But Josh never discussed his private life with anyone at Fenner's. Sam suspected that his brother would leave the family and the business without a second thought if it suited him. He had no wish to take part in the management of the fair alongside Sam, which was surprising as Josh was the eldest son. He had a singlemindedness that Sam didn't admire but sometimes envied because nobody ever talked down to Josh.

Deeply and happily immersed in fairground life, Sam kept up to date with all the latest innovations and discussed new ideas with his parents. This was why he had drifted into the position of unofficial manager – though his wife fiercely disagreed with his job description.

'Manager, my arse,' she would say in the deep-throated, crude manner that both excited and pained Sam. 'You're nothing more than an errand boy around here . . . too damned soft to stand up for yourself to those parents of yours. You've about as much go in you as flat Tizer.'

He'd given up trying to convince her that that wasn't the way it

5

was because it was inconceivable to Tania that anyone could actually enjoy the work that he did. Thoughts of his beautiful wife made Sam tense and darkened his mood. He knew she'd only married him on the rebound from someone else; and also because she had thought that life as one of the Fenner family would be an easier and more glamorous option than her previous job as a barmaid.

Being an outsider and a stranger to the ways of fair people, she hadn't realised that she would be expected to work in the family business regardless of her mood or the vagaries of the British summer. Most showmen's wives enjoyed the involvement in such a traditional and sociable trade. They were usually ardent homemakers too, with a great pride in their living-wagons.

Because Tania had made no effort to conform, she had never really fitted in at Fenner's despite the family's tolerant attitude towards her which Sam knew they adopted for his sake. Throughout their three-year marriage Tania had become increasingly discontented. If she loved him at all, it certainly wasn't with the same fierce intensity as he loved her, Sam had no illusions about that. This was a cross he had to bear because he wanted her on any terms, even though her coldness to him was so wounding.

Now, as a shower of spray blew into his face from the Water Chute, and he moved on past The Whip and The Caterpillar towards the Helter-Skelter where Tania was on duty, he could see from her glowering expression that she wasn't happy. Dressed in a low-cut blouse and tight jeans, her red hair cascading to her shoulders, Tania was a striking figure who could convey her bad temper from a distance without uttering a word. He walked towards her, bracing himself for another barrage of complaints.

'What a life!' she said in a harsh whisper as she took a young boy's money and sent him on his way with a mat.

'What's the matter this time?' he enquired patiently.

'I'm bored stiff, that's what's the matter,' she said through clenched teeth, blue eyes sparking with resentment. 'Who wouldn't be, having to stand here all day handing out mats to snotty-nosed kids on a Bank Holiday Monday?'

'You've only been doing it for a couple of hours, love,' he pointed out reasonably.

'It feels more like a couple o' years,' she informed him.

'It can't be that bad, surely?'

'I can assure you that it is,' she answered sharply. 'Bank Holidays are for having fun, not working.'

'Somebody has to work to provide that fun,' Sam shrugged.

'It doesn't have to be us.'

'Yes, it does. We have to make the most of the brisk trade and be grateful the weather didn't do the dirty on us after all.'

'You must be mad if you think I could ever feel grateful.'

'But this is our bread and butter, love, and Bank Holidays are bumper days for business,' he said. 'We take much more money than on an ordinary weekend, you know that.'

'What's the use of making money if we don't have the chance to spend it?'

'Now you're not being fair.' Sam's tone was firm. The fact that he adored her meant that she got away with murder but he wasn't standing for this. 'We have plenty of leisure time in the winter. Obviously we have to work hard and make our money in the summer . . . the same as any other seasonal business.'

'But we're part of the Fenner family – we own the fair,' she said. 'Why can't we leave the staff to do the work like other business people do?'

'Because ours is a family-run firm,' he said. 'We're working showpeople. Not company directors of some industrial concern.'

'Huh! I bet the bosses of Dreamland in Margate or the Kursaal Southend aren't flogging their guts out on a Bank Holiday.'

'I don't know what their arrangements are,' Sam said in a controlled voice.

'They'll have more sense,' Tania continued as though he hadn't spoken.

'We'll go away on holiday when the season is over,' Sam promised in an effort to please her.

'Abroad?'

'Oh, I dunno about that,' he said in a preoccupied manner because he had a lot on his mind.

'These days people go to places where it's warm and sunny, like Spain and Italy,' she said. 'Even ordinary working people who aren't in business. People with a lot less dough than we have.'

'It isn't a question of money.'

'What then?'

'I suppose it isn't something I've ever really thought about,' he said, having far more pressing matters on his mind than foreign holidays – like reorganising the staff to suit his brother, for one thing.

'You're behind the times.'

'Very probably,' he agreed to pacify her. 'But we'll have to talk about it another time. I've got a fair to run.'

'Yeah, yeah. And in the winter you'll be busy organising the maintenance.'

'These things have to be taken care of, Tania,' he said. 'But we usually manage to get away somewhere for a break.'

'Oh, yeah, to some bloody awful rain-soaked English seaside resort that's all closed up for the winter . . . where there's nothing to do but look at each other all day.'

'The entertainments probably shut down in Spain in the winter too,' he suggested.

7

'There are places further away where it stays sunny all year.' Tania was hell-bent on making her point. 'Anyway there are places abroad where it doesn't need to be hot because there are plenty of other things to do.'

'Such as?'

'Paris . . . Rome . . .'

'Blimey, Tania,' he said. 'You don't half get some fancy ideas.'

She gave him a withering look, wondering how she could have been so stupid as to marry the most boring man in Britain, a man who was obsessed with this damned funfair, and far more concerned about keeping his parents and their staff happy than pleasing his wife.

In actual fact she didn't want to go away on holiday with him anywhere, not to Margate or even Majorca. But nagging Sam and making him miserable gave her a perverse kind of pleasure because he irritated her so much.

'This is the 1960s, mate,' she said acidly. 'Times have changed. You don't have to be filthy rich or in the services to go abroad these days.' She gave him a pitying look. 'Package holidays are all the rage. But you wouldn't know anything about that, 'cause you never bother to find out what's going on in the world outside this bloody fair.'

Although Sam was inwardly smarting from her attack, he managed to appear calm because this was neither the time nor the place for an argument. 'We'll talk about this another time, okay?'

'It'll have to be, won't it?' she said irascibly, handing mats to a couple and their two children who paid their money and climbed the wooden steps into the brightly painted cone-shaped structure.

'In the meantime, how do you fancy a change of scene for this evening's shift?'

'Depends what it is,' Tania said aggressively, collecting mats and slamming them on to the pile. 'I hope you're not gonna suggest moving me to the Bingo, though? I can't stand working on that. It attracts too many old fogeys.'

'No, not Bingo.'

'What then?'

'Josh is short-staffed on the Scenic Railway,' he explained. 'I thought perhaps you could help him out later on . . . take over in the paybox so that he can work on the platform.'

'Oh . . . oh, I see.' Tania was careful not to make her pleasure too obvious and concealed it by pretending sudden concern for her current responsibility. 'Who'll look after things here, though?'

'Eric will have to do it. Josh won't have him working with him so he'll have to take over here.' Sam looked at her warily because you never knew when Tania was going to erupt into a temper. 'So – what do you think?'

'Yeah, all right, I don't mind helping out over there,' she said breezily, her wild enthusiasm hidden beneath feigned casualness. 'It'll be a change from this, anyway.'

'Right, I'll get it organised then,' he said, already moving away, his mind weighed down with fairground matters.

'Okay . . . see you later.'

So there was a God after all, she thought, her face lighting up in a smile as her husband turned away and disappeared into the crowd.

'Sorry I don't have anything smaller,' a woman punter said to Josh as she handed him a pound note.

'That's all right, love,' he said, smiling at her saucily. 'So long as it's legal tender, you won't hear me complaining.'

'Good.'

'I hope you know what you're letting yourself in for, though – going on this ride?' he said, teasing her. 'It's been known to make tough men disgrace themselves.'

'Ooh, don't!' she said girlishly, looking down at a boy of about nine. 'I'm scared to death but I can't let him go on it on his own.'

'You need a strong man to hold your hand,' said Josh, blatantly flirting. 'I'd come with you myself if I wasn't so busy here.'

'Maybe next time, eh?' She grinned, obviously flattered by his attention.

Silly cow, he thought as she walked away and was ushered on to the ride by one of the attendants. As if I'd give her a second look outside the line of business. Touching forty and with legs like tree trunks. She'll be lucky!

Chatting up the punters was just another part of the job and it bored Josh as much as every other aspect of the work. The revolting smell of fast food, the irritating throb of the generators, the constant thump of loud music . . . he loathed it all. He should have had an affinity with the business like Sam, he knew that. It was expected of the children of showpeople.

But Josh wanted a classier occupation. Something which didn't require him to get his hands dirty – his own business which he could leave in the hands of a manager when he wanted time off. A pub or small hotel, maybe. He might even open a bar somewhere warm and exotic when the right time came.

This wasn't just a dream but a serious ambition – a project he was secretly saving for and determined to carry through. Fortunately he didn't have to rely on what he earned at Fenner's to boost his savings. Thanks to some villains he knew in Hammersmith, he had a lucrative sideline that would horrify his parents if they ever got to know about it. Nothing too risky but with just enough danger to give the job an edge and earn Josh a decent wedge. Sometimes he was a look-out man for the gang; other times he'd drive the getaway car. These tasty little earners usually took place in the small hours when he'd finished work here.

His payment for these services boosted the fund he had stashed away in his living-wagon because it would have been too risky for him to use a bank. As soon as he had enough to set himself up in business, he'd be out of here. It wouldn't be next week or next month but it *would* happen. Oh, yes!

His reverie was interrupted by the return of Sam with the news that Josh's staff problems were solved for the evening.

'Tania will come and take over in the paybox so you can work on the platform,' his brother told him, looking relieved that the matter was resolved.

There was a brief pause while Josh disguised his pleasure. 'Well done, mate. I knew you'd sort something out for me,' he said in a matter-of-fact manner that masked the way he really felt. This was immediately followed by an irritating stab of conscience. Did his brother have to be quite so decent and trusting? Didn't he know that the world was full of rats? 'Thanks for getting it sorted, bruv.'

''S'all right, mate – all part of the service.' Sam grinned. 'I take it you'd sooner have Tania helping you than Eric?'

'I'd rather have *anyone* than Eric,' said Josh, managing to hide the fact that for him the day had suddenly become a whole lot brighter.

'Poor Eric,' said Sam. 'He's a good man and he really is a lot more capable than people give him credit for.'

Poor Eric nothing! thought Josh. If anyone needed pity it was Sam, if he did but know it. Josh consoled himself with the thought that at least he wasn't a threat to his brother in the family business. In fact, with Josh out of the picture, Sam would get his brother's share eventually. And good luck to him! Josh wanted no part of it.

Maddie Brown alighted from the tube at Richmond station and wondered what on earth she was going to do next. What in God's name had possessed her to come to a place that, to her had only been a name on the map of the underground until this moment?

'Why have we come here, Mummy?' asked her five-year-old daughter Clare as they emerged on to the street; Maddie was clutching her with one hand and a holdall in the other.

A reasonable question with an absurd answer, she thought. They were here because Richmond was the last station on the District Line and the farthest point from Barking that she could see when she'd stood looking at the map of the Underground on Barking station in a state of desperation, her body wracked with pain from the bruising concealed beneath her summer dress.

'I thought we'd have a day out, love,' she fibbed.

'Are we going to the zoo?'

'I'm not sure if they have a zoo here.' Maddie didn't know anything

10

about the place at all except that it was near Kew Gardens and Hampton Court which she'd once visited on a school trip.

'What do they have here then?' asked Clare. 'Is it the seaside?'

'No, darling.' Maddie searched her mind and came up with a vaguely remembered fact. 'There's a river here, though.'

'Are there boats on the water?' the little girl asked hopefully.

'Bound to be.'

'Ooh – goodie!'

They walked on.

'What's in the bag, Mum?'

'Just a few things.'

Maddie was wrestling with the problem of finding somewhere for them to stay with the few pounds she had – what was left of the housekeeping and the money she'd put by for the rent. She could still hardly believe that she'd actually found the courage to do what she should have done years ago, and what she knew in her heart was right.

It didn't *seem* right, though. As well as feeling acutely vulnerable, she was also riddled with guilt for uprooting her daughter. Such was Maddie's low self-esteem, she actually felt as though she'd committed a crime in taking herself and her child out of harm's way.

'I'm hungry,' said Clare.

'There are some sandwiches in the bag.' Thank God she'd at least had the presence of mind to bring something for them to eat; her heart pounded as she remembered how badly her hands had been shaking. She'd hardly been able to cut the bread, terrified he'd come back before they got away.

'Can I have one?'

'Yes, 'course you can, love. But let's find a park or somewhere to sit down first.'

Walking through the main street in the sunshine, Maddie noticed that there were a lot of people about even though the shops were closed for Whit Monday afternoon. Everything seemed shining bright and clean; there were elegantly dressed shop windows and people in smart clothes. A classy place by the look of it.

Following the general drift of people, Maddie found herself in a narrow alleyway flanked by quaint little shops, their fronts decorated by window boxes overflowing with spring flowers in bloom. There was a jeweller's, an olde worlde pub, a bow-windowed tea-room, several gift and book shops.

Emerging at the other end they found themselves on a promenade by the river near a beautiful bridge with wide arches and a finely modelled balustrade, its gleaming stonework reflected in the sunlit waters. Maddie guessed this must be Richmond Bridge.

'It *is* the seaside,' said Clare, her face lit with excitement.

'No, it's the riverside,' corrected Maddie, though it was an easy

11

mistake to make because a holiday feeling pervaded everything here. People in bright summer clothes were strolling in the sunshine, ice-cream sellers doing a roaring trade, pleasure boats cruising on the river. There were white-fronted hotels with lawns sloping down to the riverside where people were having tea in the fresh air. It was a world away from the council estate in Barking that had been her home until a few hours ago.

They strolled on to some public lawns and sat down on the grass where Maddie gave her daughter a cheese sandwich. She herself was far too shaken up to eat anything. Her throat was parched and she felt sick with tension. Her bones ached to the marrow. Twenty-five years old and she felt like an old woman!

'Can I have an ice-cream, please?' asked Clare.

'Finish your sandwich and we'll see,' said Maddie, keeping her voice strong. It was vital she appeared to be in control no matter how panic-stricken she actually was because her daughter needed some sort of security in these bizarre circumstances. Maddie tried to clear her muddled mind sufficiently to work out a plan of action. A place to stay must be her first priority. Maybe she could find a cheap boarding house somewhere.

Her stomach knotted at the enormity of what she'd done. She had rendered herself and her daughter homeless without any means of support. That was scary enough but the thought of going back was even more terrifying.

'Will Daddy smack us when we go home?' asked Clare, big blue eyes full of concern.

'We're not going home, love,' said her mother, the innocent pathos of her daughter's comment making her even more determined never to return.

'Was Daddy hitting you because I'd been naughty?' Clare wanted to know next.

'You?' Maddie was shocked. 'Of course not – whatever made you think that?'

'I thought it must be my fault . . . that I'd made him cross.'

Maddie slid her arms around her daughter, tears rising painfully in her throat. She held her close, stifling the need to cry out in pain as Clare's small body pressed against her own bruised chest and ribs.

Last night had been a watershed in that it had been the first time her husband had used violence on Clare. Usually she slept through it all, or appeared to. Maddie couldn't be sure how much the child had heard over the years. But last night Dave had been particularly vicious and Clare must have been woken by the thuds and thumps of her mother being thrown against the wall in the room next to hers. The frightened child had come into their bedroom only to be whacked across the head and sent back to her room while Dave continued his attack on Maddie. He never stopped beating her until his need was sated.

The moment her husband had struck their daughter was the one Maddie knew she must leave him. If he'd done it once he could do it again. That smack across the head had been nothing to what he might do later on, once he got a taste for it. She wasn't going to risk having Clare suffer as she herself had for the last seven years.

'No, of course it wasn't your fault, love,' she whispered into her daughter's golden hair. 'Don't you ever think that, do you hear me? None of what's happened is your fault.'

'Does Daddy smack you because *you're* naughty then?'

'No.'

'Why then?'

'Well . . . because things upset him and he gets angry,' said Maddie, managing to come up with a simple answer. 'But it's over now, I promise you. Forget about it. It won't happen again.'

Clare chewed her sandwich slowly, looking around her with interest.

'It's nice here, innit?' she said in the way children sometimes have of being reassuringly normal in the most abnormal situation.

'Yeah, it does seem to be a nice place,' agreed Maddie, though the glorious setting only added to her sense of loneliness. They were strangers here with no one to turn to. It seemed as though it was just herself and Clare against the rest of the world.

Looking at her daughter, her heart turned over with the painful joy of loving her. She was so small and precious sitting there with her profile towards Maddie, her tiny nose turning up, clear-cut jawline curving gently into her slender neck. She had ash-blonde hair and big blue eyes like her mother, though years of abuse had taken their toll on Maddie who was now painfully thin, eyes shadowed and sunken in her emaciated face. Living in fear had destroyed her appetite and for the past few years she'd been able to eat only just enough to stay alive.

'I like it here . . . I hope we can stay,' Clare told her.

'I hope so too.'

But they might have to move on if she couldn't find cheap lodgings here, Maddie thought. As worried as she was about finding accommodation, it suddenly seemed equally as important to provide some sort of distraction to take the child's mind off the horrors of the past twenty-four hours.

'There are some ducks on the river over there, look,' she said. 'Shall we go over and share our sandwiches with them?'

'Ooh, yes,' said the little girl in such a normal tone Maddie was heartened. She'd heard it said that children were survivors but had worried a great deal about the long-term effects on Clare of a violent father and a mother who lived in a constant state of terror. Still, she was only five. Maybe that was young enough for any damage to be repaired.

Taking deep breaths to try to release some of the tension, Maddie stood with her daughter at the river's edge, throwing bread to the ducks gobbling and splashing in the reeds beneath the fresh green foliage of a weeping willow. After a while they ambled on under the bridge, watching the pleasure boats cruising by on the undulating green water.

Music began to drift in their direction. Maddie could just distinguish Cliff Richard's hit song 'Living Doll' rising above the unmistakable hurly-burly of a fairground. Looking ahead, Maddie noticed the top of a roller-coaster above the trees. People were coming from that direction eating candy floss and holding coloured balloons. A girl of about Clare's age walked by with her parents, carrying a goldfish in a glass bowl.

'A goldfish, Mummy,' said Clare, wide-eyed with longing. 'Where did she get it?'

'I expect she won it at the fair.'

'A fair?' Clare's voice rose excitedly. 'Ooh . . . can we go to it?'

'Not now, love.'

'Go on, Mum, please.'

'Maybe later,' said Maddie, who knew she must look for a place for them to stay tonight. Had she been alone she would have settled for a park bench, a shop doorway – anything. But it was her duty to get proper accommodation for her daughter. Another reason why the fair wasn't a good idea was the parlous state of her finances. The money she had should last a few days, but only if she was careful.

'Oh, let's go now, Mummy, please.' Clare was very persistent.

'Don't keep on.'

'Can't we just have a look?'

'No.'

But when Clare's small hand clutched hers and guided her persuasively towards the music and laughter, Maddie didn't have the heart to resist. After what the poor child had been through this weekend she deserved a few minutes pleasure in the carefree atmosphere of a fair.

'Only for a little while then,' she said wearily. 'Then we have to go into town and find a place to stay. No fuss when I say it's time to go. Do you promise?'

'I promise.'

'Come on then.'

'Hurray,' squealed Clare, skipping ahead, her hair swinging.

Chapter Two

'Roll up, roll up . . . come and try your luck on Fenner's lucky Hoopla!' called Janice Fenner in a loud, rousing voice. 'Top-class prizes – no rubbish. Come on now, ladies and gents. Don't miss the chance to win a lovely ornament for your mantelpiece – a goldfish for the kids – a ten-bob note . . .'

A slim, agile woman with tanned skin and a thick mane of chestnut brown hair falling to her shoulders, Janice was distracted from her spiel by the sight of a young woman of about her own age, arguing heatedly with a child.

'Please, Mummy, please!' the little girl kept repeating.

'No.'

'But I really wanna goldfish.' The child was belligerent now. 'Let me have one . . . go on.'a

'You can't just *have* a goldfish, you have to win it.'

'Let's try to win one then,' she persisted. 'Just one go, Mum, please.'

'No, Clare.' The woman looked to be at the end of her tether, Janice thought. 'How many more times must I tell you that the answer is no.' She lowered her voice but Janice could still hear what was being said. 'I don't have any more money to spend. I said you could only go on one thing at the fair and you've been on the Boat Swings.'

'But I wanna fish to take home with me!'

Janice caught Maddie's eye and grinned. 'Kids, eh?' she said in a sympathetic manner. 'They don't half keep on when they want something, don't they?'

'She isn't usually this difficult,' Maddie said quickly because it really wasn't like Clare to act so spoiled.

'They all have their moments.' Janice looked down at a small boy by her side and tousled his dark hair affectionately. 'I know my Barney does. Drives me nuts sometimes.'

Maddie was raw with anguish and not in the mood to be sociable. In her distressed state, Clare's demands had stretched her nerves to breaking point. She was relieved when the other woman turned away to attend to her business, distributing hoops to a young couple with two children. The mother won a goldfish and the whole family shrieked excitedly.

'So who's gonna carry the latest addition to the family then?' laughed Janice, holding out a goldfish in a bowl.

'I'll take care of it,' said the woman. 'I can't trust this lot not to drop it.'

They all peered into the bowl at their new pet then went off, laughing and chattering.

Janice noticed the little girl with the sick-looking mother watching enviously. When her mother said it was time for them to go the child became really stroppy, demanding to stay to see if anyone else won a goldfish. She seemed fascinated by them.

Something about the pair touched Janice's heart. The woman was obviously in trouble. She looked terrible – ill and sort of bewildered. Why was she lugging a holdall around a fairground? They didn't look as though they'd been living rough but there was something troubling about them. Why bring the child to the fair at all if the woman couldn't afford to let her take part?

Normally Janice would have tried to persuade her to try her luck on the Hoopla. Encouraging punters to part with their money was second nature to her as she'd been doing it all her adult life. But in this instance it didn't seem right.

Instead she handed Maddie some hoops. 'Have this one on me, love,' she said, warm brown eyes smiling kindly. 'You might be lucky and win a goldfish for your little 'un.'

But Maddie was a proud woman. 'No, thanks,' she said haughtily. 'We don't need charity.'

'Suit yourself,' said Janice with a shrug.

'But the lady said we could try to win a goldfish,' wailed Clare loudly. 'I *really, really* want one and you won't even let us have a go.'

'Now see what you've done,' Maddie snapped at Janice.

'Just trying to help . . .'

'I can do without that sort of help, thanks very much,' said Maddie curtly. 'All it does is undermine my authority . . . make her think she needn't take any notice of what I say because someone else will give in to her and let her have her own way.'

'All I did was offer you a freebie. I shouldn't think that'll corrupt your child for life,' declared Janice who was a match for anyone after a lifetime on the fair, and wasn't pleased to have her gesture of goodwill misunderstood.

'Maybe not, but it doesn't help matters at this moment.'

'Why bring her to a fair if you're not gonna let her join in?' said Janice. 'It's only natural she wants to have a go on things.'

'I . . . I . . . it's none of your blasted business!' said Maddie, hot tears rushing to her eyes. She felt weak and giddy.

Janice was about to tell the snotty cow to shove off when she turned deathly white – even her lips – and swayed as though she was about to pass out. 'Oh, my Gawd,' said Janice, coming out from behind the stall and taking Maddie's arm. 'You'd better sit down before you fall down.'

Maddie ran a trembling hand over her clammy brow. 'I'll be all right in a minute.'

'You need a sit down and a cuppa tea.'

'Yeah, I think you're right,' said Maddie, too weak to argue. 'I'll go and find a cafe.'

'You're welcome to use my living-wagon.' At Maddie's blank stare, Janice added, 'A fairground term for caravan.' She pointed towards a row of them by the wooded area at the edge of the fairground. 'Barney'll take you over and show you which one it is.'

'I don't want to impose,' said Maddie feebly.

'You won't be,' Janice assured her. 'I'll come over as soon as I can get cover here.' She turned to her son. 'Take this lady and her little girl over to the wagon, then go and find your Uncle Sam and tell him I urgently need someone to look after the stall while I take a break.'

'Okay,' he said breezily.

'Thanks ever so much,' said Maddie, who was in no fit state to refuse any offer of help.

'The kids will be all right playing outside while we have a cuppa tea and a natter,' said Janice about half an hour later when she and Maddie were ensconced in the lounge area of her living-wagon, a masterpiece of careful planning with its polished walnut walls, exquisitely carved ceilings complete with cut-glass chandeliers, fitted sideboard units with glass doors, and white lace curtains at the windows. The chairs were cream-coloured soft leather and a television set stood in the corner next to a record player. 'Barney knows the fairground like the back of his hand.'

'It's ever so good of you to let us into your home like this,' said Maddie. 'I've never been so glad of a place to sit down in my life.'

'It's the least I can do,' said Janice, offering a plate of digestive biscuits. 'I didn't want to admit it at the time but you were right – I did make things worse for you with your daughter by offering you a free go when you'd already said no to her. I should have known better but I'm a soft touch when it comes to kids. Sorry about that.'

'Don't worry about it.'

'Anyway my father would have a fit if he knew I was offering freebies.'

'Your father?'

'He owns the fair,' she explained. 'I'm Janice Fenner.'

'Maddie Brown.'

'Glad to know you, love.' Janice sipped her tea, staring shrewdly at Maddie. 'You can tell me to mind my own business if you like but you look as though you could do with a friend to talk to.'

Her warmth and generosity brought a lump to Maddie's throat. 'You're right, I could, but I don't know why you would want to bother with me after I was so rude to you out there. I'm sorry.' She put a hand to her head. 'I shouldn't take my troubles out on anyone else.'

'Forget it,' said Janice. 'Like I said, I asked for it.'

'The truth is – we don't have a place to put ourselves, let alone a goldfish,' explained Maddie.

'You mean, you're homeless?'

It was a shock for Maddie to realise that this alarming word did actually apply to her now. 'Well, yes,' she was forced to admit. 'But only temporarily, I'll soon find us a place.'

'I did wonder about the holdall,' confessed Janice, giving her a close look. 'But you don't seem as though you've been sleeping rough on the streets.'

'We haven't been.' Maddie sipped some tea to moisten her parched mouth. 'I only left my husband this morning.'

'Permanently or just to make some sort of point?'

'I won't be going back.'

'Another woman?'

'No, nothing like that.'

Janice waited, chewing a biscuit slowly, careful not to be too intrusive but wanting to help this distressed soul.

Maddie was silent for a few moments, wondering whether to tell her more. Then she stood up slowly and with painful movements unzipped her dress and let it slip down to her waist, causing Janice to gasp at the sight of a body disfigured with big red and purple bruises, the skin raw and broken in several places.

'Bloody hell!' Janice swallowed hard.

'He's always careful not to mark my face,' the other woman said dully. 'In case people noticed and tried to interfere, I suppose.'

'No wonder you left,' said Janice. 'He wants locking up.'

'I feel bad about uprooting Clare from her home, though,' admitted Maddie.

'If that's what's been going on, she's better off out of it.'

'Yeah – I know in my heart that you're right,' said Maddie, grateful for Janice's support. 'It's just that . . . well, she's no security now.'

'Better off without it if that's the price he charges for supporting you.'

'She's not long started school and now she'll have to start somewhere else. When I've found somewhere for us to live.'

'Even so . . . you can't put up with that sort of violence.' Janice was adamant. 'How long has it been going on?'

'About seven years, ever since we've been married. Last night he turned on Clare for the first time,' said Maddie, replacing her dress with slow careful movements. 'I can put up with anything for myself

'. . . but there's no way I'm gonna put my daughter at risk.'

'I know it isn't any of my business but I don't think you should even consider going back,' said Janice.

'I'm not going to.' That was one thing Maddie was certain about.

'Thank God for that! It makes me shudder to think what he's done to you.' She paused, leaning forward and becoming even more ardent. 'You could have him done for assault. Why don't you go to the police while you still have the evidence to show them?'

'I've thought of doing that many times but I've never gone through with it because I know he'll somehow turn the whole thing round and make me suffer,' Maddie explained gravely. 'I'm scared he'll try and hurt my daughter to get back at me. His mind is that warped, you wouldn't believe it.'

'Sounds like a right scumbag,' said Janice. 'Someone who can do what he's done to you is capable of anything.'

'Exactly.'

'But at least you've made the break from him. That's the most important thing.'

'I can hardly believe I've actually done it.' She shook her head, remembering. 'I gritted my teeth and left after he'd gone to the pub at lunchtime for a Bank Holiday pint. I shoved some clothes into a bag and made a run for it with what's left of the week's housekeeping money and the cash I had put by for the rent.'

'Where are you from?'

'Barking.' Maddie explained why she'd chosen Richmond. 'It could have been anywhere so long as it was at the farthest end of the line. He'll never think of looking for me here. Richmond might as well be on the other side of the world, it's so remote from the people I know.'

'Same thing applies to the average Londoner, I think,' said Janice. 'We're all a bit lost outside our own manor.'

'Leaving is one thing, surviving quite another,' said Maddie, absently taking a biscuit from the plate. 'God knows what I'm gonna do without a home or an income and a child to raise on my own.'

'Have you no relatives you can stay with until you get something permanent sorted out?'

'No, there's no one.'

Maddie saw Janice's curiosity and without really meaning to began to tell her story.

The youngest child of an East End dockworker, Maddie's father had died when she was nine, leaving her mother in a state of depression from which she was never to recover. Less than a year later she threw herself under a train at East Ham station. Maddie and her three elder sisters had gone to live with their aunt who never let them forget that she had only taken them in out of a sense of duty and found their presence in her home a nuisance. When all

19

of Maddie's sisters had left home and gone their own separate ways, her aunt made it painfully obvious to Maddie that she wanted her to do the same with all possible speed.

Dave Brown – whom she'd met at a local dancehall – had seemed the answer to the prayers of a young girl starved of affection and ready for love. Maddie had fallen for him in a big way and could hardly believe her luck when he felt the same. Marrying him had seemed like a dream come true, and had, indeed, been wonderful for a brief period. His jealousy and possessiveness had been flattering at first. She'd thought it rather sweet and only natural for a newly married man to want his wife to himself.

But life soon became a nightmare as his paranoia grew to dominate their marriage. Maddie became isolated and lost all sense of her own identity. Not only did Dave regularly beat her, he drove all her friends away with his insulting behaviour. Even a harmless chat with a neighbour could result in a battering later on. If she spoke to a man Dave accused her of making a pass; if she had a conversation with a woman he thought she was entering into some sort of conspiracy against him. His rages were fearsome.

'Did you have a job before Clare was born?' enquired Janice, glad to see that Maddie had made a start on her biscuit. She needed something inside her.

'Yeah . . . I was the cashier in a grocer's shop so at least I had something to take my mind off the situation at home,' Maddie explained. 'Of course, he was delighted when I got pregnant 'cause he wanted me tied down. It got worse over the years.'

'Why did you stay?'

'At first it was because I'd always believed in marriage being for better or for worse . . .'

'But there are limits to what a woman can be expected to put up with,' interrupted Janice, enraged by this story of male brutality. 'Staying with him could have cost you your life.'

'I know – but by the time I realised that, I was in too deep. He'd destroyed all my confidence,' she explained, staring at the pattern on the carpet. 'I was a nervous wreck . . . too scared to strike out on my own.'

'What about your neighbours?'

'There were some nice people at the council flats where we lived and I made a few friends while he was out at work during the day,' Maddie said, finishing her biscuit and taking another. Talking to Janice was making her feel better. 'But he put a stop to that. They guessed what was going on and tried to help but it made things worse for me so they gave up. People thought I was crazy to stay with Dave but it isn't easy to make the break. You feel so damned worthless when someone keeps telling you you're a piece of dirt – drums it into you that you're a useless human being.'

20

'Thank God you've managed to get away from him now!'

'Yes. My heart tells me I've done the right thing but my head wonders what the hell I'm gonna do next,' said Maddie, adding defiantly, 'I'll manage, though. I'm determined to give Clare a decent life.'

'If it'll help, you can stay here for a few nights,' offered Janice.

Maddie looked at her in surprise, warmed by her generosity. Offering shelter to a complete stranger and her child seemed the most natural thing in the world to a woman like Janice.

'Are you sure?' said Maddie. 'I wasn't angling for an invitation.'

'I know you weren't, and yes, I am sure,' Janice said cheerfully. 'Barney can sleep with me and you and Clare can have the bunk beds in his room. I have bunk beds in there, just in case he wants a pal to stay over at any time.'

'It's really kind of you.' Maddie could hardly believe how much more hopeful everything suddenly seemed. 'I'd love to stay.'

'Right, now that that's settled, come and have a look around,' said Janice, rising and leading the way through a modern kitchen and down a passageway at the side of the wagon from which two bedrooms and a bathroom were accessed through sliding doors.

'Phew! Talk about all mod cons,' said Maddie, looking into the larger bedroom at the end of the wagon with its double aspect windows and fitted furniture. 'I didn't realise caravans could be so comfortable.'

'Thought fair people lived in squalor, did you?' said Janice with a hint of friendly reproof.

'No, of course not,' Maddie quickly denied.

'Don't worry, we're used to people thinking we're didicoys just because we live in caravans,' said Janice. 'If there's trouble in the town – a fight in a pub or something – they always reckon the trouble makers come from here.'

'How unfair!'

'Yeah, it is. We're not perfect but we're decent people with standards – our homes are very important to us.'

'This is really something,' said Maddie, looking around. 'The wood panelling is gorgeous.'

'It takes some polishing, believe me, but yes, we like it.' She paused, sliding the door of the bedroom back across and leading the way down the corridor. 'Mind you, not all of the living-wagons have bathrooms. Only the newer ones.'

'You have a lovely home, Janice.'

'Thank you. You must treat it as yours too while you're staying here.' They returned to the lounge.

'I can't tell you how grateful I am,' Maddie told her.

'Us women have to stick together.'

'Won't your husband mind?'

21

'I'm not married.'

'What!'

Janice roared with laughter. 'There's no need to have a heart attack about it.'

'Sorry, I just assumed . . . because of Barney, you know.'

'Oh, yes, I know all right.' Janice gave a wicked grin, her brown eyes sparkling. Her two front teeth were rather more widely spaced than normal and it gave her smile added cheek. 'I'm one of the disgraced – an unmarried mother. What a damning label, eh? They don't call the men unmarried fathers, do they?'

'No, they're usually what's known as a "bit of a lad".'

They both giggled.

'At least you haven't lost your sense of humour,' remarked Janice.

'I thought my husband had thrashed it out of me but apparently not.' Maddie finished her tea and glanced out of the window, experiencing a surge of pleasure to see Clare running around on the grass in the wooded area surrounding the wagon, laughing with Barney and some other children, the goldfish obviously forgotten. There was a good view of the fairground from here. Maddie could see the Hoopla stall and thought how convenient it must be for Janice, living so close to the job.

'So long as you've still got that you'll get by,' said Janice.

Her warmth and humanity seemed to fill the room.

'So – what happened?' Maddie enquired, knowing instinctively that Janice wouldn't mind her asking. 'Didn't Barney's father want to know when you got pregnant?'

'It wasn't like that in my case. He would have married me like a shot, it was me who didn't want to get married.'

'That's a new twist.'

'Yeah, I know it's unusual but that's me all over,' said Janice. 'I always seem to fly in the face of tradition. Much to the annoyance of my parents. People think I'm weird because my opinions don't match theirs. It's just the way I am – I have ideas of my own and I can't ignore them.'

Behind Janice's lighthearted manner, Maddie detected a woman of strong beliefs with a serious side to her nature. 'Good for you,' she said. 'Most of us just do what's expected of us because it's easier. I really admire people who stand up for what they believe in.'

'As you can imagine, my not marrying Chas caused a hell of a scandal around here at the time.'

'The stigma is just as bad within the fairground community then?'

'Oh, yeah. It's pretty general everywhere and it's all wrong, treating single women who get pregnant like outcasts.'

'I couldn't agree more.'

'Let's hope there'll be less of us about when they bring in this contraceptive pill we keep hearing about.'

22

'It'll give women more freedom.'

Janice thought about this. 'And more pressure from men to have sex,' she said.

'Yes, there is that.'

'I was lucky 'cause Mum and Dad stood by me once they knew I was serious about not getting married,' Janice explained. 'I felt terrible about bringing shame on 'em. Some people thought I was a right little tart and I know Mum and Dad were hurt. But I also knew it would be wrong for us to get married at that time. People in our community soon got used to it.'

Maddie found the story fascinating. 'Do you ever see Barney's dad?' she asked.

'Oh, yeah. We're still going strong . . . well, on and off. Chas is the only bloke for me even though we fight most of the time.'

'So if you're still together,' said Maddie, looking puzzled, 'why didn't you want to marry him?'

'Because I didn't think it was right to be forced into marriage at nineteen just because I was pregnant. Divorce is virtually unheard of in fairground circles so there would have been no way out if it hadn't worked. Neither of us was ready for marriage at that time. Chas was just a big kid himself . . . still is, for that matter.'

'Really?'

'Yeah – he's lovely with it, though, and a damned good father to Barney. Loves him to bits and they get on like a house on fire. Chas insists on supporting him financially, too. If I thought Barney was suffering because of us not being married, I'd do it. But I'm sure he isn't. I know I'm a bit way out in my ideas but I'm a good mother and my boy wants for nothing. He has two parents who love him and that's the main thing, in my opinion.'

'Chas doesn't live here with you and Barney then?' said Maddie since there didn't seem to be any evidence of an adult male living in the wagon.

'Not likely,' said Janice, her old-fashioned attitude on this point seemingly at odds with her radical modern ideas. 'I'm not having him move in unless we're married.'

'Oh?'

'Chas and I have a good relationship but it is rather up in the air at times,' she explained since Maddie was clearly confused. 'He's a travelling showman. Has his own set of Gallopers and travels about the country with 'em to different fairs. He's away at the moment actually.'

'Gallopers?'

'Carousel horses. He rents a pitch here at Fenner's for some of the season but he's away the rest of the summer. This is his winter quarters but he has his own living-wagon.'

'Does he still want to get married?'

'Not half. He'd have us spliced tomorrow if he could get me to say yes,' Janice explained. 'But Chas still has a lot of growing up to do. He's the same age as me, twenty-five, but he's very immature. Likes to go out boozing with his mates and he's an outrageous flirt. God knows what he gets up to when he's away. But what the eye doesn't see . . .'

'You feel you couldn't turn a blind eye if you were his wife?'

'Exactly,' said Janice, pushing some loose strands of hair away from her face. 'When he's ready to settle down and keep his Gallopers here permanently so that we can have a proper family life, that's the time I'll marry him.'

'It must have been hard to stick to your guns over this,' said Maddie. 'Given the way unmarried mothers are treated.'

'It would have been harder for me to take the other route.'

'You must be a very capable person.'

'I take after my mum in that respect.' Janice looked thoughtful. 'She's one hell of a woman, the mainstay of this family – and the business. Dad thinks he's in charge but she's the one who says what goes around here and he wouldn't have it any other way, truth be told. Mum lets him get away with murder because she's so sure of him. He goes out enjoying himself at night but she knows he'll never stray – not seriously anyway.'

'Your life sounds dead interesting.'

'Only because it's different from what you're used to.'

'Maybe.'

'Fairground life suits me.' Janice shrugged her shoulders. 'But I've never known anything else so I've nothing to compare it with.' She looked at the clock on the wall and stood up in a purposeful manner. 'Anyway, I have to get back to work now. Make yourself at home while I'm gone. Treat the place as your own.'

'Are there any jobs going on the fair?' asked Maddie on impulse.

'Bound to be – if you don't mind what you do,' said Janice. 'We nearly always need casual staff during the season. People come and go. They don't like the unsocial hours.'

'I'll do anything at all,' said Maddie, fired with new spirit, her blue eyes alive for the first time in ages.

'You need to talk to my brother Sam. He does most of the hiring and firing.'

'Where will I find him?'

'Try the office. If he isn't there they'll put a call out over the Tannoy for him.' They walked through the kitchen to the front door and Janice pointed towards the fair. 'The office is over there – turn left at the Ghost Train. One of my parents will be holding the fort in there 'cause there's been some sort of an argument with the woman who runs the office and she's stormed out in huff, apparently. Tell 'em I sent you.'

24

'Thanks ever so much.'

'No trouble,' said Janice breezily. 'I'll enjoy having you and Clare around.' She paused. 'You can leave her playing with Barney and the other kids, if you like. She'll be quite safe. The older children look after the younger ones here, and I'll be close by on the Hoopla stall. They'll come to me if they need anything.'

'Thank you,' said Maddie again, knowing instinctively that she could leave Clare with an easy mind.

Sam was dealing with a crisis on the Bumper Cars when he was summoned to the office over the loudspeaker.

'Two cars on the blink you say, Syd?' he was saying to the man in charge.

'That's right, boss.'

'That's about the last thing we need on a Bank Holiday Monday.'

'I'll say it is,' agreed Syd. 'Duff cars don't earn their keep.'

'I'll get the engineer to come and see to it pronto,' said Sam hurriedly, anxious to get back to the office but hoping the call didn't mean more trouble. This was proving to be an absolute bugger of a day. No sooner did he solve one problem than another arose.

'Righto, boss.'

Sam had turned and begun to walk away when Syd called him back.

'I could do with another pair of hands here later on,' he said. 'When the lads come out to play tonight there'll be a real crowd and they always aim straight for the Dodgems.'

'I'll see what I can do,' promised Sam and strode off towards the office through the crowds, wondering where he was going to find someone to help Syd.

Fenner's offices were on the top floor of a two-storey building, the lower floor being used for storage.

Maddie was sitting in reception waiting for Sam Fenner. It was a noisy whirlwind of a place currently presided over by Janice's father Vic, a burly, talkative man who had informed her that he was only looking after the office for a few hours – until he went to open the beer garden – because the woman who normally worked here had left the job in a temper a couple of hours ago.

'Walked out without even giving notice because she was asked to help out on one of the stalls,' he'd explained, puffing furiously on a cigar. 'Said she was employed as an office worker, not a fairground hand. Reckoned it was a waste of her office training.' He tutted and raised his eyes. 'Some mothers don't half have 'em. She was told when we took her on that she'd have to be versatile.'

'Oh, dear,' said Maddie.

'You got any office experience?' he asked because she had told him why she was here as soon as she arrived.

'Not really – well, I can't do shorthand or typing, but I did work as a cashier in a grocer's shop once.'

'It doesn't matter about the shorthand and typing – we have people come in weekdays to do that.' He exhaled and almost disappeared behind a cloud of cigar smoke. 'If we were to give you a job, would you be prepared to do a bit of everything? Work in here in the office and out on the fair as well if necessary?'

'Yes.'

'Even if it's chucking it down with rain?'

'Sure.'

Vic Fenner looked doubtful. 'You look a bit frail, though, love. Would you be up to it?'

'I'm as strong as a horse,' Maddie heard herself tell him.

'That's all right then,' he'd said without further ado. 'I'll call my son in. He's out on the fairground somewhere. He'll decide if we can offer you anything.'

He'd gone over to a table at the side of his desk on which stood a record player and amplifier which was piping pop music over the public address system. He made an announcement into the microphone to the effect that Sam Fenner was wanted in the office then told Maddie to take a seat while she waited.

As she did so she studied the nucleus of the fairground operation with interest. It was a hive of activity with people coming in and out for various reasons; children with messages from ride operatives, side-show workers for more prizes or small change for their float, people needing someone paged on the Tannoy. A lost child was brought in and the parents appealed to. Maddie did what she could to comfort the distressed girl until her parents arrived.

A striking woman of middle years, wearing a scarlet turban, gold hooped earrings and a long flowing dress in multicolours, swept in asking for small change. Maddie gathered from the conversation that her name was Sybil.

'Everyone seems to be giving me paper money today, Vic. I've had no end of ten-bob notes,' she told him. 'They can't wait to give me their dough to find out what the future has in store for 'em. Very little in the way of financial success if they spend their money having their fortune told, I'm thinking. But naturally, I keep quiet.'

'You'd be daft not to,' said Vic, who had greying hair and dark eyes. He was handsome in a rough, flashy soft of way, Maddie thought. The sleeves of his bright blue shirt were rolled halfway up his hirsute arms and his tie was a dazzling strip of colour. He gave Sybil a bag of coins in exchange for some notes and she hurried away, smiling at Maddie as she passed.

'She's my sister,' he told Maddie after Sybil had departed.

'A fortune teller?'

'You'd never guess to look at her, would you?' he said, chuckling at his own irony. 'It's all a load o' nonsense, o' course, but it's just a bit of fun and that's what the punters come here for – fun.' He grinned. 'Gawd knows why they wanna know what's gonna happen to 'em in the future. I've enough trouble coping with today, let alone knowing what'll happen to me tomorrow.' He smiled again, confirming Maddie's belief that he must have been stunning when he was young.

'As you say, it's just a bit of fun,' she said politely.

Before he could reply a youngish man she assumed must be Sam Fenner came in complaining about two bumper cars going on the blink and how unheard of that was at Fenner's considering how careful they were about maintenance. Having asked his father to page the engineer on the Tannoy, Sam went into an office leading off the main reception area only to be called back by Vic.

'This young lady is called Maddie and she's looking for work,' he explained to the younger man whose brilliant eyes lit up at the news.

'I hope you're real and not just a figment of my imagination?'

'Sorry?'

'I'm desperate for help,' he explained, smiling warmly. 'I need someone to take over on the Helter-Skelter so that I can move my cousin to the Bumper Cars.'

'I was thinking of getting her to take over from me here,' said Vic. 'I've things to do before I open the beer garden.'

'Yes, that's a good idea.' Sam raked back his thick hair with his fingers. 'Well, perhaps she could do a bit of each.' He looked at Maddie. 'Could you take over from my father here for now, then do the evening shift on the Helter-Skelter?'

Slightly unnerved by the speed with which things were moving, Maddie said, 'I've never worked on a fair before.'

'You look like a bright girl,' said Sam without hesitation. 'You'll soon get the hang of it.'

'I'll give it a try, but I can't start right away.'

His face fell. 'Damn.'

'I'll start tomorrow,' she offered.

'You'd be doing us a big favour if you could start now,' he said, giving her a melting look. 'Twenty-five shillings a day – cash in hand.'

'But I have to make arrangements for my little girl,' she said anxiously, and went on to tell him where Clare was.

'No problem,' he said immediately. 'She can either stay with you or play with the other kids. There's enough of 'em living on the park. She'll have a whale of a time, I promise you. Go and tell her where you are and then you can get started.'

'But . . .'

Sam was already striding towards the door. 'I'm just going over to the place where the kids play. Let's walk over together and I'll brief you on the job on the way.'

She followed him out of the office and down the stairs. On the way out of the door they met a man in overalls.

'You wanted me?' said the man Maddie assumed was the maintenance engineer.

'Problem on the Dodgems, mate.'

'Righto, boss,' said the man and walked off towards the ride, apparently needing no further instructions.

Sam turned to Maddie. 'Don't look so worried, you'll be fine,' he said reassuringly. 'The most important thing is to smile and be friendly. It's our job to make people happy. You're a natural for it, I can tell.'

'I'll certainly give it my best shot,' she said, inspired by his confidence in her. Being a stranger to praise and encouragement, she felt quite lighthearted.

Much later that night Maddie lay in bed in the bunk above Clare who had fallen asleep as soon as her head touched the pillow. Sam had been right. She'd had a great time playing with the other children. Maddie had enjoyed the work too, even if the stint in the office had been mostly guesswork and she'd only just managed to muddle through. Much to her surprise she'd also enjoyed the shift on the Helter-Skelter. The happy-go-lucky atmosphere had been infectious and she'd liked being a part of it.

Sam had come to see her several times, to check that she was managing. He seemed to be a very kind man, and good-looking too in an unsophisticated sort of way. He'd said there would be work for her for the next few days if she wanted it; Maddie had jumped at the chance.

Turning too quickly on to her side, she cried out with pain from the bruising on her ribs. Was it really only last night she'd received these injuries? It seemed so long ago; in another life. It was a different world at Fenner's.

She reflected on how the members of the family she had met so far had taken her at face value. Janice had opened her own home to Maddie, and Sam and his father had trusted her to look after the office and hand in every penny she had taken on the Helter-Skelter. These were good people. But they were also tough and she suspected that if you crossed them, you'd be made to regret it.

Rolling carefully on to her back, she watched the dappled undulating patterns on the ceiling cast by the trees outside swaying in the breeze. The fair was dark and silent now, the grounds swept clean after it had closed. Janice said that every night every last bit of litter was cleared from the site by all the stall holders working as a team.

It was a peculiar thing. Maddie had known Janice for less than a day but she felt more at home in her living-wagon than she had in a very long time. She hadn't felt as though she belonged anywhere since her father died but now she thought she could fit in here.

Nothing more than an overreaction to an act of kindness, she told herself. She had merely been offered a bed for a few nights until she got a place of her own. And work for the next few days. Nothing was promised beyond that. In a few days, when the Whitsun holidays were over, she would have to get Clare started in school. She couldn't stay on at the fair then, having the child up all hours while she herself was working in the evening.

But Barney, who was the same age as Clare, and the other fairground children seemed healthy and very well-adjusted. Janice had said something about the older children baby sitting the younger ones during term time when they had to go to bed at a reasonable hour and the parents were working in the evening. There was a very relaxed attitude towards children here. None of the adults seemed to mind having the little ones around while they were working and everyone looked out for them – unlike Dave who could only take children in very small doses and had been angry if Clare hadn't been in bed when he got home from work in the evening.

Maddie had had to keep the poor child quiet at weekends, too, because noise got on his nerves. Dave was a very tense person! Many times over the years she had tried to talk to him about it in an effort to find the reason for his uncontrollable violence, and perhaps help him to overcome it. But he had no patience for discussion and seemed to think his behaviour was normal.

Just thinking about her husband set her nerves on edge. There was something else eating away at Maddie too; despite all the years of misery there was an ache in her heart at the way things had turned out because she had once loved her husband. Now all she felt for him was loathing and fear. He must be very troubled to behave as he did.

Drowsiness washed over her, warm and sweet. For the first time in years she was able to go to sleep without being afraid of waking up. Her future was more uncertain than it had ever been before but nothing could be so bad as the certainty of Dave's relentless cruelty.

Even knowing that problems undoubtedly lay ahead, she cherished these precious moments of unaccustomed peace as she began to drift off to sleep in the knowledge that she was out of Dave's reach.

He would never find her here.

A little after midnight that night, in a council flat in Barking, Dave Brown sat morosely in an armchair, smoking a cigarette and waiting for his wife and daughter to come home.

'Bloody woman! How dare she go off, leaving me with no dinner?'

he fumed out loud to the empty room. 'The cow, the cheap little cow! I'll murder her when she does come home. She'll wish she'd never been born – oh, yes!'

It didn't occur to him that she might not come back. He simply discounted the possibility. To his way of thinking Maddie had nothing without him. No money and no place to go. It wasn't as though she had any relatives she could turn to either because she'd lost contact with them years ago. She'd be back begging him for forgiveness soon enough.

Where the hell was she, though? She had no friends, he'd made sure of that. And he'd beaten the spirit out of her so she wouldn't have the guts to stay away for long. The only way to control a woman was to wallop her, like his father had walloped his mother. And all the kids for that matter. Dave had been left with a need to be in control, to prove to himself that he was in charge. Once he let go of that control and gave Maddie her freedom, God knows what she'd get up to.

She had gone off just to make him suffer, as a protest against the beatings. Childish and typical of her! It wasn't as though he ever hurt her – well, not seriously. A sudden mental image of her bruised body hit him with a mixture of shock and pleasure. Well, perhaps he did go a bit too far sometimes but it was her own fault for making him lose his temper.

He listened to the clock ticking steadily on the mantelpiece and wondered again where she could be at this late hour. She wouldn't be walking the streets, not with the kid. The brat had always meant more to Maddie than he had.

His thoughts moved onwards. He had to be up early in the morning for work at the factory where he slaved to support his wife and child. And she was selfish enough to keep him up late so that he'd be tired at his machine tomorrow! She had no right to do it to him and would be made to pay.

Dave stubbed out his cigarette in the ash tray and rubbed his knuckles, eyes glinting with anticipation.

Oh, yes, when Maddie did come through that door, she'd be taught a lesson she'd never forget. She wouldn't dare go off a second time. And, in the unlikely event of her not returning, he'd find her. Oh, yes! He'd track her down and get his revenge.

Chapter Three

As well as the living-wagons at Fenner's Fun Park, there was also an accommodation block for seasonal workers who came from outside the area; this was always full to capacity during the summer. The living-wagons belonged to the Fenner family and a few showpeople who ran their own rides and sideshows. The wagons were situated at one side of the fairground, the flat-topped concrete units at the other.

Vic and Hetty Fenner had a house in Richmond and also a large family living-wagon on the site which they used during the season because it was more convenient. The rest of the family lived permanently in their wagons. Next to Janice's wagon – at the end of the line – was an unoccupied caravan which became of particular interest to Maddie when she was asked to stay on at the fair until the end of the season.

'Is there any chance of my renting that empty caravan?' Maddie asked Sam one morning a few weeks later when she met him on the fairground on her way back from shopping for herself and Janice. Mornings were the only time she had for chores because the fair opened at one o'clock.

'Are things not working out with Janice then?' he enquired.

'Things are fine with Janice, we're great friends,' Maddie explained. 'And because I want it to stay that way, I need my own place. I don't want to risk our getting on each other's nerves by outstaying my welcome. Anyway, Chas will be coming back soon and they'll want some privacy.'

Sam had come to expect this kind of consideration from Maddie, who had proved to be an absolute godsend these past few weeks. There was no task she'd been given that she hadn't tackled with enthusiasm and efficiency. Everything from relief work on the rides and sideshows to washing dishes in the restaurant. And she was brilliant in the reception office, answering the telephone and dealing with all the enquiries with such aplomb you'd think she'd been doing it for years. It wasn't often you came across such a willing and capable all-rounder, which was why they'd kept her on.

'Yeah, I suppose you're right,' he said, noticing how much healthier she looked lately. The vivid blue of her eyes was much more apparent now and the smoothness of her skin, lightly tanned from being in the fresh air with a sprinkling of freckles on her nose. Now that she had lost that awful skinniness, she looked pretty with her shiny blonde hair tied back to reveal her small features.

As much as he valued her as an employee, however, the decision about her renting accommodation from the firm didn't lie with him. 'You'll have to ask my parents about renting the wagon because it isn't up to me. Mum's your best bet. If you ask Dad he'll only tell you to ask her.'

She nodded in an understanding manner because everyone knew, as Janice had told Maddie that first day, that Hetty Fenner made all the decisions around here. 'Thanks for the advice. I'll have a word with her.'

'I think she's doing something in the office at the moment if you want to catch her while it's quiet before we open the fair.'

'Thanks, Sam.'

'I hope this means you'll definitely be staying until the end of the season?'

'So long as you can use me, I'll be here,' Maddie assured him.

'Great.'

Sam's friendliness towards her made her feel warm inside. She thought he was terrific. Not in any romantic sense – which was just as well because he had eyes for no one but his wife who seemed much less devoted to him, Maddie had noticed. Tania was often breathtakingly rude to her husband in public. Whenever Maddie saw them together Sam seemed to be fielding the most crushing put-downs from her. And the contemptuous way she looked at him made Maddie's heart turn over. Tania treated him like the fairground idiot instead of the person who held everything together, a rock of a man respected by everyone who worked there, as well as the regular punters.

It was odd that someone so strong and in control could allow himself to be browbeaten in this way. Still, he and Tania were probably quite different when they were on their own. It was none of Maddie's business, anyway. Strictly speaking she was employed by his parents but she looked upon him as her boss because he gave her instructions. In the same way as she trusted Janice, she trusted Sam and was enormously grateful to him for keeping her on.

'I must dash,' she said.

'See you later then,' he said and went off whistling.

'That caravan is in quite a neglected state,' said Hetty Fenner.

'I've had a look through the windows,' said Maddie. 'And it looked fine to me.'

'Oh, yes, it's perfectly habitable but it hasn't been used on a permanent basis for a few years so it'll be damp and musty inside,' she said. 'It was Sam's living-wagon before he married Tania and needed something bigger and smarter. We keep it just in case we need extra accommodation at any time for friends and relatives. But it's hardly been used and it's just been left.'

'That's no problem,' said Maddie cheerfully. 'I can soon clean it up.'

'Hmmm.' Hetty deliberated. She didn't know Maddie very well because she worked directly under Sam. But she seemed like a genuine sort and was an excellent worker. From what Hetty had heard from Janice, the poor woman had had a rough time with her louse of a husband, and needed a break. But when you were running a business you had to be realistic. You couldn't support every worthy cause that presented itself. 'But you do realise that there won't be work for you here when the season ends?'

Maddie nodded.

'So you'd just get settled into the caravan and then you'd have to move out.'

'I'm thinking of getting a job in the town for the winter,' Maddie told her. 'Bar work probably. There's bound to be a vacancy in at least one of the pubs because a lot of people are put off by the unsocial hours.'

'Are you hoping to live in?'

'No. That would be too restricting for Clare.' She looked at Hetty who would have been nondescript in appearance had it not been for the shrewd brown eyes that shone with exceptional brightness from her freckled face and were so compelling you felt drawn to her. Maddie hesitated for only a moment longer before taking the bull by the horns. 'So, I was wondering if you'd let me stay on in the wagon when the fairground is closed and I'm working outside? Provided, of course, we can agree on an affordable rent.'

'But why a caravan?'

'I need a home for Clare and the caravan just happens to be empty,' explained Maddie, eager to convince her. 'She's started at the local school and I don't want to unsettle her again in the autumn so I'm planning to stay in the area anyway. If I were to stay on in the caravan, I would be on hand for you too – if you wanted to consider me for a job at Fenner's again next season?'

'Why do you want to stay on the park, though?' asked Hetty because they didn't usually have employees living on the site out of season. 'It isn't as though you have a fairground background.'

'I like it here,' said Maddie simply. 'And my daughter's taken to it like a duck to water . . . she loves being with Barney and the other kids.' She paused, meeting Hetty's direct gaze. 'Clare is the most important thing in my life. I want her to have security and I think she feels secure here.'

Hetty leaned forward, resting her big freckled arms on the desk. She was a large woman with a shelf-like bosom and a mop of curly brown hair like Janice's, though Hetty's was shorter and dusted here and there with silver. She remained silent, still mulling over Maddie's request.

'And to be perfectly honest, Mrs Fenner,' she continued, becoming desperate when Hetty didn't reply, 'there are the practicalities to be considered. I'm on my own with a child to bring up so I have to watch the pennies. The caravan is kitted out and furnished so I wouldn't have the expense of buying stuff as I would if I set up home somewhere else.' Maddie had taken the trouble to make a few enquiries about this. 'Also, I shouldn't think the rent on a caravan would be as much as I'd have to pay on a flat or rooms in the town, even supposing I could get somewhere where children are allowed.'

'Mm. There is that.'

'I really believe I can make more of a home for Clare in a caravan than I could in a flat or bedsit.' Maddie tried to slow down, aware that she was rattling on. 'I could put my name on the council waiting list but it would probably be years before they could come up with anything.' She cleared her dry throat. 'And anything they could offer wouldn't be half as cosy as a living-wagon.'

Hetty was fifty years old, the daughter of travelling showpeople who had run a Waltzer with which they had travelled the country during her childhood, with the result that she'd never been in one place for long enough to get much of a formal education. But she'd learned enough to get by and had a sharp brain so running a business hadn't been too difficult. She had been overseeing Fenner's alongside Vic for several years before his parents had died and the fair became his officially, her own parents also having passed on by then.

It had been the summer of Hetty's eighteenth year that her parents had rented a pitch at Fenner's for the whole season and she'd fallen for Vic. She'd been determined to have him, though there was no shortage of competition for he'd been a real stunner when he was young. Much the same as Josh was now.

Being Vic's wife hadn't been easy. He was pleasure-seeking, irresponsible and work-shy if he could get away with it. But she loved him for all that and knew he loved her and their family, even though he'd rarely been at home when the children were growing up. He still preferred to be out enjoying himself with his mates than at home with his wife. But their marriage worked. He needed someone like her; someone strong who could cope with responsibility.

For all his faults Vic had his good points. He was kind-hearted and cheerful and he had a terrific sense of humour. No one could make Hetty laugh like he did. If she was off-colour or worried about anything there was nothing he wouldn't do for her.

His spending too much time in the pubs and clubs of West London had tended to upset her when they'd been younger because she'd felt hurt and excluded. But maturity had helped her to understand that he needed the relaxation of male company. Anyway, the worst he got up to was bad language and dirty jokes, she was certain of that. And it could only be a matter of time before he slowed down. The man was fifty-two.

Now, looking at this earnest young woman facing her, she saw something of herself in Maddie, a hard worker who wanted the best for her offspring. But unlike Hetty, she didn't have the benefit of a decent husband. Vic was the most gentle of men and had never laid a finger on his wife.

'I admire your honesty,' she said, impressed by the fact that Maddie had not tried to win her over with sugary sentimental reasons for wanting to rent the wagon. 'And I can see no reason why you shouldn't have the caravan to live in for as long as you need it. It's only standing there empty so you might as well make use of it. I'll have to discuss the rent with my husband but we won't charge more than you can afford.'

Maddie's face was wreathed in smiles. 'Oh, thank you, Mrs Fenner,' she said fervently. 'Thanks ever so much.'

'I'm renting you a caravan, love, not making you a partner in the business,' said Hetty in her usual down-to-earth manner, though it pleased her to see genuine gratitude.

'You couldn't have made me happier if you had,' said Maddie, rising to leave. 'I can't tell you what a load it is off my mind, having somewhere for me and Clare to live.'

'I'm sure it must be.' She threw Maddie a sharp look. 'And can we have less of the "Mrs Fenner", please? Just Hetty will do.'

'Okay, Hetty.' Maddie was thrilled because being on Christian name terms made her feel closer to the family.

'We'll fix you up with some bedding,' said Hetty, ever practical. 'You'll find saucepans and crockery in the cupboards. It'll all need a good clean but it'll be fine to use once you've done that.'

'Thank you,' said Maddie again. 'Must go . . . see you later.'

And she left the office excitedly, hurrying to tell Clare the good news.

Maddie didn't waste any time. The next morning she was up in the cool damp of dawn, working on the wagon with the windows wide open to clear the musty smell while Janice and the children were still sleeping next door. It was a huge task because the whole place needed cleaning from top to bottom.

The wagon wasn't nearly as luxurious as Janice's, and it didn't have a bathroom. There were two bedrooms but the smaller of the two was little more than a cupboard with room for nothing much except two bunk beds. Unlike Janice's thickly carpeted floors, these were covered in lino which had seen much better days.

But the place had bags of potential and a good-sized living room with an open fireplace. There was polished wood panelling everywhere, though it was badly in need of attention. Janice had told her friend to wash it down with vinegar and water before she used polish on it as it had been neglected for so long.

Despite the size of the job, Maddie had made good headway with the general cleaning by the time she and Janice walked the children to school.

'Good grief,' said Janice as they headed for the town along the riverside route, the Thames gleaming in the fresh morning light. 'You *are* in a hurry to move in there.' She chuckled. 'I hope it isn't anything to do with my personal habits?'

'Of course it isn't . . . I'm really enjoying living with you and Barney but I have to get us into our own place.'

'Only kidding.' Janice grinned. 'I admire your energy. Getting up at that hour would kill me.'

'It's the only time I have as I'm working afternoons and evenings,' Maddie explained. 'And I want it spotless before we move in. Heaven knows how long it will take me to polish that panelling!'

'I'll give you a hand tomorrow but it won't be the early shift.'

'You give Clare her breakfast and I'll expect nothing more from you. Deal?'

'Deal,' laughed Janice. 'It's bad enough doing my own polishing.'

As it happened Maddie had help from an unexpected source the next morning.

'Hello, Eric, you're out early this morning,' she said to Sybil's son, a large man with soft blue eyes and ginger hair. He appeared at the caravan door just as she was about to start polishing the panelling, an energetic Alsatian called Marlon at his side. Although the animal was one of the fairground's several guard dogs, he was also Eric's much-loved pet.

'I always get up early 'cause me and Marlon like to go out for a walk by the river before breakfast . . . not many people about then,' Eric explained in his usual slow, monotonous manner. 'I heard Janice saying you were gonna clean this place up and move in so I thought I could help.'

'It's kind of you to offer,' said Maddie, 'but I'm managing.'

'I'd like to help.' Eric was always eager to please.

'You can talk to me while I work, if you like,' she said, sensing his need of company. 'I'll make us some coffee.'

Eric bent down to the dog and fondled his head. 'You stay here,' he commanded. 'Good boy.'

'Marlon is an unusual name for a dog,' Maddie remarked as he made his way inside.

'Uncle Vic let me choose so I named him after Marlon Brando.' 'You like him then?'

'I think he's wonderful,' said Eric with childlike enthusiasm.

36

'Rock Hudson is my favourite film star,' she told him chattily.

'He's not as good as Brando,' said Eric. 'Brando's tough . . . knows his way around.'

The exact opposite of Eric himself, thought Maddie, who'd been told all about his low IQ.

'He certainly does – on the screen anyway,' she said.

He looked around, studying the walls and ceiling in the living room which had a built-in settee running along two sides, armchairs to either side of the fireplace and a table that folded flat to the wall when not in use. 'You make the coffee and I'll give this wood panelling some muscle.'

'Well, if you're sure?' said Maddie, adding jokingly, 'I don't want your mother getting on to me for taking advantage of your good nature.'

'Mum won't mind,' he said, taking her seriously. 'But you won't tell the blokes I've been doing women's work, will you? They'll laugh at me and call me a pansy if they find out.'

'Your secret's safe with me,' she said, smiling at the thought of what Janice would have to say about this conversation. She had her own ideas about a woman's role in the scheme of things and they didn't tally with the traditional ones!

'If you give me the materials, I'll get started right away.'

'Sure,' she said, handing him a tin of polish and a cloth.

Eric's slowness irritated many people who didn't have the patience to persevere with his laboured conversation. Janice had told Maddie that when her father had inherited the fair, it was in the terms of her grandfather's will that Vic should make provision for his widowed sister Sybil and her son for the rest of their lives.

This was the first time Maddie had been on her own with Eric and she wasn't finding him a problem at all. In fact, she rather liked him.

'Do you enjoy working on the fair?' she asked, pulling the table out from against the wall and putting two mugs of coffee on it for them to drink as they worked.

'Yeah.'

'Have you ever wanted to do anything else?' she enquired casually, just to get him talking and put him at his ease.

'Ooh, no, I don't wanna do anything else,' Eric said, as though the mere suggestion frightened him. 'I wanna be with Mum and the family. I won't get into trouble with them. They look after me.'

'I see.'

'Do you like it here?' he asked.

'Love it,' she told him, taking a sip of her coffee then using a polishing cloth on the other wall. 'And I'd never done anything like it before. It's hard work but there's such a cheerful atmosphere the time just flies by.'

'Funfairs are good for people,' he pronounced, rubbing steadily in circular movements. 'Because funfairs make people laugh and laughter is the best medicine.'

'So they say.'

'I heard that on the telly,' Eric said, pausing for a moment to drink his coffee.

'Do you watch much TV?'

'Not so much in the summer 'cause I'm usually working.'

'You enjoy the telly though?'

He put down his mug and resumed work. 'Yeah, I like the telly. I'm glad Mum bought a set.'

'What sort of programmes do you like?'

'Boxing . . . football . . . I watch the news sometimes an' all.'

'The news?' She was surprised.

'Mum has it on.'

'Oh, I see.'

'The telly's much better than the paper,' Eric continued.

'Why's that?'

'Not enough pictures in the paper.'

She was silent for a few moments while the significance of his remark registered. 'Can't you read, Eric?' she asked.

'Nah.'

'That must be a nuisance for you.'

'Sometimes.'

'You went to school though, didn't you?'

'Yeah, I went to school but I didn't like it.'

'That's a shame,' she said. 'What didn't you like about it?'

'The teachers were always having a go at me. I was scared stiff of 'em. Couldn't understand what they were talking about, and they used to get *so* angry.'

'Sounds awful.'

'It was, so I stopped going,' he informed her. 'I stayed at home and helped round the fair. I was happy then.' He laughed victoriously. 'Mum used to tell 'em I was ill.'

'Wouldn't you like to be able to read and write, though?' asked Maddie.

'I s'pose so – sometimes. But what's the good of wanting to? I can't do it so that's that,' he told her, standing back and looking at his work.

Not necessarily, thought Maddie, but deemed it wisest not to risk unsettling him by speaking her thoughts at this stage.

Eric might not have the sharpest intellect at Fenner's but when it came to polishing he was a whizz; his physical strength enabled him to work a great deal faster than Maddie. With him on the task, the walls were gleaming in no time at all. By the time Maddie broke off to get Clare ready for school, the place was shining.

'You've done wonders, Eric,' she said. 'I can't thank you enough.'
He gave her a wide smile and went home for his breakfast.

By the end of the week Maddie and Clare had moved into the living-wagon which smelt fresh and shone with cleanliness. Out of her wages she bought some lace curtains and pretty drapes to draw across at night. She also purchased some cheap vases which she filled with fresh flowers, and a few potted plants to add a touch of colour and homeliness.

Clare was thrilled with her new home, and loved her little bedroom. She was especially happy about living next door to Barney, and the two of them flitted from one wagon to the other, equally at home in either.

Sam was impressed with what Maddie had done. 'It's like a different wagon from the one I used to live in as a bachelor.' Maddie had invited him in to have a look one morning when he happened to be passing while she was on her way in from pegging some washing on the line. 'Well done!'

'Thank you. I'm delighted with it,' she said. 'And I'm pleased it's all done before the kids break up for the summer holidays next week. It wouldn't have got done so thoroughly with Clare around.'

'She's a great kid.'

'Yes. But her presence isn't conducive to cleaning and polishing a complete wagon in the shortest time possible.'

'No, I don't suppose it is, especially as wherever she is, Barney is too.' Sam grinned. 'Those two seem to have become inseparable.'

'Yeah.'

'Nice to see it,' he said. 'You can't beat having kids about the place.'

She'd noticed how good he was with children and was surprised he didn't have any. 'Perhaps you'll have one of your own one day,' she said jokingly. 'Or are you leaving it to Janice to keep your mother supplied with grandchildren?'

Tania would go berserk if by some mistake she fell pregnant, he thought. She found children tedious in the extreme and didn't want her life ruined by them. Her attitude upset him and he preferred not to talk about it so he just said, 'Who knows what the future might bring?'

'Fancy a coffee?' Maddie had noticed his face tighten at her question and could have kicked herself for being so intrusive.

'Yeah, I wouldn't say no to a quick one,' said Sam, sitting down at the table in the living room 'But it'll have to be really quick 'cause the rep from the fancy goods wholesaler is due in this morning and I want to talk him into giving us a bigger discount.'

'Is that the firm you get the prizes from?' asked Maddie, ever curious about the general running of the fair.

'That's right,' he said. 'I have to keep a sharp eye on their prices or they'd take all our profit.'

'All of it?' She was being cheeky.

Sam gave her a wicked look. 'Well, some of it anyway.'

'That's more like it.'

Their conversation was interrupted suddenly by a tap on the window. It was Josh. Maddie beckoned to him to come in.

'What's all this then?' he said jokingly as he came into the room 'Don't tell me my workaholic brother is skiving?'

'Not at all. I talked him into taking a coffee break,' explained Maddie, feeling uneasy for some reason in Josh's company. 'I've just put the kettle on.'

'Too bad you won't be able to stay for coffee, mate,' said Josh to Sam with a teasing glint in his eye. 'The bloke from the wholesaler's has just arrived and is waiting for you in the office. Eric just happened to see you come in here which is how I've tracked you down.'

'Oh, well – no peace for the wicked,' said Sam, rising with a good-humoured sigh and leaving.

'I'll have a coffee if you're making some, though,' said Josh, looking at Maddie in a way that disturbed her. 'I could just do with one.'

'Sure,' she said with false affability, the casual ease she felt in Sam's company noticeably absent in Josh's. 'Sugar and milk?'

'Milk and two sugars,' he said with a mocking smile, as though he knew he was making her uncomfortable and was revelling in it.

Maddie had seen him around the park and exchanged the odd few words in passing. But this was the first time she'd actually been in his company. It wasn't something she was anxious to make a habit of because he made her feel so threatened. Josh Fenner was seriously gorgeous and it was obvious that he knew it. With Sam she never felt lost for words; Josh made her feel gauche and tongue-tied.

Whereas she knew instinctively that she could trust Sam, she was equally as certain that she must be wary of his brother. Annoyingly, she wasn't able to be indifferent to him, though. Dressed in a casual shirt and blue jeans that fitted him like a second skin, he evoked feelings in her she didn't want to have – the sort of feelings she thought Dave had destroyed for ever.

'So, you're planning on staying on here, then?' he said as Maddie put a cup of coffee down on the table in front of him.

'That's right – for a while anyway,' she said, dry-mouthed and nervous.

'Lucky us.'

'Thank you,' said Maddie, smiling politely even though she knew he was laughing at her.

'I hear that you and your husband have split up?'

She wasn't surprised by his comment. In such a close-knit community as this, personal details were bound to become common knowledge. She nodded, sitting down opposite him to drink her coffee. Strip me naked, why don't you? she thought angrily, as his eyes bored into her T-shirt.

'Is it a permanent split?'

'Yes.'

'That sounds definite.'

'It was meant to.'

'Oh . . . So, why fair work?' he asked, seeming genuinely curious. 'There must be easier ways of earning a living for someone like you.'

'Someone like me?'

'Attractive – bright.'

'Working here suits me fine.' He was the most unnerving man. 'I like the atmosphere and the variety of the work.'

'They say variety is the spice of life, don't they?' he said in a manner that suggested he wasn't referring just to work.

Both Sam and Janice made Maddie feel welcome here. Josh reminded her that she was an outsider without saying anything to indicate as much. It was just something in his manner – cold and distant, whilst at the same time pushy and overtly sexual. She'd never met anyone quite so disconcerting as him before.

'I have heard that,' she said lamely, unable to come up with anything smarter. She was longing for him to leave yet wanted him to stay, too. It was dreadfully confusing!

After some more horribly stilted conversation Josh finished his coffee and got up. 'I must be off. I have things to do before we open.'

She followed him to the door, relieved to see the back of him, her confidence returning with his imminent departure.

'Perhaps we could go out somewhere together sometime, when the season is over and we don't have to work evenings?' he said, dark eyes full of promise. 'We could go up the West End, perhaps – see a film, have a meal, anything you like . . .'

She experienced a surge of pleasure and was tempted to say yes. But she was sure Josh Fenner was trouble and she'd had enough of that from one man to last her a lifetime. Anyway, there was Clare to consider.

'Thanks for asking,' Maddie said courteously, 'but I don't think so.'

'Oh.' Josh's expression hardened, eyes becoming icy, mouth turning down. He was obviously not accustomed to rejection. 'Why's that?'

'I have a small daughter to look after,' she said, pleased with herself for standing firm against his powerful charisma. 'Anyway, I'll be working evenings in the winter. I plan to get some bar work, providing I can get a baby sitter for Clare.'

41

'Surely if you organise a sitter for her while you're out working, you can do the same to go out with me?'

'I like to be at home with her when I'm not working.'

'I didn't realise that being a parent meant you had to stop doing everything else,' said Josh with withering sarcasm.

'It doesn't but it is a serious commitment, especially if you're on your own,' she said, ignoring his sarcasm.

'Apparently.'

'Clare has to be my first priority,' Maddie said evenly. 'She's had a massive upheaval and needs the security of knowing I'm there with her as much as I possibly can be, given that I have to earn enough to keep us.'

'Oh, well, you know where I am if you fancy a night out on the town anytime.' Josh's tone was casual but Maddie had a strong suspicion she hadn't heard the last of this. He swaggered out of the door and made his way down the metal steps, turning at the bottom to look up at her. 'Thanks for the coffee – I'll see you around.'

'Yeah, see you,' replied Maddie and went back inside.

Her hands were trembling as she rinsed the coffee cups at the sink. The thought that he might approach her again excited her despite herself. His reputation with women was well known around the fairground and she knew she must steer clear of him. It was very flattering, though, to be fancied by a man like Josh Fenner.

Later that same morning Maddie had another visitor at her new home.

'Tania,' she said, her heart sinking to see Sam's wife at the door because she had treated Maddie with cool indifference ever since she'd been at Fenner's. 'Come in.'

And in swept Tania, to stand with her hands on her hips in Maddie's living room. Her beauty couldn't be denied. She had a rough glamour about her in a tight-fitting cotton top and full skirt with a wide belt that emphasised her tiny waist.

'Coffee?' offered Maddie.

'Not for me, thanks. This isn't a social call.'

'No?'

'No,' she confirmed. 'I'm here to find out what your game is.'

'Game?'

'Don't play dumb with me, lady,' said Tania who saw Maddie as a serious threat to her own selfish plans.

'I'm not.'

'You know bloody well what I mean.'

'I don't – I have no idea what you're talking about.'

'I'm talking about your setting up home here on the fairground,' she said aggressively. 'I've heard that you're planning on staying here when the season's finished an' all.'

'That's right,' said Maddie. 'Why? Do you have a problem with that?'

'I most certainly do and you'll have a problem too if you stay on,' stated Tania categorically.

'Why?'

'Because there are only family and fairpeople living here out of season and you're not one of us,' Tania informed her nastily.

Maddie felt a stab of pain. Although she had received a great deal of kindness here at Fenner's she was well aware of the fact that she was an outsider. The few other families residing in the living-wagons who weren't related to the Fenner's were nevertheless considered part of the clan because they were fair people who'd known the family for years.

But despite all this, Maddie had been touched by a sense of belonging that had eluded her for so long until she'd come to live here. Janice and Sam, and even Hetty, had made her feel as though she might one day truly be at home here. She suspected that she had still to prove herself to them in some way, though. As kind as they were to her, the fact remained that she wasn't one of their own and if she stepped out of line with one family member, they would all close ranks against her.

Tania had made her realise just how tenuous her connection with the Fenners was. But she was determined not to be driven out by someone who had taken against her for no good reason.

'I'm fully aware of that,' Maddie attempted to pacify her.

'Why stay then?'

'I need somewhere to live and Hetty has been good enough to let me rent this caravan.'

'Oh, so it's Hetty is it?' snorted Tania, eyes flashing with suspicion.

Maddie looked at her, not quite sure what she was getting at.

'Who gave you permission to call my mother-in-law by her Christian name?'

'She did actually,' Maddie was able to say with confidence. 'She doesn't like being called Mrs Fenner, as you must know.'

'Mm . . . well,' said Tania, who knew she'd been petty. 'That doesn't alter the fact that you aren't welcome here.'

'That isn't the impression I've been receiving from other members of the family.'

'If you mean that husband of mine,' said her visitor, voice rising and cheeks flushed with temper, 'you don't wanna take any notice of him. Sam's too soft to say what he thinks about anything.'

'I meant Janice actually,' said Maddie evenly.

'Oh.'

'But it could also apply to Sam. He's been good to me since I've been here. He's gone out of his way to make me feel at home.'

'He would . . . the daft bugger!'

43

'Oh . . . now I get it,' said Maddie, light suddenly dawning. 'You don't like it because I invited him into the wagon for a coffee this morning. You think we're . . .'

'Oh, do me a favour, for God's sake!' interrupted Tania. 'I couldn't give a damn what that silly sod does.'

'I haven't any designs on him if that's what you're thinking.' Maddie wondered if the time Sam had spent with her during the course of their work might have been noticed and misunderstood. 'He's only spent so much time with me because I've worked on so many different things since I've been here and he's had to brief me.'

To Maddie's surprise Tania threw back her head and laughed, a rich throaty sound.

'What's so funny?' asked Maddie.

'None of your business,' she replied, dabbing at her heavily made-up eyes with a handkerchief.

'So – is that all you came for, to tell me you don't want me here?' asked Maddie.

'To tell you that you won't be wanted here by anyone out of season, whatever they say to make you think different.' Tania paused thoughtfully. 'And most of all I came to tell you to stay away from my husband,' she said, realising that Maddie had provided her with the perfect cover for the real reason she didn't want her around.

'But I've nowhere else to go,' she said. 'And I've a child to look after.'

'That's your hard luck. You shouldn't have left your husband.'

'And that's none of your business!' said Maddie, angry now.

'Maybe not but it is my business when you set yourself up where you're not wanted and start sniffing around my husband.'

'Oh, don't be so ridiculous!'

'Sling your hook,' said the other woman. 'Go back to your own kind.'

Maddie was hurt and unnerved by this attack. But she was damned if she was going to show it. 'I'm not going anywhere just to please you,' she said. 'The only reason I will leave here is if Hetty or Vic or Sam tells me to go. It's them I work for, not you, and they're very happy to have me stay.'

'I'm one of the family and that means a lot to the Fenners.'

'It doesn't mean you can order me out of my own home, though,' said Maddie. 'I pay rent for this wagon and until Hetty or Vic tells me to leave, then this is my home.' She gave Tania a hard look. 'And that being the case, I'd like you to leave now.'

'Okay, I'll go.'

'Good.'

'But there's one more thing I will say before I do.'

'Go on.'

'You've got two choices. You can either leave here of your own accord and with no hard feelings from the rest of the family, or you can stay on until they force you out with a flea in your ear.'

'They wouldn't do that. They've no reason.'

'They would, you know. I can promise you that,' Tania warned. 'I might only be a Fenner by marriage but I *am* a Fenner. And they look after their own when it comes to the crunch.'

'You're threatening to make trouble for me – is that it?'

'Just explaining the way things are around here. If you stay on, you'll regret it.'

'Then I'll just have to take that chance, won't I?' said Maddie resolutely. 'Because I won't be driven out by you.'

'Don't say I didn't warn you.'

'I won't.'

At the door Tania turned, her expression becoming frighteningly hard. 'And if you go running with tales to Janice about this conversation, you'll find out exactly what I mean about the Fenner family looking after their own.'

'Oh, get out,' said Maddie, slamming the door behind her.

But she was shivering despite the warm sunshine flooding into the kitchen and dappling the Formica worktops with patches of light. Maddie knew she had made a dangerous enemy in Tania. But why? What reason could Tania possibly have for hating her and wanting to get rid of her?

After further thought, Maddie's original theory didn't seem probable. Tania wouldn't feel threatened by Maddie as a rival for Sam's affections, not when you considered her attitude towards him. Thinking back over the conversation, it had almost been as though Maddie had put the words into Tania's mouth.

So what was the real reason Tania Fenner didn't want Maddie around? After pondering over it some more she was still none the wiser. But she was certain of one thing. She wasn't going to be driven out of her home and a job she enjoyed just because some neurotic woman had threatened her!

Chapter Four

'Ooh, look at that, Mum,' gasped Clare, breathless with awe as a glorious explosion of colour lit the night sky above the illuminated fairground.

'Yes – isn't it lovely?' enthused Maddie, smiling at her daughter who was sitting on Sam's shoulders so that she could get a better view of the firework display.

'Cor, what about that one then?' Barney was on his father's shoulders and referring to a rocket whooshing into the air and exploding loudly in a cloud of orange smoke.

'The other one was better,' declared Clare. 'It was prettier and not so loud.'

'Loud ones are great,' he retorted. 'Bangers are best.'

'I don't like bangers.'

'Girls are scared of bangers,' announced the little boy authoritatively.

'I'm not scared of them,' she protested. 'I just don't like them.'

'You *are* scared.'

'No, I'm not.'

'Yes, you are.'

'Now then, you two, that's enough squabbling,' said Chas who was a short man, not much taller than Janice, but strong and sturdy with warm smiling eyes that matched his personality, though his tar-black hair and swarthy complexion gave him a rough look. 'I thought you were supposed to be best friends?'

'It's traditional for best friends to squabble now and then,' said Janice, who was standing between Chas and Maddie. 'They love each other to bits really, though, don't you, kids?'

'S'pose so,' said Clare.

'Love's soppy,' pronounced Barney.

'Rubbish,' said Chas. 'I love your mum and I'm not soppy.'

Everyone laughed. A party atmosphere prevailed on this, the last night of the season. It was traditional, apparently, for Fenner's to make a special occasion of the closing night with rides and sideshows at reduced prices, additional stalls and live entertainment. This evening the crowds had been entertained by a high-wire act and a magician; the final event was always a firework display sponsored by

46

a well-known firework manufacturer.

There had been stalls selling toys, home-made sweets, jewellery and novelties. Maddie had been busy for much of the day making gingerbread and baking potatoes in their jackets which had gone down a storm with the punters.

The occasion was tinged with sadness for her because the end of the season meant a change of lifestyle – until next spring. She'd got used to the hectic pace of fairground life and was going to miss the music, the lights, and the constant buzz of noise and excitement.

Time had passed so quickly it was hard to believe that the summer was over. Maddie had never worked harder or felt healthier and more alive. Of particular value to her was her friendship with Janice which got better all the time. The fact that they were both single mums gave them a special bond, even though Janice had plenty of support from Chas. They helped each other with child minding and shopping, ate meals together and discussed everything under the sun. They even borrowed each other's clothes. Janice was more like a sister to Maddie than any of her biological sisters had ever been.

Clare had thrived in the sociable atmosphere and enjoyed the summer holidays, playing with Barney and the other children while Maddie was working. The teenage daughter of the family who ran the Coconut Shies looked after the younger ones and saw that they came to no harm. People helped each other here – it was that sort of a community. If Maddie was sometimes aware that she was an outsider, she was certain that Clare had no such feelings. It was as though she had never lived anywhere else.

There had been no more threats from Tania so Maddie had put the unpleasant incident to the back of her mind. Being busy had helped her to forget that she had an enemy, though Tania's hostility – which manifested itself in a deliberate lack of interest – was always present.

At this particular moment, however, Maddie was thinking ahead to the winter and how different everything would be with the fair closed. It would seem strange without the crowds; and without Hetty and Vic, who were moving into their house for the winter. She'd heard that they came to the park very often but it wouldn't be the same without them at the centre of the community in their living-wagon.

Not being able to afford to live without an income, Maddie had already found winter employment, and was starting work as a barmaid at the Fiddler's Inn in Richmond next week. She would be working the lunchtime shift and had also agreed to do some evenings on condition that she didn't have to go on duty until she'd got her daughter ready for bed. Janice had agreed to have Clare in with her and Barney on the evenings that Maddie was working.

But now the fireworks had come to the end with a splendid tableau.

FENNER'S FUN PARK – 1960 lit the sky in a dazzling display. There was a roar of applause from the crowds and the children were almost beside themselves with excitement.

'You didn't enjoy that, did you, kids?' teased Chas as he and Sam lifted them to the ground.

'We did,' came their joint reply.

'Is there anything else to come?' asked Barney, who was in the mood for the celebrations to go on all night.

'No, that's it,' said his mother.

'Oh,' he said, downcast. 'I want something else to happen.'

'And it will, son,' said Janice with a smile in her voice. 'It begins with B.'

'B for Bumper Cars?' he said.

'No, B for bed,' corrected his mother, laughing.

'For you too, Clare,' added Maddie, resting her hands on her daughter's shoulders.

Both children took a dim view of this and protested loudly.

They found a powerful ally in Chas. 'You can't put 'em to bed yet,' he said looking from Janice to Maddie. 'They'd never get to sleep after all that excitement. They need time to wind down.'

'Good old Dad,' cheered Barney.

'Hurray for Uncle Chas,' added Clare who had become a very outgoing child under the influence of fairground life.

'We're all gonna have a drink before we tackle the clearing up,' said Chas.

'Can I have a Coca-Cola, please?' asked Barney.

'I'm talking about the adults.' Chas looked down at the children with a deadpan expression. 'You two don't want any pop, do you?'

'We do,' said Barney.

'No, you don't.' Chas was deadly serious. 'I heard you couldn't stand the stuff.'

The children stared at him warily, Clare looking so fair against Barney's dark looks.

'We do like pop,' she said solemnly.

Chas roared with laughter, his white teeth flashing against his dusky skin in the neon lighting. ''Course you do. I never knew a kid who didn't.' He tousled both the children's hair. 'I really had you worried for a minute, didn't I?'

'Nah, I knew you were only teasing,' said Barney who adored his fun-loving father.

'We wouldn't leave you out,' said Chas.

'I'd like to see you try and leave Barney out of anything,' said Janice. 'Your son takes after you ... he's got more front than Windsor Castle.'

The children thought this was hilarious and joined in the laughter.

'Come on, Chas, let's go and get some drinks,' said Sam as there was a general drift towards the beer garden which had a small covered area for wet days and chilly evenings like this. 'Or we'll never get served.'

Having taken the order for drinks, the two men departed and the children went off with their friends. There were people everywhere, standing around in groups chatting; punters, fairground staff, members of the Fenner family. Glancing around, Maddie spotted Vic, Hetty and Tania talking to the trapeze artiste, his lavish sequined costume now covered by a coat. Eric and his mother were chatting to the magician, an elderly trouper of the old school who'd held the audience spellbound by making doves vanish then reappear under his top hat. Josh was in conversation with Fenner's senior engineer on the edge of the crowd.

The air was spiced with the chill of autumn, earthy dampness rising as the evening advanced, the air tinged with smoke. People had dispensed with summer clothes in favour of sweaters and coats. Maddie was wearing a duffel coat over her jeans.

'Chas is a quite a comic, isn't he?' she remarked to Janice.

'A complete nutcase,' said her friend. 'He hasn't got a serious bone in his body.'

'You know that isn't true,' said Maddie in friendly admonition. 'He obviously takes his responsibilities towards Barney very seriously.'

'Yeah, I s'pose so.'

Maddie had taken an instant liking to Chas when he arrived back at Fenner's at the wheel of an enormous truck with his Gallopers dismantled and loaded on to it, his living-wagon attached to the back. 'Clare thinks he's wonderful,' she added.

'I told you, he's a wow with all the girls.'

'You seem to enjoy having him around, anyway,' she said because Janice and Chas really sparked each other off. They were always joshing but were obviously devoted.

'I'm making the most of it. He's off again soon.'

'Oh . . . but the season's finished?' said Maddie, puzzled.

'For us – yeah. But there are quite a few short-term fairs around in October, in various parts of the country,' Janice explained. 'He's going up north next week.'

'The kids'll miss him.'

'Me an' all.'

'Do you ever fancy going with him when he goes travelling?'

'No, not really. Anyway, I wouldn't wanna cramp his style.'

'I don't think you would be,' said Maddie. 'He's obviously nuts about you.'

'I've told you – Chas is the world's biggest flirt. He could win prizes with his chat-up lines.'

'It doesn't mean anything.'

'Maybe not – but who knows what he gets up to when he's away?'

'I don't think you really believe he gets up to anything you wouldn't approve of,' insisted Maddie. 'I've never seen a couple so good together as you two are.'

'You haven't heard us quarrelling.'

'I have,' grinned Maddie. 'I live next door, remember.'

'So you know that it isn't all sweetness and light.'

'What relationship is?' asked Maddie. 'But I still say you're right for each other. You're mad not to marry him.'

'As I've told you before – when he's ready to settle down and live in one place and behave like a grown up, then I'll marry him.'

'But don't travelling showpeople do it all their lives – taking their wife and children with them?' queried Maddie, who had learned about the various different types of fairground life since she'd been at Fenner's. 'I get the impression that travelling around is their way of life and they wouldn't be happy doing anything else.'

'That's probably true of some of them,' said Janice. 'But it isn't as though Chas would have to come out of the fair business just because he stopped travelling. He could stay here at Fenners running his Gallopers.'

'Mmm.'

'He could even join the firm if he wanted to,' Janice continued. 'Mum and Dad think the world of him and would love to have him in the company.'

'But he doesn't want that?'

'No.'

'It's difficult when you both want different things.'

Janice nodded. 'If he were to stay here on a permanent basis, he could still take the Gallopers off every now and again to the fairs that he particularly enjoys. I wouldn't mind that. But as it is now he's away for most of the season.'

'And you'd rather stay here?'

'Yeah – 'specially now that Barney's started school,' she said. 'I don't want his education ruined 'cause his parents are on the road for months on end. I know it works for some people but I don't want that for him. So I don't see any point in us getting married if Chas's away for most of the time. I'd rather leave things as they are.'

'I can see your point.'

'And Chas is a crafty bugger. If I were to marry him his way, he'd have the best of both worlds,' said Janice. 'He'd have all the comforts of married life and still be able to live the bachelor life while he's away. Out every night after work, chatting up any girl he fancies . . .'

'You don't know that.'

'No – but if he really loves me, he'll stay home with me and Barney.'

'It works both ways,' Maddie pointed out. 'He probably thinks that if you really love him, you'll do things his way.'

'Yeah.' Janice grinned. 'We're as stubborn as each other when it comes to it so it's probably just as well we're apart most of the time. At least it stops us from killing each other.'

Maddie shivered. Janice was only joking but those words reminded her of how close Dave had come to doing just that to her. She could still see his face when he was hitting her: features twisted with rage. She could feel his rough hands on her; smell his nicotine breath. Then the horror of what had come after, because violence always excited him sexually. She shivered at the thought of what he'd do to her if he ever found her again. This didn't come to mind so often now but when it did, the terror was all-consuming.

'What's up?' enquired Janice. 'You've gone all quiet.'

'Nothing.'

'It's that husband of yours, I bet.'

'You're right.'

'Forget him,' said Janice. 'He's bad news and past history.'

'I know,' said Maddie, but it wasn't easy to forget someone as menacing as Dave.

Sam and Chas returned with a tray of drinks and some crisps for the children who appeared from nowhere at exactly the right moment. The conversation was soon light and easy and Maddie was able to cast out her dark thoughts.

'Where's your other half, Sam?' asked Chas casually, taking the head off his pint.

'Around somewhere,' he said, glancing around. 'She was talking to the trapeze artiste the last time I saw her.' He paused, nodding towards the crowd. 'She's over there, with Josh.'

It was the sort of social gathering where people moved around and mingled. The children disappeared again, Janice wandered off to talk to a distant male cousin, Sam went to join Josh and Tania, and Chas turned away to chat to some men Maddie didn't know, leaving her alone. She wasn't on her own for long, however.

'I've been meaning to have a word with you, dear,' said Sybil, still in her fortune teller's costume, hair hidden beneath her turban, a coat over her long dress. Her make-up was copious – lipstick a bright scarlet shade and her cheeks liberally daubed with rouge. In ordinary clothes she was nothing special to look at – plumpish with straight brown hair and a freckled face. Maddie had barely recognised her the first time she'd seen her out of costume.

'Oh?'

'I heard you'd got a job off the site for the winter and I just wanted to say that if ever you're stuck for a baby sitter while you're working, you can always call on me,' said Sybil. 'I know you're fixed up with Janice but if she can't do it at any time, you know where I am.'

'Why – thank you very much.' Maddie was really touched. 'That *is* kind of you . . . I'll bear it in mind.'

'We all have to do what we can to help each other, and you do

51

your share,' Sybil said. 'I'm very grateful to you for being so patient with my Eric. I know he can try the patience of a saint.'

'He doesn't try my patience,' said Maddie and meant it. 'I think he's rather sweet actually.' She recalled the number of odd jobs he'd done for her in her wagon since they'd first struck up a friendship that time he'd helped polish the wood panelling. 'And a very useful man to know.'

'Eric's very good with his hands.'

'I always get the impression there's more to him than meets the eye.'

'What . . . up top, you mean?'

'Yeah,' said Maddie thoughtfully. 'Some of the things he comes out with are quite surprising.'

'Is that why you've offered to teach him to read?'

'It was only a casual suggestion,' said Maddie, who'd mentioned it one day when she'd been chatting to him. 'I wasn't being all that serious.'

'He seems to have taken it seriously.'

'That's good,' said Maddie. 'I only have the most basic education myself but I'm willing to help him if he wants me to. Clare's learning to read and I'm helping her. I thought perhaps Eric and I could give it a try with some of her easy reading books – when the season has finished and there's more time.'

'It would be wonderful for him if you could get him to understand.'

'Even if he just grasps the basics, it could change his life.'

'Not half!'

'But I expect you tried everything when he was a kid, didn't you?'

Sybil shook her head. 'I'm ashamed to say that I didn't,' she said, looking sheepish. 'I thought if the teachers couldn't make him get the hang of it, then what chance did I stand, a woman without much of an education herself? I suppose I thought he was a hopeless case so far as anything academic was concerned.'

'Poor Eric.'

'Yeah . . . he hated school to the point where it made him ill,' said Sybil sadly. 'He used to be physically sick every morning on school days. They said he was mentally retarded. He'd always been a bit slow but I didn't think he was that bad. Anyway, the kids laughed at him and the teachers despaired of him. It was torture for the poor boy. He was always running out of school at playtime and coming home to me in tears.'

'He told me he didn't like school – I didn't realise it was that bad.'

'I couldn't bear to see him in such a miserable state,' said Sybil. 'So I let him stay home . . . fobbed the authorities off by making out he was ill. When the war came there was a lot of disruption and it was easier to get away with something like that. People thought you'd been killed or evacuated if you didn't turn up somewhere.'

'So, he didn't go to school at all then?' said Maddie.

'Only for the first couple o' years,' Sybil admitted. 'I suppose I should have been firmer with him and made him go but it was breaking his heart – and mine. And he wasn't learning anything except how to be a nervous wreck.' She paused thoughtfully. 'Maybe if his dad had lived we could have got something done for him . . . but he was killed in action in France in 1940 – when Eric was eight.'

'That's a shame.'

'You wouldn't get away with keeping a kid off from school these days, o' course,' continued Sybil sagely. 'Too many officials snooping around checking up on you.'

'Yeah.'

'Anyway, dear, if you do manage to find the time to spend with him on this reading lark, I'd be ever so grateful, and I'll do anything I can to help him at home,' she promised. 'I know he's a grown man but he's still my boy and I want the best for him.'

Maddie grinned. 'Perhaps you can have a look in your crystal ball to see whether or not it's going to work.'

Sybil frowned. If she ever did see anything other than her own reflection in her crystal ball she'd probably die of shock. She respected the fact that some people had a genuine gift but she herself had never had a psychic experience in her life. Strictly speaking that made her a fraud but she considered what she did to be entertainment like everything else on the fair. And it wasn't as though she did serious consultations. She simply told people what they wanted to hear while they were out enjoying themselves at the fair: that they were going to find romance, or have some happy experience. She was always positive, always sent them away smiling. That was the whole point.

Like her brother Vic, Sybil had been brought up to fairground life and had done various jobs on the park. It was only when the fair reopened after the war that she'd decided to set up as a fortune teller because she thought she was old enough to be convincing by then, and it appealed to her theatrical inclinations. No one was ever likely seriously to challenge her supposed powers because everybody recognised what she did as just a bit of fun. Like the horoscopes in the magazines, the things she forecast could apply to anyone.

'Not a good idea,' she said, making a joke of it. 'If I saw that it wasn't gonna work, you might not want to try.'

'That's true enough,' agreed Maddie. 'Anyway, once I get settled into a routine with the new job, I'll arrange something definite with Eric. We'll have to fit it in between my shifts.'

'And don't forget to let me know if you're stuck for someone to look after young Clare at any time. Me and Eric usually go out for a couple of drinks on a Saturday night but I'll give it a miss if you need me.'

'Thanks, Sybil.'

The evening's activities were drawing to a close. Last orders had been called at the bar and the crowds were dispersing. While waiting for the public to clear the grounds, members of the Fenner family were beginning to gather near the beer garden, finishing their drinks and chatting. Sybil and Maddie went to join them.

'Well, I reckon that's a good note on which to close the season,' said Sam.

There was a general murmur of agreement.

'I suppose we'd better get the clearing up organised,' said Hetty.

'I think that's our cue to go and put the kids to bed, Maddie?' laughed Janice.

'Crafty cow,' said Chas, teasing her.

'I don't blame her,' smiled Tania, unusually jovial.

Josh joined the party and astonished Maddie by making a great fuss of her.

'Well, how's the best-looking woman this side of the river?' he asked, slipping a casual arm around her shoulders.

'If I see her, I'll ask her,' she answered, causing a ripple of laughter.

'Ooh, she's sharp tonight,' he grinned, removing his arm and turning to look at her without quite meeting her eyes. 'But seriously, now that the season's finally over and we're not slaves to the job every night of the week, how about us having a night on the town together?'

The others looked on with an air of detached interest.

Having already made her feelings clear on this subject to Josh some time ago, Maddie was surprised that he'd brought it up again so publicly.

'Don't be coy,' he said when she didn't reply. 'You'll have a good time, I can absolutely guarantee it.'

'Go on – say yes to him, Maddie,' urged Janice delightedly. 'Go out with him and sting him rotten! He's a proper old skinflint. He stashes all his dough away somewhere.'

There was a roar of lighthearted agreement.

'The moths lay their eggs in his wallet,' said Chas.

'Stop trying to put the girl off,' said Josh, seeming to take it all in good part. 'Anyway what's wrong with saving for the future?'

'Nothing, son,' declared Hetty, who wouldn't hear a word against Josh, even in jest. 'Take no notice of 'em.'

'How about it then, Maddie?' he urged.

She was feeling most uncomfortable. She had a horrible suspicion that this whole thing was being staged by Josh for the benefit of the family, and had nothing to do with her at all except that she just happened to be the only young, unattached female in the company.

54

'Stop embarrassing the girl,' admonished Sam who could see that Maddie was uneasy.

'She's not embarrassed, are you, babe?' said Josh, slipping his arm around her again.

''Course I'm not.' Maddie was in a very awkward position. To reject him out of hand in front of everybody would be embarrassing for them all – and he knew that.

'I'll look after Clare if you wanna have a night out,' offered Sybil.

'Thanks for the invitation, Josh,' she said politely, forcing a smile. 'But I'll have to see how I get on with the new job.' She was careful not to commit herself or appear rude in front of the others. 'I'll have to concentrate on that for a while – see how much free time I get.'

'That's right, Maddie,' said Sam jokingly. 'Keep him guessing.'

'I'm not put off that easy,' said his brother. 'I'll keep on at you until you do say yes.'

'Make sure you give him a run for his money, Maddie,' laughed Sam.

She was saved from further comment because the group began to disperse. Sam headed for the office to check that all was secure there, having deposited the takings in the underground safe just before the firework display. Hetty and Vic went to organise the clearing up with Sybil, Eric and Chas, though some of the staff had already started sweeping the grounds.

Maddie and Janice found the children and headed for the living-wagons.

'Can you look after Clare for a couple of minutes, Janice?' asked Maddie on impulse. 'There's something I have to do.'

'Okay.'

Hurrying back into the fairground, she found Josh near the Scenic Railway, talking to some male employees.

'Can I have a word in private?'

'Sure.' He moved away from the men. 'What's on your mind?'

Maddie was not a strident woman. But being a single parent had forced her to be more assertive than she used to be, and she didn't like being taken for a fool. 'Don't you *ever* use me like that again,' she said coldly.

'I don't know what you're talking about,' he said innocently, as though he wasn't in the least bit concerned.

'What was it all in aid of anyway?' she wanted to know. 'That nonsense just now.'

'It was just a bit of fun.'

'There was more to it than that.'

'I honestly don't know what you mean.'

'Oh, yes, you do,' she said. 'I don't know what your game is but I do know that that performance was put on for the benefit of your family.'

'All I did was ask you to go out with me sometime.'

'No – what you did was make sure the family heard you ask me to go out with you,' she said, tears of humiliation prickling beneath her lids. 'I went along with it so as not to embarrass them but don't you ever put me in a position like that again.'

Without waiting for him to reply, she turned and marched towards her caravan. Was his male ego so inflated that he had to illustrate his ability to date women in public? she asked herself. But if that was the reason for the curious incident, why would he risk having her turn him down in front of everyone, as she had done? He hadn't seemed in the least bothered by that.

There was more to this than mere vanity. She sensed that Josh didn't really fancy her at all, but was merely pretending to. He was trying to use her for reasons of his own, she was certain of it. It was all very sinister and Maddie didn't like it one bit!

Chapter Five

The cheerful clamour of fairgoers was replaced by the resonant tap of hammer on nail, and the clink and grind of metal as the rides and sideshows were overhauled. The smell of fresh paint was a noticeable successor to the pungent whiff of hamburgers and hotdogs as artwork and signwriting were meticulously repainted on some of the rides. The structures looked forlorn, Maddie thought, without the cars and carriages which were stored away for winter – metal shutters pulled down on the sideshows.

By the time the russet blaze of autumn on the riverside had darkened into winter and chilling November mists hung over everything, she had settled into her job at the Fiddler's Inn. It was an olde worlde pub run by a middle-aged couple called Pat and Bob Robinson with whom she got on very well. The pub had once been a coaching inn and the decor reflected this with abundant horse brasses, dark wood finishings and faded sepia photographs of the premises in earlier times adorning the walls. Since it was in the centre of the town, there was a bustling atmosphere which Maddie enjoyed, even though it didn't have quite the same vibrancy as a funfair.

As well as her work at the pub, she also did a few hours a week in the office at Fenner's. Although the business wasn't trading, the maintenance work created paperwork, with materials to be ordered and tradesmen's wages to be paid. There was also a certain amount of administration concerning the new season next year as promotions were planned and new attractions considered by the family.

Maddie was always looking for ways to repay the Fenner family for saving her from destitution, and was only too happy to make time to give Eric a reading lesson each week. These took place in her wagon in the late afternoon on her off-duty evenings. To make the lesson more palatable, Maddie made a social occasion of it by inviting Eric to join her and Clare for tea afterwards. His learning to read helped Clare too and the whole thing was a great success.

Because he had been written off as an idiot all his life, Eric had accepted this as fact and felt no embarrassment about having reading lessons at such a late stage. At the beginning, Maddie despaired of him as a pupil. But with a little time and a great deal of patience he gradually began to grasp a few easy words. The real breakthrough came when he became able to decipher simple words in the newspaper. He came on in leaps and bounds after that because, contrary to popular belief, Eric had a hunger for knowledge about the world around him which came from watching television, Maddie suspected.

The dark winter nights in the wagon – when she wasn't on duty at the pub – were blissful. No matter how bitter the weather or how loudly the winds howled outside, she and Clare were cosily ensconced by the fire with the curtains drawn and the calor gas lights casting a pale glow over everything. Maddie even managed to buy a secondhand television set out of her wages.

Her traumatic life with Dave gradually began to recede into the past. Fear of his finding her became less of a gnawing worry and more a hovering shadow – constant but peripheral – though a sudden unfamiliar noise in the night could still give her palpitations.

Her friendship with Janice continued to flourish, even when Chas returned from his travels and spent a lot of time in Janice's home. He was such a friendly man, Maddie never felt as if she was intruding.

Josh made no further approach to her and she put the incident at the firework party out of her mind. Until he came into the Fiddler's Inn one evening in November about half an hour from closing time . . .

'We don't usually see you in here,' Maddie remarked as she served him.

'No. Drinking on my own doorstep isn't normally my style.'

'Can't let yourself go if you're too close to the family, eh?' she said lightly.

'Something like that.'

'So, what brings you here tonight then?' she enquired pleasantly because it was her job to be sociable to the customers.

'I was practically passing the door on my way home and thought you might like a lift,' he explained casually.

'Really?' she said, unable to conceal her doubts because he wasn't the sort of man you normally associated with unselfish behaviour, even in such a small measure as this.

'Don't worry. You'll be quite safe,' he assured her with a knowing look. 'I'm not planning on making a detour down any dark lanes.'

'In that case, thank you very much,' Maddie accepted graciously.

On the way home they talked generally and he told her he'd been to see some mates in Hammersmith. Inevitably they got on to the subject of the family and he said he thought she must have the patience of a saint to spend time teaching Eric whose slowness drove him round the bend. Maddie said she didn't find him a problem, all the while wondering what Josh was up to and half expecting him to make some sort of a move on her.

58

When they got home, he helped her to get the sleeping Clare from Janice's wagon into her own bed next door, something that Janice or Chas and Maddie normally did between them. He then accepted her invitation to stay for coffee. They had a superficial conversation and he left without making a pass.

The same thing occurred on several other occasions over the next few weeks. Josh would appear at the pub just before closing time with the offer of a lift home. *And nothing ever happened between them.* Either the warning she'd given him on the night of the firework party had hit home, or he had lost any interest he might have had in her in that direction. Neither of these explanations satisfied Maddie, though, because she judged Josh Fenner to be more complex than that, and still suspected that there was a lot more going on behind those sultry dark eyes than anyone knew about.

Because he was Janice's brother Maddie didn't feel able to discuss the situation with her. Naturally, Janice had wanted to know if there had been any developments after Josh's public display of interest, but Maddie just laughed it off – said they were just friends. As solid as their friendship was, she got the distinct impression that she would be shown blood was indeed thicker than water if she spoke in a derogatory manner about Josh.

So she let things go on as they were, hoping – very much against her better judgement – that he might eventually show some genuine interest in her. Despite all her doubts about him, Josh was the most exciting man she had ever met. He was entertaining company, too, when he wasn't showing off.

Christmas with Dave had always been a particularly harrowing time for Maddie because his temper had been made even more vicious by booze and an increased amount of time at home.

This year it was different. No longer at the mercy of his moods, Maddie was able to anticipate the festive season with pleasure and share her daughter's excitement during the run-up, when she and Barney became almost manic with eagerness.

Christmas morning was magic. Clare and Maddie went next door to Janice's so that the children could open their presents together. It brought tears to Maddie's eyes to see her daughter so happy, and to feel that they were both among friends.

Maddie and Janice cooked Christmas dinner together in Janice's wagon where it was eaten with much joviality, Chas's lively banter adding to the fun. In the late afternoon Maddie and Clare prepared to depart because Janice, Chas and Barney were going to Hetty and Vic's for a get-together.

'Why don't the two of you come with us?' suggested Janice.

'I wouldn't dream of intruding on a family party,' said Maddie tactfully.

'Don't be daft,' said Janice. 'Mum and Dad would love to have you.'

But Maddie didn't want to overstep the mark. No matter how kind Hetty and Vic were to her, she wasn't one of their own. She couldn't help feeling a pang of envy for Janice being part of such a close-knit family, and was immediately ashamed because the Fenners – excluding Josh and Tania – had given her more than anyone could expect in the way of hospitality and friendliness.

'Thanks for asking, but no . . .'

'Do come, Maddie.'

'I'd feel awkward – not being family.'

'There'll be other people there besides family,' said Janice.

And all long-established fairpeople, thought Maddie, which was almost as good as a blood tie. But she said, 'You go and enjoy yourselves. Clare and I will be fine, honestly. We'll stuff ourselves with sweets and have another drool over our presents . . . watch some TV maybe.'

'But you'll be here all on your own at the park,' Janice pointed out. 'Everyone will be having a knees up at Mum's place.'

'I wanna go with Barney,' said Clare, who had been listening to all this.

'The kids will have a great time,' said Janice, looking from Clare to Maddie. 'Christmas night is the one night of the year we break all the rules and let Barney stay up till he drops.'

'Please come with us, Auntie Maddie,' begged Barney.

'Not this time, Barney,' she said firmly. 'We'll see you tomorrow.'

Clare was still a bit down in the mouth when they went next door to their own wagon. But a forage through her Christmas stocking and another look at her presents soon cheered her up. Maddie gave the fire a good stir with the poker so that a warm orange glow flickered over the room that was prettily decked with home-made paper chains, a small Christmas tree shining in the window.

Maddie was helping Clare to dress the doll she'd given her for Christmas when the sound of Marlon barking broke into the silence outside, indicating a visitor – or intruder – to the site. She could feel the deafening thud of her own heart as a car door slammed out there.

Who would want to visit a closed fairground on the evening of Christmas Day? she asked herself. Her imagination ran wild with the thought that Dave had somehow tracked her down.

Peering nervously through the curtains into the darkness, she could just make out a blue Ford Zephyr parked outside in the dim glow of the fairground lighting.

'Josh!' Hot relief surged through her as she opened the door to a rush of cold air. 'You nearly gave me a heart attack.'

'Sorry.'

'What brings here?' she said. 'I thought you were at the party.'

'Mum sent me to get you,' he explained, looking devastating in a dark overcoat with a white shirt showing at the neck.

'But . . .'

'No buts. I was told not to take no for an answer,' he explained. 'Mum was expecting you to arrive with Chas and Janice. She was quite upset when you didn't turn up.'

'I wasn't invited.'

'She just assumed you'd take the invitation for granted.'

'But it's a family gathering,' Maddie reminded him.

'Family and friends,' he corrected in a jovial manner. 'So go and get your coat – and your daughter's. My life won't be worth living if I go back without you.'

'I . . .'

'Look – Mum won't enjoy herself knowing that you're here on your own. I don't think you want to be responsible for spoiling her Christmas, do you?' He looked down at Clare who had already put on her coat and was standing by the door with the fur-trimmed hood pulled up over her head. 'Your daughter's all ready, so now we're just waiting for you. Come on . . . chop-chop. Put a warm coat on, though – it's brass monkey weather outside.'

More deeply touched than he could possibly imagine by this gesture of friendship from his mother, Maddie went to get her coat.

It was a lively party with food and drink in abundance and dancing to the latest hits on the record player in Hetty's front room. The furniture was pushed to the side of the room and people were dancing rock 'n' roll style. Maddie danced with Chas and Sam, and even Janice. When the mood changed to a more smoochy rhythm with Elvis Presley's 'It's Now Or Never', Josh swept her into his arms and held her close. He'd been making a fuss of her all evening.

She couldn't remember ever enjoying a party more than this one, and Clare was having a wonderful time.

'What were you thinking of, staying in your wagon on your own?' admonished Hetty when Maddie was in the dining room helping herself to some cold turkey and pickles.

'I didn't realise I was invited to the party,' she explained.

''Course you were invited,' said Hetty. 'It goes without saying.'

'Thank you,' said Maddie gratefully, warming even more to her.

The party went on until after midnight. Josh insisted on driving Maddie and Clare home because Chas was giving some other people a lift in his car. Clare fell asleep on the way and Josh carried her inside. It was after she'd settled Clare into bed that Maddie received a late Christmas present. Josh gave her a goodnight kiss at the door which both pleased and startled her.

The man could be as charming as he was hateful but when he

behaved as he had tonight, he was irresistible. She lay awake for a long time looking back on a truly wonderful Christmas Day. Instead of thinking of Josh with doubt and suspicion, her thoughts were soft and full of hope. He really was the sexiest man!

Lying in bed beside her sleeping husband, Tania reviewed the day with a great deal less pleasure. In fact, Christmas was a complete waste of time so far as she was concerned. It was all right for people who wanted to be up to their ears in turkey fat and stuffing all morning, but that held about as much appeal for Tania as being marooned on a desert island with only Sam for company.

The Christmas night party had been the only bit of light relief and that had been completely ruined for Tania by Maddie Brown who seemed determined to worm her way into the Fenner family despite Tania's warning. Josh had his own reasons for paying the stupid woman so much attention but Tania didn't like the way that was going at all.

And she wasn't going to put up with it! The time had come for Maddie Brown to go. She'd been given the chance to leave of her own accord and she hadn't taken it. So now she would be given no choice in the matter. Tania's heart beat faster with malicious excitement as she worked out her plan.

The Christmas spirit seemed to be continuing on into Boxing Day and spreading through the family, Maddie thought, when Tania knocked on her door the next morning to invite her and Clare to a pre-lunch get-together.

'It's just an impromptu affair . . . a few drinks and some nibbles,' she explained, smiling. 'Just come as you are. No need to dress up.'

'I'd love to come, thank you, Tania,' said Maddie, warmed by this gesture of friendship from a woman she'd previously regarded as an enemy. This really was proving to be the season of goodwill!

All the family were there despite such short notice, even Hetty and Vic who'd been notified from the telephone in the office.

'This has been the best Christmas I've ever had,' Maddie told Sam.

'Really?'

'Yeah, I can't remember ever enjoying myself as much.'

'I'm so pleased,' he said because he'd grown genuinely fond of Maddie. She'd been in such a bad state when she'd first come to Fenner's, and it was good to see her so healthy and enjoying life. 'And what about Clare?'

'Need you ask?'

'No, not really.'

Being a lunchtime occasion, the party was much less exuberant than the affair of the previous night. No music or dancing; just small-talk and drinks and little dishes of crisps and nuts. Maddie was in terrific form, positively bubbling as she mingled with the other guests. Bonhomie seemed to surround her in great warm clouds. Josh told her she looked lovely, Janice said that having Maddie and Clare around was the best thing that had happened to her in ages, and Sybil said it was a miracle what Maddie had done with Eric. She added jokingly that his burgeoning reading skills were a mixed blessing because he commandeered the newspaper and drove her mad asking her what the words meant that he hadn't yet mastered.

The weather was cold but bright and the children were in and out of the wagon, especially Barney who wouldn't be separated from the new bicycle he'd had for Christmas; he was tearing about all over the park on it.

'What have you called the dolly you had from Santa, Clare?' asked Sam, smiling at the child he had grown to regard with affection.

'Mary.'

'That's a pretty name.'

'She can cry,' said the little girl, pressing the doll's tummy so that it made a wailing noise. 'And wet her nappy.'

'That's amazing.'

'Yes, it is.'

Sam was so busy paying attention to Clare, and the other guests were so involved in enjoying themselves, that nobody noticed Tania slip out of the wagon. When she returned a few minutes later she hadn't been missed.

Maddie was at home getting the tea ready that afternoon when there was a knock at the door. To her amazement she found herself facing a furious Tania with Sam by her side.

'You've taken it,' she shrieked at Maddie. 'You've stolen my gold bracelet!'

'Calm down, Tania,' admonished Sam. 'You don't know that Maddie's taken it.'

'I do know,' she sobbed, blue eyes hot with tears. 'Who else could it be? No one from the family would take it and she was the only outsider at the party this morning. It was definitely in our wagon just before people started arriving – on the shelf in the kitchen. I took it off while I was preparing the food and forgot to put it back on in all the excitement of everyone arriving. When I looked for it this afternoon it wasn't there.'

'I've taken nothing of yours,' denied Maddie, hurt by the accusation.

Tania looked at Sam. 'Surely you don't believe her?'

'Perhaps you've just mislaid it, dear,' he said, devastated by this development because he had trusted Maddie completely. 'Maddie wouldn't do a thing like that.'

'I don't even wear jewellery,' she said in a strangled voice. 'And I certainly wouldn't want someone else's.'

'Don't come the innocent with us,' shouted Tania. 'You stole it to sell it. It would fetch a good price.'

'I have never stolen anything in my life,' said Maddie, face burning and a terrible sick feeling growing in the pit of her stomach as the seriousness of this accusation struck home. She looked at Sam. 'You must believe me.'

'I'm sure Maddie's telling the truth,' he said to his wife. 'Let's go back indoors and have another look for it.'

'It's her wagon we should be looking in, not ours,' declared Tania.

'Be my guest,' invited Maddie, eager to prove her innocence. 'Come on in . . . search the place. I've nothing to hide.'

'That isn't necessary . . .' began Sam.

'It bloody well is,' said Tania, stamping through the front door which led into Maddie's kitchen. 'I want my bracelet back and this is where we'll find it.'

Attracted by the sound of raised voices, Clare, who had been watching an ice skating show on television, hurried to her mother's side. 'What's happening, Mummy?' she asked, sounding frightened.

'Nothing for you to worry about, love,' she said, slipping a reassuring arm around the child's shoulders. 'You go back into the living room and watch the TV.'

'Tania, this really isn't on,' said Sam as his wife followed the child into the other room and began looking under cushions on the sofa and pulling out the sideboard drawers.

'No, let her carry on, Sam,' said Maddie. 'If this is what it takes to clear my name, I'd rather she did.' Maddie wanted there to be no lingering doubts about her innocence. She turned to Tania. 'Feel free to go through my things . . . all my clothes, everything. Then perhaps you'll be satisfied.'

Maddie and Sam followed Tania along the passageway to the bedroom area where she went through Maddie's wardrobe, Sam apologising all the while for this gross intrusion of privacy.

'Trust you to take her side,' said Tania, scowling fiercely at him. 'You've never had the guts to speak out.'

'Happy now?' said Maddie as the search of the wagon was complete.

'I haven't quite finished yet,' pronounced Tania as they went back into the living room and she prepared for the grand finale of this convincing piece of theatre. 'I know you've got it hidden in here somewhere.'

She went to the small cupboard on which the television stood and knelt down, peering inside and feeling around with her hand.

'Bingo,' she said triumphantly, standing up and waving a gold bracelet. 'I knew it was here somewhere. You'd got it well hidden, tucked away there in the corner, but not well enough, you rotten little thief!'

Maddie was speechless, realising with the dull thud of certainty that she had been set up by Tania. The invitation to the lunchtime get-together had not been a friendly gesture at all but just a part of her evil strategy. She must have slipped out of the party and planted the bracelet, knowing that Maddie wouldn't lock the wagon because the children were in and out.

'You put it there,' she blurted out. 'You came in here and planted it with the deliberate intention of making trouble for me.'

'That does it,' screeched Tania whose performance would have won her a standing ovation on the West End stage. 'Not only is she a thief but a liar as well.' She turned to Sam. 'I want her off this site.'

'Oh, Maddie,' he said in a quiet voice, pale with shock. 'Don't make things even worse by making dreadful accusations like that. I'm disappointed enough in you as it is. I honestly would never have believed it of you.'

'I did *not* steal that bracelet, Sam,' she said. 'I swear to you.'

'But it was here,' he said gravely. 'Here in your wagon.' He spread his hands in a gesture of hopeless bewilderment. 'We've just watched Tania take it out of your cupboard.'

With a sinking heart Maddie realised that to continue along these lines would only worsen the situation for herself. 'I don't know how the bracelet got there,' she said. 'All I know is that I didn't put it there.'

Sam's heart told him that Maddie was speaking the truth but the evidence was here and his wife was pressurising him to take action.

'I'm so sorry, Maddie,' he said, voice gruff and clipped. 'But I can't overlook something as serious as this.'

'I should bloody well hope not,' shouted Tania.

He gave her a warning look then turned back to Maddie. 'I'll have to tell my parents,' he said grimly. 'It's them you rent the wagon from so they will decide what action to take.'

'But I didn't do it, Sam, honestly.' She was distraught.

'I'm sorry, Maddie, but the evidence says otherwise,' he said.

'Why are you apologising to a common thief like her?' demanded his wife.

'Oh, give it a rest, Tania,' he said wearily. 'I'll deal with it.'

'You make sure you do an' all,' she said, throwing Maddie a triumphant look.

'I trusted you, Maddie . . . we all did,' said Hetty when she came to Maddie's wagon on the evening of that same day, having been told what had happened. 'And this is how you repay us.'

'I didn't do it, Hetty,' she said.

'How did the bracelet find its way into your cupboard then?'

'Someone else must have put it there,' Maddie told her in a firm tone. 'Someone who wants to make trouble for me.'

'I assume by that you mean my daughter-in-law since she was the one who both lost and found it,' said Hetty through tight lips.

Maddie thought of telling Hetty about Tania's threat. But the extent of the Fenners' family loyalty was becoming all too horribly clear to her. Just a hint of an accusation about one of their number would cause them to close ranks even more firmly against her. She thought it safest to say nothing.

'My daughter-in-law isn't the easiest person to get along with, I know,' said Hetty. 'But she wouldn't do a thing like that.'

'If you say so,' said Maddie evenly.

'I'd thank you not to suggest such a thing,' said Hetty.

Maddie knew that she was damned whatever she said. Tania had made sure there was no way she could prove her innocence.

'I'm very disappointed in you, Maddie,' continued Hetty sadly.

'And I'm very disappointed in you for thinking such a thing of me,' she replied.

Hetty swallowed a lump in her throat. It was hard to believe ill of Maddie but the proof had been conclusive. She looked at Clare who was standing close to her mother looking ashen-faced and tearful. This was one of the most painful jobs Hetty had ever had to do. No wonder Vic had left it to her. 'I wouldn't see that little mite out on the street,' she said, shifting her gaze back to Maddie. 'But I have to ask you to be out of here as soon as possible.'

'Fair enough.' Maddie stood up, head held high. She was deeply hurt but determined not to let this injustice destroy her. 'But as I've paid rent until the end of the week and this is still my home, I'd like you to leave now.'

The other woman looked at her with a mixture of anger and admiration. There was a quiet gallantry about Maddie that touched Hetty's heart. Until this afternoon she would have staked her life on her integrity. But evidence was evidence and thieves weren't welcome in their community.

'I was going anyway,' she said in a subdued tone, and left without another word.

Maddie closed the door after her then cradled her daughter in her arms, suppressing her own tears so as to be strong for Clare who was to be cruelly uprooted yet again.

Leaving Chas with Barney, Janice called in to see Maddie later that evening when Clare was in bed and asleep. Maddie made some coffee and they sat to either side of the fireplace.

'I'll miss you,' said Janice.

Maddie gave her a sharp look. 'I'd like you to be honest with me, Janice. Do you think I took the bracelet?'

66

'Give over.'

'Thank God for that!'

Maddie made no reference to Tania. Janice was sympathetic but this was a very awkward situation for her. So far as Maddie knew, Tania wasn't a particular friend of Janice's but she *was* her sister-in-law and it wouldn't be fair to ask Janice to take sides. They both carefully avoided the question of how the bracelet had come to be found where it was.

'I wish there was something I could do,' said Janice, chewing her lip and sighing. 'But Mum's adamant about your going and I can't convince her otherwise. It's a rule they've always had at Fenner's about . . . er . . .'

'Not having thieves on the premises?' Maddie finished for her.

'You know I don't believe you're a thief,' said her friend emphatically. 'But anyone caught fiddling so much as a penny piece is always sacked on the spot.' She paused. 'I don't think Mum really believes you took the bracelet, either. But she has to stick to the rules. Tania wants you out and she is Sam's wife . . .'

'I wouldn't want to stay here with a slur like that on my character, anyway.'

'I don't blame you either,' said Janice. 'But where will you go?'

'I'll ask Bob and Pat if we can have a room at the pub until I get something permanent sorted out.'

'At least it's a roof over your head.'

'Yeah, and living on the job does have its advantages,' said Maddie. 'I won't need to worry about baby sitters for Clare.'

'Poor little thing.' Janice shook her head sadly. 'Poor Barney too. They are both gonna be devastated.'

'I can hardly bear to think about it,' said Maddie.

The two women looked at each other uncertainly, the atmosphere delicate and charged with emotion. Maddie might have been able to hold back her tears had Janice not come over to her chair and put an arm around her shoulders. But that sympathetic gesture opened the floodgates.

'We'll stay in touch,' said Janice, who was crying too.

'You bet we will,' said Maddie with a brave smile, but it was little comfort to someone with such a bleak future.

'Why on earth did you get rid of Maddie Brown?' Josh asked of Tania the next day as the two of them sat in his car, parked in a deserted lane just outside Kingston.

'Because you were making too much fuss of her,' she said candidly.

'But we agreed I should pay her plenty of attention,' he said. 'While the family think I'm chasing Maddie Brown, they won't be curious about who I'm really seeing.'

'I know we agreed,' she said. 'But at the party on Christmas night you seemed to be enjoying it a bit too much for my liking.'

'Rubbish!'

'Giving the woman a lift home after work at the pub and staying for coffee with her so that you're seen leaving her wagon late at night is one thing, Josh. Even a goodnight kiss at the door of her wagon for the sake of appearances is okay. But you were practically snogging with her at the party!'

'*I was not.*' Josh was emphatic. 'I danced with her, that's all.'

'You were all over her.'

'I had to make it seem genuine or there would have been no point.'

'Mm. I suppose so,' she reluctantly agreed.

'Maddie must have been wondering what I was up to because I never try anything on with her when we're on our own,' he said.

'It doesn't matter what she thinks.'

'Oh, but it does,' said Josh. 'She once accused me of using her. We don't want her to work out what I'm using her for, do we? In case she tells the others. That's why I've been trying to keep her sweet.'

'Well, she won't be around any more so you won't have to bother.'

'That's true. But we're losing the best diversion we could have had,' he said. 'Maddie was very useful to us.'

'I'm glad she's gone.'

'It was going a bit far, though, getting her thrown out for a crime she didn't commit.'

'How else could I shift her?' said Tania. 'The rest of the family think she's the best thing since hamburgers hit British shores – or at least they did until I put the boot in.'

'I still think you should have left well alone.' Josh had quite enough on his conscience without being responsible for making someone homeless too. 'She *has* got a kid to look after and it won't be easy for her to find somewhere to live.'

'Sounds to me as though I got shot of her just in time,' said Tania. 'Seems like you're starting to fancy her.'

'You know you're the only woman for me,' he said, and it was true, though no one was more surprised about this than Josh was. He'd never felt like this about a woman before. He'd always been in control of his feelings and was used to being in command. But he was helpless against his passion for Tania. He'd tried to give her up several times and failed. Josh wasn't used to being uncomfortable with himself. He'd been born bad and he liked the feeling. Had Tania been married to anyone but his brother, Josh's peace of mind wouldn't have been disturbed. But even he couldn't rest easy in the knowledge that he'd been having an affair with his brother's wife since last spring. But despite his compunction, he couldn't face the pain of giving her up. Pain for a woman? Josh Fenner? It was the craziest thing!

'Yeah, I do know that, really,' she said, leaning her head on his chest. 'I just wish we could be together all the time. These snatched meetings aren't enough for me.'

'Me neither,' he said.

'I'm sick of lying to Sam,' she said. 'It's a wonder he believes my stories about going to see a girlfriend. But it doesn't seem to occur to him to doubt me.'

'Sam's a good bloke.'

'I know that,' she said because the fact was undeniable.

'Decent and trusting.'

'That's probably why he doesn't suit me,' she said. 'Because he's good.'

'The opposite to you.'

'Being bad is what you and me both do best, Josh,' she said. 'That's why we can't leave each other alone. That's why I can't help being rotten to Sam.'

'You should take it a bit easier on him, you know.'

'You're a fine one to talk,' she said lightly. 'You're not exactly doing him any favours.'

There was a brief hiatus as Josh reeled from another stab of conscience. 'I know that and I'm not proud of what we're doing.'

'Neither am I but these things happen . . . it's life.'

'If only you'd never married him.'

'I wouldn't have got to know you then.'

'There is that.'

'I want us to go away together *so much*,' she said snuggling closer to him.

'And we will, I promise you,' he said, kissing the top of her head. 'Just as soon as I get enough dough together, we'll be off to somewhere faraway. It'll be Spain here we come.'

'I can't wait.'

'Nor me. But in the meantime let's find somewhere a bit more private, shall we?'

'What a good idea!' she said.

Chapter Six

Clare didn't seem very well when Maddie collected her from school one afternoon a few weeks later.

'What's the matter, love?' she asked when they got back to their room at the pub, a draughty attic overlooking a tiny backyard which had beer crates stacked around the walls. The room was inadequately heated with an ancient gas fire which devoured Maddie's shillings and left a lingering smell of gas even when it was turned off.

'Nothin',' said Clare.

Maddie put her hand to her daughter's brow to see if there was any sign of a raised temperature but her skin felt normal. 'Have you got a tummy ache?' she asked.

The child shook her head listlessly; she was very pale and seemed on the verge of tears.

'Headache?'

'No.'

'If you're not feeling well, I need to know,' Maddie coaxed gently. 'So tell Mummy where it hurts.'

'Well, it is a sort of tummy ache,' her daughter admitted, sounding desolate. 'And it hurts because Barney doesn't like me any more.'

'Whatever makes you think that?' asked Maddie, tensing.

'He doesn't want to play with me at playtime,' she said. 'And he says I can't go to his place to play with him after school any more.'

'Oh, love!' Her daughter's suffering cut far deeper than Maddie's own pain at being cast out of the Fenner clan.

'Why doesn't he like me any more?' Clare asked. 'What have I done?'

'He does like you and you haven't done anything,' said Maddie, her throat constricted with love.

'Why won't he play with me then?'

'I think it's something to do with the grown-ups in his family,' Maddie tried to explain. 'It has nothing to do with you or Barney.'

'But he was my best friend – even though he is a boy.'

'I know.'

'I thought his mummy was your friend, too.'

'She is.'

Maddie could understand its being difficult for Janice to have

Clare at her place to play, given the circumstances. But she couldn't imagine Janice being cruel enough to tell Barney to steer clear of Clare at school as well. But someone must have told him to do this to Clare as a way of twisting the knife in Maddie. Surely the boy wouldn't have had the guile to behave like that of his own accord?

'I want to go home to our wagon,' said Clare in a small voice.

'It isn't our home any more, darling.' Maddie held her daughter close.

'But I miss Barney and Auntie Janice and Eric and all our friends.'

So did Maddie, *dreadfully*. She was grateful to Pat and Bob for renting her the room. They were good people and did their best to make their lodgers comfortable, giving them the use of their own kitchen and living room. But Maddie and Clare were just lodgers and it didn't feel like home. There was nowhere for Clare to play. Maddie missed the fairground atmosphere too. Even in the depths of winter there was still a feeling of camaraderie there.

But all of that was over; they had to move on. 'So do I, love,' she said. 'But we can't go back there, I'm sorry.'

'There's no one to play with here.'

That was true. The pub was in a busy shopping street and the occupants of the shop-flats were all business people with not a child among them.

'I know,' said Maddie sympathetically. 'But it won't be for too long, I hope. I'm trying to find somewhere better for us to live.'

'Will it have somewhere to play and children living next door?'

'I'll do my best.'

How in God's name was Maddie going to find somewhere suitable on what she could afford? Decent rented accommodation in her price range was practically non-existent in the Tories' 'never had it so good' London. She'd added her name to the council housing list as soon as she'd left Fenner's but, being relatively new to the area, she was in for a long wait.

'I wish Barney hadn't gone off me,' said Clare wistfully.

Maddie's empathy with her daughter was so intense, she could hardly bear it. But she was angry, too. Furious that her child was being punished as the result of an injustice to herself. Admittedly the evidence against her must have seemed convincing to anyone who didn't know the truth but she couldn't help feeling betrayed by the Fenner family collectively. Even Eric and his mother had put their allegiance firmly on the side of the family, albeit they'd both seemed genuinely sorry to see her go and had made a point of coming to the wagon to say goodbye – somewhat awkwardly – and to thank her for her helping him.

If she'd thought there was the slightest chance of clearing her name, Maddie would have left no stone unturned to do it. But her word against Tania's was worthless so far as the Fenner family was concerned. So she and Clare must remain outcasts from the people and way of life they had come to love.

'He hasn't gone off you,' said Maddie. 'I can promise you that.'

Clare brightened slightly at this. 'Will he be friends with me again soon then?'

God, this was heartbreaking. 'I don't know, love,' said Maddie. 'But you've got other friends, haven't you?'

'Yeah – but I like Barney best.'

A change of subject seemed vital at this point. 'Let's forget about Barney, shall we, and have some tea?'

'Don't want any.'

'I've got some of your favourite chocolate cake . . .'

'I'm not hungry.'

'Not even for a little piece?'

'Well . . .'

'I'll go and get us both a piece,' said Maddie determinedly.

As she made her way down the creaky old stairs to the rambling kitchen on the floor below, Maddie knew it would take more than chocolate cake to compensate Clare for the loss of a friend. And all because Tania had taken against Maddie. Hurt me if you must, you evil cow, she said silently, but not my child!

'What on earth is the matter with you, Barney?' Janice, Barney and Chas were having hot buttered teacakes for tea, the red coals from the Aga casting a warm glow throughout the wagon. It was a bitterly cold January day and dusk was already falling over the fairground. 'You've been going about with a face like a flagpole for days.'

'Nothin'.'

'Cheer up then and eat your tea,' she said in her usual forthright manner. 'Your long face is enough to put us all off our food.'

'Not hungry.'

'Just eat what you can then.'

Barney was fed up. Nothing had been right around here since Boxing Day. He didn't know the details but there had been a big argument between Aunt Tania and Clare's mother, and Clare had moved away because of it. No one told him anything. When he'd asked his mother what exactly had happened she'd said it was nothing a little boy need know about. And when he'd asked if Clare could come over and play after school his mother had looked peculiar – as if she was going to cry – and said it wouldn't be a good idea for Clare to come to the fairground again because things were difficult, whatever that was supposed to mean.

Seeing how upset Clare had been when he'd told her, he'd decided it would be easier to avoid her altogether in case she asked if she could come home with him again. And since he'd been avoiding her, he'd had a horrible sick feeling in his stomach.

72

Something else was worrying him too – something strange he'd seen Aunt Tania do on Boxing Day. He'd not told anyone about it because everyone seemed to be in such a bad mood lately. Curiosity now finally got the better of him.

'You know if you take something that belongs to someone else it's called stealing?' he said in a questioning manner.

'Yeah?' confirmed Janice.

'What's it called when you give something to someone else without them knowing about it?'

Janice and Chas stared at him curiously.

'What – like a present?' said Chas, spreading jam on a toasted teacake.

'Well . . . sort of. But you don't wrap it up like a present and you don't exactly give it to 'em.'

'What *are* you talking about, boy?' asked his mother.

'I mean when someone puts something in someone else's wagon . . . hides it somewhere, like when you play Hunt the Thimble, but nobody is actually playing the game?'

'What's all this about, Barney?' Janice looked worried. 'You haven't been hiding things for a prank, have you?'

'Nah, not me.'

'Who has, then?'

'Aunt Tania.'

'What!'

'She went into Clare's wagon and put something in there.'

'How do you know this?' asked Chas.

'I saw her.'

A grave parental glance was exchanged.

'When was this, Barney?' enquired Janice.

'On Boxing Day when you were all in Uncle's Sam's wagon at the party. I was outside riding my bike and I saw her go into Clare's place.'

'What makes you think she was hiding something in there?' asked Janice, her heart racing at the implications of this new development.

'I saw her do it.'

'How?'

He stayed silent, afraid he'd be in trouble if he said any more.

'This is very important, Barney,' his mother informed him.

'We must know, son,' said Chas. He liked Maddie and Clare and had been almost as upset as Janice when they had left.

'You won't tell me off if I tell you what I did, will you?' he said warily.

'You'll be in dead trouble if you don't,' his mother said quickly. 'So stop messing about and spit it out, for goodness' sake.'

'I crept up to the front door of the wagon after her,' he explained. 'I thought Clare must be in there and Aunt Tania had gone to find her and tell her off for not being at the party.'

'And?' prompted his mother.

'She'd left the door open so I could see through the kitchen into the living room. She was looking round at first, she had something shiny in her hand . . . then she put it in the cupboard under the telly,' he said. 'I ran away when I saw that Clare wasn't there. I thought I'd be in trouble with Aunt Tania for following her. She's always cross.'

You certainly would have been in trouble if she'd known you were there, thought Janice wryly. God knows what she would have threatened you with to keep your mouth shut about what you'd seen. 'You're sure about all this, aren't you?' she said.

'Oh, yeah,' he said, his mood lightening as a telling off didn't seem to be forthcoming. But he was a bit too premature about this as it happened.

'Why the hell didn't you tell us this before?' bellowed his mother.

'Dunno.'

'You should have told us,' shouted Janice. 'People have been hurt because you kept this to yourself.'

'You've been in a bad mood and I thought you'd tell me off for spying on Aunt Tania.'

'Leave the boy alone, Janice,' admonished Chas. 'He wasn't to know it was important.'

'No, o' course you weren't, Barney,' said Janice in a kinder tone. She stood up purposefully. 'Finish your tea. I'll be back later.'

And she hurried from the wagon.

Janice looked at her sister-in-law across her living-room table, wondering how someone who had so much could be mean-spirited enough to rob a woman less fortunate of the little she did have. Tania had a devoted husband she didn't deserve, a luxurious home and plenty of money to spend on whatever she liked. While Maddie was living in a poky little room in a pub because of Tania's malice!

'There are two ways we can do this,' declared Janice. 'Either you go and tell my mother that you planted your bracelet in Maddie's wagon with the deliberate intention of making trouble for her, or *I'll* do it for you.'

'What!' exclaimed Sam, his eyes wide with shock. 'What on earth are you talking about?'

'It's true, I'm afraid.'

'Don't listen to her,' said Tania dismissively, but Janice could tell by the guarded look in her eyes that she wasn't as calm as she was pretending.

Janice went on to tell them what she knew.

'And you believe Barney . . . a six-year-old boy?' said Sam.

'In this case, yes, I do.' She looked at her brother solemnly. 'Come on, Sam, don't tell me you didn't find it hard to believe that Maddie had taken the bracelet?'

'I don't deny that . . . but to accuse my wife of deliberately planting it. Well, really, Janice, that's going too far in the name of friendship.'

'It's true,' she said again, looking directly at Tania. 'Isn't it?'

'Don't be ridiculous.'

'I know you were friendly with Maddie, Janice,' said Sam in a warning tone. 'But Tania is your sister-in-law, for heaven's sake.'

'That doesn't give her the right to do what she did to Maddie and make us all behave like monsters towards her. Tania has abused her position in the Fenner family.'

'You're deranged,' said Tania.

'Why would my wife want to do a thing like that anyway?' asked Sam, glaring at his sister.

'That's been puzzling me too,' said Janice. 'And the only thing I can come up with is that she must have thought you were getting too friendly with Maddie and wanted her out because she was jealous.'

Sam tutted. 'Oh, really, this is crazy. Tania hasn't got a jealous bone in her body. She knows I'd never even look at another woman.' He turned to his wife. 'Isn't that right?'

'Of course it is,' she said.

'The reason why she did it doesn't concern me – my friend being wrongly accused of theft does.' Janice looked at her sister-in-law. 'Well, as I told you just now, you can either go and tell Mum the truth yourself or I shall go and see her – with Barney.'

'Hetty wouldn't take the word of a child,' said Tania.

'Barney wouldn't have the nous to invent a story like that and she knows it,' said Janice. 'He isn't old enough.'

'Children are known for their vivid imaginations,' said Sam.

'About ghosts and monsters and stuff maybe – but he wouldn't make up something as bizarre as that,' said Janice.

'He has done,' insisted Tania.

'He has not – my son is telling the truth and I'm going to see to it that Maddie's name is cleared.' She threw Tania a hard look. 'With or without your co-operation.'

'Do what you like,' she said.

Janice stood up and marched to the door. She had just opened it to a blast of cold air when Tania called her back.

'All right – so I did plant the bloody bracelet in her wagon,' she admitted, injecting a sob into her voice.

'Oh, Tania, how could you?' gasped Sam.

'I was only doing what any wife would do,' she lied, looking at him pleadingly. 'I was protecting my marriage. Maddie Brown was after you. She was trouble from the minute she arrived.'

'You're wrong,' said Sam, aghast. 'Maddie didn't have any ideas

75

about me. We were just friends . . . workmates.'

'She fancied you rotten.'

'Oh, grow up, for God's sake,' said Janice. 'Maddie has just escaped from a bad marriage after years of abuse. I don't think she wants any man at the moment, let alone a married one.'

'Janice does have a point, dear,' said Sam.

Tania remained silent.

'Well, you're going to have to get used to having her around again because I'm going to make sure she gets the opportunity to come back,' said Janice. 'Though I'm not sure if she'll want to after the way this family has treated her.'

'Poor Maddie,' said Sam.

'Poor Maddie?' shouted Tania, throwing him a furious look. 'You're sorry for that cow. I knew she'd got to you.'

'Don't be tiresome, Tania,' he said irritably. 'You've nothing to worry about so far as Maddie and I are concerned.'

'You two can sort your marriage out later,' intervened Janice. 'What I want to know is – do I go to see Mum or will you do it, Tania?'

'I'll go,', she said, scowling.

Maddie's stomach churned when she saw Hetty come into the pub that evening while she was working behind the bar. What was she going to blame her for now? she wondered bitterly, her mouth dry with nerves as Hetty walked over to her.

'Evening,' Maddie said politely. 'What can I get you?'

'Can you take a break?' Hetty asked, looking worried. 'We need to talk.'

'Oh.' Maddie was taken aback. 'I'll have to find out if it's convenient,' she said coolly, troubled by the grim expression on Hetty's face. 'If you'd like to go and sit down, I'll join you when I've checked with the boss.'

'Thanks, love.'

'So, what's all this about?' Maddie asked a few minutes later, putting a gin and tonic on the table for Hetty and one for herself. 'I take it this isn't a social call?'

'No.'

'Something's happened?'

'I'll say it has!' She told Maddie about events at Fenner's. 'There are no words to tell you how sorry I am for putting you through such an ordeal.'

'It *was* an ordeal too.' Although Maddie was relieved beyond words, a mere apology wasn't going to wash away all the pain she and Clare had been through. 'It still hurts like hell to think that you doubted me.'

'You've every reason to be upset,' said Hetty, shaking her head and tutting. 'But put yourself in my position. It wasn't so much a question of us doubting you as being faced with the evidence. I mean, who would have thought that Tania – or anyone – would have done such a thing?'

'I knew she must have done it because there was no other explanation,' said Maddie. 'But I agree with you, it was an extraordinary thing for anyone to do.'s

'She's been a very silly woman.'

'Silly isn't the word I'd use,' said Maddie. 'What she did was nothing short of wicked. You've no idea what I've been through over it. And it's thoroughly unsettled Clare.'

'I feel so ashamed,' said Hetty.

Maddie believed her. 'You were put in a very difficult position,' she said in a more forgiving tone.

'Yes, I was. And all because Tania thought there might be something going on between you and Sam,' said Hetty. 'The silly cat! Everyone knows that he wouldn't look at another woman.'

'I wouldn't get involved with a married man anyway,' said Maddie pointedly.

''Course you wouldn't, love,' said Hetty wholeheartedly. 'We all know that. I just can't understand what Tania was thinking of.'

Neither could Maddie. 'Well, what's done's done,' she said. 'We can't turn the clock back.'

Hetty swallowed her drink, her brown eyes full of admiration for this courageous, hardworking woman who seemed to have taken so many knocks in her short life. Hetty had only just managed to stop herself from smacking Tania's face on hearing her confession. Her daughter-in-law wasn't her favourite person at the best of times even though she kept her true feelings hidden out of deference to the fact that Tania was Sam's wife.

She'd come close to telling Tania the truth today, though. By God she had! But she'd managed to restrain herself and instead given her a thorough trouncing for using her position in the family to such evil effect. She'd dared her to do anything like that again and demanded that she apologise to Maddie personally.

'No, we can't.' Hetty finished her drink and sighed. 'But we can take up where we left off, with you and Clare back at Fenner's.'

'I don't know if that's a good idea . . .'

'We've all missed you, love.'

'And what happens when Tania starts to get some other daft idea into her head?' Maddie sensibly enquired.

'She won't harm you again,' said Hetty. 'She wouldn't dare. One hint of trouble and you come and tell me about it.'

'I'm still not sure . . .'

'Look, I know an apology isn't enough to make up for what we've done to you.' Hetty paused, appealing to Maddie with her eyes. 'But it's a start.'

'I appreciate that.'

'Tania isn't all bad,' said Hetty who had been given a skilled performance by her. 'She's very misguided, that's all.'

Knowing that Tania was a spiteful bitch who would stop at nothing to get her own way, Maddie was reminded yet again of the Fenner family bond. Hetty would feel compelled to defend a serial killer if she was related to them. And she would never admit their failings to anyone outside the family because of her strong sense of loyalty.

'I bet Tania doesn't want me to come back,' said Maddie.

'I shouldn't think she does but it isn't up to her,' said Hetty. 'Vic and I make the decisions at Fenner's.'

Despite the tense atmosphere Maddie couldn't help but smile.

Hetty immediately caught on. 'All right, so Vic doesn't get much of a look in when it comes to decisions,' she said, grinning.

'I think that's the way he likes it.'

'And I think you're getting to know us rather well.' She gave Maddie a shrewd look. 'You're more than a match for Tania, you know. Don't stay away, Maddie,' she urged, reaching across and taking her hand. 'Give us a chance to make it up to you.'

'But Clare and I are outsiders,' she pointed out. 'This business with Tania has proved that.'

Hetty thought about this. 'You weren't raised in the fair business, and you aren't family, it's true,' she said, looking at Maddie. 'There's nothing any of us can do to change that. But that doesn't mean we don't want you with us. You fitted in well and we'd all love to have you back.' She gave a wry grin. 'Excluding Tania, o' course.'

Maddie grinned.

'You can give as good as you get, Maddie,' Hetty told her. 'So long as it's a fair fight.'

'I know.'

'And there's another reason you have to agree to come back . . .'

'What's that?'

'Janice will skin me alive if I don't get you to agree!'

Maddie gave a smile that lit up her face, melting away the anguish that had dogged her this past few weeks.

'You'd better tell her I'll be back tomorrow, then,' she said happily. 'It's my day off so I'll start clearing my things out of here after I've taken Clare to school in the morning.'

'I'll get one of the boys to collect you in the car.'

'There's no need,' said Maddie, independent to the last.

'You thinking of piling your stuff on to a barrow and wheeling it through the streets then?' asked Hetty with friendly sarcasm.

'I can get a taxi.'

'Do you think I'd have you pay for a cab when both my sons have cars?' she said. 'Not bloomin' likely!'

★ ★ ★

In the event it was Sam who came to the pub in his estate car the next morning and helped Maddie load her belongings into it. She was particularly grateful because the weather was bitter. The wind was piercing and dark skies promised snow.

'I don't know what got into Tania,' he said on the way to Fenner's after apologising profusely to Maddie. 'I mean, you and me – the idea is absolutely ludicrous.'

She was unexpectedly piqued, and that *really was ludicrous* because she wasn't interested in Sam in that way. She guessed that her reaction was due to hurt pride.

'Absolutely,' she said.

'So – are we mates again?'

'We always were so far as I was concerned,' she said. 'But I don't want Tania on my back every time I have to speak to you about anything in the line of work.'

'You won't have any more trouble from her,' Sam assured her. 'She knows now that there is nothing like that between us.'

'Good.'

The ground was icy and the wheels of the car crunched as they rolled into the fairground.

'It'll be freezing in my wagon,' said Maddie, shivering. 'As it's been empty since Christmas.'

'I don't think it will be, you know,' he said with a smile.

Maddie didn't have time to wonder what he meant because as soon as they drew up outside her wagon, Janice appeared from inside and rushed over to her.

'Welcome back!' she said, hugging Maddie as soon as she got out of the car. 'I'm so pleased to see you. The place has been like a morgue without you.'

'And I'm glad to be back,' said Maddie, overwhelmed with emotion. She'd not thought she could be this glad to be anywhere.

'You two go inside,' said Sam with typical consideration. 'I'll bring the stuff in.'

'Thanks, Sam,' said Maddie.

When she stepped inside she was greeted by a rush of warmth and the smell of something cooking.

'I popped in and lit the fire earlier on,' explained Janice.

'That was thoughtful of you.' Maddie wrinkled her nose. 'What's that lovely smell?'

'I've made you a stew,' Janice explained.

'Oh, that *is* kind of you.'

'It wasn't all kindness,' said her down-to-earth friend to ease an emotional moment. 'Mum told me it was your day off so I've invited myself to lunch – and there'll be enough left for the kids when they get in from school. I think we'd better let them have their tea together on Clare's first day back, don't you?'

Maddie smiled in agreement. 'Is Chas joining us for lunch?'

'No. He's gone to see a mate . . . and he'll be gone all day,' Janice explained. 'So we can have a good old gossip.'

'Smashing.'

'Back to normal, eh, kid?'

Maddie stood where she was in the centre of the living room, tears of joy rushing into her eyes. She would never have imagined that a caravan could feel so much like home.

'Oh, Janice, it's so good to be back.'

'Yeah,' she said, sniffing into her handkerchief. 'No one would have blamed you if you hadn't come, after the way we treated you. I'm so sorry.'

'It wasn't your fault,' said Maddie. 'Anyway, that's all in the past.'

'Thank God for that,' said Janice, blowing her nose. 'I'll make some coffee. All this emotion is wearing me out.'

Maddie grinned. She might be on the outside of the Fenner family but she'd rather be here than anywhere else.

Tania's welcome was much less warm.

'I've come to apologise,' she announced grudgingly when she came to see Maddie that evening after Clare was in bed.

'You don't sound particularly sorry.'

'I'm not,' she admitted with sullen hostility. Her brash beauty was awesome, Maddie thought, bright red hair especially stunning against a black polo-necked sweater, a tan sheepskin coat thrown casually around her shoulders.

'You've only come because Hetty said you should, haven't you?' guessed Maddie.

'Hetty *and* Sam,' she said. 'Anything to get them off my back.'

Maddie almost laughed at Tania's complete and utter selfishness. 'It was a terrible thing you did . . . don't you feel any remorse?'

'No.'

'You really are a bitch of the highest order, aren't you?'

'If you say so. I was only looking out for what's mine,' she said. 'I warned you what would happen if you didn't leave of your own accord.'

'You certainly did.'

'Anyway, I was told to come and apologise and that's what I've done,' she said. 'Bloody people. Anyone would think *I* was the outsider around here to hear them talk.'

'Aren't you worried that I might tell someone about your attitude?'

'Do what you like,' challenged Tania. 'The worst they can do is have a go at me. They wouldn't make me leave because I'm family. Anyway, Sam won't hear a word against me.'

Maddie was puzzled. 'Why are you so worried about someone stealing him from you then, if you're so sure of him?'

Tania's expression changed to something not quite as strong as fear, more a fleeting moment of unease. 'You can't be too careful where men are concerned,' she said. 'They're all susceptible if it's laid on a plate for 'em.'

'Charming!' was Maddie's answer to that.

'Don't you get all high and mighty with me, mate. This is a fairground community you're living in, not some la-di-da street in Richmond. We speak our mind here. If you don't like it, why don't you bugger off?'

'You'd like that, wouldn't you?' said Maddie, 'Well, I'm sorry to disappoint you but I'm not moving from here again, no matter how difficult you make it for me.'

'I don't like you and I don't want you around,' said Tania. 'But I'm not planning on making any more trouble for you.'

'Really?'

'Yes, really. Just so long as you don't start messing about with my husband.'

But her words didn't ring true. 'You know that Sam isn't interested in me.'

'Do I?'

'Yes, I believe you do,' said Maddie slowly; she was suddenly convinced.

'Proper little mind reader, aren't you? You should team up with Sybil. Fortunes told and minds read.'

'What are you really afraid of, Tania?' asked Maddie, eyes narrowed on the other woman. 'Why am I such a threat to you?'

She didn't reply for a few moments and Maddie could almost hear her working out her reply. 'As an unrelated, unattached woman, you are a distracting influence on my husband,' she said at last.

'Rubbish!' said Maddie.

'Why would I lie about it?'

'I don't know,' said Maddie ponderously. 'I really don't.'

She *did* know that Tania was lying, though. She also suspected that there was a darker side to all this than was apparent, and was filled with a sense of foreboding.

As she slipped back into her old routine at Fenner's, Maddie was able to put Tania to the back of her mind, something that was made easier because everyone else seemed so pleased that she was back. The freezing weather meant that people didn't stand about chatting outside so it was easier to avoid someone, too. Josh was pleasant to her but oddly distant, and didn't resume his habit of collecting her from work at the pub. Maddie had no idea why and wouldn't dream of asking.

Eric resumed lessons with her though not quite so often now that he'd mastered the basics and was able to work on his own.

The cold weather lasted throughout January with bitter winds that howled across the fairground, and rain that pounded on the wagons and formed miniature lakes on the ground. An unusual silence hung over the park as the maintenance work ground to a halt because of the weather conditions. Against this unnaturally quiet atmosphere came the reassuring sounds of everyday living – dogs barking, the bang of a dustbin lid, the slam of a car door, an occasional snatch of dialogue as a wagon door opened briefly. Maddie loved it here whatever the weather.

When the snow came in February it was like living in a world apart even though the men got busy with shovels to clear the paths so that they weren't cut off. Much to the delight of the children, school closed for a couple of days and they spent the time playing in the snow. Everyone put titbits out for the robins and blue tits who came close to the wagons in search of food while cut off from their natural resources.

Walking back to her wagon from the fairground office one afternoon when a carpet of snow still lay on untrodden ground, Maddie was struck by the beauty of the scene. An orange sun burned low in the sky behind the skeletal trees, wisps of smoke spiralling from the wagon chimneys into the glacial air.

One frosty evening when most of the snow had gone, Maddie left Clare with Janice as usual and set off to go to work at the pub. She walked along the riverside, the pale yellow lights of Richmond Bridge reflecting on the black waters in long beams. She made her way into the well-lit town and through the main shopping area, the shops closed and streets practically deserted on this bitter weekday evening, except for a gang of noisy youths roaming the streets in search of amusement.

Noticing a woman standing on a street corner, Maddie tensed when she realised it was Tania. Hoping to avoid her, she slowed her pace, expecting Tania to move on, guessing that she was waiting for someone.

Even as Maddie braced herself for a meeting since she had to pass her to get to the Fiddler's Inn, a car stopped and Tania got in. Maddie stood still in her tracks as she recognised the car, her heart beating fast as she watched Tania lean over and embrace the male occupant. The man was Josh!

Of course! How could she not have seen it before? Those unexpected bursts of attention Josh had given her had never come to anything because they'd only been for show, so that no one would suspect what he was really up to. Maddie had been used as a decoy. Tania had seen Maddie as a threat *not for Sam's affections but for Josh's*. That was why she'd wanted her out!

How blind she'd been not to have seen something that now seemed so glaringly obvious. Oh, lord, she said silently, poor Sam.

82

As the car rolled away, Maddie cast out any naive hope that what she had just witnessed was an innocent meeting between brother and sister-in-law. No, what she had seen was an assignation. Typical of those two to be arrogant enough to meet in such a public place so close to Fenner's.

Maddie could have throttled the pair of them. Sam didn't deserve this, not someone as thoroughly decent as him. In the fury of the moment she wanted to confront Josh and Tania with what she'd seen and threaten to tell Sam if they didn't stop this awful betrayal.

But she knew she mustn't meddle in such an emotional minefield which was, after all, none of her business. These things happened and it wasn't her place to be judgemental. But when you'd been used – even evicted from your home – it was difficult not to overreact.

Eventually she decided no good could come from her telling anyone what she had seen. Maybe it was just a fling that would burn itself out and Sam need never know? After all, what he didn't know couldn't hurt him.

Sam was her only concern in this and she hoped to God that he never discovered what was going on between his beloved wife and his brother. A thing like that could destroy him!

Chapter Seven

As the weather softened into spring and the riverside became lush with fresh new vegetation, a great burst of energy swept across the fairground. Tarpaulins were peeled away, shutters opened and cars put back on the tracks ready for another new season.

Until she'd come to Fenner's, Maddie had never given a thought to what went on behind the scenes at a funfair. Now she knew what a huge amount of planning and organisation went into it. The amount of capital tied up in the rides was immense too. New additions were not made lightly. The pros and cons were carefully weighed up and meticulous costings made before the purchase of any new ride or sideshow.

Other major expenses also fell to the proprietors. This year they had to have the grounds completely resurfaced before the new season, and this really cost them.

'It isn't as exciting as spending money on a new attraction but it has to be done – it's vital to public safety,' Hetty remarked to Maddie one morning just before the new season when they were both in the office. 'Uneven ground is dangerous.'

'It would be ironic if someone braved one of the white-knuckle rides only to have an accident on the ground afterwards.'

'The rides just give an illusion of danger,' said Hetty. 'The punters have more chance of getting hit by a meteorite on the way here than coming to harm on any of our rides. Whereas dodgy ground is an actual hazard, which is why we have to fork out and have it resurfaced every so often.'

'The fairs I used to go to as a child always seemed to be grassy.'

'Travelling fairs usually are 'cause they take place on commons and heaths – for a limited period only,' said Hetty. 'We have to have a hard surface here. Grass wouldn't stand a chance with thousands of feet tramping all over it day after day for months on end. We'd all be up to our ankles in mud.'

'Yeah, I suppose we would.'

'We've had an expensive time lately what with the resurfacing and the purchase of our new ride.'

All winter the family had been toying with the idea of buying a new attraction and had finally gone ahead and exchanged the Water

84

Chute for a more modern one with steeper drops and a tunnel for extra thrills. It was very impressive with its bright blue structure, fountains and multicoloured cars.

'I reckon that the new Fenner Falls is gonna be a real hit with the punters,' said Maddie.

'It had better be, the amount of money we spent on it. Vic and Sam saw it at a trade exhibition and fell for it right away,' Hetty explained. 'I wasn't sure if we should buy it because I didn't think there was anything wrong with the Water Chute we already had. But they both seem to think that this one has a lot more commercial potential. So I agreed to it in the end.'

'You have to move with the times, don't you?' said Maddie.

'In this business – not half.'

'Amazing new things seem to be happening everywhere,' remarked Maddie. 'What with the contraceptive pill going on sale, and rumours about the Russians sending a man into space for the first time soon.'

'Makes you wonder what they'll come up with next, dunnit?'

'Sending a man to the moon, perhaps?'

Hetty laughed. 'Now you're being fanciful. I don't think we'll ever see that, love,' she said. 'Not outside of story books.'

'You never know,' Maddie smiled.

'Things are changing, though,' said Hetty chattily. 'People have more money to spend on entertainment these days but they also have more to choose from than they used to. In the old days we didn't have so much competition. Now there are Bingo halls and bowling alleys, as well as the television to keep people away from the fair.'

'Surely people wouldn't stay at home to watch the box instead of coming to the fair?'

'Teenagers wouldn't. But parents of young children might not be so keen to take the kiddies to the fair if the weather was looking dodgy and there was something good on the telly.'

'The place was packed out last season,' Maddie reminded her.

'It was – and we do all right, don't get me wrong. I'm just saying that it pays to be aware of the competition.'

'Maybe Janice and I should do some sort of special promotion to launch the new season,' suggested Maddie jokingly.

'Such as?'

'I dunno . . . Perhaps we could hire some costumes and go out on the streets in fancy dress to remind people that Fenner's is here. Let 'em know what we have to offer. I know you've already done a poster promotion but this would be something a little bit different.'

'It's a very good idea,' said Hetty.

Maddie hadn't been serious at first but the fact that Hetty obviously was fired her with enthusiasm. 'It would be a bit of fun and it would get the new season off to a good start.'

'I'm all in favour,' Hetty said. 'If you're willing to do it.'

'I'm willing,' said Maddie. 'And I'm sure Janice will be too.'

And so it was that on Easter Saturday morning Maddie, Janice and their offspring went among the shoppers in Richmond's busy streets dressed as a pink rabbit, a clown and two little Easter Bunnies, each with a sash bearing the name of Fenner's Fun Park draped across their fronts.

Causing a lighthearted stir with their eye-catching attire, they chatted to people and distributed leaflets advertising Fenner's many attractions. Maddie hadn't had so much fun in years.

Leaving the pub to work full-time at the fair until the end of the season, Maddie had to take her chances about finding employment again in the autumn. She couldn't expect Pat and Bob to guarantee her a job for next winter, though they said that if they did need someone at that time, they would love to have her back.

Even though business wasn't particularly hectic at Fenner's between Easter and Whitsun when trade really gathered momentum, there was plenty for Maddie to do. Although she was kept busy in the office, she worked out on the fair, too: filling in on the Helter-Skelter, Kiddies' Speedway, Ghost Train – anywhere.

For a few days she even wore a mermaid costume and sat in a tub of water outside the simulated underwater grotto owned by a travelling showman who rented a pitch from Fenner's and whose assistant had gone down with flu. It was a wonder the poor girl didn't have double pneumonia, Maddie thought, earning her living in such a damp and chilly way. It was great fun but she wasn't sorry to return to more comfortable duties.

Whitsun passed busily and Maddie entered her second year at Fenner's. The summer advanced at a hectic pace with never two days the same.

On the morning of August Bank Holiday Monday, she walked from her wagon to the office in the sunshine, thinking how pleasant life was and how convenient it was to be living on the premises. It was a relief to go to work knowing that she could keep an eye on Clare who was playing with Barney and some of the older children in the garden Maddie had made behind her wagon.

This morning there was a palpable air of expectancy on the fairground as people prepared for the day's business – checking floats, replenishing prizes, chatting among themselves. The weather was warm and humid with a hint of storminess. Like all fairpeople on a Bank Holiday Monday, Maddie was almost paranoid about wanting it to stay fine.

'Well . . . are you ready to do a roaring trade?' she said lightly to Janice as she passed the Hoopla stall where her friend was pinning prize ten-shilling notes on to wooden blocks.

'Not half . . . should be a good day if the weather holds.'

Maddie looked up, shading her eyes from the hazy sun and watched a procession of white, grey-tinged clouds floating across the sky. 'Looks quite promising, so let's keep our fingers crossed.'

She went on her way, counting her blessings. She had a comfortable home, a job she enjoyed, and a beautiful daughter she was now able to bring up without the constant threat of violence. The thought inevitably reminded her of the past, dimming the brightness of her mood. But only briefly because she really was beginning to feel safe in this enclosed community.

She found herself wondering if Dave had found someone else. A good-looking bloke like him wouldn't have any trouble, surely? He might be happier with a different partner and not violent. She'd always had the impression that it was only her who drove him to it.

As her thoughts returned to her current surroundings and she approached the Chairoplanes, she was glad that the Fenners – in their determination to keep abreast with modern times – hadn't dispensed with popular old favourites like this one of which Maddie had always been fond.

She instinctively slowed her step at the sound of raised voices drifting through the open door to the central structure, a multicoloured masterpiece of hand-painted patterns. It was inside here that the engine was housed.

'I'll check this ride myself today, Eric,' Josh was saying with the impatient edge to his voice that was always present when he spoke to his cousin. 'That way I know it's been done properly.'

'I always check it properly,' came Eric's protest. 'I used to do it every day when Sam was in charge of this ride.'

'But you don't do it now that I've taken over, do you?' said Josh who hadn't suddenly been fired with diligence towards his work, and merely wanted Eric out of his way because he was in a foul mood due to a hangover. His cousin's irritating presence made him feel worse.

Having learned so much about the daily routine of the fair, Maddie knew that the shackles and bolts that held the chains to the framework of the Chairoplanes had to be checked every morning before the fair opened for business. Regular safety checks on all the rides were standard procedure. She also knew that Eric had been doing these routine checks since he was a boy and everyone trusted him to do things properly because fairground machinery was the one thing he did know about.

Although the Chairoplanes were staffed during business hours, overall responsibility for them had been added to Josh's list of rides recently because Sam was too overworked to deal with them. Maddie had heard that Josh was none too pleased to have his workload increased.

'I know what I'm doing,' insisted Eric whose progress with the written word had made him slightly less ready to be browbeaten. 'Sam's always trusted me to do the job.'

'It's a wonder there hasn't been any accidents then, innit?' said Josh.

Maddie had almost come to a halt, listening. Her heart turned over to hear this. Did Josh have to be so cruel?

'No, it isn't,' said Eric in his slow but persistent manner. 'I know how to check the rides. I've been workin' on 'em all my life. Anyway, Sam sent me over to do it for you.'

'Look, mate,' said Josh, and Maddie perceived a slight moderation of his tone as he struggled to keep his temper, 'I know you mean well but I don't need any help, thanks.'

'But Sam says I've to check the chains to save you doing it.'

'I don' t need you so bugger off!' said Josh, losing his temper.

'I take my orders from Sam.'

'Oh, for God's sake,' roared Josh who thought, anyway, that his brother was far too fussy about safety checks. 'Don't you ever take the hint – you cretin?'

There was a silence during which Maddie could picture Josh's fury. 'I suppose my brother sent you over here to do the check 'cause he thinks I won't bother to do it, is that it?'

'Dunno,' said Eric. 'I'm just doing what I'm told.'

'Oh, give me strength.' Another long silence. 'Look, mate, if you really want to do something to help me, you can go across to the newsagents' and get me a packet of fags and a newspaper.'

'That isn't what Sam told me to do.'

'Well, it's what *I'm* telling you to do so bloody well go and do it,' ordered Josh. 'Here's the money for twenty Players and a *Daily Mirror*.'

Maddie moved on out of earshot. God, Josh was arrogant! Every so often her fury at the way he was deceiving Sam reached unbearable levels and this was one of those times.

Because she knew that he and Tania were lovers, it seemed odd to her that it wasn't obvious to everyone else, considering their tendency to exchange intimate glances. But, of course, any tenderness between them that was perceived by others was simply attributed to family affection.

Her heart went out to Sam. Although a part of her thought he ought to know what was going on, she dreaded his finding out. She couldn't bear to think of what it would do to him if Josh and Tania went off together, which she supposed might happen.

None of my business, she reminded herself firmly, as she continued on to the office.

The weather stayed fine and the Bank Holiday crowds poured into the park. By mid-afternoon the place was heaving, queues trailing from every ride and sideshow and the ice-cream sellers barely able to keep up with the demand.

Aware of the vivid scene beyond the office window as she answered the telephone, kept people supplied with small change and made various announcements on the public address system, Maddie wished she could be working outside. As the afternoon advanced towards evening her wish was granted. Sam appeared with instructions for her to take over on the House of Mirrors while the assistant took a meal break.

'We'll lock the office for the time being,' he said.

The sun was still warm and the sky cloudless as Maddie picked her way through the crowds. The colour and noise were overpowering, shrieks and bawdy laughter rising above the beat of rock 'n' roll music. Maddie had made sure there were enough records in the pile that would play automatically while the office was unattended.

She took her place in the paybox of the House of Mirrors. 'Come on, folks, come and see another side of yourself in our special mirrors. You can be as tall or short as you like,' she called through the microphone, though people didn't need much persuading to go on anything today.

During a rare moment without customers she stood back mentally and absorbed the atmosphere, the sights and sounds seeming to register with more clarity than usual: kiddies in the Boat Swings squealing at every dive, lucky punters carrying soft toys they'd won on the Shooting Range or Coconut Shies. A Fun Park this truly was. For a few hours on a Bank Holiday Monday afternoon people could trade their troubles for a brief spell of magic.

Just seconds later her happy mood was shattered. A sudden movement overhead turned her blood to ice. What she saw was so horrific, she couldn't take it in. A human missile – trailing metal chains – was flying through the air in her direction.

My God, one of the chairs has come away from the Chairoplane frame, she thought. Even as the realisation came, a hush spread across the fairground. Stunned, Maddie watched the chairbound person land face down with a crunch on the concrete. Chaos immediately ensued. People appeared at the scene of the accident as though they had dropped from the sky.

Pushing through the crowds with the idea of assisting, she managed to get near enough to see that the crumpled figure on the ground was a boy with short brown hair – he looked to be in his early teens. Chains were tangled about him, the yellow Chairoplane seat on top of him. He was ominously still.

People were running, pushing, screaming and coming from

everywhere. Maddie was almost knocked over in the crush. A human wall surged forward. She struggled to hold them back as panic prevailed and she feared the boy would be trampled.

Then, suddenly, Sam was by her side, taking control. He told the crowd to keep back and received an immediate response. Obviously upset but remaining calm, he told Maddie to go and call an ambulance. Then he got down on his knees to do what he could for the boy.

Managing to get through the crowds to the office, Maddie dialled 999 with a shaky hand. Even as she asked for the ambulance, she had a terrible suspicion that it was already too late.

She was right. The lifeless body of fifteen-year-old Anthony Smith – who'd been at the fair with his mates – was carried into the ambulance covered in a blanket. It was thought that he had died instantly and wouldn't have felt any pain.

Shock waves reverberated throughout the grounds as news of the tragedy spread. Fear turned to anger and whipped the crowds into a frenzy. Sam made an announcement on the Tannoy to say that the fair would be closed for the rest of the day.

Not everyone left. Some people were making their anger plain and crowding around the office demanding an explanation for the accident. Police officers and safety inspectors were quick to arrive followed soon after by the press.

Vic was whey-faced, chain smoking and muttering about there never having been a fatal accident at Fenner's before. Hetty did what she could to calm the dead boy's mates before they drifted away. The police had gone to notify Anthony Smith's parents.

'Poor devils,' she said to Maddie and Janice as everyone gathered in the office. 'That's every mother's worst nightmare . . . the police at the door to tell you you've lost a child.'

All the men of the fair did what they could to help but Sam was the one who took charge. Calmly and efficiently he dealt with the police, safety inspectors, reporters and the lingering crowds. Maddie thought he was wonderful. Efficient but kind, calm but caring, Sam Fenner really was one hell of a man.

What a black day this had turned out to be, though. Maddie was sick with horror. Seeing a young boy plunge to his death was something that would stay with her for ever.

'Will the fair be closed tomorrow?' Maddie enquired of Janice later that same evening as they had a cup of cocoa in Maddie's wagon. Clare was asleep in bed and Barney was next door with Chas.

'I should think so – as a mark of respect. But a seasonal business like ours can't really afford to close for long.'

'No, of course not.'

90

'I'm not sure if anyone will want to risk any of our rides once the story hits the papers, anyway,' said Janice. 'Public confidence is bound to be at an all-time low after something like this.'

'There'll be those who'll come out of morbid curiosity, I suppose,' said Maddie. 'To have a look at where it happened.'

'Unfortunately I think you're right.' Janice sipped her cocoa and smoked a cigarette. 'That poor boy . . . those poor parents. I keep thinking of how I'd feel if it was Barney.'

'I've been thinking the same thing about Clare,' said Maddie.

'There'll be an official enquiry, I suppose,' remarked Janice.

'Will the firm be taken to court for negligence with regard to safety precautions, do you think?'

'Probably.'

'Oh, dear.'

'Poor old Eric,' said Janice, inhaling deeply on her cigarette. 'He must be feeling dreadful. He's worked on the rides all his life – knows everything there is to know about them, for all that he's slow in other ways. This just goes to show that you can never rule out human error no matter how careful you are.'

Maddie said sharply, 'Eric? What's he got to do with it?'

Janice gave her a puzzled look. 'Well, everything,' she said. 'Didn't you know – the accident was Eric's fault?'

'What!'

'He checked the Chairoplanes this morning but obviously didn't do the job properly.'

'Are you sure he did it?' asked Maddie, remembering the conversation she had overheard that morning.

'Yeah, 'course I'm sure. Sam sent him over to do the job for Josh.'

'Did Josh actually say that Eric had checked the Chairoplanes today?'

'I suppose he must have,' said Janice. 'That was what Chas said, anyway. The men have been talking about it. Apparently, Josh is blaming himself for trusting Eric with the job. And Sam is blaming himself for telling him to do it. But there was no reason not to trust him since he's been doing jobs like that for yonks.'

'Hmm . . .'

'Maddie, what's the matter?' asked Janice. 'You look miles away.'

'Nothing,' Maddie said, distractedly. 'It's been a terrible day, that's all.'

'You can say that again,' Janice agreed. 'I hope I never have to live through another one like that.'

As soon as Clare had gone out to play the next morning, Maddie went in search of Josh. She found him sitting on the steps of his wagon smoking a cigarette.

'You and I need to talk.'

'Do we?' he said absently. She could see how tired he was, face bloodless, eyes red and shadowed with fatigue. He didn't deserve to have slept last night either.

She nodded. 'Can we go inside?'

'Be my guest,' said Josh lazily, getting up and leading her up the steps.

'This isn't a social call,' she explained, sitting in a black leather armchair in his living room. His home was stylish with expensive furniture and glossy fittings but it was impersonal and lacked homeliness. It was very untidy, too, with newspapers scattered around, ash trays overflowing and dirty tea-cups everywhere.

'No?' He looked at her, drawing hard on a cigarette.

'I'll come straight to the point,' she said. 'I know that it wasn't Eric who checked the Chairoplanes yesterday.'

His eyes became alert but he didn't lose his composure. 'Oh, really?'

'Yes, really,' she said. 'It was you who did it, or were supposed to.'

His face hardened. 'I don't like what you're suggesting,' he said.

'And I don't like what you're doing to Eric. Making him take the blame for something for which you were responsible.'

He stood up. 'Get out of here . . .'

'I heard you telling him you would do the safety check yesterday morning,' Maddie persisted. 'I was standing near the Chairoplanes when you and Eric were inside the engine room. You sent him to the newsagent's . . . to get him out of your way because he was getting on your nerves.'

Josh was silent for a moment, smoking. 'You didn't actually see who checked the ride, did you?' he was able to say with confidence because the job hadn't actually been done by anyone.

'No.'

'Well, don't come to me with some cock-and-bull story then.'

'I heard what you said to Eric . . . I heard you tell him that you'd check the chains.'

'So, why isn't he saying anything about it then?'

'Because he doesn't have the confidence to stand up for himself against you.'

'Balls!'

'He looks up to you even though you treat him like something you've trodden in,' Maddie continued determinedly. 'He admires you but he's scared of you too. Anyway, he knows no one would believe his word against yours as he's supposed to be simple . . .'

'He *is* simple, there's no supposed to be about it,' declared Josh. 'And, yes, you're right . . . no one would take his word against mine, in much the same way as they wouldn't believe you rather than me.' He paused. 'So get out of here before I lose my temper.'

Maddie stood up. But she had no intention of letting Eric be

92

blamed for something he hadn't done, particularly something as serious as this. She felt compelled to use any means at her disposal to clear his name. Maddie knew only too well the misery of false accusation.

'What happened yesterday morning, Josh?' she asked, without expecting an answer. 'Did you think it wouldn't matter if you skipped the safety check for once . . . or did you have other things on your mind and not do it properly?'

'Get out.'

'I'm going,' she said, walking towards the door with him behind her. She turned there and looked him straight in the eye. 'But there is something you should know before I do.'

'Ooh, goodie,' he said with blistering sarcasm, his mouth twisting into an ugly smile. 'Do tell me – I'm all ears.'

'I know about you and Tania.'

Her words rang in the electric silence. Josh wasn't smiling now. His expression was grim as he pulled her back inside and closed the door.

'What are you talking about?'

'I know that you're sleeping with her.'

He was clearly disconcerted while pretending indifference. His eyes were fixed on her face. Even when he was at fault he maintained an air of disdain that made others feel as though they were in the wrong.

'Reckon yourself to be some sort of a clairvoyant, do you?'

'Nothing as complicated as that,' said Maddie, standing her ground. 'I saw you together months ago. I've known for ages the real reason why Tania wanted me out of Fenner's. It certainly wasn't because she was worried about Sam and me.'

'Proper little smart arse, aren't you?'

'No,' she said. 'But I am capable of putting two and two together.'

'All right, so you're in possession of certain facts,' he said smoothly. 'But proving them is another matter altogether.'

Maddie studied her fingernails, feeling her confidence ebb slightly.

It would be all too easy to be outfaced by him because, as the eldest Fenner son, he had all the power. But she was determined not to be. She couldn't stand by and see Eric's reputation destroyed just when he had begun to earn some respect as a result of being able to read.

'I know that. But people are inclined to believe the old saying about there being no smoke without fire,' she said levelly. 'And if you don't come clean about who was responsible for checking the Chairoplanes yesterday morning, I shall make sure people get to know about you and Tania.'

'You wouldn't!'

Actually he was right, she wouldn't if she could possibly avoid it because the last thing she wanted to do was to hurt Sam. This was merely a bargaining point.

'I would,' she bluffed.

'You bitch!'

'What you're doing to Eric is wrong,' she said, ignoring his insult. 'He's had more than enough humiliation in his life. He really doesn't need this. I won't let you use him as your scapegoat.'

'You can't prove anything.'

'No, but Sam and the family will begin to wonder about you and Tania if the idea is planted in their minds – they won't be able to help it once the allegation has been made. It's only human nature. When they remember her little scam at Christmas, they'll begin to wonder why she *really* wanted to be rid of me and the penny will eventually drop.'

'Why don't you mind your own business?'

'Probably because I've been cursed with a sense of fair play,' she said. 'Eric's had enough trouble. I'm not going to let him take this on his shoulders as well.'

'Trouble! Eric?' said Josh cynically. 'He doesn't know the meaning of the word.'

'I don't know what gives you that idea.'

'He's very well looked after by the family, and protected by us all. He doesn't feel things like the rest of us. People will make allowances for him having made a mistake.'

'Because he's two horses short of a Carousel?'

'Exactly.'

'He isn't so thick that he doesn't feel pain,' Maddie retorted. 'There's actually a lot more to him than you give him credit for. He's been a laughing stock around here for long enough.'

'Just because you've taught him to do what the rest of us were doing by the time we were seven, that doesn't make him normal.'

'He isn't the brightest man in London,' she agreed. 'But he's as normal as you or me.'

'Oh, get out.'

Maddie held up her hands. 'I'm going.'

'Good.'

But she stayed where she was to make one final point. 'If I hear that you've done the decent thing and owned up to what really happened yesterday, by the end of today, I'll say nothing about you and Tania.' She paused, looking at him hard. 'If not, I shall not only make it known that you were to blame for the accident, I shall tell Sam what I know about you and her, too . . . and don't think I'll enjoy it because I won't. The last thing I want to do is to hurt Sam. But if you leave me no choice . . .'

'Oh, get out of here, woman, before I throw you out,' growled Josh.

Maddie left his wagon in a state of turmoil, not knowing which way this would go. She would just have to wait and see what the next few hours would bring and pray that Josh wouldn't force her into a position where she had to hurt Sam.

Josh watched Maddie from the window as she walked towards the office, a slim figure in a T-shirt and jeans, hips swaying, straight blonde hair blowing in the breeze. She was a good-looking woman in a natural kind of way. He might have been tempted if he wasn't already fixed up in that direction. But being in love with Tania consumed him completely and left no room for anyone else.

God only knows where it will end, he thought. She was pressing for them to go away together and he wanted that too. But he couldn't bring himself to make the final public declaration that he knew would destroy his brother, and his parents.

So Josh had been fobbing her off with a story about wanting more money behind him to set himself up in business, rather than admit that he was too much of a coward to have Sam find out about them. Tania was fond of pointing out that they could just go and leave a note for him – they needn't be around when he read it. Oddly enough this didn't help soothe Josh's guilty conscience.

Why was he so bothered about this particular misdeed when he'd managed to reach his thirties without being unduly troubled by remorse? Perhaps running away with his brother's wife was a low trick even for him. That was the trouble with blood ties, they encouraged illogical feelings and cramped your style.

Tania had the right idea. She didn't give a damn about anyone. Completely self-centred, she didn't even pretend to any finer feelings. He knew that if it suited her to drop him, she wouldn't hesitate. While this had its painful side, it also excited Josh. It had always been her sheer callousness that attracted him to Tania. She was demanding and selfish – and he just couldn't get enough of her. As she had often said, they were two of a kind.

This latest stunt of his took some beating, though – passing the blame for a fatal accident on to his cousin. But it hadn't seemed such a terrible thing to do at the time. Josh's reasoning had run along the lines that the family would be easier on Eric than they would on him because everyone always made allowances for Eric.

And, after all, it would be the business that would be in trouble with the authorities, not Eric personally. It had just seemed so much easier to go along with the idea that he had checked the Chairoplanes, since Sam was under that impression anyway. The fact that Eric was too daft to challenge Josh made it even simpler.

He had been seriously hungover yesterday morning and had given the safety check a miss as he quite often did. The shackle had snapped from wear and tear on the metal which would have been noticed had he carried out the inspection.

Weighing up the dilemma from his own perspective – as usual – Josh decided that his best bet would be to get Eric out of trouble rather than have the other scandal break. Maddie Brown didn't seem like the sort of woman to make idle threats.

But how was he going to vindicate his cousin without destroying his own reputation? He certainly had no intention of admitting the truth: that he'd cold-bloodedly let Eric take the blame. There must be a way of doing this so that Josh Fenner didn't come out of it looking too much of a bastard.

A boy was dead because of his negligence and he'd tried to pass the buck, which made him the worst kind of vermin. Josh knew that only too well. But there was no need for anyone else to know. There had to be a way around this; it was just a question of giving the matter some serious thought.

Chapter Eight

The shock of the accident hung over Fenner's like the shadow of doom. Everyone felt bad about it, from Hetty and Vic down to the part-time casual labourers. Just working for the Fenner organisation made you feel guilty about the boy's death, or so it seemed to Maddie.

Still, at least Eric had been vindicated and the real culprit was now known, even though he'd managed to come out of it relatively unscathed. The way Josh had turned the whole thing to his own advantage was almost beyond belief.

'Josh was trying to protect the reputation of the fair – that's why he said that Eric had checked the chains on the Chairoplanes,' Janice said to Maddie the next day.

'Am I missing something here?' she said. ''Cause I don't understand.'

'Apparently Josh thought it would look even worse for the firm if one of the sons of the family was known to be at fault since they really should know better,' she explained. 'So he let everyone believe that Eric had done the job as Sam had told him to do. But he couldn't go through with it – decided it was best to tell the truth.'

'But he *was* going to let Eric take the blame,' said Maddie, astonished that this didn't appear to be bothering Janice.

'Well, yes – but only briefly and for the good of the family business,' she said, leaping to her brother's defence. 'Poor old Josh was in such a state after the accident, he wasn't thinking straight.'

'I shouldn't think Eric was any too calm, either.'

'A boy is dead because of Josh – how do you think that makes him feel?' her friend said curtly. 'Anyway, he's put things right for Eric now. And I've told Josh he mustn't be too hard on himself about the accident.'

'You have?'

'Of course.' She gave Maddie a sharp look, not caring for her critical tone. 'It was an accident. Okay, so Josh wasn't as thorough as he might have been, but we're all only human. Anyone can make a mistake.'

'Mmmm.'

'There's no point in Josh's making his life a misery over it,' Janice said briskly. 'He obviously thought he'd checked the ride properly.

No one would *want* to cause an accident.'

'Of course not.'

'Dad's given him a real bollocking and he's got the safety inspectors on his back. He doesn't need the rest of us turning against him.'

'No.'

'None of it will bring the boy back anyway,' Janice continued sadly. 'The important thing is to make sure that nothing like that ever happens again.'

'Yeah.'

'We'll get enough stick from outside over this, Maddie. We need to stand together inside the fairground. The authorities will be down on us like a ton o' bricks – and it's only right and proper that they should. Dad reckons he'll be taken to court.'

'Your dad will?'

'As the owner of the business, the responsibility is his.'

'I wonder what'll happen?'

'He'll be very heavily fined, I should think. We're insured for this sort of thing but I don't know if it'll cover the loss of business we'll undoubtedly suffer.' She paused, looking sheepish. 'I know it seems hard even to think about such things when a boy is dead because of an accident on one of our rides. But life goes on and bills still have to be paid.'

'You can't be certain that business will drop off.'

'Would you go to a fair where there'd been a fatal accident?'

'People soon forget . . . they'll get their confidence in us back, eventually,' said Maddie.

'Eventually being the operative word.' Janice paused, her eyes glazing over. 'Still, we're lucky – we can work to regain our reputation. Mr and Mrs Smith can't ever get their son back.'

'That's a fact.'

Janice sighed. 'It's enough to make you feel like getting a job in a sweet shop where the worst harm you can do anyone is give 'em a humbug short of a quarter.'

'Mmm.'

'But you have to do what you do. And we're in the fair business.'

'Exactly.'

'In actual fact, our rides will be safer than ever after a thing like this. Safety checks will be even more stringent from now on. The authorities will make sure of that.'

'People will soon realise,' said Maddie.

'We'll have to make sure that they do. Put something in the paper to reassure them.'

'Good idea,' said Maddie.

The subdued atmosphere at Fenner's continued. Business picked up slightly after the predictable drop immediately following the accident, but people still didn't come in such large numbers.

There were plenty of people in Trafalgar Square one Sunday in September, though, for the biggest ban-the-bomb demonstration ever seen in London. An ardent supporter of worthy causes, Janice decided to take advantage of the fact that the fair was quiet and have time off to join the protest. Having arranged with Chas to look after the children, she persuaded Maddie to join her.

Although a little apprehensive about going, Maddie was soon infected by the spirit of the demonstration when she and Janice joined the crowds in Trafalgar Square to be met by singing and chanting. She'd never experienced anything like it before – this great outpouring of enthusiasm and camaraderie that swept through the vociferous crowds in a warm enveloping tide, inspiring everyone in its wake to believe in what they were doing. They sang songs, cheered the speakers and made new friends. It was wonderful!

But things turned ugly later on when some of the demonstrators staged sit-down protests and the police struggled to arrest them. Suddenly all hell was let loose with people pushing and shoving in all directions.

Maddie was knocked to the ground and forced to stay there because of the army of feet moving around her. Hot and breathless, she struggled to get up only to be knocked down again. A loud cry of pain was torn from her as a heavily booted foot trod on her hand.

'Thank God I've found you,' said Janice who'd heard the cry and managed to reach her friend and drag her to her feet. 'You all right?'

'Just about – I think,' she said, moving her fingers to make sure no bones were broken. 'I thought I was gonna be trampled to death, though.'

'It's getting a bit scary now,' said Janice. 'I think it's time we left.'

Scuffles between police and protestors were breaking out all around them and it took ages to get to the tube station through crowds whose mood had turned sour.

But they arrived back at Fenner's with no harm done except a badly bruised hand for Maddie. For what it was worth, she was glad she'd let Janice talk her into going, especially as on this day the Russians exploded another bomb in their test series.

The fair didn't regain capacity crowds for the rest of the season. Even the special closing night with novelty acts and a grand firework display lacked its usual magic.

But time passed and life went on. This autumn there wasn't a job for Maddie at the Fiddler's Inn but she found employment in another pub nearby. Vic Fenner was taken to court and heavily fined for negligence with regard to public safety. The case was given a great deal of publicity but at least it highlighted the fact that routine safety checks would be a lot more thorough in future.

Sam managed to get an interview with an understanding reporter on the local paper to emphasise this point and reiterate their deep regret about the boy's death. While Hetty was undoubtedly the head of the business, Sam was its strength.

Maddie was especially sensitive to her position as a non-family member during this traumatic period. This feeling of being on the periphery wasn't caused by any lack of friendliness on the part of the family. It was simply Maddie's perception of the close personal bond within the family members at their time of trouble, something which she did not share.

Another winter passed and another new season got underway. The accident wasn't forgotten but its impact did begin to recede with time, and things seemed to get back to normal. Maddie found herself more involved in the administration of Fenner's and worked closely with Hetty and Sam, taking on new responsibilities in the office. Janice couldn't abide any sort of office work, Tania didn't have any aptitude for it, and none of the men were interested. If Sam was in his office it was usually because he was on the telephone.

Autumn came again and Maddie began her out-of-season working routine, though this year she managed to get a job at the Fiddler's Inn for the winter.

On the afternoon of Boxing Day 1962 it started to snow, creating a festive scene with snowflakes falling and fairy-lit Christmas trees shining through the wagon windows. Clare and Barney were hoping the snow would settle. Their wish was rather too generously granted as it happened; by tea-time there was a substantial covering and the next morning it was still snowing heavily.

Paths disappeared, hedges were buried and roads became impassable. A few days later a blizzard of fine snow crystals banked into drifts, making conditions even more hazardous. When it did eventually stop snowing, the temperature plummeted and the existing snow froze over.

At first the big freeze was fun, especially for the children. But snowball fights began to lose their appeal when temperatures remained stubbornly near freezing point. The thaw in the New Year was short-lived and everyone at Fenner's forgot what it was like to feel firm ground underfoot.

Despite the misery of coping with everyday life in temperatures that defied all forms of heating and forced people to go to bed fully dressed, there was an enjoyable sense of community at the fairground. Maddie and Janice joined forces against the merciless weather, sharing the contents of their food cupboards to save battling against the elements to get to the shops as often as normal. Janice, who had learned to drive at an early age so that she could help shift fairground vehicles, drove the children to school in Chas's

Ford Consul, once the schools re-opened and roads were useable again.

Shopping became a community thing at Fenner's during these abnormal conditions as people did what they could to help each other. Maddie even forgot about the tension between herself, Josh and Tania. That had been less noticeable anyway since Maddie had told Josh what she knew, presumably because they were afraid to make their hostility towards her too obvious for fear she'd spill the beans. Whether or not they were still having an affair, she didn't know; she tried not to think about it.

It was early-March before the temperature finally rose above freezing point after a winter that was said to have been the coldest in Britain since 1740. During that harsh period, Maddie never once questioned her own judgement in bringing her daughter up in a caravan on an amusement park. Surrounded by the warmth of true companionship, in a wagon as cosy as any brick dwelling, she knew it was right for them both.

By the late spring, however, doubts began to creep in when Clare changed from a sunny-natured little girl into a sulky eight year old obsessed by personal hygiene and reluctant to go to school.

'I don't know what's got into her,' Maddie confided to Janice. 'Her personality seems to have altered completely.'

'Not so happy, huh?'

'That's the understatement of the decade.'

'Oh, dear.'

'She used to be such a contented and chatty child,' Maddie continued. 'Now I can hardly get a word out of her. And she used to love school. Now she'd do anything to get out of going. Tummy ache, a sore throat . . . she'll try anything to stay at home.'

'I presume you've tried asking her what's the matter?'

'I've asked her till I'm blue in the face but she's keeping her lip buttoned.'

'Perhaps she's finding it difficult to keep up with the lessons now that they're out of the infants and doing some serious learning,' suggested Janice. 'Could be that she doesn't want to admit it.'

'I'm sure it isn't that,' said Maddie because Clare was very quick on the uptake.

'No, I suppose not,' agreed Janice. 'She always strikes me as a bright kid.'

'Then there's this thing she's got about cleanliness.'

'Cleanliness?'

'Yeah. She'd shower a dozen times a day if I'd let her.' Although there were toilet and washing facilities in the caravan, Maddie and Clare had to go to the other side of the fairground to the accommodation block for a bath or a shower. 'And given what that

101

entails for us, it makes her behaviour even more puzzling.'

'Do you think it's connected?'

'It all seemed to start at about the same time so I think it must be.'

'I'll have a word with Barney,' offered Janice. 'He might know if anything's happened at school to upset her.'

The next day, Janice had some rather distressing news for her friend.

'There are some girls in their class whom Clare is keen on, apparently,' said Janice. 'You know what little girls are for following their peers . . . and boys too for that matter.'

'And?'

Janice bit her lip. 'Barney said that one of the girls – someone called Annie Wright – is a right little bully. She rules the roost among the girls, apparently.'

'Bullying?' said Maddie, her heart aching for her daughter. 'I should have guessed.'

'Don't jump to conclusions,' advised Janice. 'You don't know for sure. You need to get Clare to talk to you about it.'

'I know. And at least I have a clue as to what I'm dealing with now. I'll have a chat with her about it at tea-time.'

'I promise I won't do or say anything to embarrass you in front of your friends, or get you into trouble at school,' Maddie said to her daughter, 'but I must know what's upsetting you.'

Clare stared at her mother across the table in silence, her blue eyes like sad moons in her freckled face, blonde hair tied back in a pony tail. She pushed her half-eaten beans on toast aside and stared at her lap.

'Now, come on, love,' coaxed Maddie. 'This has gone on for long enough. Something is obviously bothering you.'

Silence.

'I think it has something to do with a girl called Annie Wright.'

Clare drew in her breath, as though just hearing the name frightened her.

'Who told you?' she asked.

'Never you mind,' said her mother. 'Just tell me what's going on.'

'Nothin'.'

'We both know that isn't true.' Maddie recalled the frequent hand washing and the many trips to the showers. 'Has she been saying that you're not clean or something?'

Another gasp, as though the mere suggestion caused her pain.

'Why not tell me all about it, Clare,' said Maddie gently. 'I might be able to help.'

She stared into her lap for a while then looked up slowly. 'Annie says I'm a dirty gypsy,' she blurted out in a rush, her voice quivering before she collapsed into violent sobbing. 'She says I'm dirty and smelly 'cause I don't live in a proper house. Oh, Mum, I'm not dirty, am I?'

'Of course you're not,' said Maddie, getting up and leading her daughter to the sofa where she sat her down and cradled her in her arms, feeling the slim little body shuddering against her own. Maddie's eyes were bright with tears. Clare was so young to be coping with such torment. 'It's a wonder you haven't worn your skin out with all the washing you've been doing lately.'

'Barney says I'm not a gypsy . . . he isn't either,' she sobbed, voice thick with distress. 'He says that we're just fair people.'

'That's right,' said Maddie.

'But Annie says I *must* be a gypsy if I live in a caravan, and she doesn't want any dirty gypsies in her crowd.'

'Shush! There, there,' soothed Maddie.

When Clare had calmed down and her crying had subsided, Maddie explained a few things to her. 'True gypsies aren't dirty. They're cleaner than the rest of us, or so I've been told.'

'But I still don't want to be one,' wailed Clare, eyes wide with horror.

'And you're not,' her mother assured her firmly. 'We live in a caravan on a fairground because it suits us to do so. All our friends are here.'

'Oh.' Clare still sounded doubtful.

'You like living here with Barney and Auntie Janice next door, don't you?'

'Yes, but I don't want people to think that I'm dirty.'

'Would you want to move away from all our friends here?'

'Well, no . . .'

'Because if you're really unhappy here, I shall find somewhere else for us to live,' said Maddie, and meant it. If this way of life was going to upset her daughter in the long-term then she would move heaven and earth to get them a place in an ordinary street.

'I love living here,' said Clare in a more decided manner. 'But I don't want to be different from the other children in my class. I wanna be in Annie Wright's crowd.'

'This Annie must be very special for you to want it so much?'

'It isn't Annie that I like. But all my friends go around with her now, and if she won't let me be in the gang, I won't have anyone to play with.'

'What about Barney?'

'He's a boy. He's my best friend at home – but at school girls play with girls.'

'Well, these girls should be proud to be your friend,' said Maddie with feeling. 'And by the time I've finished, they will be.'

'Will you get my dad back then?'

Maddie's heart lurched. 'Don't tell me you have to have a dad to be in Annie's crowd?'

'She's got one,' said Clare solemnly. 'She says all decent children have them.'

Annie Wright will be asking hers for protection if I ever get my hands on her, thought Maddie, but only said, 'She doesn't know what she's talking about, love.'

'I have got a dad, though, haven't I?' said Clare uncertainly.

'Well, yes . . .'

'Why doesn't he live with us?'

'Because . . . well, because grown-ups sometimes stop being friends with each other. And that's what happened to your dad and me.'

'Oh.' Fortunately this explanation seemed to satisfy the girl and she didn't enquire further. She appeared to have forgotten Dave's violence, which wasn't too surprising since she had been very young at the time and it was three years ago. It was a huge relief to Maddie. 'Perhaps we could get another one.'

'I can't promise you that,' said Maddie with a lump in her throat. 'But I can promise you that Annie Wright will stop being mean to you.'

'Can you?' she said, snuggling against her mother.

'I certainly can,' said Maddie with feeling.

Janice listened to her account of what had been happening to Clare over coffee in Maddie's wagon the next morning when they got back from school. 'This Annie sounds a right little horror!'

'Not half.'

'A typical product of uninformed parents,' said Janice. 'As I told you when you first came here, there are a lot of ignorant people around who confuse us with gypsies – and not proper gypsies at that.' She paused, sipping her coffee. 'If they bothered to think about it, they'd realise that we're business people earning an honest living.'

'Barney doesn't seem bothered about what the other kids think?'

'It's different for him. He was born to the fair and proud of it,' said Janice. 'It's in his blood, I suppose. He can't wait to work with his dad on the Gallopers.'

'So I've heard.'

'Anyway, I suppose you're gonna rush up to the school and tell 'em what's going on?'

'Not at this stage.'

'It isn't always the answer because the teachers can't control what happens after school,' Janice pointed out. 'And this Annie Wright sounds like a right little heathen to me . . . the sort to make trouble for Clare for snitching on her – away from the teacher's watchful eye.'

'That's what I thought,' said Maddie. 'Which is why I'll only get the teachers involved as a last resort. I've come up with a much better idea.'

'Oh?'

'How do you fancy helping me to put on a party – the best party anyone in Clare's class has ever been to?'

'Party?' Janice grinned uncertainly. 'It isn't anyone's birthday.'

'No, but it is Whitsun this weekend – three years since Clare and I first arrived at Fenner's,' said Maddie. 'That's a good enough excuse for a party, I reckon.'

'You bet it is.'

'Whit Monday will be too busy on the fair for us to take a couple of hours off. So how about Saturday?' she suggested. 'I'm sure Sam can spare us for a couple of hours in the afternoon before the evening crowds start pouring in.'

'When he knows the reason why we want the time off, I'm sure he'll agree,' said Janice. 'He thinks the world of Clare.'

'Yes, he does,' agreed Maddie, feeling a sharp pang of unexpected emotion that she didn't really understand. 'I'll go and see him about it right away.'

Clare's friends from Meadow Road Juniors had never been to a party like this one before – with tea in the sunshine on a long table outside a caravan decked with balloons blowing in the breeze. It wasn't eating alfresco in itself that was so exciting so much as what was on the menu. Hot dogs, hamburgers, chips – with toffee apples and candy floss to follow. Later on they each had an ice-cream that they chose themselves from the van. And as if all of that wasn't enough, they were each allowed to have a go on two things on the fair.

There was a general fascination with Maddie's caravan.

'It's like a real house inside – only more fun,' said one child.

'Reminds me of holidays,' said another.

'I wish I lived at a fair,' said someone else.

Annie Wright, a plump child with dark hair and brooding eyes, proved to be a proper brat. She spent the whole time telling tales on the other children in an effort to get the attention she was missing because Clare and Barney – residents of this wonderland – stole the show.

The guests were mostly girls with a few of Barney's friends to create a balance. Maddie had done the thing properly and sent out party invitations. She had even taken the precaution of speaking to Annie Wright's mother outside the school to make sure that Annie could come.

Sam had been wonderful, arranging cover for Maddie and Janice. It had been Sam who had suggested giving the party guests free rides.

Maddie didn't feel bad about robbing her meagre savings to fund the party because she considered it vital to her daughter's well-being. Some people might say she had resorted to cheap tactics to achieve her end, in that junk food and fairground rides were guaranteed to impress the under-nines. But if that was what it took to end Annie Wright's reign of terror, then so be it. If you didn't have the traditional trappings to use in the fight against class distinction you were perfectly entitled to use any means at your disposal, in Maddie's opinion.

'Can I come and play with Clare again some time, please, Mrs Brown?' asked one little girl as the party neared its end.

'Yes, of course you can, dear,' said Maddie, beaming.

Up until now, Clare hadn't wanted anyone but Barney and the fairground children to play with when she was at home. But she was growing up. It was only natural she would want to broaden her circle of friends. Somehow, though, Maddie didn't think anyone would ever replace Barney as her most special friend even though he was a boy. And she hoped not because they were lovely together.

'Well, I think we can count that as a success, don't you?' said Janice when the last child had been collected.

'Definitely.'

'Clare'll have 'em eating out of her hand at school from now on,' said Janice. 'Kids are fickle little buggers and Annie can't come up with anything to match that.'

'The lengths we go to for our kids,' laughed Maddie.

'If a trip to the fair is what it takes to win friends and snub bullies . . .'

'The party was just a way to break down the barriers and give Clare a chance to assert her own personality,' said Maddie more seriously. 'I hope they'll like her for her own sake now, not just because they fancy a trip to the fair.'

'Those who are worth having as friends will,' said Janice.

'Yeah.'

That night Clare fell asleep as soon as her head touched the pillow. Maddie was in rather a happy frame of mind herself too – until she remembered Clare's recent remarks about her father. Just the idle chatter of an eight year old, forgotten almost as soon as the words were uttered? Probably. But Maddie sensed trouble in the future as Clare inevitably became more aware of things and wanted to know about her father.

On the evening of Whit Monday Dave Brown was sitting at a table in his local pub with his female companion, a woman of his own age whom he'd been seeing for the last few months. She worked at the same factory as he did. He thought she was quite tasty, a bottle blonde with nice eyes, big tits, and very few sexual inhibitions. He quite fancied her but she meant nothing more to him than that. He

106

saw her on a regular basis for companionship and sex.

'What's up with you tonight, Dave?' she asked, sipping a gin and tonic. 'You've hardly said a word all evening.'

'I don't feel like talking.'

'You might at least make the effort . . .'

'What do you wanna talk about?' he said without interest.

'I dunno. What everyone else is talking about, I suppose – the Profumo scandal.'

'Not that again.'

'We could talk about what's been on the telly lately, then . . . anything,' she said. 'But if you're just gonna sit there staring into space all night, I might as well go home.'

'Go if you want then,' he said indifferently. 'I'm not stopping you.'

'Don't be daft,' she said quickly because Dave was a good-looking bloke and she fancied him rotten even if she did find his peculiar moods a bit frightening. 'I just thought we could have a chat, friendly like – but if you're feeling quiet . . .'

'I am.'

'I'll shut up then.'

'Good.'

She looked away, sipping her drink. Dave Brown was odd, there was no doubt about that. He could be on a real high one minute and in the depths the next. It was no wonder his wife had walked out on him – he must be murder to live with. He certainly had a mood on him tonight; God knows what had rattled his cage. She never even tried to fathom out what was going on behind those flinty dark eyes that had a harshness about them she found exciting – because it was his body that interested her. He certainly didn't have anything to recommend him in the personality department.

He was terrific in bed, though. Brutal – just the way she liked it. Anyway, she wasn't exactly spoilt for choice. Unattached men weren't thick on the ground when you'd turned thirty. She was only back in circulation herself because her marriage had broken up. Oh, well, he doesn't want to talk so I'll shut up, she thought, and amused herself by watching the other people in the crowded bar enjoying themselves.

Dave's black mood was caused by the fact that today was Whit Monday – it was three years to the day since he'd last seen his wife and daughter. Disappeared into thin air! Not a word in all that time. For months after Maddie left he'd expected her to be there when he got home from work in the evening. When he found the flat empty once more he would fly into a rage and kick the walls and bang his head against them until it hurt. It was a wonder he hadn't given himself a brain haemorrhage. All Maddie's fault. She'd made him crazy!

Nowadays he didn't expect her to be at the flat when he got home, not after all this time. But he never stopped wanting her back. He cried a lot in the privacy of his own home. Wanted to weep now with the sheer hopelessness of the situation. He felt sick with frustration and fury. If he ever did get her back, he'd make damned sure she never dared stray again.

He'd go anywhere to find her if only he had a clue as to her whereabouts. Thoughts of his daughter crossed his mind occasionally but only fleetingly because she meant nothing to him. It was Maddie who preoccupied him to the point of obsession.

'Hey, Dave – what's all this about?' his companion was saying. Lifting his hand to his face, he realised that his cheeks were wet with tears.

'Nothin'.'

'Don't upset yourself, love,' she said sympathetically, rummaging in her bag for a handkerchief which she handed to him. 'Things can't be that bad.'

He looked at her, hating her because she wasn't Maddie, and wanting to beat the living daylights out of her because of it. He was too depressed to feel embarrassed and took the handkerchief to wipe his face.

'Thanks.'

''S all right.'

'Shall we go back to my place?' he suggested pointedly because he needed to blank out the pain of wanting Maddie.

'Yeah, if you like.' It was a bit early but she didn't mind. It was better than watching everyone else have a good time.

They left the pub and walked back to Dave's flat, the evening air soft with early summer. He was holding her hand but it could have been the hand of a stranger for all it meant to him.

Where are you, Maddie? he cried within himself. I'll get you back one day if it's the last thing I ever do!

Chapter Nine

The 1963 season was coming to an end. Time for Maddie to look for winter employment again.

'If only Fenner's had an all-year-round attraction, I wouldn't have to go job hunting every autumn,' she remarked lightly to Hetty one morning when they were working in the office together. 'Because you'd need me here, I should think.'

'No question about that,' said Hetty, pulling out a drawer in the filing cabinet and looking into one of the files. 'But by its very nature ours is a seasonal business.'

'It doesn't *all* have to be seasonal, though, does it?' said Maddie impulsively.

Hetty looked up. 'How do you make that out?'

'We could have indoor Bingo.'

The older woman took off her reading glasses and peered at Maddie. 'Whatever's given you that idea?'

'Bingo halls are competition, you've said so yourself,' Maddie pointed out. 'So – if you can't beat 'em, why not join 'em? We already have Bingo on the fairground so why not enlarge it, put it under cover and have it open all year round? A pavilion type of building, possibly with space for some other indoor activity – ten-pin bowling, for instance.'

'Hey, slow down, love. You're getting carried away.'

'It makes sense when you think about it, though.'

Hetty pondered the idea. 'Where would we put a pavilion?'

'You could use some of the ground you rent out to independent traders during the season,' suggested Maddie eagerly. 'Then you'd have the added advantage of its paying its way all the year round, instead of just in the season.'

'Mmm . . . there is that. But putting up a pavilion isn't a simple matter. There's the question of planning permission for starters.'

'That shouldn't be a problem as it would be situated on an existing fairground,'said Maddie, unable to stem the tide of her ideas. 'It isn't as though you'd be building a Bingo hall in the middle of a residential area.'

'I s'pose not.' Hetty still seemed doubtful. 'But Fenner's has always been a traditional summer funfair. I'm not sure if I fancy the idea of opening all year round.'

'Perhaps you could put a manager in to run it if you and the family didn't want to work through the winter,' said Maddie. 'And I could look after all the paperwork from this office.'

'I'll mention it to Vic and Sam and the others,' said Hetty, struck more by Maddie's enterprising nature than the idea itself which she feared might change the whole nature of their business. 'But don't hold your breath, love. Apart from anything else, there's the expense.'

'If what I've heard about Bingo halls and ten-pin bowling is true, it would be well worth the investment.' Maddie gave a wry grin, realising that she had totally overstepped her position as an employee. 'Honestly . . . the lengths some people will go to to create a job for themselves!'

Hetty smiled, her face a mass of wrinkles and laughter lines. 'I don't blame you for looking out for yourself, especially when you've a nipper to bring up on your own.'

'Seriously though,' said Maddie, 'I really was thinking of the firm.'

'I believe you – thousands wouldn't.'

'Anyway, my luck's in again this year,' said Maddie. 'Because I think there's a job for me at the Fiddler's Inn.'

'I'm glad about that,' said Hetty, putting her specs back on and turning her attention to her work, the subject of the proposed Bingo hall closed for the moment.

'What are you doing when you finish here?' asked a man called Alan King who'd been flirting with Maddie all evening over the counter of the Fiddler's Inn. He'd become a regular customer during the summer months when she hadn't been there, apparently, and was a big spender. Maddie had heard that he was the owner of a thriving modern garage and service station in Twickenham and had recently bought a house in the Richmond area.

'Going home,' she replied.

'Bit boring, innit?'

'No, not really.'

'Don't you need to unwind and relax before you go to bed?'

'Yeah, and I do that with a hot drink by the fire.'

His penetrating grey eyes rested on Maddie's face. She thought he was probably in his mid- to late-thirties. Good-looking with clean-cut, masculine features. 'Why not come up the West End to a club with me?' he invited. 'It'll be more fun than drinking cocoa on your own, I can promise you that.'

I bet you can, she thought, but said, 'Thanks for asking but I have to go straight home.'

'But I know you don't have a husband to go home to.' He paused, raising his eyebrows. 'I checked with Bob.'

'I do have a little daughter, though.'

'Who's looking after her now?'

'A friend.'

'Might that friend be persuaded to stay with her for a while longer if I make it worth their while financially?'

His attractiveness was rather contrived, she noticed. He was well-groomed and expensively dressed in a continental-style suit, with chunky gold cuff links and rings on his fingers. But Maddie felt herself responding to him, mainly because it was so good to feel fancied again. Chat-up lines went with the job for any barmaid but Alan seemed genuinely keen on her.

She had come a long way in terms of increased confidence since leaving Dave. She had proved that she could stand on her own two feet, hold down a job and provide for herself and her daughter. But her awareness of her own sex appeal had been practically non-existent, especially since the blow to her ego caused by Josh's pretended interest. Being still quite young, she did sometimes feel the need for physical passion even though she was extremely wary of it.

'I wouldn't be prepared to ask her at such short notice,' Maddie said firmly. 'I'd like to come – but not tonight.'

'What about your night off then?' Alan's eagerness was heady stuff after years of celibacy.

'Maybe.' She couldn't commit herself to anything definite yet because of Clare.

'Playing hard to get, eh?'

'No harm in making you put some effort into it.' Maddie grinned. 'But as it happens I'm not trying to do that. I just can't make plans to go out myself without first making arrangements for my daughter to be looked after.'

'Yeah, I understand,' he said with a melting smile. 'But . . .'

A sudden influx of customers meant Maddie had to leave the conversation unfinished while she attended to them. Immediately things calmed down at the bar, she was asked by Pat to go to the kitchen to help with a large order for sandwiches.

'I want a word with you,' said Pat, a smart, gregarious woman of about fifty with tinted red hair and round green eyes.

'The sandwiches . . .'

'All taken care of,' she said, glancing towards another member of staff who was busy at the kitchen table. 'That was just an excuse to get you out here for a quiet word before you commit yourself to anything.'

Maddie looked puzzled.

'With Alan King,' Pat explained. 'He's obviously after you. Looks to me as though you wouldn't say no to him either.'

'What's wrong with that?'

'Nothing. But he's a wrong 'un, love,' Pat said, her expression darkening. 'I thought you ought to know that before you agree to do anything you might later regret.'

'He's only asked me out for an evening.' Maddie was indignant because the flirtation was fun and she didn't want it spoiled. 'I don't need a character reference for that.'

'You'd be wise to steer clear of him altogether,' warned Pat.

'He's married – is that it?'

'Not that I know of,' she said. 'But I do know that he's a crook.'

'A crook!' Maddie was incredulous. 'Oh, really, Pat!'

'It's true.'

'How do you know?'

'You get to know a lot of things in the licensed trade.'

'But you and Bob seem quite friendly with him?'

'Only in the line of business. It's our job to be sociable to punters whoever they are,' the landlady pointed out. 'And he's a damned good customer. But when it comes to his taking a personal interest in one of our staff, I consider it my duty to intervene.'

'But he's a businessman,' said Maddie. 'The owner of a big garage.'

'That's just his legitimate front.'

'What does he do exactly that's so terrible?' Maddie wanted to know.'

'I don't know what he's up to at the moment but he'll be involved in something dodgy, you can bet your sweet life on it. His service station will be a cover for something a lot more lucrative than the straight motor trade.'

'How can you be so sure?'

'He's a known face in Fulham where Bob and I used to run a pub. Everybody knows about him, including the Old Bill. They've been trying to nail him for years but Alan's too cute for 'em – makes sure they never get enough evidence to convict him.'

'Oh.'

'Look, the last thing I wanna do is spoil anything for you,' said Pat, observing Maddie's disappointment. 'I could see you were enjoying having him chat you up and I don't blame you – Alan's a good-looking bloke. But if you've any sense, you won't get mixed up with the likes of him.'

'Just my luck,' sighed Maddie. 'I get some gorgeous man after me and he turns out to be a villain.'

'What you do outside of working hours is none of my business, o' course,' said Pat. 'But I couldn't have rested easy in my bed if I hadn't let you know the sort of man Alan King is.'

'He seems so nice, too.'

'A perfect charmer,' agreed Pat. 'And he'd know how to treat any woman he took out, I bet. But he'll go down one of these days and anyone he's seeing could be implicated.'

'Yeah, you did right to tell me.'

'Someone better than Alan will come along for you, one of these days.'

Maddie doubted it. Romance always seemed to elude her.

'Thanks for the warning anyway,' she said in a manner that indicated she would make up her own mind about Alan's invitation.

But when he repeated it a few nights later, Maddie made it clear that she wasn't interested in seeing him outside working hours. Had she not had Clare to consider she might have been tempted by the excitement that a fling with him would undoubtedly bring. But her maternal instincts prevailed when it really came down to it.

One thing in particular that really impressed Maddie about Fenner's was the efficient way the men of the fair dealt with trouble on the fairground – without involving the police whenever possible.

Never was their expertise more commendable than on the evening of the last day of the 1964 season the following year when a crowd of local Mods arrived en masse and parked their chrome-sided Lambretta motor scooters on the edge of the fairground.

Dressed in a strangely contradictory manner with smart short-jacket suits but ripped parka coats, they were noisy but harmless, riding the dodgems and testing their skills on the Shooting Range. But when some out-of-town Mods decided to try their luck at Fenner's too, on this special night of reduced prices, the mood became ugly as the youths began to taunt each other and fights broke out.

Maddie was finishing something in the office before going out on to the fair in time for the fireworks, unaware that anything untoward was happening outside, when Sam rushed in and asked her to sound the signal for trouble. This entailed blowing a whistle into the microphone so that it could be heard throughout the fairground.

This done Maddie locked the office and went outside to look for Clare who was with Barney and the other children. Passing the Dodgems, she found herself right in the path of the marauding youths. Turning, she was confronted by the rival Mods coming the other way. She just managed to get out of their way by darting to one side.

People were screaming and hurrying towards the exits as fear spread among the punters.

'Don't leave now and miss the fireworks,' Maddie urged them. 'The management will soon get this matter cleared up.'

Some took notice of her, others continued on their way. An eerie silence fell as one by one the rides stopped operating at the sound of the whistle. As Maddie watched – along with crowds of punters – the men of the fair, accompanied by dogs on leads, pushed through the Mods and stood between the two rival groups. Sam was leading with Josh, Chas, Eric with Marlon, Vic and a crowd of fair workers behind him. These men had plenty of muscle they would use if they had to, and the dogs were trained to obey them.

'Come on, lads, on your way,' said Sam in an even but commanding tone. 'If you must fight, go and do it somewhere else.'

There was a lot of shouting and he was told – in strong language – to mind his own business.

'You're on our property which makes it our business,' he said.

'Get out of our way and you won't be hurt,' ordered one of the youths. 'We ain't got no quarrel with you.'

'This is a family funfair and there are women and children around,' continued Sam, holding the lead of a straining Alsatian. 'Not the place for a stylish bunch of lads like yourselves. Wimbledon Palais is more your scene. So on your way.'

'Bugger off or we'll set the dogs on you!' shouted Vic, face plum-coloured with rage, eyes bulging.

'Leave it to me, Dad,' said Sam, moving in front of his father to protect him. He stared at the Mods. 'So, what's it to be – do we let the dogs loose or will you leave quietly?'

After some angry discussion the youths began to head back towards their Lambrettas, muttering among themselves.

Seeing Sam so strong and in control did astonishing things to Maddie's libido and she found herself reeling from the shock. Telling herself she didn't need those sort of complications, she composed herself and went over to the men. 'Well done, you lot,' she said.

'You should have left it to the young 'uns, Vic,' admonished Hetty who appeared with Janice and the children.

'Give over, woman,' he said. 'Think I'm too old to look after my own fair?'

'You could have got hurt.'

'By a crowd of teenagers? Don't make me laugh,' he retorted. 'If the day ever comes when I stand back from a bunch of boys still wet behind the ears, I'll call it a day and put my head in the oven.'

'Not in our oven, you won't,' she said, but she was smiling.

'Well, I thought you were all heroes,' said Maddie.

There was a general roar of agreement from the women, then everybody began to talk at once, relieved that the altercation hadn't developed into anything more serious.

'We can't let a gang of lads upset the last night of the season, can we?' said Sam.

There was a wholehearted response from everyone – except Josh who seemed very preoccupied, Maddie noticed.

'Come on then, everybody, let's get this show back on the road,' said Sam in rousing tones.

Maddie was about to turn away when she saw a look pass between Josh and Tania who was standing on the sidelines. It was so piercingly intimate that it startled her, and she knew for a fact then that their affair was still going strong.

Within minutes the rides were all running again and the fair was back to normal. Clare and Barney were arguing about who was the hero of the hour.

'My dad was the bravest,' said Barney.

'Uncle Sam was,' said Clare.

'They all did their bit, so stop quarrelling,' Maddie intervened. 'It'll soon be time for the fireworks.'

'Yippee!' whooped Clare.

Maddie smiled. Her daughter had seemed much more settled and content since that awful business with Annie Wright.

Later that night when all the festivities were over, Josh sat alone in his wagon, smoking a cigarette, drinking whisky and mulling over the appalling situation he was in. He was in love with a woman with whom he could have no future, despite Tania's views to the contrary.

To her it was simple; they should leave Fenner's and make a new start together somewhere else – end of story! Sure Sam would be hurt, but it wasn't as if there were any children involved. Sam was a grown man and all adults had to take knocks at some time in their life. He would get over it.

Tania had lost touch with her own relatives years ago, and didn't know the meaning of family ties, even the tenuous ones of a man like Josh who had always made a point of keeping his distance from the family in an emotional sense.

More than anything else in the world, he wanted to make his life with Tania – to have children with her and grow old with her. Even his plans to buy a bar in Spain had been overshadowed by his all-consuming attachment to her.

Thank God the fair season had come to an end. He'd hardly seen her except in passing during the summer months. Working long hours in a family environment, neither of them could get away without its being noticed.

With the fair shut down for winter, clandestine meetings would be possible again. But Josh had to make a decision. He couldn't go on as they had been, loving her and not being able to share his life with her. It was crushing him.

Earlier that evening when the Fenners had united against the Mods, he'd felt the strong tug of family loyalty. This piercing reminder of its existence had saddened Josh because – while recognising it as a priceless thing – it was a burden to him, something he had fought against all his adult life.

He wanted to be free to do as he liked and be with the woman he loved. And that meant going away and cutting himself off forever from the family who would, understandably, disown him.

But compunction is a powerful force. As besotted as he was with

Tania, he knew he couldn't do it. His conscience simply wouldn't allow him to take away his brother's wife.

'But you've already taken me away from Sam,' she had reminded him when he'd spoken of his doubts. 'Us going away isn't gonna make much difference. I don't love him and he knows it.'

'He'd sooner have you, knowing that you don't love him, than not have you at all,' Josh had said. 'Anyway, I don't think he could cope, knowing it's his brother you're in love with. I know I would find it impossible if it was the other way around.'

But Tania had said they must forget about Sam and get on with their own lives. Lately she'd been threatening to tell Sam the truth if Josh didn't do what she asked.

'You'd be forced to go away with me then,' was her reasoning. 'Because we'd both be outcasts.'

Josh didn't mind being an outcast; he'd always been the odd one out in the family anyway. But the thought of Sam learning about him and Tania was unbearable. He knew it would break his brother's heart.

So what was he to do? As things couldn't go on as they were and he wasn't prepared to take his brother's wife away from him altogether, he would have to go away without Tania; take the money he'd saved and make a new start somewhere else – on his own.

For a moment he toyed with the idea of leaving now, *this instant*, just disappearing without telling anyone. But he couldn't do that. He was every kind of bastard but even he couldn't sink that low. Quite apart from the pain that would cause Tania, he couldn't just walk out of his mother's life without a word of warning. She didn't deserve that. No mother could have done more for her children than his had, and, for all that he didn't deserve it, she had always favoured him above Sam and Janice.

But Josh was in a mess and he had to do whatever it took to resolve it. With him out of the picture, Tania might settle down to life with Sam even though she didn't love him. She wasn't the sort of woman to want her independence. She wasn't self-reliant like Maddie Brown. Tania needed a man to lean on.

Josh decided to arrange to meet her and tell her of his plans before he said anything to the family. His stomach churned at the thought of her reaction to the news but it was the only solution. When he was about to leave, he would tell the family he was going; he'd say he wanted a change from fairground life, which was perfectly true. This way no one need ever know about him and Tania.

It occurred to him that Tania might tell the family about the affair to get him ostracised from Fenner's out of revenge for his leaving without her. But if she did that she risked losing her own place in the family. And Tania was far too fond of comfort and regular meals to jeopardize that.

Making the decision to go didn't make him feel any better but at least he had a definite plan now. The first thing to do was to arrange a meeting with Tania . . .

Two days later Sam left the office and walked back to his wagon, feeling pleased with himself, having just booked a table for two this evening at one of Richmond's classiest riverside hotels. Tania deserved to be pampered now that the season was over and they had more time for leisure.

Dusk was beginning to fall, the sound of workmen's voices echoing in the damp evening air hazed with patchy mist. He'd finished work for the day and the maintenance workers were just packing up. Tania should be back from her shopping spree in the West End by now, he thought, smiling at the thought of the treat he had in store for her. She always went up the West End to buy clothes as soon as the season was over as there wasn't a chance to do anything much besides work during the summer.

He was disappointed to find that she wasn't home when he arrived because he was eager to tell her what he had planned. His high spirits took even more of a dive as he wondered if she would actually be pleased about what he'd done. She could be very offhand about the most carefully planned treat. Still, that was just her way and all part of her charm. A sweet nature wouldn't suit Tania.

Removing his coat he drew the curtains across the windows, put some coal on the fire and the kettle on the stove for tea. The wagon felt dismal without Tania's presence even though he knew she would be home soon. Sam switched on the television for the early-evening news and sat down in the armchair with a cup of tea to await his wife's return.

The news was dominated by the Labour Party's narrow victory in yesterday's general election after thirteen years of Tory government. He wondered vaguely what sort of a Prime Minister Harold Wilson would make as he appeared outside number ten, Downing Street smiling victoriously. He seemed a genuine enough sort of a bloke but politicians usually did – until they got into power.

When the news had finished and there was still no sign of his wife, Sam hoped she wasn't going to be much longer because she would want plenty of time to get herself all glammed up for their posh night out.

When Maddie got home from her session at the pub that evening and went to collect Clare from Janice's, Sam was there – in a state of high anxiety.

'Tania hasn't come home,' Janice explained to Maddie. 'And Sam's working himself up into a state about it. I've told him not to worry.'

'She should be back by now,' he said and Maddie could see how worried he was; lips tight, face tense.

'You know what Tania's like,' said Janice. 'She often goes out without you and gets back late, doesn't she?'

'Yeah, but . . .'

'Remember, she doesn't know you have a surprise planned for her so wouldn't think it important that she should get back at any particular time.'

'She wouldn't stay out this late on a shopping trip,' said Sam, chewing his bottom lip. 'The shops will have closed hours ago.'

'Perhaps she called to see a friend and got chatting,' suggested Maddie, suspicion filling her with dread.

'I've phoned all her friends that I know of,' said Sam, 'and none of them has seen her today.'

'Well, I'm sure there's a simple explanation,' said Maddie soothingly.

'Maybe.' Sam looked unconvinced.

'Have you asked everyone on the park if they've seen her?' asked Maddie, glancing towards the other wagons and noticing that Josh's was in darkness and his car wasn't there.

'No one's seen her since this morning, and I haven't asked Josh 'cause he isn't there. He hasn't been around all day. He'll be in a pub or club somewhere, making the most of his free time.'

'I saw him go into his wagon on my way to work,' said Maddie, remembering. 'He seemed to be in rather a hurry.'

'He must have just popped back to get something because he wasn't there when I came over from the office,' said Sam. 'Anyway, never mind about him . . . it's Tania I'm worried about.'

Knowing what she did about Josh and Tania, Maddie was beginning to get a terrible sinking feeling in the pit of her stomach.

'Has Clare been all right while I've been out, Janice?' she asked, turning her mind to her own concerns.

'Fast asleep in Barney's room. You can leave her there till the morning, if you like. To save disturbing her.'

'Thanks, Janice, I will.'

'Don't all stand about talking, then. Sit down and I'll make some coffee.'

'Not for me, thanks, sis,' said Sam grimly. 'I'm going out looking for Tania.'

'Where?'

'Round the town . . . at the station . . . anywhere,' he said. 'I can't just stay here doing nothing.'

'Shall I come with you?' offered his sister, looking at Maddie. 'You'll look after the kids, won't you?'

''Course I will.'

'There's no need for you to come.'

'But she could be anywhere, Sam,' said Janice. 'My bet is she's met up with a friend and they've gone to a restaurant. Tania's just making the most of the season being over.'

'Not this late,' he said gruffly. 'Something must have happened to her.'

Sam was like a different person tonight, observed Maddie. This wasn't the calm and collected man who ran the fair so efficiently, a man who solved problems and defused trouble on a regular basis. This was someone tortured with worry for a woman who wasn't worthy of his love.

'Now don't start imagining things,' said Janice to calm her brother. 'She'll have forgotten the time, that's all.'

'If she doesn't show up soon, I'll have to notify the police.'

'Stop panicking, for God's sake! She'll turn up.'

Maddie was much less sure about that. The signs pointed to the one thing she had dreaded ever since she'd learned about Tania and Josh – that they'd gone off together for good. It seemed odd that no one else had made the connection. It obviously hadn't occurred to Sam and Janice that Tania and Josh might be together.

''Course she'll turn up,' Maddie said to Sam with fake confidence.

The situation became more serious the next morning when Tania still hadn't appeared. Sam contacted the police who came to Fenner's to take details before mounting a search. Hetty and Vic were notified and came straight over. Questions were being asked about Josh's whereabouts, though still no one suggested the unthinkable. Everybody seemed to think that he and Tania both being missing was coincidental.

Maddie was beginning to wonder if she ought to tell Sam what she knew to stop him fearing that Tania had been abducted. But the poor man was wretched enough as it was. How could she tell him about his wife's adultery?

That afternoon something happened that shook the Fenner family to its very foundations, and made everything else pale into insignificance . . .

A woman's body answering to Tania's description was found by some quarry workers at the bottom of a ravine on the edge of a quarry near Hanleigh Woods in Surrey. Sam was required to go with the police to the mortuary to identify the body. His father went with him. No one actually believed that it was Tania. It couldn't be. Things like that just didn't happen to people like them!

Maddie telephoned Pat to say she couldn't go into work that evening. She thought the family needed her. They were in a dreadful state, waiting for Sam and his father to come back. Maddie felt pretty awful herself, but being unrelated considered it her duty to be strong for them.

119

They all gathered in Janice's wagon, awaiting the men's return. Hetty, Janice, Sybil, Eric and Chas sat around talking while Maddie made pot after pot of tea. She gave the children something to eat and they went next door to her caravan to watch the television.

When they finally heard a car draw up outside, they all rushed to the door. Maddie's heart was thudding. She might not be family but she still felt their pain.

Only Vic got out of the car, looking grim. There was no sign of Sam.

'Well, was it . . . ?' ventured Hetty.

He nodded. 'Yeah, I'm afraid it was Tania,' he said.

There was a shocked silence.

'Where's Sam?' enquired Hetty in a trembling voice.

'At the nick.' Vic's voice shook. 'They need him to help with their enquiries.'

After a short silence while this shocking news registered, there was a general outcry. Maddie thought Hetty was going to pass out and eased her gently into a chair.

'Helping with their enquiries?' she said, her voice distorted with anguish. 'That's just a polite way of saying they think *he* had something to do with her death.'

'Of course it isn't,' said Maddie.

'They think he murdered her.' Hetty was deathly white.

'No they don't,' said Maddie.

''Course they don't,' echoed Janice. Everyone else seemed stunned into silence.

'Then why are they keeping him at the police station?'

'I suppose it's because they need to talk to the next-of-kin when someone dies unexpectedly,' said Maddie. 'It's probably just routine.'

But she was deeply worried. There were things she could no longer keep to herself.

Chapter Ten

By the time Sam got back from the police station that evening, Maddie had gone home to put Clare to bed. While making it clear that she was at hand if they needed her, she'd deemed it wisest to retreat slightly from the family circle, sensitive to their need for privacy.

Janice popped in later on with the news that no charges had been laid against Sam who had a rock solid alibi. He'd been at the fairground all day yesterday and plenty of people could vouch for that.

'Are the police treating Tania's death as murder then?' Maddie enquired.

'It seems to be a question of "Did she fall or was she pushed?"'

'My God!'

'There doesn't seem to be any doubt that she died from the fall – it's a very steep drop apparently,' explained Janice, brown eyes dull with worry. 'But the police don't think she was there by herself. The implication is that someone might have deliberately pushed her to her death. Hanleigh Woods is a favourite spot for lovers.'

'Oh, dear.'

'Yeah,' said Janice grimly. 'Looks like my sister-in-law had been playing away.'

'Sam must be devastated.'

'He is, the poor love. Mum's in a right old state about it an' all.' Janice sighed. 'If Josh was here it would help. A family needs to be together at a time like this.'

'Mmm.'

'He's certainly chosen his time to go swanning off.'

'You've no idea where he is, then?'

Janice shook her head, tutting. 'We don't even know where to start looking. He's always kept quiet about his mates – they're dodgy types you wouldn't wanna bring home, according to Sam. So we've nothing to go on. Mum's tried a few of the pubs in Hammersmith that we know Josh uses but nobody seems to have seen him for the last few days.'

It seemed incredible to Maddie that the family hadn't put two and two together about Josh and Tania. But as she reminded herself, he was often away when the fair was closed for the winter, and it simply wouldn't occur to this close-knit family that any of their number would break the rules in the way that Josh and Tania had. If Janice ever found out what Maddie had kept to herself for so long, she'd probably see it as a betrayal – not only of Sam but of the whole family.

The information as it stood at the moment suggested to Maddie that Josh had pushed Tania to her death then gone on the run. His being in such a hurry when she'd seen him yesterday made that theory even more feasible.

But Maddie didn't really see Josh as a murderer. Arrogant and cruel, yes. But a killer? She shuddered inwardly, remembering once reading somewhere that anyone could be capable of murder under certain circumstances.

One thing was certain, though. It was only a matter of time before somebody made the damning connection. The police would certainly start to probe deeper if Josh didn't turn up soon. Better that Sam heard the painful facts from Maddie herself than be humiliated by the police.

'Josh will be back when he's ready,' was all she could think of to say to her friend.

Maddie hardly slept that night. She thrashed about between the sheets rehearsing the awesome task that lay ahead of her the next day . . .

Being Sunday there was no school. As soon as Clare had gone out to play with Barney, Maddie went to Sam's wagon and knocked on the door.

'I'm so sorry about Tania,' she said as he ushered her inside, seeming relieved that she was alone.

He looked terrible: ashen-faced, eyes bloodshot and darkly shadowed.

'I'm glad I've caught you on your own,' she said, perching uneasily on the edge of an armchair in his living room which had Tania's stamp all over it, crudely glamorous rather than homely. It had contemporary leather furniture in a garish shade of blue, luxurious red carpet, gilt-edged mirrors and an abundance of vases and ornaments.

'Not an easy thing at the moment, catching me alone,' he said, his voice thick with grief. 'Everyone seems to think I'll pine away if I'm left for more than five minutes. They'll all come piling back in before long.'

'They mean well,' said Maddie. 'You're lucky to have such a caring family.'

'I know.' Sam sighed. 'There are times when you can have too much of a good thing, though.'

'I can imagine.'

'Tea – coffee?'

'No, thanks.'

'Oh.' He looked at his watch and she knew he wanted her to go. 'I . . . I appreciate your coming to see me with your condolences. It's kind of you but . . .'

'You'd like to be on your own?'

He gave her a wry grin. 'I knew you'd understand, Maddie.'

Each word he uttered was torn from the depths of his anguish and she hated herself for having to add to his pain.

She stood up, rigid with tension. 'The thing is, Sam,' she began hesitantly, 'I didn't just come to say how sorry I am.'

'Oh?'

'There's something else . . .'

'Can it wait until things have calmed down a bit?'

'It can't, I'm afraid.' She ran her fingers through her hair nervously. 'There's no easy way to say this . . .'

'Get on with it then,' he said wearily. 'I'm not in the mood for a long drawn out discussion.'

'I feel I must tell you, before the police start to work things out . . .'

He gave her a close look, his attitude softening as he realised that something was really bothering her. 'Out with it, Maddie.'

'I've heard that the police think Tania was at Hanleigh Woods with a man?'

'That's right,' he confirmed miserably.

'I believe that man was Josh.'

'Josh?'

'Yes. He and Tania were having an affair,' she blurted out. 'It's been going on for some time.'

Sam didn't reply, just stared at her in disbelief.

'Don't be ridiculous!' he said at last.

'I only wish I were being ridiculous,' she said. 'But, unfortunately, it's true.'

'No!'

'I'm afraid so,' she continued. 'It was the reason Tania wanted me out of Fenner's. She thought Josh was paying me too much attention.'

'Rubbish! She did that because she thought *I* was getting too fond of you.'

Maddie shook her head. 'I'm so sorry, Sam. But with Tania's death being treated as suspicious, I feel duty bound to tell you the truth about what's been going on. I shall have to tell the police what I know anyway.'

His face was bloodless. 'I think you'd better tell me everything.'

She told him the whole story then, including the way Josh had been forced to take the blame for the Chairoplane accident because of what she knew.

'You even used the information against him . . . but you didn't tell me?'

'It was the only way I could make him do the decent thing,' Maddie explained, spreading her hands in a helpless gesture. 'I couldn't just stand by and let him destroy Eric.'

'You saw fit to let him carry on betraying me, though,' said Sam, voice gruff and clipped with emotion. 'All this time they've been deceiving me. *You knew* . . . and kept it to yourself.'

'I didn't want to hurt you. I hoped the affair would run its course and you'd never have to know.'

'That bastard brother of mine!' he said, almost choking on the words. 'I've always known he didn't give a damn. But this . . .'

'Perhaps he really did love her?' suggested Maddie. 'Such things do happen.'

'*Love*! You talk to me about *love*!' Sam's voice rose in anger. 'He had no business to love another man's wife, let alone his brother's. There are such things as loyalty and *self-control*.'

'Did you never suspect anything?' asked Maddie. 'I mean . . . in all that time, Tania must have given some sort of indication.'

'It wasn't in her nature to be content so I was used to her coldness towards me. She always wanted more than I could give her,' said Sam. 'And, yes, to be perfectly honest, I did suspect she was seeing someone. But I tried not to think about it. I hoped it would fizzle out. I never dreamt it was my brother – *my own flesh and blood*.'

Maddie stood still with her arms by her sides as he continued.

'And now the bastard's killed her and run away because he's too much of a coward to stay and face up to the consequences of what he's done.'

'You don't know that he killed her. That's a very serious allegation.'

'It's obvious to me now that I know what's been going on,' said Sam. 'My wife's dead and her lover's gone missing. It speaks for itself.'

She didn't say anything.

'And you, Maddie – all this time you've known what was going on and you didn't tell me,' he said. 'That really hurts.'

'Look at it from my point of view,' she urged him. 'It was a very delicate and personal matter. I didn't think it was my place to meddle in other people's lives. If you were my brother, I might have felt I had the right to interfere. But I am, after all, just an employee here.'

'You're more than that, *much more*, you must know that. You're a part of our community – a family friend.'

Despite the appalling circumstances, his words warmed Maddie.

'I'm glad you think of me in those terms,' she said. 'But even as a family friend, discretion seemed the wisest thing.'

'You protected them.'

'*No, never!*' she cried emphatically, cheeks flaming at the accusation. 'I was protecting *you* – trying to save you from pain. I didn't have any time for Josh or Tania. I hated what they were doing. It hurt me just to think about it. It's you I care about, Sam. You're the reason I've kept it to myself all this time, because I couldn't bear to see you hurt. You're a very dear friend. I thought I was doing the best thing for you.'

'Well, you weren't.' His tawny eyes were harsh and sad. He seemed like a stranger. 'If I'd known what they were up to, I might have been able to do something about it. Now she's dead and it's too late.'

'I can understand you being angry and upset. I'm so sorry.'

'And so you bloody well ought to be!' he said, his face twisted with pain. 'My God, Maddie, I could kill you for not telling me! So just get out of here and leave me alone.'

Hurt beyond words, she said, 'Don't blame the messenger, Sam. I'm not the one who betrayed you. Whether you believe it or not, I only had your best interests at heart.'

Then she left.

Maddie was half expecting a torrent of abuse from other members of the family when they heard the secret she had guarded for so long. But as no one said anything to her about it she assumed that Sam had decided to keep it to himself. She was grateful to him for this even though she still believed she had done the right thing.

When Josh's absence continued, the awful truth began to dawn on everyone, especially as the police emphasised their eagerness to question him about recent events at Hanleigh Woods. Everybody at Fenner's was warned of the serious consequences of not notifying the police if he contacted them.

Although nobody seemed to know about Maddie's prior knowledge, it was now generally assumed that Josh had been with Tania at the quarry when she had 'fallen'. He was believed to be on the run. His continued absence pointed to his guilt, and the family was devastated, though the official verdict was an open one.

'I'd have soon sorted out that cow Tania if I'd known she was cheating on Sam,' Janice said to Maddie.

'She wasn't doing it on her own,' Maddie pointed out.

'Josh is a man, though, in't he?' she said, protective as ever of her sibling. 'They've no will power when it comes to sex. It's the way they're made and they can't help it.'

'Even so . . .'

'Don't think I'm condoning his behaviour 'cause I'm not,' Janice was keen to point out. 'I could murder him for what he's done. This has broken my mother's heart as well as Sam's. Josh has always been the apple of her eye.'

'Mmm.'

'Not any more though,' said Janice. 'She says she wants nothing more to do with him now she knows what he's been up to.'

'Poor Hetty,' said Maddie.

People poured into the cemetery from all over the country for Tania's funeral. Not because she had been popular but because she was Sam's wife and he was very well liked in fairground circles. Because there was such a crowd, they had the gathering afterwards in the fairground restaurant.

'Quite a turnout,' remarked Maddie as she and Hetty and Janice worked together in the restaurant kitchen, trying to meet the huge demand for sandwiches.

'They've come as a mark of respect to Sam – nothing to do with Tania,' said Hetty. 'I've only laid on this do for his sake. She could have gone to her grave without a single mourner for all I care – the bitch!'

'Now then, Mum, don't upset yourself,' said Janice.

'I made allowances for her because of Sam – put up with her laziness, even defended her when she made trouble for Maddie,' continued Hetty, voice rising with emotion. 'And all the time she was committing adultery within the family!' She paused and sucked in her breath. 'And as for Josh . . .'

'He's still your son.'

'Sam's my only son now,' she said, turning to them so that Maddie could see the raw pain in her eyes. 'Josh is no longer a son of mine.'

'You know you don't mean that,' said Janice with feeling. 'If he does turn up you'll feel differently about him.'

'Josh isn't welcome here any more.' Hetty was adamant.

'Whatever he's done, he's still your son and my brother.'

'Only by blood.'

'I thought that counted for everything in your book?' said Janice.

'And it always has done until now. There's nothing I wouldn't do for my kids, you know that. If Josh'd robbed a bank or committed fraud, I'd have stood by him. But he's split our family – destroyed his brother and betrayed us all with his mucky goings on. And he hasn't even the guts to stay and face up to it!' She grimaced. 'Ugh! It makes me feel sick just to think about it. It's the complete disregard for other people's feelings that gets me – the sheer immorality of it. I brought my kids up to be decent people. I don't expect them to repay me by doing something like Josh has been doing within our family. It's not far short of incest.'

'They weren't related by blood,' Janice pointed out.

'Moral incest then.'

126

'None of us is perfect.' Janice was broad-minded and fond of both her brothers which meant her loyalties were divided. 'I don't suppose I've always come up to your expectations.'

Hetty's tired brown eyes softened as she looked at her daughter. Watching her, Maddie realised how deeply she felt for her children.

'I admit I was disappointed when you got yourself pregnant – and even more upset when you wouldn't get married to give your child a decent start in life.' She paused. 'Even now I'd like to see you and Chas married – for young Barney's sake if not your own. I never did like the idea of your being an unmarried mother, and I don't like it now.'

'Attitudes are changing towards that sort of thing.'

'The stigma is still there, though. And your modern ideas won't change that. You can hold your head up all you like, but you won't change the way people feel about things.'

'The day will come when women in my position won't be made to suffer.'

'Maybe it will – but it hasn't come yet. But you've got your own way of doing things and I've had to accept that.' Hetty's eyes filled with tears as she stood with the butter knife poised, looking at Janice. 'What I'm trying to say is . . . I'm not disappointed in you, love. Quite the opposite.'

'Really?'

'Yeah, really,' she confirmed. 'However much I'd like you to be married, I'm proud of you for sticking to your principles. You're true to Chas even though you're not married to him, and you're a damned fine mother to young Barney.'

'Oh.' Janice was taken aback because the Fenners weren't much given to sentimental speeches. Her eyes glistened with tears. 'Thanks, Mum, that means a lot to me.'

Maddie turned away and concentrated on slicing the ham. Being on the outside of such deep-felt affection was a very lonely feeling.

When Maddie got back from work at the Fiddler's Inn on the night of the funeral, Clare was asleep next door at Janice's so Maddie left her where she was until the morning.

This was quite a regular occurrence but the place always felt empty when her daughter wasn't there. Tonight the emptiness was particularly noticeable. It had been an emotional day for everyone, a real family occasion that Maddie couldn't help feeling excluded from at certain times.

Her loneliness was exacerbated by the fact that Sam hadn't spoken a word to her since their last meeting. She'd thought she was immune to pain after the regular agony she had received at Dave's hands. But knowing that Sam thought badly of her was surprisingly hurtful.

She had agonised over it until her head ached. Maybe she had been wrong not to tell him what she knew? He certainly seemed to think so. But at the time it had seemed the right thing to do – and still did if she was honest.

Sitting down in the armchair with a mug of cocoa, Maddie intended to watch the television until the epilogue with the idea of reaching exhaustion before going to bed. With everything that had been happening lately, she was finding it difficult to sleep.

Sam sat in his armchair by the fire in his wagon, glad to be alone after the strain of being sociable to people at the funeral. He appreciated their kindness in coming but felt distant from them – from everyone. But the solitude he had welcomed turned to a feeling of desolation as the aching stillness of the caravan without Tania in it enveloped him. Worse was the awful realisation that this was for always. Never again would he hear her voice, smell her special scent or feel her presence in their home – it would be just his home from now on.

Up until now the fact of her actually being dead hadn't seemed real. He'd been numb – living in a curious state of limbo between the death and the funeral when ordinary everyday life had been replaced by the official paperwork of bereavement, funeral arrangements and entertaining a stream of visitors who came to pay their respects. Now that that was over, the fact that she had gone was a harsh reality; he had to face up to never seeing her again.

Normally a moderate drinker, today he'd had more than he could comfortably handle to help him through the ordeal, the effects of which had now worn off, leaving him feeling even more depressed. Sam went over to the sideboard and poured himself a comforting glass of whisky, wondering which hurt the most: Tania's being dead or Tania's being unfaithful? He decided on the former. While she'd been alive there had always been the chance of making their marriage work.

It was only since he'd known about her affair with Josh that he'd admitted to himself that their marriage had been in serious trouble for a long time. He'd been afraid to confront her with his suspicions in case he lost her altogether. Hoping that whatever was going on would come to its natural end, he'd pretended not to notice her distant attitude towards him. He now presumed that their increasingly rare lovemaking had been endurable to her only by imagining that he was Josh.

He held his head, hardly able to bear the pain – pain he'd been spared for so long because of Maddie. Maddie . . . Somewhere in the jumbled haze of memory was a blurred vision of her face when he'd turned on her for not telling him what she'd known. She'd looked wounded but not defeated. Her mouth had been set firmly, head held high. 'Don't blame the messenger,' she'd said, vivid blue eyes dulled by hurt but still retaining a gleam of spirit. 'I only had your best interests at heart.'

In retrospect Sam could see that this was true, and compunction was now added to his grief. He finished his drink and poured another, the soothing effect dulling the misery of his thoughts. He'd had no right to behave as he had towards Maddie, shouting at her and then deliberately ignoring her.

The truth was, he couldn't bear to look at her because she reminded him of things he didn't want to think about. And that wasn't fair. It wasn't Maddie's fault Sam had been betrayed by his own wife and brother. She'd just been an innocent bystander who'd been drawn into the sordid affair simply because she happened to have seen them together. She didn't deserve any of it. The least he could do was apologise.

Looking at his watch and seeing that it was past eleven o'clock, Sam got up and went outside, peering down the line of caravans to Maddie's on the end to see if the lights were still on. They were. She was up so he would make his apologies now, while it was on his mind. He wasn't drunk exactly but he'd had enough to affect his judgement. In his mellowed state it seemed vital that he make his peace with Maddie now! He needed to see her.

She was in her dressing gown when Sam arrived at her door.

'Oh, sorry . . . you're just going to bed,' he said cautiously.

'It's all right, I'm not sleepy,' she said evenly. 'So come in.'

He did as she asked and Maddie offered him coffee, noticing the strong whisky scent drifting from him.

'I've come to apologise,' he said when she'd given him a cup of coffee and they were sitting to either side of the fire.

'Oh?'

'I realise now that I was right out of order to have a go at you for not telling me about the affair. I'm *so sorry*.'

'That's okay.' She gave him a warm smile because he seemed genuinely repentant, and it was such a relief to be friends with him again. 'I won't pretend I wasn't hurt by your attitude but I think it was probably a natural reaction to what I had to say. That was about the last thing you wanted to hear on top of everything else.'

'I'll say! This is the worst time of my life.'

A wave of tenderness towards him swept through her. 'I'm sure it must be.' She paused. 'I didn't know what to do. But I knew that if Josh didn't come back soon, everyone – especially the police – would start to make the connection between him and Tania. I thought it best you were prepared.'

'I realise that now.'

'Obviously, if I'd known all this was going to happen, I'd never have kept it to myself for all that time.'

'None of us can see into the future.' Sam managed a faint smile. 'Except perhaps Aunt Sybil, and that's debatable.'

Her answering smile was brief. 'Maybe it was doomed to end in tragedy anyway.'

'We'll never know.'

Maddie sipped her coffee. 'I wonder what's happened to Josh?'

'Don't waste your time worrying about a murderer on the run.'

'Don't be like that, Sam,' she said. 'None of us knows what happened that day.'

'If he isn't guilty of something, why isn't he here?'

'I don't know.'

'*I'll* be charged with murder if I ever see him again, I know that much,' said Sam, eyes dark with rage. 'And I won't just be under suspicion either.'

'Oh, Sam,' she said, worried. 'This isn't you talking. I can't imagine you ever being violent to anyone.'

'I'm not normally a violent man, it's true,' he said. 'But something like this is bound to bring out the worst in anyone.'

'I suppose so,' she agreed, sad to see him so changed.

'It's knowing I'll never see Tania again that hurts so much,' he said, his deep voice cracking. 'If I could only have her back, I'd forgive her for being unfaithful to me – I could forgive anything just to see her again.'

'It's natural you should feel like this. It's still early days,' said Maddie, at a loss to know how to comfort him.

'I can't imagine ever feeling any different.'

'You will, though.' Maddie's tone became harder. 'We all do.'

He looked at her, cheeks flushed from the fire, straight blonde hair falling to her shoulders and shining in the gaslight. He knew from Janice that Maddie had had a bad time with her violent husband but didn't know much else about her background. 'You lost someone then?'

'My parents died within months of each other when I was nine,' she explained, and went on to tell him what had happened and about the hard-hearted aunt who'd taken her in. 'Marriage to Dave seemed like paradise after that. Little did I know when I married him how it would turn out!'

Sam couldn't imagine anyone wanting to hurt Maddie. Who in their right mind would want to injure someone as tender and gentle as her? She seemed so warm and lovely at that moment.

'You're a fighter,' he said approvingly.

'You have to be if you've a child to look after. You can't give in to the bad things that happen. You have to find a way through them – get on with things.'

'I suppose you do,' he said, and there was no mistaking the wistfulness in his voice.

130

'You regret not having children, don't you?' Maddie dared say because it seemed right to encourage him to talk.

He nodded. 'Tania wasn't ready to start a family, or so she said. Now I know that it was because she didn't want to have children with *me*.'

'You can't be sure of that, Sam,' Maddie pointed out emphatically. 'It could have been that she didn't want children with anyone. Not every woman wants to have babies.'

'It seems obvious to me that *I* was the problem.'

'You're making too many assumptions, and torturing yourself in the process.'

'You're probably right.' He paused, looking at her. 'I've been torturing myself wondering if they were planning to go away together?'

'You're bound to think about things like that.'

'Do you think they were?'

She gave him a direct look. 'I honestly don't know, Sam.'

'But you think they might . . .'

She was hesitant to talk about something so painful to him.

'I'd really value your opinion.'

'Okay . . . I think it's odd that they didn't go off together a long time ago,' she said. 'I mean, isn't that what people usually do when they're having a serious affair?'

'Don't ask me – I've never been involved in anything like that.'

'It had been going on for years to my knowledge, so it wasn't just a fling. Doesn't it strike you as strange that they didn't go away together? There must have been some reason why they stayed – something that stopped them from making that final break.'

'Perhaps it would have been better if they had gone off,' Sam said bitterly. 'It would have saved a lot of lies and deceit.'

'Maybe – but it's happened this way and there's nothing we can do to change it. The only person who knows what happened that night is Josh, and unless he comes back we'll never know.'

'I'll kill him if he does!'

'You wouldn't kill anyone,' said Maddie. 'It just isn't in you.'

'It's all such a mess.'

'It won't always feel like this,' she said, overwhelmed by the warmth of her compassion for him. 'You'll come through this, you'll see.'

'You're such a comfort to me,' he said, the harshness gone from his voice.

'I hope I am. You've been good to me since I've been at Fenner's and I'd like to repay you.'

'There's no need – but I'm glad of your company.' He paused, sighing, and put his empty cup down on the coffee table. 'Anyway, I'd better be off so that you can go to bed.'

Maddie nodded. 'I have to be up early. Clare's sleeping over next door and I like to be in there in time to wake her for school.'

Sam stood up and moved towards the door. She followed.

'If there's anything I can do, you only have to ask,' said Maddie, reaching up and kissing his cheek in a gesture of friendship.

Her skin felt warm and smooth against his. Amid all the pain and tackiness of his wife's adultery, Maddie shone like a beacon, honest and true. Beautiful, too. In a less glamorous way than Tania, but lovely none the less.

'I don't want to be alone tonight,' he heard himself say, slipping his arms around her and drawing her back into the room.

'I know you don't,' she said softly. 'And you've no need to be . . .'

Sam opened his eyes and stared into the pale light of dawn, feeling wonderfully at peace for a few lovely moments. Until he became conscious of a dull insistent hammering inside his head, the unmistakable throbbing of overindulgence. Memory quickly followed, causing waves of the blackest despair. Tania was dead, Josh was missing. God, why had he woken up? He longed to escape into sleep again but knew that wouldn't be possible because he was too wakeful.

As he shifted around, he brushed against something beside him – *someone beside him*. What the hell was going on? Maddie . . . *of course*. He remembered with a deep sense of shame that it was Maddie. Surely he wouldn't have, would he? He had – he bloody well had! What was happening to him? Had he lost all sense of decency along with his wife? And on the day of Tania's funeral, too. He couldn't believe it. But it all came flooding back to him on a great rush of remembered pleasure. It had been wonderful! *Absolutely fantastic*! He could still feel the sweetness of Maddie, smell the scent of her next to him.

The reality of it was appalling, though. He'd taken advantage of a good friend like her. Sick with self-disgust, he sat up slowly and turned to the woman beside him, lying on her back, sleeping peacefully. His heart was heavy with guilt but he felt unbearably moved by her, too. She looked so lovely, her fair hair spread out over the pillow.

Careful not to disturb her, Sam got out of bed and fumbled into his clothes in the half light. Then he left the wagon like a guilty teenager who's just cheated on his steady girlfriend.

Maddie woke up with a start to the insistent clanging of the alarm clock. She'd slept like a log and felt rested and renewed. Luxuriating in blissful memories of last night she turned to Sam, registering his absence with a piercing sense of shock.

Maddie felt different within herself and knew that something more important than just sex had happened to her last night. You couldn't

132

do that with someone and not feel different, of course. But this was more, *much more*. She wanted Sam beside her – always.

For God's sake, woman, she admonished herself, the man's wife was only buried yesterday. He needed someone, *anyone*, last night and you were there for him. There was nothing more to it than that.

Forcing her mind towards practicalities, she got out of bed, slipped into her dressing gown and put the kettle on for a pot of tea. Wishing – much against her better judgement – that Sam was here to share it with her. Maybe one day, she thought . . .

If Chas was living on the site and his car available, Janice often drove Clare and Barney to school, especially if it was raining which it was this morning – a fine penetrating drizzle gently seeping into everything. Maddie went along too because she enjoyed seeing her daughter through the school gates.

On the way back, Janice brought up the subject of Chas's imminent departure; he was taking the Gallopers up North to a series of autumn fairs in the next day or so, and would be away for about two weeks.

'I'm not looking forward to his being away,' she confessed.

Maddie was surprised to hear this because Janice was so independent and accustomed to Chas's not being around. 'That isn't like you.'

'It isn't, I know, but I feel as though I need him with me just now. It's been such a strain lately, with everything that's happened.'

'Why not go away with him then?' suggested Maddie. 'It'll be a break from here.'

'I don't want Barney to miss school,' said Janice. 'And I'd rather not leave him with Mum and Dad because they have enough on their plate at the moment, worrying about Josh.'

'Leave him with me then,' offered Maddie. 'The spare bunk bed in Clare's room is always available.'

Janice seemed doubtful. 'It's nice of you to offer, Maddie, but I'm not sure.'

'I'll take good care of him.'

'I know that,' she said loudly and with emphasis. 'But I've never left him with anyone for more than a day before.' She paused. 'Anyway, who would look after them both while you're at work?'

'Sybil. I shall have to ask her to sit with Clare while I'm at work if you're gonna be away anyway, so she can have them both,' said Maddie. 'She'll be delighted. She's always dead keen to sit with Clare on the odd occasion when you aren't able to have her.'

'Are you sure you wouldn't mind?' asked Janice, warming to the idea now she was getting used to it. 'Barney can be a bit of a handful.'

'Of course I don't mind,' said Maddie truthfully. 'It'll give me a chance to pay you back for all you've done for me.'

'I could certainly do with a break from this place,' admitted her friend.

'Well, the offer's there if you want it.'

'Thanks ever so much,' said Janice. 'You're a good friend. I don't know what any of us would do without you.'

'It works both ways,' said Maddie, and really meant it.

Because Janice was going to visit her parents that morning, she declined Maddie's offer of coffee. Maddie had just let herself into her wagon when Sam came to the door.

'I've been waiting for you to come back from the school,' he said when she had ushered him inside out of the rain.

'Oh?' said Maddie, in a non-committal tone because she felt awkward.

'About last night,' he said as she took off her wet anorak and hung it up on a hook just inside the front door.

'Yes?'

'It shouldn't have happened and I'm really sorry about it.'

'There's no need to apologise.' Maddie had mixed feelings about Sam's attitude. On the one hand she was glad he'd had the decency to come and tell her that he hadn't taken what had happened for granted. On the other hand his apology seemed to diminish the importance of it somehow.

'It must have been the booze,' he said. 'I don't usually have that much.' He shook his head. 'I felt so ashamed of myself this morning, I didn't know what to do. That's why I rushed off. God knows what you must think of me?'

Seeing him standing there, squirming with guilt, she realised that this was just what she could have expected of Sam, who was a gentleman through and through. She found herself wanting to put her arms around him and embark upon a re-run of last night. And was immediately taken aback by the intensity of her desire. She'd always liked Sam but this was something else altogether.

'I think you're an ordinary human being and not a saint,' she said. 'And I don't think any the less of you for what happened so there's no need to feel bad.'

'But I do . . .'

Maddie could have told him that she'd cherished every moment of last night and thought she was falling in love with him. But now wasn't the moment. Sam was full of raw grief and time must pass before he would feel anything for another woman. Last night had been a one off. If anything was to grow between them it would happen naturally. If they ever slept together again it would be for love and not just comfort, Maddie promised herself that.

'I don't remember anyone twisting my arm,' she said lightly.

'Well, no, but I still feel awful.' He shifted from one foot to the other, looking sheepish.

'Look – I'm your friend and you needed me last night. There's no more to it than that. I knew that at the time and I haven't read anything more into it.'

'I know that,' he was keen to assure her. 'But it was so wrong of me . . .'

'You've had a really rough time this last week or so and the funeral must have been hellish for you,' she said softly. 'So . . . you'd had more to drink than you're used to and you behaved out of character. Let's just forget all about it and not let it spoil our friendship.'

'Okay.'

Maddie thought he looked relieved but couldn't be sure.

'Stop worrying about it,' she said because he still looked troubled. 'It was just one of those things that happen.'

'It isn't that I didn't – that I don't . . . I mean, you're a very attractive woman.'

'Stop making things worse, Sam,' she said with an understanding smile. 'It happened and it's over. Let's say no more about it.'

'Thanks, Maddie,' he said, moving towards her then stepping back because a casual embrace no longer seemed appropriate.

'Fancy a coffee?'

'No, I'd better go and make a start,' he said. 'I've got a team of tradesmen to see to. I'm a bit out of touch with what's happening on the park . . . with everything else that's been going on.'

'See you later then.'

'Yeah.'

On the way out he passed Janice on her way in. She'd come to tell Maddie that she'd decided to take her up on her offer. She was going away with Chas and leaving Barney behind.

Because her emotions were heightened by what had happened with Sam and her changed feelings towards him, Maddie felt close to tears at this news. It was as though, in trusting Maddie with her child for two weeks, Janice was setting a seal on their friendship. Maddie was touched.

Chapter Eleven

Maddie enjoyed looking after Barney. A double helping of youthful exuberance brought a new sense of fun and vitality into her life, which was much needed after the gloom of recent tragic events. Being busier meant she had less time to dwell on her changed feelings towards Sam, too.

Barney was so accustomed to being with Clare and Maddie he was completely at ease in their home. Occasionally he and Clare got a bit wild, usually if it was raining and they couldn't go outside to play after school. With reserves of energy needing to be expended, they would argue over the slightest thing – even something as trivial as the number of baked beans on their plate at teatime. Insults and blows would be traded but at the first sign of any intervention from Maddie they would behave as though they'd never had a cross word.

She took them out whenever she could – to Richmond ice rink or the cinema. If the weather was fine they would go walking in Richmond Park or by the river.

They were more like brother and sister than friends. They squabbled as a matter of course, closed ranks against Maddie should she reprimand either of them, and were totally inseparable.

'Are Barney and I cousins?' Clare asked her mother one day.

'No.'

'Why do we call each other's mothers Auntie then?' she wanted to know.

'Because we're all good friends and it's a friendly thing to do,' said Maddie. 'But you're not actually related.'

'Shall we pretend to be cousins, Barney?' suggested Clare eagerly.

'If you like,' he said casually.

'Fab!'

Everything was 'fab' with these two lately, along with the rest of Meadow Road Juniors from what Maddie could gather. The latest teenage jargon and Beatlemania seemed as strong with primary school children as it was with teenagers. Clare and Barney were great fans of the Fab Four and were glued to the television set in the hope of seeing them whenever the new television show Ready, Steady, Go came on.

Maddie guessed that Clare's need to have Barney as a surrogate cousin was as a result of her friends at school talking about their families. She could see no harm in the childish pretence which was just a phase her daughter would grow out of.

It was Christmas Eve and Dave's local pub was packed to the doors. A haze of cigarette smoke hung over the crowds who were singing along with Cilla Black to 'You're My World' which was belting out from the juke box.

Dave had had a good few whiskies and was well into the party spirit, especially as he'd got himself fixed up with a new woman for Christmas, a tasty brunette who worked on the checkout at the supermarket. He'd been seeing her for the last few weeks after chatting her up while she'd helped him pack his shopping. She was a divorcee who knew her way around and liked a good time. Ideal for a man who didn't want complications.

'I'm having a smashing time, Dave,' she shouted to him above the noise of talking and laughter as the song came to an end.

'Me, too,' he said. 'There's a good crowd in here tonight.' He drained his glass and pointed at her empty one on the table. 'Same again?'

'Yes, please.'

'I'll probably have to wait to get served,' he said, looking at the crowd around the bar, 'so I might be a little while.'

'Don't worry,' she said in a thick, slow manner because she'd had a good few gins. 'I'll still be here when you get back.'

He fought his way to the bar through the mass of people and waited his turn, happy and mellow with drink. The only way to cope with Christmas was to make sure you weren't sober. All the talk about it being the season of goodwill was a load of rubbish in his opinion. It was nothing more than an excuse for a booze up for most people.

Finally managing to get the barmaid to take his order, he waited, idly glancing along the bar. His heart took a sudden leap as he found himself mesmerised by the profile of a woman with blonde hair. It was Maddie! Maddie was here in this pub! He couldn't believe it. His wife was just a few yards away from him. Drinks forgotten, he pushed his way across to her.

'Maddie,' he said, touching her arm.

'Here, what's your game?' said the woman, turning to face him so that he could see quite plainly that she wasn't Maddie.

'Oh, sorry.' He moved back. 'I thought you were someone else.'

'You watch what you're doing with my wife, mate,' said the man she was with, glaring at Dave.

Fuelled by disappointment and alcohol, white-hot rage scorched through him. He clenched his fists ready to punch the man. He wanted to smash his face in, and hers for not being Maddie. But the man towered above him and had a jaw as solid as a cliff-face.

'Sorry, mate,' said Dave, opening his fists and raising his hands in a conciliatory gesture. 'It was a genuine mistake.'

'You watch it,' said the man. 'I won't overlook it a second time.'

Back at the table Dave's companion noticed his change of mood. 'What's the matter?' she asked. 'Did they short-change you at the bar or something?'

He put his hands under the table to stop himself from physically lashing out at her here in public. Such was the strength of his violence, he *needed* to hit someone – *needed* to feel the power of being in control, to demonstrate his superior strength. He swallowed some whisky to calm himself. Okay, so it hadn't been Maddie this time. But she was out there somewhere, and he'd find her. By God, he would! One of these days she'd be made to pay for what she'd done to him.

And in the meantime he had an accommodating companion to help take his mind off things. This one had been given the gentle touch so far. Maybe it was time to change all that. Yes, later on he'd show her what a big man he really was. The thought immediately made him feel better.

'I'm all right,' he replied, drinking more whisky and joining in the singing as it started up again.

Christmas was quieter than usual that year at Fenner's. There was the usual gathering at Hetty and Vic's on Christmas night but the festive spirit was noticeably absent among the adults, though the children were as ebullient as ever. Hetty's sparkle was missing, Vic was subdued, Sam was drinking too much, and Janice and Chas were at loggerheads.

Only Sybil and Eric seemed the same as ever. He was thrilled with the cowboy novel Maddie had given him for Christmas. In his enthusiasm to improve his new reading skills, he'd become an avid consumer of Westerns and was now able to read them for pleasure, albeit slowly.

''I'll never be able to thank you enough for helping him to learn,' Sybil said to Maddie while they sipped gin and tonics against a background of Sandie Shaw's latest hit from the record player. 'It's changed his life. He may not go far from the fairground in the physical sense but he can travel the world in his imagination now.'

Maddie was delighted. She was also pleased to see the back of Christmas, even though she had enjoyed it vicariously through Clare. There was too much sadness about somehow.

In the New Year, Maddie found herself cast in the role of agony aunt to several members of the family . . .

Janice stormed into her caravan one day in January to let off steam about Chas. This particular issue reared its head quite regularly, and was the cause of their falling out over Christmas.

'He's still refusing Mum and Dad's offer to come into the business,' she fumed. 'He's agreed to stay at Fenner's all season this year with the Gallopers if Josh still isn't around, as a stand in for him . . . to help out generally around the park. But only as a temporary arrangement. He won't commit himself beyond the coming season and says he won't join the firm under any circumstances.'

'Oh, dear.' Maddie had learned to be circumspect when there was a war raging between Janice and Chas; to agree with her friend's complaints about Chas usually turned Janice against Maddie in his defence.

'And he wonders why I won't marry him,' she raged. 'He's still behaving like a seventeen year old. That man is so damned immature!'

'He must have a good reason for not wanting to join the firm?'

'Oh, he's got his reasons all right,' said Janice. 'He says it'll only lead to trouble between him and the family. He enjoys being his own boss and wants to stay that way. We all know what the real reason is though, don't we? He wants to go off travelling with his bloody Gallopers!'

'But if being a travelling showman is in his blood . . .'

'But it isn't in *my* blood, is it? I don't wanna go carting around the country for a great chunk of the season.' Janice was on the brink of angry tears. 'And neither do I want a husband who is. If he came into the business with Mum and Dad, we could have a proper family life.'

'We've been over this before,' said Maddie. 'And we agreed that you both want different things.'

'But we don't, not really,' said Janice. 'We're both showpeople . . . we both want a fairground life. It isn't as though I'm asking him to go into a different line of business or anything.'

'There is that,' said Maddie. 'But if neither of you is prepared to back down, you'll have to come up with some sort of a compromise.'

'That man makes my blood boil!'

With passion as well as fury, thought Maddie, or she'd have given up on him long ago. 'You'll find a way round it between you . . . eventually.'

'I don't see how.' Janice sipped the tea Maddie had given her, seeming calmer. 'But I feel a lot better for having talked to you about it. I always feel better when I've had a chat with you.'

'A problem shared and all that,' said Maddie, glad to have been of help.

The next morning she heard the other side of the argument when Chas paid her a visit while Janice was out shopping.

'I enjoy being my own boss, you see,' he explained over a cup of coffee. 'I love Janice to bits. I'm very fond of her family, too. And that's the way I want it to stay.'

'You think you'd fall out with them if you joined the firm?'

'Bound to, I'd say.'

'Not necessarily.'

'Very likely, though. I mean, I've got my way of doing things, they've got theirs,' Chas said. 'I like to run my own operation. I've been travelling all my life and running the Gallopers since my dad died.'

'Mmm.'

'I've agreed to stay at Fenner's all summer this year because of Josh not being around, but that's not enough for Janice. Oh, no!'

'You can see her point of view, though,' said Maddie.

'I'm not asking her to go on the road with me – as much as I'd like that – because I know she doesn't want to,' he said. 'So I can't see why we don't get married and carry on as we are, with me away for some of the time. We've managed to stay together all these years. My being away hasn't split us up.'

'If Janice gets married, she wants a more settled life and you can't blame her for that,' said Maddie. 'Especially with Barney to consider.'

'Barney is one of the reasons I want to keep my own business,' said Chas proudly. 'I want it to be Chas Baxter & Son one day.'

'That's understandable, but I'm not going to take sides. You both have valid reasons for wanting different things. Only the two of you can work it out.'

'Yeah . . . I know. But it's good to talk to someone who doesn't go through the roof when I put my point of view.'

'It's easy for me to stay calm because I'm not involved,' said Maddie. 'I can look at the problem objectively.'

'Yeah, I s'pose so.' He sipped his coffee. 'Thanks for listening.'

'A pleasure.'

Chas finished his coffee and left, saying he felt a whole lot better.

The next one to confide in Maddie was Hetty . . .

'I'd give anything to see my eldest boy come walking back across that fairground,' she said, gazing out of the office window one day in early March.

'I thought you'd disowned Josh,' remarked Maddie, getting some invoices into order ready for filing.

'Yeah . . . well, we all say things we don't mean when we're upset, don't we?'

'True.'

'He's still my son whatever he's done. He bleeds, I bleed.' Hetty turned away from the window and looked at Maddie, the light picking out the grey streaks in her hair and the new lines around her eyes and mouth. 'You feel things for your kids no matter how old they are, you know. It doesn't stop when they grow up.'

'I can imagine.'

'In some ways it's worse when they're adults 'cause you sometimes have to watch 'em mess up their lives and there's not a damned thing you can do about it.' She sighed and shook her head. 'I was hurt for Sam because of what Josh had done to him. But I feel for Josh too. Not a day goes by when I don't wonder where he is . . . if he's all right.'

'I'm sure.'

'I wouldn't admit that to the others, though,' she said.

'Why not?'

'I suppose it's because Josh has let the family down – especially me because I brought him up,' Hetty explained. 'I can tell you how I *really* feel because you're not one of my kids. I don't have to set you an example. Because I still love Josh doesn't mean I'm condoning what he did or letting my standards slip.' She pressed one large, rough-skinned hand to her heart, eyes bright with tears. 'But it hurts right in there, Maddie. No matter what I've said about Josh, missing him feels like a bloomin' great stone weighing me down.'

Swallowing a lump in her own throat, Maddie put her hand on Hetty's arm. 'You wouldn't be human if you didn't feel that way about your own son.' She paused, removing her hand. 'I think the others miss him too. Except Sam, of course.'

'Sam.' Hetty frowned. 'Poor boy. He's really let the whole sorry business get to him.'

'So I've been hearing,' said Maddie because it was common knowledge at Fenner's that Sam was drinking too much; they were all worried about him. He'd been in the Fiddler's Inn the worse for drink the other night. She'd had to send him home in a taxi.

'That bloody Tania,' cursed Hetty. 'If she'd not dropped her knickers outside the marriage, Josh would still be here and Sam wouldn't be drinking himself senseless.'

'It takes two to make an affair,' Maddie pointed out.

Hetty gave another deep sigh. 'Yeah, you're right. It's a mother's instinct to protect her own even when she knows they've done wrong.'

'Blaming anyone isn't going to help Sam anyway.'

'You're right about that an' all,' agreed Hetty. 'I wish there was something I could do to bring him out of this trough he's sunk into. I've talked to him till I'm blue in the face but he just doesn't seem able to pull himself together. God knows what's gonna happen when we open for the season and are really busy, if the mainstay of Fenner's is nursing a hangover for most of the day.'

'I feel sorry for him,' said Maddie.

'So do I, but sympathy isn't gonna help him. It's time he snapped out of it. He'll do himself no good this way.'

Maddie nodded.

Hetty gave her a thoughtful look. 'I've had an idea, love,' she said. 'Do you think you could have a word with him?'

'Me?'

'He might listen to you. All of us in the family have had a go at him, even Sybil, and it's not made a blind bit of difference. He might take notice of you.'

'Because I'm not family?'

'Yeah, that . . . and because you've a way with you that brings people out of themselves – makes them want to talk about their troubles.'

'I have?'

Hetty nodded. 'You're not afraid to give it to 'em straight either,' she said. 'If you were to have a few strong words with Sam he might just hear what you have to say.'

'I'd rather not interfere in something that isn't my business.'

'You'd be doing me a great favour.' Hetty gave her a persuasive look.

'But it isn't my place . . .'

'Please, love.'

Hetty looked so desperate, Maddie caved in. 'Okay, I'll give it a try,' she said. 'But don't pin too much hope on it. He'll probably be furious and send me off with a flea in my ear.'

Which was exactly what did happen.

'I don't need this,' growled Sam the following afternoon; Maddie had timed her visit carefully so that he'd have slept off his hangover. 'So just go away and leave me alone.' His tawny eyes were raw, a dark growth of stubble making him look unkempt. 'Go on, Maddie, bugger off. I'm not having some woman telling me how to live my life.'

She winced at the black despair in his eyes. She didn't want to be tough on him but the gentle approach certainly wasn't going to shake him out of this. 'Your *life* . . . ? You call this coma you're in a *life*?' she exclaimed.

'So – I'm making things easier for myself with a little anaesthetic,' he said. 'What's it got to do with you?'

'Okay, so you've had a treble blow,' said Maddie, ignoring his remark and forcing herself to continue with this painful lecture. 'You lost your wife and found out she'd been cheating on you. And as if that wasn't enough, her lover turned out to be your own brother.' She moistened her lips and made herself go on. 'These are dreadful things to have to come to terms with.'

'I'm glad to hear you admit it.'

'But it's no excuse to let yourself go.'

'I haven't . . .'

'Oh, for goodness' sake, just look at yourself,' she interrupted, casting a disapproving glance over his unshaven appearance: hair wild and uncombed, shirt crumpled. 'You're a bloody mess.'

'I'll be all right when I've had an Alka Seltzer,' said Sam, putting his hand to his head.

'You mean you'll be feeling well enough to start working on tomorrow's hangover as soon as the pubs open tonight.'

'As I've just told you, what I do is my own business,' Sam replied curtly.

'If you carry on with this routine of boozing every night and sleeping it off for most of the next day, you'll end up drinking all the time before very long.'

'Rubbish!'

'It happens, and it'll happen to you if you don't pull yourself together.'

'No prizes for guessing who's behind this visit of yours,' Sam said irritably. 'If I hear one more person telling me to pull myself together, I swear I shan't be responsible for my actions. Everybody's at it – Mum, Dad, Janice, Aunt Sybil . . . and now you. What is it with you people that you can't leave a man alone?'

'Apart from caring a great deal about you, your parents need you – the business needs you,' said Maddie. 'You're the strength of Fenner's and they rely on you, you know that.'

'I'm here, aren't I?' he said gruffly. 'I haven't walked out and left them like someone else I could mention.'

'They'd be better off without you here if this is how you're going to carry on,' said Maddie, angry now.

He went to the kitchen and returned with a glass of something she assumed was Alka Seltzer which he drank sitting in his armchair, still frowning with the pain of his headache.

'What's so terrible about finding comfort in booze?' he asked. 'People have been doing it ever since the stuff was invented.'

'Nothing – within reason. But you seem to have embarked upon a crash course in self-destruction.'

'So what if I have? Being drunk beats being sober any day.'

'How would it be if we all just gave up when something bad happened to us?' Maddie reproved him. 'The whole world would consist of drunken drop outs, that's what. Everyone has to cope with something that seems beyond them at some time or another.'

At last he had the grace to look shamefaced. 'Not everyone has your grit, you know.'

'You have plenty of it, though, if you'd only let it come to the surface.' Maddie's voice was rising in exasperation. 'You have to stop running away. You have to face the pain and get on with your life.'

'Oh . . . do stop going on about it!' Sam looked really pained. 'Please!'

But she felt duty bound to carry on. 'I've always respected you and admired the way you held things together at Fenner's – solved the problems, listened to what the staff have to say. There isn't anyone here who doesn't feel the same as me. But none of us is going to feel that way this season unless you get yourself sorted. Don't let yourself down.'

'Why should you care?'

'A good question.' Maddie looked at her watch and stood up purposefully. 'Well, I've said my piece. It's up to you what you do about it. I have to collect Clare from school now so I'll leave you to wallow in self-pity on your own.'

'Good!'

At the door she turned and gave him a hard look. 'And while you're looking back on the woman you thought was so wonderful, and thinking how dreadful life is without her, it might be an idea to remember the appalling life she led you.'

'She didn't . . .'

'Oh, but she did and you know it! I used to cringe at the way Tania behaved towards you in public. She might have been different when you were on your own, but I doubt it. Tania didn't make you happy when she was alive. Don't let her destroy you now that she's dead.'

Sam's face was like thunder. Maddie thought for a moment he was going to come after her and hit her. But that wasn't his style.

'Get out of here,' was all he said in a dull voice.

Maddie knew she'd gone too far with Sam and couldn't get it out of her mind. She was so worried she left for work a few minutes earlier that evening and called in at his living-wagon first.

'My turn to apologise,' she said, noticing that he was freshly shaved and wearing clean clothes; he looked smartly casual in a Fair Isle sweater and jeans. 'I was out of order this afternoon. I'm sorry.'

He managed a half smile. 'You're a big bully, Maddie Brown,' he said jokingly. 'But you didn't say anything I didn't deserve. I'm sorry I've been such a pain lately.'

'Am I hearing this right?' Maddie could hardly believe the change in him.

'You are.'

'Thank God for that.' She gave him a close look. 'You going out?'

He nodded.

'Oh.' She tried to make her voice light but her concern was obvious.

'Don't worry, I'm not going on the booze. Well, no more than a sociable pint,' he said. 'There's a pub in Brentford that has a pool table. I thought I'd take Eric down there later on. He enjoys a game. He's not a bad player, as a matter of fact.'

That was more like the Sam she'd grown to know and love. 'That's a nice idea,' said Maddie, cautiously optimistic that he'd turned the corner now.

'Might as well make the most of the spare time,' he remarked conversationally. 'There won't be too many chances to go out of an evening once the season starts.'

'That's a fact,' she agreed, turning to go. 'Must dash. See you.' She smiled warmly at him.

'See you, Maddie.'

One day in the spring of 1965 the children came home from school bursting with the news that the Beatles were going to be filming in the Richmond area the next day. Maddie and Janice thought it was just a rumour but the children were quite certain; the information had come from one of their classmates at school who had an uncle who worked at Twickenham Studios, where the film was being made. He had heard about the team going out on location in Ailsa Avenue, St Margaret's.

Clare and Barney begged their mothers to take them to see if they could catch a glimpse of their heroes, who were now international superstars.

'It isn't far – only on the other side of the river,' Clare pointed out excitedly. 'Please let's go and have a look.'

'Be a sport and let us go, Mum,' Barney said to Janice.

And so it was that Maddie and Janice found themselves among the crowds of screaming fans as the four famous pop stars were filmed getting out of a Rolls-Royce and going up to four separate front doors and entering four ordinary terraced houses for the opening scenes of their second film *Help*. This normally quiet suburban street became a cauldron of excitement as the fans went wild and police struggled to control them.

'Well – was it worth it, kids?' asked Janice later as they drove home in the Mini she had recently bought from her savings.

'Cor, yeah!' said Barney.

'Fancy seeing the Beatles *in real life*,' said Clare.

'Yes, it was very exciting,' said Maddie, glad that they had made the effort because she'd enjoyed it too.

As it happened the Beatles weren't the only celebrities the children saw in person that spring . . .

Even though life was hectic and spare time at a minimum once the season was underway, Maddie and Janice made the time to take them down river to Runnymede one Friday in May to see if they could catch a glimpse of royalty. In a meadow near the spot where the Magna Carta had been signed, the Queen was to dedicate an acre of wood and grassland to the American people in memory of President Kennedy who had been assassinated in Dallas in 1963.

Quite a crowd had already gathered by the time they got there but they managed to get near enough to the barriers to see the royal party when they finally appeared. Having given the Queen and the Duke of Edinburgh the once over, Clare wanted to know who the pretty lady with the two children was.

'That's the President's widow, Jackie Kennedy,' explained Maddie, filled with admiration for this slim, elegant woman who had borne the tragedy with such dignity.

'What are the children's names?' enquired Clare, having been given brief details of the Kennedy situation, or as much as Maddie thought necessary for a ten year old.

'John and Caroline,' Janice informed her, also admiring the glamorous woman who, as First Lady, had led the world of fashion with her stylish dress sense.

Among the trees a simple memorial of Portland stone was placed, carrying the late president's famous declaration in his inaugural speech. Maddie was moved by this tribute to a man who had been much loved by the British people.

Clare was also affected by what she had seen but in a different and unexpected way.

'It's sad about those Kennedy children's father, isn't it?' she said that night as Maddie tucked her up in bed.

'Very sad.'

'They won't see him again then?'

'No.'

The little girl thought about this for a while then said, 'What does my father look like?'

Maddie was taken aback. 'He's got dark hair and dark eyes.'

'Is he good-looking – like Paul McCartney?'

'He doesn't look like Paul McCartney,' said Maddie. 'But he is good-looking.'

'I could see him, couldn't I?' said Clare. 'I mean, he isn't dead?'

'No, he isn't dead,' said Maddie, becoming very tense; she had long dreaded something like this.

'Can we go and see him then?'

'I don't think that's a very good idea, love.'

'Why?'

'Well . . . it just wouldn't be, that's all.'

'Because you don't like him?'

'Have I said that?'

'You said something once about the two of you not getting on.'

'I also said that these things sometimes happen to grown ups.'

'Did he go away?'

'No. We did.'

'We went away and left him . . . on his own?' Clare sounded outraged.

'I had to take you away.'

'You made us leave him,' she said with a blistering note of

accusation. 'It's *your* fault that I never see my own father!'

Maddie knew the moment had come to tell her daughter as much of the truth as she thought Clare could take. She was old enough for some sort of an explanation about her own background.

'I had to leave your father because it was dangerous for us both to stay with him,' she replied carefully. 'He used to hit me.'

'You must have done something bad to make him do that.'

'No, I didn't.'

Clare then astonished Maddie by bursting into tears and sobbing loudly.

'Hey,' she said, bending down and drawing her into her arms. 'What's brought this on?'

'Everybody else has got a dad,' she said, voice thick with tears. 'Even Barney. And you won't even let me see mine.'

'It's my job to do what's best for you until you're old enough to make your own decisions,' said Maddie, holding her close and stroking her hair. 'And you have to trust me to do that.'

'Will I ever see him?' asked Clare when the tears had finally abated and Maddie was wiping her eyes with a handkerchief.

'When you're grown up, you can make up your own mind.'

This seemed to calm her and Maddie was saved from further questions by her daughter's exhaustion. She just couldn't stay awake any longer. The next morning Clare seemed to have forgotten all about it.

Maddie knew she hadn't heard the last of the matter, though. It might not be mentioned tomorrow or next week but this was a subject that wasn't going to go away.

'Do you think I ought to take her to see her father?' Maddie asked Janice on the way back from school in the car.

'Absolutely not!'

'How can you be so sure?'

'I saw the state you were in when you'd just escaped from the bastard, remember? I saw the bruises.'

'Of course you did,' said Maddie, remembering that extraordinary day.

'I reckon if you go anywhere near him, you'll get more of the same.'

'I've no intention of going back to him,' Maddie made it clear. 'But I am wondering if I should let Clare get to know him – under supervision. I wouldn't let her be alone with him.'

'I wouldn't let her within a mile of him if she was mine,' said Janice. 'It's too risky.'

'That's why I haven't done anything about it,' sighed Maddie. 'But I've always known I'd have to see him again sometime.'

'Why?'

'Because I just walked out leaving everything up in the air. I'll have to end it properly one of these days.'

'Only if you want a divorce,' said Janice in a decisive tone. 'And that could probably all be done through solicitors.'

'I expect I'd go to see him personally if anything like that ever came up. I've let things drift on rather than have to think about them.'

'You might want to get married again sometime,' said Janice. 'You'd have to get rid of him legally then.'

'There's nothing like that in the offing at the moment.'

'But you're still a young woman. You're bound to meet someone eventually.'

'Dave's probably found someone else by now and if he wants to file for divorce he can't because he doesn't know where I am.' Maddie paused, biting her lip. 'I feel bad about not doing things properly.'

'I should think it's difficult to work out what's right and proper when someone's beating the shit out of you,' said her friend cynically.

'I mean, after I'd left . . . perhaps I should have contacted him to let him know that we were all right? But I've always been so terrified of his finding us, I didn't dare get in touch in case he got any clue as to our whereabouts and started looking for us.'

'A good enough reason for not getting in touch,' said Janice. 'And it still applies. Because if he did find you, he'd make your life a misery again. Men like him don't change.'

'I won't argue with you about that. It's just that . . . well, this business with Clare has set me thinking.'

'Her curiosity about him will probably pass,' said Janice. 'You know what kids are like for phases and crazes. If she wants to get to know her father when she's grown up and is more able to defend herself from him, that will be her decision.'

'I still feel guilty, though.'

'Guilty?' Janice was astounded. 'For protecting yourself and your daughter from some moron who gets his kicks from thumping the living daylights out of his own wife and child?'

'Put like that, it sounds crazy.'

'It *is* crazy.' Janice pulled up outside her wagon and turned to Maddie with a serious expression on her face. 'Look, I know it isn't as simple as I'm making it sound. But you've nothing to feel guilty about, honestly – so forget him.'

'I'll try,' Maddie said, but it wasn't easy to forget a man like Dave Brown.

Chapter Twelve

When Maddie answered the telephone in the office one day in the summer, the caller's voice sounded vaguely familiar.

'Can I speak to Vic Fenner, please?'

'Certainly. Who's calling?'

'It's personal.'

'Oh . . . one moment while I connect you to him,' she said, putting the call through to the extension in the beer garden where Vic was finishing the lunchtime shift.

One morning a week or so later, the same person called again and Maddie still couldn't put a name to the voice. Vic happened to be in the office at the time so he took the call there.

'Oh, it's you again – and the answer is still the same. I thought I made it clear to you when we spoke before that I'm not interested in selling.' Maddie couldn't help hearing what Vic was saying while she filed some correspondence. There was silence while he listened for a moment. Then: 'No, it isn't a question of money – I won't sell for any price you care to name.' Another long pause. 'No!' His tone hardened dramatically. 'I certainly am *not* using tactics to get you to raise your offer. How many more times must I tell you? It isn't for sale. *Not now, not ever.* So there's no point in your contacting me again.'

The receiver was slammed down. 'Cor, dear me! Some people just won't take no for answer, will they?' muttered Vic.

'Somebody trying to buy your car?' Maddie enquired casually because Vic's 1948 Jaguar was his pride and joy, a collector's car much coveted by other enthusiasts.

'No, it isn't my motor he's after,' he said. 'The bloke wants to buy the business.'

'What!' Maddie blurted out, fearing for her job and her home.

'Don't worry, I'm not sellin',' he assured her determinedly.

'That's a relief!'

'It's nothing new. We've had plenty of offers for it over the years,' he said chattily. 'It's a valuable site, being big and by the river.'

'Do the offers come from people in the fairground business wanting to open another outlet?'

'No. They usually come from businessmen wanting the land,' Vic

149

replied. 'This latest offer is from a man who wants to put a hotel on the site.'

Maddie's jaw dropped. 'But there's been a funfair here since early in the century.'

'Exactly,' said Vic. 'And there'll be one here until the end of it if I have anything to do with it.'

'It must be a bit tempting, though, if they offer you a good enough deal?'

'Not to me, ducks,' he said, walking towards the door. 'I'll never sell this fairground. *Never, ever.*' He stopped at the door. 'I'll be over at the beer garden if anyone wants me. I'm expecting a delivery from the brewery.'

'Okay.'

A few evenings later a large crowd of rowdy, foul-mouthed youths descended on Fenner's, rampaging through the fair, terrorising punters with their vile language and violent presence.

The men and the dogs finally removed them from the fairground but not before substantial damage had been done to Fenner's reputation as well as to their property. Hot dog stalls were overturned, glasses smashed in the beer garden and broken bottles thrown on to the floor of the Bumper Cars.

This incident was far more threatening than the invasion of the Mods. They had only been a problem because they'd been in conflict with each other. These hooligans came as enemies of the Fenner family, with the deliberate intention of ruining their business. More worrying still was the fact that they came again the following weekend.

'The bloke who wants to buy us out is behind it,' Janice told Maddie.

'You reckon?'

'No doubt about it,' she said. 'He's bringing louts in from other areas and paying 'em to make trouble on the fairground with the idea that Dad will give in and agree to sell to him. The man's admitted it in so many words.'

'Really?'

'Yeah. Apparently he went to see Dad in the beer garden yesterday and asked him if he was ready to reconsider his offer. When Dad told him again that he wasn't interested in selling, the bloke warned him to expect more trouble.'

'That's terrible!'

'Bloody Alan King,' fumed Janice. 'I know what I'd like to do to him.'

'Alan King?' Maddie finally put a name to the voice on the telephone.

'You know him?'

'Yes, I do. He asked me to go out with him one night at the Fiddler's. Pat told me he was a villain so I turned him down.'

'He sounds like an evil bugger to me,' said Janice worriedly. 'He'll stop at nothing to get this piece of land . . . even put us out of business if necessary.'

'Could he do that?'

'Oh, yeah. The punters won't come near if the place gets a reputation for trouble,' she said. 'The only sort of people who'll turn up then will be yobs looking for a fight and with no intention of spending any money.'

'Are you sure it isn't just local boys looking for mischief?'

'Some of them probably are local,' she said. 'But King will have recruited the rest from other places. It's far too violent and well organised for it to be just local lads out for a bit of fun.'

'Surely he'll call them off when he realises that your dad isn't going to change his mind?'

'I'm not so sure . . .'

Unfortunately Janice's doubts proved right. Every few nights the trouble-makers arrived in hordes while the genuine customers stayed away. To make matters worse someone tipped off the local paper who sent a photographer along.

LOCAL FUNFAIR BECOMES TROUBLE SPOT AND MAGNET FOR RUFFIANS was the destructive headline, accompanied by action pictures of the louts struggling with the fairground men who were trying to remove them.

'That'll do wonders for business, that will,' said Janice with heavy irony. 'It won't be worth opening at all soon.'

'Shouldn't the police be called in?' said Maddie.

'Dad won't do that,' said Janice. 'If people get to know that the coppers are here every few nights, it'll make things even worse. As well as scaring the punters away, it'll highlight the trouble to local residents who might then claim that the fair is giving the area a bad name, and try to get us closed down.'

'And, of course, Alan King couldn't care less about that because he only wants the land – not the business.'

'Exactly. That's why it's best for us to let our men deal with the unwelcome visitors in the usual way.'

'When I mentioned involving the police, I meant with a view to their nicking the organiser,' Maddie explained.

'They wouldn't do anything unless we could prove it's King who's behind it,' Janice wisely pointed out. 'Obviously he would deny any involvement – even though he's admitted it to Dad. It would just be Dad's word against his. And you won't get any of those louts opening their mouths and dropping King in it. They'd be too scared of getting their legs broken by one of his minders.'

'Not a very positive outlook then?' said Maddie gloomily.

151

'No, not really – but all isn't lost yet,' said Janice. 'It's just a question of keeping our heads and holding out against King.' She frowned. 'Trouble is, the whole thing is really upsetting Dad and making him ill.'

'I've noticed how strained and pale he's looking.'

'I'm really worried about him – so is Mum. He's so strung up and isn't sleeping.'

'As if your parents haven't had enough trouble – with Josh not here, too.'

'Don't remind me,' said Janice. 'Still, there's nothing we can do about the present crisis except sit it out until King gets fed up with it and realises that Dad means what he says.'

But Maddie had a sudden brainwave which made her think that perhaps there was something that could be done!

'I told you Alan King was a crook, didn't I?' said Pat when Maddie went to see her at the Fiddler's Inn later that morning. 'I bet you're bloomin' glad you didn't get involved with him?'

'Not half!'

'He doesn't come in here any more,' said Pat. 'And I'm not sorry. He was a good customer but we can do without his sort.'

Maddie gave her a sharp look. 'I remember you said you don't know exactly what King does besides running a legitimate garage business. But I wondered if you might have any suspicions?'

'Plenty, but that's all they are – suspicions. Why?'

'Well, we can't prove to the police that he's behind the trouble at Fenner's but if we could find out what other mischief he's up to, maybe we could make sure the law got to know about that,' explained Maddie. 'I mean . . . if he was a guest of Her Majesty, he couldn't be making trouble for Fenner's.'

'But how would you find out for sure what he's up to?'

'I was hoping you might have some ideas about that, being as you've known him for a long time,' Maddie explained. 'That's why I came rushing over.'

Pat shook her head. 'I think you've stumped me on that one,' she said. 'Short of bribing one of his heavies for information, which would be nigh on impossible, or keeping his garage under surveillance . . .'

'You think whatever he's doing, he's doing it from his garage, then?'

'Oh, yeah. It's bound to be connected with cars in some way because that's his line of business . . . what he knows about.'

'Dealing in stolen ones?'

'Something like that. Could be car radios or new parts he's getting through the back door of a car factory somewhere. Though that seems a bit small-time for Alan. He's strictly big-time. So cars seem the most likely option, and he wouldn't be dealing in clapped out old bangers either!'

'How to find out for sure so that we can tip off the police, though?' pondered Maddie. 'That's the big question.'

'You could always do what the coppers do . . . keep watch on the place.'

'How can we when we're all working well into the evening?'

'If he is dealing in stolen cars, he probably shifts them under cover of darkness when there's no one much about – after you've finished work at the fair.'

'Pat, you're a genius!' said Maddie.

'It's the most ridiculous idea I've ever heard!' protested Sam. Maddie had waylaid him in his office when she got back from the pub.

'Do you have a better one for getting Alan King off our backs?'

'Well, no, but . . .'

'I know it's a longshot but your family business is being destroyed by King and your father is becoming ill because of it,' she said. 'We can't just sit back and do nothing.'

'I *don't* sit back doing nothing,' Sam reminded her. 'I'm out there in the thick of it every night, dealing with the thugs.'

'I know you are and it's very brave of you.' Maddie was totally sincere. 'But it doesn't stop them coming back – it isn't a solution – and it isn't doing any of you men any good. In fact, it's doing none of us any good. My nerves are in tatters . . . I'm living in fear of those hooligans going near the living-wagons and hurting somebody. The children in particular.'

Sam shot her a look. 'That won't happen so you can stop worrying about it,' he said in a firm tone. 'They won't go near the wagons. It's the fair they want to destroy.'

'Who knows what they'll do? They could lose control and cause real damage.'

'That isn't going to happen,' Sam said earnestly, 'I promise you.'

'I don't think you're in a position to make such a promise since you're not dealing with normal decent people,' she said. 'You're dealing with a power freak like King and the morons he employs to wreak havoc on our fair.'

'All right, you have a point,' he said. 'But surely you don't really believe that our sitting in a car for hours at night, watching King's service station, will achieve anything.'

'It might.'

'Apart from anything else, how are we supposed to stay awake after working all day?'

'We'll take it in turns to sleep,' she said. 'Anyway, we won't stay all night.'

'No, Maddie, it isn't on.'

'Okay, if you won't do it I'll ask Chas, or even Janice,' she threatened. 'I was going to ask her before I approached you, actually. But I thought some male muscle might come in handy in an emergency. She can drive a car and Chas will look after the kids while we're gone.'

'Oh, no. You're not going out on the streets all night with Janice.' Sam was adamant about that. 'Two women meddling with hardened criminals? I'm not having that. I'll go myself or with Chas or Eric rather than let you do that.'

'We wouldn't be meddling with criminals, we'd be watching them, that's all,' Maddie pointed out. 'And as this is my idea, I want to see it through – whoever I go with.'

'I wouldn't sleep a wink knowing you were out there . . .'

'Then you'll have to come with me, won't you? 'Cause I'm gonna do it one way or another,' she told him categorically. 'I'd do it on my own if I had a car. But you can't do surveillance properly without one.'

'Surveillance, eh?' he said lightly. 'Someone's been watching the TV.'

'Chance would be a fine thing at the height of the season.'

'Only kidding.'

'I should hope so, too.' Maddie looked at him hard. 'But don't change the subject. Are you on for this or shall I go and ask Chas?'

He gave an eloquent sigh. 'What time are we leaving on this fool's errand?'

'As soon as we've finished here.'

'I must be out of my mind.'

'So must I,' said Maddie, smiling. 'But better to be mad than complacent. Anything's worth a try if it's gonna help us see the back of Alan King's thugs.'

'True.'

'Oh, and Sam . . . '

'Mmm?'

'Janice and Chas will have to know about it 'cause I'll be asking them to look after Clare, but perhaps it might be best if we don't say anything to your parents until we get a result. No point in raising their hopes on the strength of a longshot.'

'You're right,' he agreed. 'But I doubt if we'll be able to keep it from them. They'll hear us coming and going.'

'There is that. But let's keep quiet for as long as we can. We might hit the jackpot tonight.'

'You never know your luck,' said Sam, but he didn't think they would get a result in a month of Sundays let alone on the first night.

Maddie poured coffee from a flask into a plastic cup and handed it to Sam.

154

'Ooh, lovely,' he said. 'I might have known you'd come prepared.'

'I thought I'd better bring a few things to keep us going,' she said, throwing him a Mars Bar. 'Didn't want to have to listen to you moaning on about being hungry or thirsty.'

'Charming,' he retorted, but there was a smile in his voice.

It was nearly midnight and they were in Twickenham, ensconced in Sam's car which was parked on the corner of a side street near where it joined the main road. They were almost opposite King's Motors which was near a small parade of shops. From their vantage point they could see anything that went in or out of the premises, an impressive property with a wide modern forecourt, stylish showrooms and large workshops at the side.

Tucked away in the shadows among the other cars parked on the street, they were completely inconspicuous.

'Nothing seems to be happening over there,' Maddie observed.

'No.' Sam stared ahead of him. 'I told you we'd be wasting our time.'

'Stop being so negative and give it a chance,' she said. 'We might have to come every night for weeks before we see anything useful. Whatever's going on, King wouldn't be fool enough to do it every night in case it was noticed.'

'There is that,' he agreed. 'I don't fancy doing this every night for weeks, though.'

'You've no stamina.'

'My stamina is being seriously challenged by thoughts of my comfortable bed.'

Maddie laughed; her mood was surprisingly lighthearted – almost adventurous. 'I know what you mean.' She wiped some condensation from the windscreen with a piece of rag and glanced up at the star-studded sky from which a clear moon was radiating a pearly glow. 'It's a lovely night, though. I wouldn't fancy doing this job in the winter.'

'You'd do it in a blizzard if you thought it was necessary.'

'Naturally.'

'Just as well it isn't winter then, 'cause I'd be bound to get roped in.'

'Definitely,' she joked. 'I'd need a big strong man in case the crooks got nasty.'

'Now she tells me.' He bit into his Mars Bar. 'So how come you know this King geezer, anyway?'

'He made a pass at me one night when I was working at the pub.'

'And . . . ?'

'Pat didn't like the idea of my getting involved with him because she knew that he was a crook. Lucky for us she told me that, as it turned out. At least we've got something on him. And the chance to get him out of our hair.'

155

'Albeit a slim one.'

'Pessimist.'

'Sorry.'

'You're as keen to get Alan King sorted as I am, don't deny it.'

'I wouldn't dream of denying it. It's the method I find doubtful,' he said, but there was levity in his tone. 'I can't help thinking there must be an easier and surer way.'

'We could threaten to go to the police about his bent activities if he doesn't call off his yobs. But as we don't know what those activities are, we'd look pretty stupid. Whereas if we can find out what he's up to . . .'

'I understand what you're saying, Maddie, so you can stop trying to convince me.'

'If we do manage to pull this off, the bad publicity would be disastrous for any would-be hotelier in the area,' she continued. 'Even when he came out of prison he'd be unlikely to want to start again here.'

'You've got it all worked out.'

'I've thought a lot about it since I realised there was something we could do.'

They fell silent, looking thoughtfully ahead of them into the main road which was well lit by street lamps. The atmosphere between them felt intimate suddenly.

'Would you have got involved with King if you hadn't found out he was dodgy?' Sam enquired casually.

'I don't know about involved, as such, but I probably would have gone out with him.'

'Really?'

'Don't sound so surprised. He's a good-looking bloke – and I'm a normal woman,' Maddie said. 'If it hadn't been so risky, I wouldn't have minded a night out with him just for the fun of it. It's years since I've had a date.'

'Me too.'

'I don't suppose you're short of offers,' she said. 'A man like you – part of a long-established business – you're a good catch.'

'You make me sound like a salmon.'

She laughed softly. 'Oh, Sam, you know what I mean. Anyway, fairground men are often very attractive to women. Even when they're not as well connected as you.'

'Are they?'

'It's the magic of a fair that does it, I suppose. Because you're doing something out of the ordinary.'

'It isn't our amazing sex appeal then?'

'It's all part of the same thing. It's that strong, earthy, outdoor look that gets the women going.'

'I like it, I like it – keep going.'

'Stop fishing for compliments!' It was so good to hear Sam joshing again after months of aching depression. Even though he no longer drowned his sorrows in drink, he wasn't the man he'd been before Tania's death. He was cheerful enough on the surface but it was obvious to anyone who knew him that he was just putting up a front. Tonight, though, he seemed different. 'I'm not going to feed your male ego.'

'Why not? I think it's an excellent way of passing the time and trying to keep awake,' he said, chuckling.

'It's nice to hear you laugh.'

'Yeah?'

'Yeah. It doesn't happen often enough,' she said. 'But you do seem to have been coping better lately.'

'I daren't do otherwise with you around,' he said with a wry grin. 'I still haven't recovered from that last trouncing.'

'Oh, dear,' said Maddie, remembering. 'I did come on a bit strong, didn't I? But I had to get tough. It was the only way to drag you out from under.'

'Why . . . why did you have to get tough?' he asked more seriously.

'Because your mother asked me to talk to you. She was worried about you.'

'But why did you agree to do it when you knew I'd give you a hard time?'

'What are you getting at?'

'I mean, why put yourself out when you don't have to? Why teach Eric to read and make Josh own up to his part in the accident on the Chairoplanes? Why did you feel you must protect me when you knew Tania was cheating on me – and why are you out on the street in the middle of the night trying to save Fenner's family business when you could be at home in bed? You don't have to do any of this. None of it is your responsibility.'

'If the fair goes out of business and the site becomes a hotel, I'll be jobless and homeless,' Maddie pointed out.

'That isn't the reason you're doing it, though, is it?'

'No.'

'Why then?'

'I'm not sure,' she said. 'Probably because I care about you as a family. I know that, strictly speaking, I'm an outsider but I have more of a sense of belonging with you lot than I've had anywhere since I was nine years old.'

'Don't you ever feel as though you'd like the other sort of life – a nine to five job and a home in an ordinary street? The sort of life you were brought up to?'

'No.'

'You sound very sure.'

'I am,' she said. 'I feel totally involved in the funfair world. It

157

interests me. I feel I have a lot to offer.'

'And you have,' he said. 'You practically run the office these days.'

'I get so deeply engrossed in the job, I always feel sad at the end of the season when I have to find work somewhere else.'

'Must be a nuisance for you.'

'Still, that's life. I can't afford not to have an income all year, not with a daughter who's growing faster than a weed in wet weather. It won't be long before Clare'll be wanting all the latest gear to wear and I don't want her to miss out because I'm on my own.'

'Her father should be helping you to support her,' said Sam.

'He probably would if he knew where we were. But if I let that happen neither of us would be safe.'

'You've plenty of people around you to protect you from him.'

'I'd still rather not risk having him know where we are.'

'He must have really scared you for you to prefer to go it alone when he could be helping you financially.'

'He did more than just scare me. He made me into a complete nervous wreck. The mere thought of seeing him again makes me feel physically sick.' Maddie turned to Sam, drawing comfort from the firm line of his profile visible in the pale glow from the street lights. 'So it's bar work for me in wintertime ... unless you can offer me year-round employment at Fenner's?'

'There's no way we can do that, I'm afraid.'

'You could if you were to open an indoor attraction – like a Bingo hall and bowling alley under one roof.'

'What a good idea!'

'I think so. I mentioned it to Hetty once. She said she'd talk to you and Vic about it but I never heard any more about it.'

'She never said anything to me about it,' Sam said thoughtfully. 'Probably decided it wasn't on. Mum and Dad like things the way they are, with us closing up completely in the winter.'

'That was the impression I got.' Maddie laughed. 'It comes to something when the hired help not only drags you out in the middle of the night to save your business but suggests you expand to provide her with employment too!'

'As I've said to you before, you're much more to all of us than just the hired help,' he said gravely. 'Surely you know that?'

'Yes, I do know . . . sort of,' said Maddie staring into her lap so that he wouldn't see the tears that had rushed into her eyes. 'I was only kidding.'

'I'll have a chat with Mum and Dad about the Bingo hall idea,' he said. 'But I don't think they'll go for it.'

'Neither do I. Anyway, we have to solve the current problem before making any plans for the future of the firm.'

'You're right there.' He yawned. 'You sleep if you like. I'll keep watch.'

'No, I'm okay at the moment,' she said. 'You have a nap first. I'll wake you when I can't keep my eyes open any longer.'

The time passed uneventfully. They stayed until about three o'clock then drove back to Richmond.

'You were right . . . we did waste our time,' Maddie said on the way.

'Never mind, better luck tonight, eh?' he said, sounding positive.

'You mean, you'll come again tonight without putting up a fight?' she said in astonishment.

'That's right,' Sam assured her. 'We've only just begun.'

'Well, you've certainly changed your tune!'

'Maybe I can see some sense in the idea after all.'

Although that was true and Sam was now keen to follow Maddie's plan through, he had enjoyed their time together. In fact, during the last few hours he'd felt happier than he had in ages. It was odd. The way his life was at the moment, the last thing he'd expected to feel was pleasure – what with being terrorised by louts every few nights, worried to death about his father's health, tortured still by memories of his wife's death and adultery, and being kept from his bed to spend the night in a draughty car. But being with Maddie had been wonderful.

'Perhaps you've got a taste for detective work – being out on the silent streets at the dead of night and all that?' she laughed.

'Maybe.'

'We should set up a sideline as private investigators.'

'I haven't got the constitution to be up half the night on a regular basis.'

'Nor me,' she said, yawning, feeling very close to Sam at that moment.

They continued with their nightly vigil for the next week without a result, both sleeping late in the morning to remain functional. As Sam had predicted they were unable to keep their nocturnal activities from Hetty and Vic who heard them coming home in the early hours.

'You be careful,' warned Hetty when she discovered what they were up to. 'From what I've heard that Alan King is dangerous – a real nasty piece of work.'

'They know what they're doing,' said Vic who was in such a state about the trouble King was causing he was past caring who stopped him – so long as someone did.

'It's no job for a woman, though,' said Hetty. 'Why don't you get Chas to go with you, Sam? And let Maddie stay home in bed.'

'What! I'd be a dead man if I left Maddie behind,' he said, glancing at her.

'He would too,' she agreed.

They all laughed, even Vic. Nothing seemed quite so bad when Maddie was around.

'We can't keep this up for ever if we don't get a result,' said Sam a few nights later while they were on watch.

'I know.'

'But you're not ready to give up yet?'

'Not likely.' Even though Maddie hated to admit it, the lack of sleep was beginning to tell on her. There were times during the day when she felt lightheaded and muddled with tiredness. 'Bags I have first kip now, though. I'm shattered.'

She put the seat back and was asleep as soon as she snuggled under the blanket, waking with a start to find Sam nudging her.

'Things are happening,' he whispered. 'There's a new-looking Jaguar slowing down across the road.'

They both had their eyes glued to the sleek vehicle moving noiselessly along the road and almost coming to a halt by the service station.

'Damn, it's gone past!' said Maddie.

'It's turned into a side street just past King's place.'

'Must be one of the residents coming home late, then.'

'Mmm, I suppose so.'

They were both disappointed. But a few nights later – at about the same time – a Rolls-Royce passed by and turned into the same side-street, followed soon after by a Bentley.

'There must be a lot of rich people living around here,' commented Maddie. 'Yet it doesn't seem all that classy.'

'Not Rolls-Rolls type of classy anyway,' muttered Sam.

'It must have its share of rich residents, though,' said Maddie. 'You need to have a few bob to afford one of those cars.'

Sam opened the door.

'Where are you going?'

'Wait here, I won't be a minute.'

'Sam . . . ?'

'Stay where you are, Maddie, and keep the doors locked.'

He disappeared into the shadows, returning a few minutes later grinning broadly. 'I think we've got him!' he said excitedly.

'You think the posh cars are stolen?' she suggested.

'That's right. There's a rear entrance into King's workshops that backs on to a piece of waste ground. I think they're taking the cars in the back way and driving them along another turning, having changed the number plates. That's why we've only seen them going one way.'

'Are you sure?' she said. 'I mean, the cars could belong to people who live in those houses around there.'

'No. I'm certain they're in the workshops having something done to them,' said Sam. 'Why else would the lights be on?'

'I see – that's even better.'

'I couldn't see inside, though, 'cause the windows are too high.'

'Why would anyone be working in a car workshop at this hour if it was all legal and above board?'

'My guess is that the cars are going in with one number plate and coming out with another – a false one,' he said. 'As well as forged documentation.'

'That's terrible!'

'I reckon King is running a high-class operation in quality stolen cars,' he said. 'He's employing people to steal 'em from the West End and having 'em brought down here to be adapted for sale. Because the garage doesn't have any houses backing on to it, no one notices them coming and going at night. He'd needs to shift 'em sharpish and wouldn't take the risk of having them in there during business hours.'

'How would he get official documents forged?' Maddie wondered aloud.

'It wouldn't be difficult for a man like King – he'd have plenty of contacts.'

'How would his people find the cars to steal?'

'Off the street where they're parked while people are at the theatre or a restaurant. Or even from outside their houses in places like Mayfair and Knightsbridge. The West End is teeming with class cars.'

'When I heard King was dodgy, I didn't think he was a master criminal.'

'He's that all right,' said Sam. 'He's probably got a team of experienced car thieves working for him.'

'You think so?'

'Yeah. It's no accident that his garage backs on to waste ground, either.'

'You reckon he bought the place with stolen cars in mind?'

'I'm certain of it,' Sam said. 'He's probably working with bent car dealers abroad who have customers waiting for the cars. And as the motors cost him nothing beyond the wages of the blokes who steal 'em and the false number plates and documents, just think of the profit he's making. It's no wonder he can afford to build a riverside hotel.'

'Shall we go to the police with what we know? If they keep watch on the place for a few nights, they'll catch 'em at it.'

'This isn't quite the moment to go to the coppers,' he said. 'I want to make absolutely sure first. We need to get a closer look.'

Sam drove the car into a turning on the other side of the main road and parked in the shadows. From here they had a good view of the back of King's garage. They had to wait awhile but their patience was eventually rewarded. The workshop doors opened and the Jaguar rolled out, followed a bit later by the Rolls-Royce.

'They're taking them to the coast ready to ship abroad, I bet,' said Sam.

'The sheer greed of the man!' said Maddie, enraged. 'Not content with a lucrative legitimate business, he has to steal from decent people who've worked hard for what they have. And to cap it all he tries to get his grubby hands on land belonging to someone who doesn't want to sell. The sooner the police know about this the better!'

'Yeah, I think we've enough to go on now,' said Sam. 'They might have to watch the place for a few nights but once they see what we've seen, it'll be all over for Alan King.'

They reported the matter at the nearest police station and were assured that the matter would be looked into. Tiredness was swept away by the heady rush of success.

'You've been great,' said Sam as they got back into the car.

'No more than you have.'

'You set the whole thing up.'

'I just happened to be the one in possession of certain facts.'

'You were right to persist with the idea until I agreed to do it.' Sam leaned across and put his hand on Maddie's. 'Thanks for everything you've done for me and the family.'

'Thanks aren't necessary,' she said. 'Let's just pray the police follow it up.'

'We'll have to hope for the best about that,' he said. 'It's in their hands now.'

It was almost dawn by the time they got back to Richmond and – despite all the excitement – nature had taken its course and Maddie's head had fallen on to her chest from sheer exhaustion. She came to with a start as they turned into the fairground.

'What the hell's going on?' Sam was saying.

Her eyes snapped open to see the lights on in all of the wagons and an ambulance driving off the site.

'Trouble,' she muttered.

'Looks like it.'

As they drew up outside Sam's caravan, Janice came out of hers – fully dressed – and rushed over to them. Even in the dim light they could see how distressed she was.

'It's Dad,' she informed them gravely, her voice shaking. 'Mum's gone in the ambulance with him. I'm going to the hospital in the car. Chas is with the kids.'

'What's wrong with him?' asked Sam, his voice quivering.

'He collapsed,' she explained. 'They think he's had a heart attack!'

162

Chapter Thirteen

Exhausted and tense as she waited for news from the hospital later that morning, Maddie felt as though every one of her nerves had been individually severed when the telephone shocked her with its shrill ringing.

With a pounding heart she seized the receiver only to find that it wasn't the call she was expecting. Instead it was the secretary of a charity who wanted to confirm the details of the fun afternoon for children in care – an annual event at Fenner's when the youngsters were entertained free of charge.

'It's always the last Friday in August,' Maddie informed her. 'A final treat before they go back to school.'

'What time?' enquired the woman, who explained that she was new to the job.

'From two o'clock until four on the fairground with tea in the restaurant afterwards,' Maddie informed her.

'And all free of charge?'

'That's right.'

'Wonderful!'

'The kids seem to think so.'

The woman asked a few more questions which Maddie answered. 'We'll look forward to seeing you on the day then,' she said with an air of courteous finality, anxious to leave the line clear for news of Vic. 'If you have any more queries, don't hesitate to contact us again.'

'I must say, I think it's a very generous gesture and much appreciated by the association,' said the woman who was obviously in a chatty mood.

Maddie was almost too weary to speak. 'I think it's a nice idea too,' she said, managing to sound normal. 'Fenner's has been putting on these special afternoons for many years, I believe. Long before I came here to work anyway.'

'Very commendable.'

'I'll pass your comments on to the family.' Would the woman never go? 'And we look forward to seeing the children on the day.'

'Thank you. Goodbye.'

''Bye.'

Forcing herself to stay awake, Maddie applied herself to her duties, removing yesterday's takings from the underfloor safe where the money was stored overnight. Having entered the cash in the ledger and got it ready for the bank, she then replaced it in the safe until two of the men were available to take it to the bank as was the usual procedure. This done she telephoned their ice-cream suppliers with an urgent order, dealt with a salesman from a confectionery firm and contacted their regular bakers about a shortfall on their delivery of hot dog and hamburger rolls. She then telephoned the senior barman – who lived off the site – and arranged for him to come in early and take over in place of Vic in the beer garden. She also found provisional cover for the Hoopla stall in case Janice wasn't back by the time the fair opened.

She was just wondering what to do about Chas's Gallopers when he walked into the office with Sybil and Eric.

They were looking grim but not hopeless, she noticed with cautious optimism. 'I've been going mad waiting for news.'

'It *was* a heart attack,' said Chas. 'Quite a serious one, apparently.'

'Oh, God,' said Maddie, reeling from the blow. 'I suppose that will have been brought on by all the aggro Alan King's been giving him.'

'It can't have helped,' agreed Sybil.

'I'll sort that bugger out for making my uncle ill,' said Eric, dancing about with his fists clenched. 'He'll be in hospital as well as Uncle Vic when I've finished with him.'

'Calm down, son,' said his mother. 'Alan King's already been sorted, from what I've heard.' She turned to Maddie. 'Sam told us that you got a result last night.'

Maddie nodded, her jubilation forgotten in the worry about Vic. 'But not soon enough.'

'Not to save Vic from the heart attack,' said Sybil. 'But knowing the problem's solved should help his recovery.'

'That sounds hopeful.'

'It was meant to be. He's still very ill but he's out of danger now, and the doctors seem to think he'll pull through.'

'Thank God for that!'

'Anyway,' Sybil continued solemnly, 'Alan King isn't entirely to blame for my brother's illness.'

'No?'

'Mum and Aunt Hetty think it's all the fags he smokes,' chipped in Eric.

'And the boozin' and stayin' out till all hours,' added Sybil. 'Vic'll have to change his ways if he does get through this or he'll be back in hospital again in no time – that or the morgue.'

'Don't say that,' said Chas, looking stricken.

'Well, he's had a warning,' Sybil said sagely. 'He might not get a second one.'

'He'll be all right so long as he looks after himself,' said Chas, who couldn't bear to think about the alternative.

'Working here will be out of the question,' Sybil warned. 'For a while anyway.'

'I can't imagine Vic not being around the fair,' said Maddie. 'He might not be Fenner's hardest worker but he'll be lost if he isn't involved.'

'That's all very well,' said Sybil, shaking her head. 'But if he wants to stay alive, he'll have to change his ways.'

'Hetty's already talking about retirement for them both,' Chas said to Maddie.

'That's a bit drastic.'

'She's talking about moving into their house permanently,' he said. 'And if she can persuade Vic to retire or semi-retire, she'll stay at home to keep him company.'

'To keep an eye him, you mean,' said Sybil.

'Well . . . whatever.'

'They'll have to hand the business over to Sam officially,' said Sybil.

'That won't be a problem for him since he already runs the fair,' Maddie observed.

'That's true.' Sybil sighed. 'I dunno – the family members in the firm seem to be dwindling lately. First we lose Josh and Tania, now Vic and Hetty. Where will it end?'

'Don't worry, I'm sure it'll work out for the best,' said Maddie in her usual positive manner.

'It's finding people with the same dedication as family that's the problem.' Sybil looked at her. 'There aren't many about like you.'

'That's very flattering but I'm sure it isn't true.'

'Well . . . be that as it may, dear,' Sybil went on, 'we have a message for you from Sam. He says you are to make sure that you have a rest before the fair opens. You can't keep going all night and all day without any sleep.'

'I haven't got time to rest,' said Maddie, but she was touched by Sam's thoughtfulness, especially when he had more serious matters on his mind.

'Yes, you have,' insisted Sybil. 'I'll look after the office. You go and have a lie down before you fall down.'

'What about Sam?' said Maddie. 'He's been up all night too.'

'Don't worry about him,' said Sybil. 'He'll grab some shut-eye in a chair at the hospital.'

'If you're sure you don't mind covering for me, perhaps I had better do what he says or I'll be fit for nothing later on.'

'Off you go then,' said Sybil.

After arranging for Chas and Eric to take the cash to the bank, Maddie left the office and went home to bed. The caravan was very

165

still and silent without Clare who had gone to the ice rink with Barney and some of the older children, this being the school summer holidays.

Despite her exhaustion she found it difficult to sleep. Not so much because of the clatter outside – delivery vans coming and going and people talking and shouting to each other around the fairground as they prepared for the day's business – but because she was wondering how Hetty was going to make her hedonistic husband change his way of life!

Hetty had always considered herself to be rather a brave person, able to take most things in her stride. She didn't stand back and leave it all to the men when Alan King's thugs invaded the fairground; she was out there cheering Fenner's men on and giving those scallywags a tongue lashing.

But sitting by her husband's bedside, sick with terror at this close encounter with mortality, she began to doubt her own courage. Vic was sleeping and the doctors seemed fairly optimistic about his chances but his condition was still serious and he looked awful, his face bloodless and shining with sweat. Every wheezing breath he took might be his last, she feared.

Something debilitating had happened to her in the early hours of this morning when he had cried out in pain then slumped unconscious to the floor, having got out of bed for something from the medicine cabinet for what he'd thought was indigestion. Although she'd tried not to show it to the others, she'd felt physically weak ever since – impotent against the fear that had taken such a hold on her, unable even to stand up without feeling faint. It was particularly distressing for someone normally so robust, especially as there didn't seem to be a damned thing she could do about it.

Until now, the nearest thing Vic had had to an illness was a hangover. Trust him to go for the big one and scare us all to death! she thought. He had never been a model husband – far from it, in fact. But they had a good marriage and even after all these years she still loved the old bugger, and couldn't bear the thought of losing him.

She was so deep in thought she hardly noticed her son and daughter slip quietly into the room. But when their comforting presence did register she felt a surge of warmth and gratitude for their support these last few hours.

'I've had a chat with the doctor, Mum,' said Sam in a low voice, sitting down beside her.

'Oh?' She turned to him, afraid of what he might say.

'It's all right,' he said, giving her hand a reassuring squeeze. 'He said that Dad's condition has definitely stabilised, and they're hopeful of a recovery.'

'It doesn't look like that from where I'm sitting.' Hetty turned doubtfully back to her husband.

'These medical people know what they're talking about,' Janice reassured her.

'They'll tell you anything to stop you asking questions,' Hetty fretted, unreasonable because she felt so vulnerable and afraid.

'I'm sure that isn't true,' her son answered gently. 'And it isn't like you to be so negative.'

'You're quite right, it isn't,' she said, shaking her head as though to dispel a sense of doom. 'But he looks so ill, and . . . I suppose I'm just not used to it, him being such a fit man all his life.'

'Doctors aren't given to offering people false hope,' Sam pointed out, full of sympathy for his mother who had been knocked sideways by this. 'So we have to believe them when they say that Dad stands a good chance of getting better.'

'Yeah, I know.'

'Anyway the good news is they're confident enough to suggest that we should take a break now and go home for a while.'

'I'm not going anywhere while your dad's like this,' said Hetty, who had been given the use of a relative's room as Vic was so ill.

'I should go and have a lie down, though,' said Sam. 'Then you'll be on form when he wakes up.'

'We'll see.'

'Will you be all right while I go back to the fairground to check that everything's okay? Dad would want me to do that.'

''Course I'll be all right. You need to get some sleep an' all, you were up all night.' His mother frowned, gathering together her muddled thoughts. 'You and Maddie did a good job. Your dad will be proud of you. Tell her from me that she's a diamond.'

'I'll tell her . . . if she hasn't collapsed from exhaustion,' said Sam, managing to smile. 'She was left holding the fort on her own until Chas and the others went back.'

'We're lucky to have her,' said Hetty. 'There aren't many people outside the family you could trust with your business.'

'I know,' he agreed.

Hetty looked at Janice. 'You go home with Sam, love.'

'No. I think I'll stay with you for a bit longer.'

'As you wish.'

'I won't be gone long,' said Sam. 'But ring the office if anything untoward happens and I'll come back right away.'

His mother nodded; she was thinking about the missing member of her family. 'Josh ought to know what's happened.'

''Course he should,' agreed Sam, his voice becoming hard. 'But as we've no idea where he is or how to contact him, there's nothing we can do about it, is there? We certainly can't ask the police to find him for us.'

167

'Hardly!'

Sam got up and stood behind his mother with his hands on her shoulders. 'Don't worry, Mum, you've still got Janice and me.'

'And glad I am of it, too,' she said, reaching up and putting her hand on his. 'You've both been wonderful. I don't know what I'd have done without you.'

But she ached for Josh to be here with them too. Where was her eldest son? He should be with his family at a time like this.

Dressed only in a pair of shorts, a deeply tanned Josh was stretched out on a lounger in a shady corner of the balcony of his seaview apartment in Marbella, keeping cool in the heat of the afternoon. A gentle breeze rustled through the palm trees below in the lawned gardens of the apartment complex, the sun glinting on the turquoise shimmer of the kidney-shaped swimming pool, deserted in the intense heat of a Spanish summer afternoon.

Many of the residents of these luxury apartments were foreign business people like Josh who lived here all the year. They didn't feel the need to subject their bodies to the blistering Spanish sunshine at siesta time in pursuit of a tan with the same relentless dedication of the sun-starved British holiday-maker. The few people who were in the gardens were sitting in the shade.

Staring out over the sea, Josh was smoking a cigar and reflecting on his situation. He had made it. He now had everything he'd wanted for most of his adult life: money, independence, his own business, and a luxury home in an idyllic setting far away from the restricting confines of the family.

He'd had no trouble finding a business in his price range on arriving on the Casta del Sol. The lease on a British-run bar that traded all year round had been on offer. Having the cash immediately available had made it a smooth transaction. These days Josh went to work in smart clothes and employed reliable staff so that he could take time off as he wished.

Time off to do what, though? Drink alone in the town's bars? Go to a holiday-makers' disco to pick up a woman for a one-night stand? Stay here in the apartment on his own? Some choice! He didn't have any mates here in Spain and there was no woman in his life. He didn't want there to be – *ever*. No one could replace Tania, the love of his life.

Hot tears swelled beneath his eyelids. He blinked them back instinctively because men of his sort didn't cry, not even in private. Josh still couldn't think of Tania without wanting to weep. She should have been here with him. It would all have been so different if he hadn't made a mess of everything.

He felt alarmed, suddenly and for no apparent reason; a shiver ran up his spine as a vivid mental image of his mother came into his mind. His heart beat faster from fear. Of what? Something was wrong at home, he could sense it. Panic scorched through him. He was nauseous and sweating.

Guilty conscience, mate, he told himself, sceptical about the existence of psychic phenomena. You're going to be haunted by feelings like this for the rest of your life because you know it was wrong to walk out on your mother without even leaving a forwarding address – and unforgivable not to get in touch to let her know that you're safe.

Fraught with tension, he went inside to get a cold beer from the fridge. The marble tiles felt cool and soothing to his feet. Restlessly wandering into the lounge with its white walls and Mediterranean furnishings – cane chairs with brightly patterned cushions and an intricately carved Spanish dining table with high-backed chairs – he went over to the telephone on the wall and picked up the receiver, replacing it almost immediately.

It was no use, he couldn't speak to anyone at home, not even to find out if all was well. He just didn't have the courage. Anyway, there were no words that could excuse what he'd done. He'd run away from trouble like the coward he was, and in so doing had broken family ties for ever. There was no going back for Josh. He'd made his bed, as his mother would say. He found himself smiling affectionately at the thought of her shrewd brown eyes and sharp sense of humour.

Sam had inherited Hetty's strong character. Janice too, up to a point, though his sister was no angel. She'd given their parents a whole lot of grief by getting pregnant and refusing to have any part of the most common solution to that sort of trouble. Josh himself took after the old man – pleasure-seeking and irresponsible. Still, not everyone could be as naturally decent as Sam. His brother . . . Josh's heart twisted at the thought of what he'd done to him.

No, a clean break was the best thing for everyone. No explanations, no prodding of old wounds or hurt for any of them. Let them forget him. They had their life and he had his – the sort of lifestyle he'd craved for so long. He'd thought it would feel different when he got it, though.

He went back out on to the balcony, feeling miserable and ashamed. He looked at his watch, longing for the hours to pass until it was time to go and open the bar for the evening session. As least work helped him to forget what a thoroughly wretched human being he was.

Sam came rushing into the office one afternoon a couple of weeks after his father's heart attack, waving the local newspaper.

'Alan King's been arrested,' he told Maddie, putting the paper down on the desk in front of her. 'For stealing cars, dealing in stolen goods, forgery – the lot.'

169

'Wow!' she said, scanning the report which was on the front page together with a picture of King.

'It's all down to you,' he said.

'We did it together,' she corrected him.

'It was your idea.'

'I can't deny that.' Maddie laughed. 'Glad I twisted your arm now?'

'Not half.'

'So – no more visits from rent-a-mob for us then?'

'No. I think Alan King's gonna have more pressing things on his mind than trying to build a hotel on our site, don't you?'

'Yeah – like how long he's gonna be spending in prison.'

'Exactly.'

Janice came into the office for some small change and was told the good news.

'Brilliant! Mum and Dad will be really chuffed.' She smiled. 'Well done, you two.'

'We're just glad our stint of night duty is over,' said Sam, smiling at Maddie.

'You can say that again! I don't know about needing matchsticks to prop open my eyes while that was going on – it felt like I needed a couple of very large logs.'

'Things seem to be looking up in general,' remarked Janice. 'With Dad getting a bit better every day.'

'Any news about when he'll be coming out of hospital?' asked Maddie.

'Quite soon, according to Mum.'

'He won't be coming back to work this season, though,' added Sam.

'If at all. Mum's still talking about retirement.'

'I can't imagine Vic agreeing to that without a fight,' commented Maddie.

'The old rogue wouldn't mind retiring if he could still do all the other things that are bad for his ticker, like being out till all hours smoking and drinking,' said Sam. 'But Mum isn't having any of that so he'll miss the company if he doesn't come back to work.'

'His illness has really frightened her,' said Janice. 'She's terrified that he might have another attack.'

'It's shaken Dad up too,' said Sam. 'Though he'd never admit it.'

Janice picked up the newspaper. 'Can I take this to show Chas?'

''Course you can.'

'If I can find him, that is. Since he's been helping on the fair generally, he's not so easy to track down.'

'He's been a real asset to us since Josh left, though,' remarked Sam. 'We need him more than ever now that Dad's laid up.'

'Yeah.' His sister's voice was warm. 'Chas is all right.' She took

170

some bags of copper and silver from Maddie, handing her some notes in exchange to keep the books straight.

'You busy on the Hoopla stall?' enquired Maddie conversationally.

'Yeah, quite steady.'

'Good.'

'It's a real help being able to leave Barney to look after it for a few minutes,' said Janice. 'I wouldn't leave him for long while he's still so young but at least I can go and have a pee without having to ask for cover.'

They all laughed.

'He enjoys helping you, he was telling me all about it,' said Maddie.

'Oh, yeah, he's a natural with the punters, just like his dad. I wouldn't let him work with me on the stall if he didn't enjoy it,' said Janice. 'But he loves it and it's extra pocket money for him, too. You're not supposed to let kids of his age work but it's more like fun for him so I don't worry about it. And the children don't know what to do with themselves in the summer holidays anyway.'

'That's why I let Clare help with the balloon selling and toffee apples,' Maddie said. 'To keep boredom at bay.'

The telephone began to ring just as one of the maintenance staff came into the office with some queries, and someone brought a lost child in for safe keeping until her parents could be found, reminding them all that there was work to be done.

Janice and Sam went back outside and Maddie returned to her work feeling pleased about the arrest of Alan King. She didn't wish harm on anyone but she did like to know that justice was being done.

171

Chapter Fourteen

Hetty and Vic moved into their house permanently when he came out of hospital, and she stayed at home to look after him. It seemed strange for their living-wagon to be empty during the season, although they would still use it occasionally for special fairground events, and when Vic was feeling well enough for them to help out.

In their absence, Sam, Janice, Chas and Maddie ran the fair together. Chas agreed to stay at Fenner's indefinitely but still wouldn't accept a partnership in the firm.

In October Janice and he took the Gallopers to the Nottingham Goose Fair and other autumn fairs around the country, leaving Barney in Maddie's care as they had last year, so that he wouldn't miss school. Having no leanings towards academia, he was thoroughly miffed not to be going on the trip with them but was told he'd have to wait until he'd left school before he could join them.

Pat and Bob at the Fiddler's Inn found a place for Maddie again that autumn. With all the functions they had booked at the pub up until Christmas, they needed extra staff. It was when things were quiet in January and February that they couldn't guarantee her employment.

However, something happened that autumn to make Maddie think this might be the last winter she would have to find work off the park . . .

Sam suggested that the four of them go out for a meal together one evening when Janice and Chas returned from their travels. Partly as a treat because they had all worked so hard during the season and partly to discuss business, he said. The outing was arranged for one of Maddie's off-duty nights and Sybil was enlisted to sit with the children who were both asleep in Janice's wagon, to make things simpler.

They went to a pub with a restaurant on the river near Runnymede – one of the new steak houses that were all the rage. It was done up in nautical style with anchors and pictures of boats adorning the walls. The foursome were all looking smart, the men in suits, the women in mini-dresses.

'This is all very nice, Sam,' remarked Janice after a certain amount of small talk. 'But what's it all in aid of?'

'I thought we ought to have a general discussion about the business and some ideas I have.' He looked at Maddie. 'I have included you because you're just as involved as we are.'

'Naturally,' said Janice and Chas nodded in agreement.

'All my suggestions will be subject to Mum and Dad's approval, o' course,' he said. 'They're still the guiding force of the business even though I'm now officially in charge.'

There was a general murmur of agreement from the others.

'I know it's a bit early to be thinking of next season. But I think we have to face the fact that – even if Mum and Dad do come back – it will only be part-time. Dad's a lot better but he still has to watch his health.'

'As I understand their intentions, they'll be on hand to help out whenever we need them but they won't be there all the time any more,' said Janice.

'Maybe it's all for the best,' said Sam. 'They've worked hard all their lives, they should have some time to themselves.'

Nobody could argue with that.

'Anyway,' he continued, 'Mum and Dad aren't forward thinkers but my way of doing things is different.'

'I'm not sure I like the sound of that,' said Janice.

'I hope you'll like my proposals because I think of us four as a team.' He looked round the table, his gaze resting first on Chas. 'I know you want to retain your independence so I'm not going to ask you to join the firm.'

'Right.'

'But I need to know if I can rely on your staying at Fenner's next season and continuing to work for us in a general way,' Sam went on. 'I know you've said you will but I have to be absolutely sure. I mean, if you want to go off travelling with the Gallopers, I'll have to find someone else I can trust. And I need to know where I stand on this so I can plan ahead.'

Chas thought about this. He'd always been a free spirit. But, much to his surprise, he'd enjoyed being part of the team at Fenner's, and seeing more of Janice and Barney had been great. It had been a good business arrangement, too, because Fenner's had waived his rent for the pitch as well as paying him for taking responsibility for several other rides. They had also provided him with assistance on the Gallopers so that he was free to attend to his other duties around the fair.

'Yeah, you can count on me, mate.'

'The same arrangement as we had last season?' said Sam.

'Suits me.'

'Great,' said Janice, sipping her wine and smiling at Chas.

'Now we come to Maddie.'

'Me?' She was puzzled. She hadn't expected to be the subject of discussion.

'Yes, you,' he confirmed. 'Over the years that you've worked for us you've taken on an increasing amount of responsibility.'

She nodded.

'So, I think it's time we put you on a proper salary instead of paying you by the day,' he said. 'You'll get an increase too when you start with us next season.'

'Wow!' she said, beaming. 'Thank you . . . very much indeed.'

'You're not being given anything you don't deserve.'

'I'll second that,' said Janice.

Sam took a long gulp of wine. 'Now we come to the final and most dramatic suggestion,' he announced mysteriously.

They waited expectantly.

He looked at Maddie. 'On several occasions you've suggested that we build a pavilion and keep it open all year round.'

'That's right, but your parents never fancied the idea.'

'No, because they want things to stay the same as they've always been,' he said. 'But now that they've handed over to me officially, I want to do things my way. Frankly, I think we're going to have to move with the times to stay in business. In days gone by there wasn't much to compete with the fair, it was the most colourful and exciting entertainment around. But as we all know there have been a great many changes in the leisure industry even since I was a boy. Now there are discos, clubs, coffee bars . . .'

'. . . Bingo halls, bowling alleys,' Maddie finished for him.

Sam smiled. 'Exactly. We could have one or the other in a pavilion-type building.'

'Why not both?' she suggested enthusiastically. 'Then we'd be catering for a much wider age group.'

'It's a question of space,' he said. 'Both activities require a great deal of floor space.'

'True,' agreed Maddie, who could hardly contain her excitement about this project. 'But the fairground isn't used to its full capacity at the moment. There's a great deal of ground wasted around the edges of the site. And we could afford for some of the sideshows to be a bit closer together without causing any problems at all. With a little reorganisation, I think you'd be surprised.'

'She's got a point,' agreed Chas.

'It's a thought,' said Sam. 'Anyway, that part of it can be sorted out later. The important thing for the moment is to establish whether or not we are all in favour of a new attraction that we'd keep open all year round?'

'I can see the sense of it from a commercial point of view,' said

Janice cautiously. 'But won't it mean that we'll all be working during the winter?'

'For some of the time, yes. But it would be staffed so that we would get plenty of time off.'

'I'll be straight with you, Sam,' said Janice. 'I don't wanna be tied to the job like we are all through the season.'

'I don't think any of us do,' he said. 'Which is why I wanted to discuss this project with you all before taking the idea to Mum and Dad.' He turned to Maddie. 'Obviously if it does come to fruition we'll need you to work for us all year round because there'll be plenty to do in the office. But I don't think we'll hear you complaining about that.'

'You certainly won't!'

'Well, I'm all in favour of the idea so long as we're not gonna have to work flat out like we do in the summer,' said Janice. 'I want some time to do other things.'

'I'll second that,' said Chas.

'We can arrange things to suit ourselves so far as that's concerned,' said Sam. 'If we put a manager in, that should take the pressure off.' He turned to Maddie. 'We'd have to keep the office open but you wouldn't have to work nearly such long hours as you do in summer.'

'That's no problem to me, anyway,' she said. 'I'm used to working during the winter.' She paused. 'But tell me – would the pavilion be licensed?'

'I hope so. I'm going to apply for one.'

'A pavilion with Bingo, bowling and a comfortable bar?' said Maddie. 'Sounds like a real money spinner to me.'

'Yeah, it does sound like a winning combination,' Sam agreed, voice rising with enthusiasm. 'Always supposing we can get Mum and Dad's approval since it will take a lot of money to set up.'

'It would pay for itself very quickly, I should think,' Maddie commented.

'I wonder if there'll be any local opposition to our opening a Bingo hall-cum-bowling alley?' remarked Janice.

'There are sure to be restrictions about the style of the building,' said Sam. 'I imagine it would have to be pretty tasteful. But because we're already a fairground offering similar entertainments, I shouldn't think there'll be any real problem. It isn't as though there are any private houses near us.'

'I think we should go for it,' said Chas.

'Count me in, too,' Janice agreed.

Sam looked at Maddie and grinned. 'And as it was your idea in the first place, there's no need to ask you.'

She smiled in reply.

'The next step is to put the idea to the parents,' Sam proposed.

'If they do agree, how long will it take?' asked his sister.

'Well . . . we'll get the plans drawn up. Then we have to get planning permission, so that'll take a while. But I'd like to have Fenner's Leisure Pavilion ready to open at the end of the next summer season at the very latest,' he announced.

'Sounds about right to me,' said Maddie.

'Well, I think that just about concludes the business part of the evening,' said Sam. 'So let's forget all about Fenner's for a couple of hours and enjoy ourselves.'

'I'll drink to that,' enthused Janice.

Maddie was having a wonderful time. For someone whose social life was normally limited to serving in a bar, an evening out like this was a real treat. She was wearing a black mini-dress she normally wore for work at the pub which looked good with her blonde hair.

Being so comfortable in the company she was with, she positively sparkled, making jokes and having fun. They were all still laughing when they got back to Fenner's in Sam's car.

'Anyone fancy a coffee?' Maddie invited casually, having checked with Sybil that Clare was fast asleep. Maddie had had a few drinks and didn't want the evening to end.

'Not for me, thanks,' said Janice. 'I'm heading straight for my bed.'

'Me too,' said Chas.

'I'll join you for a coffee, Maddie,' said Sam.

'Good. I'm not tired enough to go to bed yet.'

'G'night both,' said Janice. 'See you in the morning.'

''Night,' said Maddie. 'I hope the kids don't wake you up too early.'

'Don't worry. I'll send 'em in to you if they do,' she laughed.

Maddie and Sam sat by the fire, drinking coffee and chatting. He commented on how attractive her home was now, casting an approving eye over the rich red carpet, curtains in autumnal shades and subtle light fittings.

'I've done my best to make it homely on my limited budget.' She gave him a wicked grin. 'Still, who knows what I'll be able to afford next year when I get my salary increase?'

'I don't think it will quite run to a bathroom extension,' Sam said. 'But it'll help with everyday things.'

'Don't mention a bathroom extension or you'll have me in tears.'

'Why is that?'

'About the only thing I've got against this caravan is the lack of a bathroom,' Maddie explained. 'We manage well enough with just a washbasin and toilet but it's a real drag having to go across to the accommodation block for a shower, especially on cold winter mornings.'

'Well, you don't look too bad on it,' said Sam, thinking how attractive Maddie looked, clear blue eyes sparkling, cheeks prettily suffused. 'In fact, you look wonderful.'

'Flattery will get you everywhere,' she said, glowing. 'You're not so bad yourself . . . quite the toff tonight in your smart suit.'

He did look overwhelmingly sexy tonight, she thought, with his eyes warm and approving of her, tie loosened, hair ruffled.

'Thanks. I thought I ought to make the effort given the company I was in.'

'The evening was lovely,' she said softly. 'Thank you.'

'My pleasure.'

Realising how much she wanted to go to bed with Sam, and sensing that he wanted it too, Maddie felt awkward and began to talk about the proposed pavilion to defuse the passion now palpable in the air. Finding it increasingly difficult to make intelligent conversation, she asked Sam if he would like another cup of coffee. He said he would.

As she leaned across to get his empty cup from the coffee table beside him, he touched her arm. She stood still with her heart racing, his touch burning through the sleeve of her dress.

'Oh, Maddie,' he said, standing up and sweeping her into his arms.

She melted against him, completely in thrall to her feelings for him. But in that last second of rational thought before impulse took over she realised the risk she was taking – this could mean either the loss of their friendship or the possibility of its developing into a more serious relationship.

'This isn't a good idea, Sam,' she said, drawing back.

'Sorry, I thought you . . .' He was aroused and breathless.

'I do, but I don't want it to happen just to round off the evening because we've both had a few drinks.'

'Oh.'

'Last time it happened because of grief,' she said, voice quivering. 'If it happens again I want it to be for the right reasons.'

'I understand.' Sam struggled with disappointment and frustration. The purely masculine side of his nature urged him to persist and to hell with the consequences. But Maddie meant more to him than that. She wanted something profound from him – *she deserved nothing less than total commitment* – and he didn't feel able to give her that. How could he make a true commitment to anyone when he couldn't get Tania out of his system? Damn her!

'It's all right, Sam,' said Maddie, sensing his turmoil. 'I know you can't make any promises to me at the moment.'

'I care for you – a lot,' he said. 'But I'm just not ready for a love affair.'

'So let's just carry on being friends then, shall we?' she said.

'Yeah, okay . . . I'm sorry.'

177

'Apologies are unnecessary . . . it was as much my fault as yours,' she said, suddenly wanting to be alone. 'But I think it's probably best if you go now.'

'Yes, I think you're right,' said Sam, putting his coat on and making for the door.

After he'd gone, Maddie sat in her chair staring into the dying embers of the fire and mulling over her feelings. She felt confused; stronger for having refused him but empty and disappointed too. Had she given in to her feelings, she would have been setting a pattern for the future. Sex with no strings could have become a habit simply because they were together so much and attracted to each other. Whatever they had it was worth more than that.

Knowing that she had done the right thing didn't ease the empty feeling, though. She wanted Sam – *so much*!

Sam was also feeling confused as he got into bed. He was very fond of Maddie and fancied her rotten. But love? That was a different thing altogether and something he didn't know if he could feel again for any woman. Because he cared for Maddie, he didn't want her to have to accept second best. She'd suffered enough at the hands of one man; Sam didn't want to risk hurting her by entering into something he wasn't sure about. Maddie deserved better than that. But, by God, he had wanted her with a ferocious passion tonight.

In future, situations like the one this evening mustn't be allowed to develop. It had been lovely being with Maddie, sharing her pleasure in the happy occasion. He felt so alive and happy when he was with her.

But if he was to retain her friendship, he must think of her only as a friend and colleague. A depressing prospect indeed.

Chapter Fifteen

Hetty was beginning to think that fate hadn't dealt her and Vic such a cruel blow after all . . .

Immediately after his heart attack – when she'd been so acutely vulnerable and convinced he was about to drop dead at any moment – she'd forced herself to accept the depressing fact that their lives would never be the same again.

But as time passed and a new pattern emerged, she realised that this wasn't such a bad thing. After a period when Vic had seemed old and feeble, he gradually became stronger. With a healthier diet and regular exercise – which he took in the form of gentle walking – he lost his wheezy chest as well as some of his excess weight. There was always a threat when someone had a dodgy heart, of course, but his general health was better than ever. Since boozing until all hours in clubs was no longer an option, he spent more time at home, too.

Being forced to submit to the limitations of his illness was especially hard for someone like Vic – a man's man who would rather be dead than seen to be under his wife's thumb. At first he'd rebelled against the new regimen; he'd been difficult and bad-tempered, and Hetty had borne the brunt.

'For God's sake, leave me alone, woman,' he'd roared at her when she'd found him in the garden shed with a glass of whisky and a cigar, which she'd immediately confiscated. 'I'm better off dead if you're gonna take away all my pleasures.'

For a while he'd complained bitterly about the food she'd been advised to give him, too. 'What's this rubbish you're dishing up?' he said of the salads she served at midday instead of the enormous plate of meat and vegetables he'd been used to prior to the heart attack. 'Are you trying to starve me to death or something?'

As for the late nights in drinking clubs – which he'd insisted on taking up again in a perverse attempt to deny his illness, even though he got tired more easily these days and was in no fit state – they had come to an abrupt end after an attack of severe chest pain in a club one night which had frightened them both and resulted in a serious warning from his doctor.

Hetty had given her husband a real trouncing over it. 'Have you got a death wish or are you just plain stupid?' she'd fumed.

'Stop nagging.'

'You're bloody selfish, I know that much, Vic Fenner,' she ranted. 'I don't know why I don't just wash my hands of you . . . let you get on with it.'

'I wish you would.'

'Right, I will. Go ahead and kill yourself if that's what you want,' she said, on the verge of tears from sheer frustration. 'Ignore your responsibilities and leave me to cope with life on my own, when you could have a good few years ahead of you if you'd only look after yourself.'

'You've got this whole thing out of proportion.'

'I have not. I'm facing up to things and it's time you did the same.'

It hadn't been an instant surrender. But as Vic's health continued to improve and Hetty's confidence grew sufficiently for her to vary his diet, he complained less about his temperate lifestyle. When the doctor said an occasional glass of beer wouldn't hurt him, Hetty encouraged him to go out to the pub for a spot of male company. The men he got talking to at the local weren't such a bad influence on him as the hardened whisky swiggers who'd been his buddies in the clubs.

Hetty went with him sometimes. In fact, they re-discovered each other as companions and went out together quite often. The following spring they began to take regular day trips to the coast, and even the races on occasion. They had the best of both worlds, in Hetty's opinion; they retained their involvement with the fair and helped whenever they were needed as the new season got underway, but they weren't tied to it every minute as they used to be.

After grave reservations about the new Fenner's Fun Pavilion – which was due to open in the autumn ready for the winter – Hetty was rather excited about it now that it was a fait accompli. But it was a relief not to have to shoulder the burden of responsibility for this huge project.

The best part was knowing that the business was safe in Sam's hands. Hetty was proud of the way he handled himself now that he officially held the reins. She liked the way Janice and Chas supported him, too. And Maddie, of course. Sometimes Hetty sensed something special between Sam and Maddie. But nothing seemed to come of it, much to her disappointment for she would welcome Maddie into the family with open arms. Sam was probably still clinging to the memory of Tania. The fool!

But now on this June afternoon, as Hetty sat in the garden with a cup of tea while Vic snoozed in a deckchair, she realised that the telephone was ringing indoors and hurried inside to answer it. It was Maddie asking if Hetty and Vic could go over to the park for a few hours later on to help out. They were short-staffed, especially in the beer garden.

'Of course we'll come, love,' said Hetty, delighted to be asked.

Although she was thoroughly enjoying her newfound freedom, she needed to be in demand occasionally.

That September of 1966 seemed to herald the end of an era for Maddie when Clare and Barney started at secondary school, especially as they were in different schools now.

With the change of school came other alterations. Clare became more independent, made friends further afield, got home from school later in the afternoon. She made her own way and was horrified at the mere suggestion of being accompanied by an adult. She and Barney walked part of the way together, then went their separate ways.

Although all of this was probably quite normal for someone of Clare's age, there were other personality changes that made it seem to Maddie as though her daughter's childhood had ended prematurely. She became moody and uncommunicative. She no longer confided in her mother and was incredibly difficult at times – fiercely rebellious and would disagree with Maddie almost as a matter of course. Some of her temper tantrums were quite alarming!

'I suppose we'll have to expect that sort of thing now,' said Janice one wet morning just after the season had ended when Maddie told her all about it over a cup of coffee in the office. 'Our kids are growing up. They'll be twelve next birthday. Soon be Tampax time for Clare.'

'Yeah – at least I've managed to talk to her about that.'

'Good.'

'But the change in her is so drastic and sudden, I'm wondering if it's more than just growing up? One day she was her usual loving self, the next she was a behaving like a sulky teenager.'

'She soon *will* be a teenager.'

'She's still got a while to go yet,' said Maddie. 'I know she's showing all the classic symptoms of adolescence but this seems too early and too extreme.'

'I'm sure the change in her is nothing to worry about,' said Janice. 'She's always her usual sweet self with me.'

'Yeah, saves all her bad temper for me!'

'That's typical . . . Mum's the one to take the flak.'

'I realise that but Clare and I have always been so close, being only the two of us,' said Maddie. 'Then suddenly she's fighting with me over every little thing, from what clothes she should wear to what I give her to eat.' She paused. 'The worst part is, I can feel her reaching out to me from somewhere deep inside but I can't get near her any more. She's shut me out.'

'It'll pass.'

'Is Barney showing any of the signs of adolescence?'

'Not really, not yet,' said Janice. 'But no doubt he'll start getting stroppy when his hormones go on the march.'

'I can't imagine Barney ever getting into a strop about anything,' said Maddie because the lad in question was the most easygoing of children.

'He has his moments like anyone else,' said Janice. 'But I've no complaints. He seems to have inherited his father's even temper.'

'Mmm.'

Something about Maddie's expression made Janice frown. 'Oh – now I understand why you're so worried. You're afraid Clare might be going to take after her father . . .'

'Well, she does have his blood and she does seem to have developed a filthy temper all of a sudden.'

'That doesn't mean she has a violent streak though.'

'No, of course not. But she's not the sweet girl she once was and I'm really worried about her.'

'I'm sure it'll pass, love,' said Janice, responding to her friend's mood with sensitivity. 'Try not to worry.'

'As things are at the moment, I don't feel in control of her.'

'Inevitable as they grow up, I should think,' said Janice, who was making light of it in an effort to calm Maddie's fears; she sipped her coffee thoughtfully. 'On the subject of Clare's father – has she started asking about him again?'

'Yes, she has. She seems very interested in our life before we came to the fair.'

'She's at an age to be more curious now, I suppose.'

The conversation was interrupted by the arrival of the foreman of the building team working on the pavilion, a ruddy-faced man wearing yellow oilskins that were dripping with rain.

'Can you get on the phone to the electrician, please, love?' he asked Maddie. 'Ask him if he's gonna honour us with his presence today.'

'Not turned up again?'

'No, he hasn't . . . and the wiring is only half finished.'

'That isn't good enough!'

'You can say that again,' he said in a gravel voice. 'Tell him he isn't the only sparks in the world and if he isn't here by midday, I'll give the job to someone else. That should get him off his arse.'

'Will do.'

As he left, the two women turned to the window and watched him walk towards the shell of the pavilion, hazy through the rain mist.

'It's really beginning to take shape, isn't it?' said Maddie.

'Yeah.' Janice stared across the closed and shuttered fairground to the bungalow-style-building on the edge of the site, still without windows and doors at the moment. 'It'll seem funny having punters around in the winter.'

Maddie nodded.

'Must seem funny to you not having to go to the pub to work?' said Janice.

'Wonderful is the word that springs to mind,' Maddie answered buoyantly. 'There's nothing quite so comforting as a steady, year-round job when you've a child to support.'

'It must be hard doing it all on your own.' Janice gave a wry grin. 'I must admit I've never been too proud to stop Chas paying his share towards supporting Barney even though I wouldn't be bullied into marriage.'

'Chas wouldn't have it any other way.'

'You're right there,' agreed Janice.

'Talking about money,' said Maddie chattily as she looked through her book for the electrician's telephone number, 'I feel a bit of a fraud for drawing my salary at the moment because there isn't very much to do with the fair being closed. Until the pavilion opens, all I have to do is organise the materials for the fairground maintenance, keep the paperwork straight, and make sure the builders have everything they need.'

'Make the most of it! You'll probably be rushed off your feet when it all opens.'

'I'm really looking forward to it,' said Maddie. 'I love my job.'

Their conversation came to a temporary halt while she made the call to the electrician, repeating the foreman's message and adding a similar one of her own on behalf of Fenner's. The man promised to be there within the hour.

'So – now you have the work side of your life organised,' said Janice, 'what about doing the same with your lovelife?'

'What lovelife?'

'Exactly. You need a man.'

'You make me sound like a bitch in season.'

Janice roared with laughter. 'We're all animals under the skin . . . we all have an instinct to mate. Even if, as human beings, we are more civilised about it and like the whole thing wrapped up in love and marriage and all that stuff.'

'Really, Janice,' said Maddie in a tone of friendly reproof.

'There's no need to be coy about these things – not these days,' her friend said. 'This is 1966. It's becoming perfectly acceptable for sex to be enjoyed by women as well as men.' She paused, grinning. 'Not that I waited until it became acceptable – I always have thought it was great.'

Maddie laughed. 'Not everyone is lucky enough to find the right partner.'

'No, I s'pose not.' She shot Maddie a look. 'What about Sam?'

'What about him?'

'You two would be great together,' Janice said. 'He has a soft spot for you.'

'Has he said anything?'

'He doesn't have to,' Janice said casually. 'You can see it in the way he is when you're around, the way he looks at you sometimes.'

Maddie wasn't prepared to talk about her feelings for Sam. One hint of a possible romance and Janice might try to help things along – with the very best of intentions. But Maddie's friendship with Sam, which she believed was a love affair in the making, was too important to expose to the possibility of outside intervention.

'I think you've misread the signs,' she said quickly. 'Sam's still in love with his wife. There isn't a woman on earth who can match Tania in his eyes.'

'To be perfectly honest, I think you're right,' Janice agreed gloomily. 'He always was potty over the woman, even though she treated him like dirt. It was a case of "treat 'em mean, keep 'em keen," I think.'

'Whatever the reason, he was besotted.'

'*Was* being the operative word,' said Janice. 'Tania is dead! Being in love with her memory isn't healthy.' She paused. 'Still, Sam is basically very down to earth. He'll come out of it eventually.'

'I hope so, for his sake,' said Maddie. 'It's been two years.'

'That long?' said Janice.

'Yes,' said Maddie. 'Tania died in 1964.'

'Blimey! Where does the time go?' remarked Janice.

Maddie was wondering the same thing. It didn't seem a year since that last near miss with Sam, since when their relationship had been determinedly platonic, both of them carefully behaving as though nothing had happened.

It was surprising how well they got along, considering the fact that they were physically attracted to each other. Maddie's love for him was almost too much to bear at times, though. The only thing that enabled her to carry on working with him was the belief that when he finally freed himself from the emotional chains that bound him to Tania, he would be hers.

Occasionally she thought it might be easier if she left Fenner's altogether. But she couldn't do that. Even apart from the fact that she wouldn't want to uproot Clare, such a move would be a blow to the firm since Maddie had made herself as near to indispensable as anyone could be. She'd surprised herself with the number of skills she'd learned and the responsibilities she'd taken on: bookkeeping, making sure the firms's bills were all paid on time, staff wages, promotional work, personnel matters, and there was no ride or sideshow on the fair on which she couldn't work with confidence.

Her involvement in the pavilion project had been more or less one hundred per cent. Sam had sought her opinion at every stage, along with Janice's and Chas's. Between them they had discussed every aspect at length, including design and decor, opening hours and staffing. Although they were planning to employ a pavilion manager, Maddie was going to do the overall administration from the general fairground office. She had also agreed to do relief work in the pavilion if necessary.

Now that Sam had control over the pay and conditions of the workforce he was an exceptional employer, tough with the lazy and uncommitted but keen to reward hard work and loyalty. A few months ago, as a token of appreciation of Maddie's commitment to the firm over a number of years, he'd arranged for a bathroom extension to be added to her living-wagon, at Fenner's expense. It was bliss not having to trek across the fairground every day in all weathers with toilet bag and towel. The Fenners had been good to her and she wouldn't repay their generosity by leaving just because she was a victim of unrequited love.

'You tell me,' said Maddie now in answer to Janice's question about the time. 'But speaking of time, the firm is paying for mine at the moment so I'd better get on and do some work.'

'Yeah, I must get on too,' said Janice. 'I have to go shopping for sports gear for Barney.'

'What it is to be a lady of leisure, eh?' Maddie smiled.

'I'm making the most of it,' Janice laughed. 'I have a feeling that once the pavilion opens, I'll have precious little spare time. I know there's gonna be staff but I'm bound to get roped in somehow.'

'Don't pretend you wouldn't hate it if you weren't involved.'

'Course I'd hate it. I just don't want to have to work every night of the week, that's all.'

'And you won't have to,' said Maddie. 'Not unless there's some dire emergency, like a flu epidemic among the staff.'

'Yeah, yeah, I know.'

'I can't wait to get the whole thing underway,' enthused Maddie.

'I'm looking forward to it too,' agreed Janice. 'I'm planning on being a whizz at bowling.'

Fenner's Fun Pavilion was bright, brash and unashamedly commercial. It shone out like a seaside pier through the dark winter trees on opening night at the end of November, the shocking pink neon signs and coloured lights a dazzling contrast to the ghostly outlines of the closed winter fairground. It was an attractive building, white-rendered with a red tiled roof and timber cladding as a finishing touch. After dark it was a welcoming sight.

It had opened with a flourish, a great deal of hype and plenty of incentive for the public to give it a try. There were free first-night games in both the Bingo hall and bowling alley and cheap drinks in the bar. They had done an extensive leaflet drop and Maddie

185

managed to get the local paper to do some editorial to back up their advertisement on a page dedicated to the pavilion, with everyone connected with the building of it placing congratulatory advertisements.

'Pity about the weather,' said Sam as family and friends gathered in the bar to celebrate opening night, the rain beating against the windows.

'This is one time the rain isn't our enemy,' said Vic, smartly dressed in a suit especially for the occasion. 'We're not at the mercy of the elements for this project. Bingo and bowling are just the things for a wet night.'

'The rain might keep people at home, I meant,' said Sam.

'Doesn't seem to be keeping many of them away tonight,' Maddie commented as people piled in.

'You're right,' said Hetty, looking at the crowds packing into the bar, which was well-lit and contemporary in style with modern furniture and jazzy carpet.

Clare and Barney appeared, wanting to know when they could have a try at bowling. Vic reached into his pocket and gave them some money.

'Go and get in the queue like everyone else,' he said. 'We don't want to upset the manager by giving you preferential treatment.'

'And we don't want to be in trouble with the law for having children in the licensed part of the premises either,' said Janice. 'So off you go.'

'I'll go and see about getting them a game,' said Chas.

'I'll come with you,' Eric offered.

'You crafty pair – you can't wait to have a go yourselves,' Janice teased them lightheartedly.

'Come on, kids,' said Chas, and they bounded off after him.

'Bless 'em,' said Hetty. 'I'm going to have a game of Bingo later on.'

'Me too,' Sybil agreed.

'Before you all disappear, I'd like to propose a toast,' said Sam.

They all stood with glasses raised, looking at him.

'To Fenner's Fun Pavilion,' he said. 'To its success.'

Glasses were raised.

'And to the person who actually dreamt up the idea in the first place,' he said, giving Maddie a melting smile. 'To Maddie.'

The atmosphere was warm and enveloping, the love she felt for every one of these dear people was almost overwhelming. She gulped back the tears and said jokingly, 'So if it isn't a success, I'd better leave town sharpish?'

'Don't you dare,' said Sam.

Maddie was well established in her new working routine by the New

Year. The day began for her when the previous night's takings were brought over to the fairground office from the pavilion safe for her to enter and bag up for Sam and Eric to take to the bank. While the manager dealt with all the pavilion organisation and staff matters, Maddie ordered everything he needed for the bar and coffee shop. He took on the staff, Maddie saw to their wages.

She certainly earned her salary but her workload was only a fraction of what it was in the summer. As long as she got everything done she could suit herself about her hours, which meant she was able to be in when Clare got home from school even if she sometimes had to go back to the office later. Most of her evenings were her own but she helped out if she was needed in the pavilion bar or coffee shop.

There was no doubting the success of the new venture. The takings spoke for themselves, especially in the run-up to Christmas. Even in the traditionally slack trading months of January and February the pavilion still drew the crowds. Maddie thought its success lay in the fact that it appealed to all ages and was excellent value for money. It was cheerful, comfortable and relatively inexpensive.

Ironically, now that she was able to be home in the evenings with her daughter, Clare was at an age to value the company of her friends above that of her mother. She either seemed to be at the homes of school friends or over at the bowling alley with Barney. They would watch people play for hours, their own games being limited by the amount of their pocket money. Too many freebies didn't help children develop a responsible attitude towards money.

On her twelfth birthday, Clare didn't want a party so Maddie – with Janice for support – took her and a group of friends to the ice rink and then out to tea afterwards. There were eight girls and Barney.

'I'm glad she invited him. I wasn't sure if she would as it was a girlie thing,' said Maddie to Janice afterwards.

'I wondered if he'd want to go, the only boy among all those girls,' said her friend. 'But he seems to have had a whale of a time. He's obviously gonna take after his dad in that direction.'

'I'm glad they stayed friends after they changed schools.'

'I suppose they'll drift apart as they get older but they don't seem to be doing so at the moment,' said Janice. 'They're more like brother and sister than ever.'

'Yes,' agreed Maddie, feeling a sharp unexpected pang because she'd never intended Clare to be an only child. Oh, well, you can't have everything, she thought.

One evening in March 1967 in the living room of a small flat in Barking a woman lay on the floor, having been badly beaten by Dave Brown with whom she'd been living for the last year. She'd lost consciousness briefly when her head hit the floor but was now in a dazed state with Dave's voice filling her ears.

'Get up, you silly cow!' he shouted.

'All right,' she said, tasting blood from her cut lip. 'But don't hit me any more, Dave – please . . . no more.'

'You're pathetic.'

'I'm hurt . . . really hurt this time,' she said weakly. 'Help me up . . . please?'

He dragged her to her feet and stared into her bruised and grazed face. 'It's your own fault,' he said. 'You asked for it.'

Why? What had she done? So far as she could remember she had done nothing to warrant this latest attack other than express an opinion about a television programme that didn't coincide with his own.

'I didn't mean to upset you, Dave,' she said humbly.

Hearing her own pitiful voice, she could hardly believe that she'd once been a confident woman. At the time she'd met Dave in a pub one night, she'd been self-assured and enjoying life. A twenty-five-year-old single woman, she had earned her own living by working in a dress shop in the West End; she'd had her own little flat in Canning Town and had answered to no one. Then, when she'd been seeing Dave for a few months, she'd made the mistake of letting him talk her into moving in with him. In a very short time she'd become an unpaid housekeeper and punch bag with no job. She'd lost hers because she'd become unreliable on account of regular beatings which left her unable to work for several days at a time.

Why she stayed with him was a mystery to her. She could only put it down to a complete loss of confidence and the fact that most of the time she was in too much pain to go anywhere. She'd lost her own home and income, so where would she go? There was only her parents' place in Colchester and she didn't want them to know about the mess she was in. They'd be horrified. They thought she was doing well and that her new address was an upmarket move. She was careful only to visit them on the rare occasions when she didn't have any visible bruises.

'Don't do it again,' said Dave, his voice guttural with anger. 'Don't you dare upset me.'

'Why . . . why are you so cruel to me?' she asked, tears running down her face.

'You have to be punished when you do wrong.'

'But I didn't even realise I'd *done* anything wrong.'

'If you annoy me, you've done wrong. And stop snivelling. It makes me sick to look at you.'

Something happened to her in that moment. A flash of spirit returned long enough for her to speak out. 'I annoy you just by breathing, apparently.'

'When you talk rubbish, yes.'

'You shouldn't take it out on me because your wife left you,' she said in a moment of real daring. One of the few things she did know about Dave's past was that his wife had walked out on him. He was obviously still obsessed by her.

'Don't you dare mention my wife!' he said, hitting her around the head again, his eyes glazed and unnatural-looking.

Her head was ringing and she could hardly breathe from the pain but she managed to say, 'It's no wonder she walked out on you if *this* was what she had to put up with.'

He grabbed hold of her and rammed her against the wall, staring into her face, his mouth turned down at the corners, eyes wild with rage. 'You're not fit to utter Maddie's name,' he said, pulling her away from the wall before smashing her against it again. 'Do you understand me. Do you? Do you . . .'

'I understand, Dave,' she said, returning to her former meek state.

'Good,' he said, fist crunching against her cheek one last time before he left her to stagger to the sofa. 'I'm going down the pub . . . see you later.'

Oh, no, you won't, mate, she said silently as the front door slammed shut, suddenly making a decision. Somehow she must find the strength to leave this flat before he got back. She had finally faced the fact that the man was mentally unbalanced and by staying with him she was putting her own life at risk.

Dragging herself to her feet, she limped to the bathroom and wiped the blood from her face with a cold flannel, wincing from the pain and barely able to see out of one eye because it was so swollen.

In the bedroom she packed some things into a suitcase, wincing with every movement. Taking only the belongings she could comfortably manage, she carried the case into the hall and put it down while she took her raincoat from the peg and slipped into it. Pausing by the telephone, she dialled a number.

'Hello, Mum, how are you?' She listened to her mother. 'Me – I'm fine. Actually . . . er . . . something's come up and I need a place to stay for a while . . . just until I find a new flat. I wondered if I could come home for a few days?'

Checking the housekeeping money in her purse to make sure she had enough for the fare to Colchester, she walked through the front door, slamming it shut after her, relieved that she wouldn't be coming back here – *ever again*. She pitied any woman who got involved with Dave Brown!

Chapter Sixteen

Spring was definitely in the air, Maddie noticed as she walked from the office to her living-wagon for tea one March afternoon. Its special scent pervaded everything, the breeze gentle on her face and the sunshine gleaming on the newly polished cars now in place on the rides for the start of the season next week.

Tea-time with her daughter was the highlight of Maddie's day, or had been until Clare had become so difficult. These days you could cut the atmosphere between them with a knife. But being a determined sort of person Maddie continued with the ritual in the hope of getting back on to their old footing.

Her working day wouldn't be so well ordered once the fair opened, she thought, and neither would she have the evenings to herself. She looked forward to the challenge, though; the start of a new season was always exciting.

Eric was walking towards her with Marlon at his heels. 'Going home for tea?' he enquired in a friendly manner.

Maddie nodded. 'You been for a walk by the river?' she said, because she knew that was one of his favourite pastimes.

'Yeah . . . it's lovely along there in this weather. Marlon enjoyed himself, didn't you, boy?' He looked adoringly at the dog, fondling his head.

The animal threw himself at Maddie, panting and wagging his tail. She patted and stroked him until Eric gave him the command to sit. She and Eric chatted generally, mostly about books because he had recently become a reader of children's adventure stories as well as cowboy books.

Barney came ambling towards them carrying his school bag.

'Hello, Barney,' said Maddie.

'Hi.'

'Had a good day?'

'It was all right.'

'Clare's not with you today, then?' she said because he and Clare often met up along the route and arrived home together.

'No.'

'She'll be chatting to her friends, I expect.'

'Probably.'

'It's just as well she's late . . . it'll give me time to get the tea ready.'

Barney nodded then moved on and disappeared into his wagon. Maddie asked Eric if he'd like to join her and Clare for tea.

'Thanks for asking but I'd better not,' he said. 'Mum'll have tea ready for me.'

'Another time, perhaps.'

'Tomorrow,' he suggested with childlike enthusiasm.

'It's a date.' And Maddie went into her caravan smiling.

She made sandwiches and toasted some tea cakes but delayed making the tea until Clare actually arrived. She's late today, thought Maddie, glancing out of the window without much concern. Heaven knows what these girls find to talk about. They're together all day at school and still they hang about nattering on the way home.

Half an hour later she was beginning to get anxious. She didn't remember Clare mentioning anything about staying on at school today for any extra-curricular activity. With a nagging ache in the pit of her stomach she went next door to ask Barney if he knew of any reason why Clare would be late home from school. He said he didn't.

By six o'clock Maddie was really worried and by seven she was desperate, especially as she'd telephoned the homes of all of Clare's friends and none of them had seen her since they'd come out of school together. She'd not walked part of the way with them as she usually did. Apparently she'd said she had to go back into school for something and she'd catch them up, but hadn't done so.

'She'll have gone to a mate's house,' said Janice, trying to conceal the fact that she too was beginning to feel uneasy now.

'But I've tried all her friends and she's not with any of them.'

Maddie had been out searching the streets on the school route. She'd also been to the school but everyone had gone except a teacher taking the drama club. No one there had seen Clare.

'You don't know every girl she's friendly with,' suggested Janice.

'I know most of them,' said Maddie in a strangled voice. She felt sick and had to keep rushing to the toilet. 'Oh, Janice, what could have happened to her? Supposing she's been abducted!'

'Maddie, love,' cried Janice, 'keep a grip – don't let your imagination run wild.'

'These things happen,' Maddie persisted. 'You only have to read the paper to know that. Kids get taken by perverts every day of the week.'

'It's still a rare occurrence, which is why it makes news when it does happen.'

'Surely she wouldn't go off with anyone she didn't know?' said Maddie, throat dry and constricted. 'She knows she mustn't. I've drummed it into her often enough.'

191

'Exactly,' said Janice. 'She's a sensible girl and soon she'll come strolling along as bright as a button. You know what kids are like for forgetting the time.'

But they both realised that this didn't carry much weight.

'I'm not waiting any longer,' said Maddie. 'I'm going to call the police.'

The concern for Clare at Fenner's was almost a tangible thing. Everybody wanted to help. Pavilion staff, fairground workers already here for the new season and maintenance men joined the family in the search. Maddie was persuaded to stay at the park in case Clare came back or telephoned. Sybil and Janice stayed with her by the phone in the office to offer moral support. Hetty and Vic came over as soon as they heard – eager to do what they could.

Having to supply the police with a photograph of her daughter so that the bobbies on the beat had her description made the horror of the situation seem even more real. Maddie thought she had known fear before. But the black terror of her concern for Clare was indescribable.

'Please don't let her be hurt,' she muttered to herself over and over again.

At eight o'clock there was still no news. Nor at nine or ten. Maddie was beside herself and as time passed without a new development the police couldn't hide their concern. This was obviously not just a case of a girl being late home from school for some ordinary reason.

'They think she's dead, don't they?' Maddie said to Sam. 'They're looking for a body.'

'You mustn't think like that,' he said firmly. 'Clare will be all right. You have to keep believing that.'

But where was she? That was the question in all of their minds. If she hadn't been abducted she would have come home by now.

Eric offered to stay by the telephone in the office just in case Clare tried to get in touch. He obviously really wanted to do this so Maddie didn't argue. She didn't feel able to go to bed and no one was insensitive enough to suggest that she should. Although she felt torn inside and unable to escape her own troubles, she was aware of the needs of the others and insisted that they go home and get some rest. Hetty and Vic stayed on the site in their caravan for the night to be close at hand if they were needed.

Sam insisted on staying with Maddie.

'There's no need,' she said in a cracked voice. 'You go home and get some sleep. I'll be all right.'

'If you think I'd leave you alone at a time like this then you don't know me very well,' he said, sitting down on the settee in her living room.

'Well, if you're sure then,' she said, finding his presence as comforting as anything could be in the circumstances.

'Sit down,' he ordered as she paced the room. 'You're making me giddy.'

'Sorry . . . I can't keep still.' She walked out of the room to the front door.

'Maddie, where are you going?'

'To look for her,' she said, voice rising hysterically. 'I can't just stay here doing nothing!'

Sam went after her, gently pulling her back inside. 'There's no point in your doing that now . . . not in the dark,' he said. 'Anyway, you need to be here in case she comes back.'

'Yeah, I suppose you're right,' she said dully. 'But I feel so helpless.'

'We all do,' he said. 'But all we can do for the moment is wait.'

'I know.'

She made tea for them both then perched stiffly on the edge of an armchair.

'I know that you can't possibly relax but why don't you try to lean back in the chair a little?' Sam suggested. 'There's no sense in being more uncomfortable than you have to be.'

Maddie moved back slightly but still sat bolt upright, rigid with tension.

'We're experts at staying up half the night, aren't we?' he said to give her something else to focus on. 'We had enough practice when we were trying to nail Alan King.'

'God, yes.' She put her hands to her head. 'That seemed like such a big drama at the time.'

'It was.'

'It was nothing compared to this.'

'No.'

She made more tea which neither of them really wanted. Sam didn't offer to do it for her because he knew she needed to occupy herself. He himself felt quite ill with dread for he had grown fond of Clare over the years and his empathy with Maddie was total. Her pain was his pain, it was as simple as that. He would do anything to take away her anguish but only good news would do that. All he could do now was be with her to comfort her and make sure she knew that she wasn't alone.

Maddie's face looked ashen against her black sweater, her eyes red and swollen. Sam felt murderous towards whoever had taken Clare, for as more time passed without news it was becoming increasingly likely that someone had taken her.

'Shall I get you a pillow from the bedroom so that you can lie back?' he suggested.

'No, thanks,' Maddie replied vaguely.

'I wouldn't mind one,' he said, hoping to encourage her to do the same.

She went to the bedroom and came back with a pillow and a blanket for each for them. They both lay back in silence; the only sound was the gentle put-put of the little blue and yellow flames in the coal on the fire.

'It's always been just Clare and me,' she said suddenly. If talking did nothing else it helped her to lie still. She was so tense her muscles ached and her nerves were painfully raw.

'Even before you left your husband?'

'Oh, yes,' she said. 'Dave never had any interest in her . . . he wasn't interested in me either, not as a person. He just wanted someone to bully and abuse.'

'That's sad.'

'Dave's a sad character.'

'He's barking mad from what I've heard.'

'Maybe he is. He certainly isn't normal by ordinary standards.' Maddie fell silent for a while then said, 'Clare's my life. I can't imagine being without her.'

'I can understand that.'

'This is the worst thing that's ever happened to me, Sam.'

'I'm sure it must be,' he said. 'They say parental love is unimaginable unless you have kids of your own.'

'Yeah.' Her voice was dull and lifeless. 'Being a parent means always being vulnerable – your child's pain is your pain.'

'Lots of joy, too, though?'

'Oh, yes!' Maddie's voice lifted. 'Lots of that.' She paused thoughtfully. 'There hasn't been much joy between Clare and me lately, though – we haven't been getting on.'

'Really?'

'She's been that hostile towards me you wouldn't believe. I think it's hurt her as much as it's hurt me although she'd never admit it. I don't know what's been the matter – I've tried every way I know to put things right but I just couldn't get through to her.'

'You can make it up when she comes back,' he said in a deliberate attempt to seem positive.

Maddie got up suddenly, the awfulness of the situation becoming unbearable again. 'Where is she?' she moaned, rushing over to the window and peering out into the darkness. 'Where the hell *is* she?' She began to sob and her voice became distorted. 'Please, somebody, find her safe. For pity's sake, find her. Don't let anyone harm her.' She clenched her fists and began laughing and crying simultaneously, stopping abruptly when Sam slapped her face.

'Sorry, Maddie,' he said, wanting to weep himself from sympathy.

'It's all right, I shouldn't have lost control. I just don't know what to do, Sam. I really don't.'

He put his arms around her and eased her gently down on to the settee beside him, holding her against him until her sobbing subsided

194

and she seemed calmer. They leaned back without speaking. Eventually she dozed off in his arms.

In the pale light of dawn she awoke and the nightmare continued. The grinding ache inside her seemed to drag her downwards. Her mouth was so dry she could hardly speak.

'Oh, Sam,' she said, turning to him. 'What are we going to do?'

'We're going to wait and pray and hope,' he said.

Barney woke with a start that morning after sleeping only fitfully with a tight knot of apprehension in his stomach. He dreaded getting up for fear of what would greet him.

Slowly, he forced himself out of bed and padded down the passage to the living-room window at the front of the wagon. He peered warily through the curtain. Oh, no! There was a police car outside the office already. What a nightmare this was turning out to be, he thought, hurrying back to bed and pulling the covers over his head.

'Come on, Barney, up you get,' said his mother grimly a bit later. 'How many more times do I have to call you? You'll be late for school if you don't shift yourself.'

Peering at her over the top of the covers he could see that she looked terrible. Her face was pale and tight-looking, her eyes red from crying.

'Is there any news of Clare?' he asked, following her into the kitchen in his pyjamas.

'No.'

His heart turned over. 'What . . . no news at all?'

'I'd have told you if there was, wouldn't I?'

'All right, keep your hair on,' he said, and retreated hurriedly to the bathroom before he copped it for being cheeky.

His father had stayed the night. He always slept in Mum's bed when there was a crisis. Over breakfast Barney's parents were discussing Clare's disappearance.

'How's Maddie this morning?' asked Chas, buttering some toast.

'How do you think she is?' replied Janice, who'd hardly slept a wink and had gone next door to see her friend first thing this morning. 'The woman is demented with worry. Who wouldn't be?'

'I know what you mean.'

'I'll kill the bastard who's got young Clare if I ever set eyes on him,' said Janice, her voice quivering with rage. 'I'll tear the bugger limb from limb.'

'We don't know for sure that anyone's got her,' argued Chas.

'What other explanation can there be?' said Janice bitterly. 'The child wouldn't just disappear unless some sick bugger's taken her.' She lit a cigarette with trembling hand. 'I daren't think what he might have done to her.'

195

'Stop torturing yourself, love,' said Chas, but he was grey with worry himself.

'These perverts are capable of anything. They do terrible things then murder their victims,' she ranted as though he hadn't spoken.

'Murder!' spluttered Barney.

Janice looked at him quickly, noticing his pallor and the anxiety in his eyes which looked suspiciously wet. 'We don't know if that's what happened, love,' she said. 'But we have to be realistic. Clare has been missing for too long for it to be just a simple case of her going to a friend's house and forgetting to let her mother know about it.'

'Yeah,' said Barney glumly.

She looked out of the window. The police were talking to Maddie and Sam over by the office.

'I expect they've got a search underway now that it's light,' said Chas, following her gaze.

'Good job an' all.'

'Excuse me,' muttered Barney, rising and heading for the door.

His mother called after him, 'Hey, where do you think you're going?'

'To my room to get my school bag.'

'But you've not eaten anything.'

'Not hungry.'

'You must have something to eat, son,' said Janice, her voice warm with concern. 'I know you're worried about your best friend but you'll feel poorly at school if you don't have any breakfast at all. It's a long time till dinner.'

'I'll be all right.'

Janice was too weary to argue but she wrapped some buttered toast in greaseproof paper and forced him to take it to school with him. 'Just to stop you feeling faint.'

As Barney crossed the fairground with his school bag slung over his shoulder, he passed Clare's mother talking to the policemen. She looked worse than his own mother, grey-faced and funny round the eyes. Snippets of what was being said drifted over to him – something about dragging the river further down stream.

His heart pumped horribly. This whole thing had got completely out of control. There was nothing else for it. He would have to break his promise before things got any worse. Sick with dread and bracing himself for the roasting of a lifetime, he ran back home.

'Barking!' exclaimed Maddie, tears of relief running down her cheeks as she stared dumbfounded at Barney. 'My daughter is in Barking?'

'I don't know if she's still there now,' he explained nervously. 'But that's where she went yesterday after school. She caught the train . . .

she's been saving her pocket money for the fare and any other expenses that might come up.'

'To Barking?' muttered Sam who had been with Maddie in the office when Janice and Chas had come in with their ashen-faced son – just after the police had gone.

'It's on the District Line . . . the same as Richmond,' said Barney helpfully.

'I know what line it's on, thank you, Barney,' said Maddie, still in a state of shock.

'She's gone there to find her father,' said the boy, cheeks flaming in his pale face.

'You knew this and let us all go through hell, thinking the worst?' shouted Janice, cuffing him round the ear.

'I had to . . .'

'You *wicked, wicked* boy,' fumed his mother. 'Not only have you driven Aunt Maddie almost to a nervous breakdown, and worried the life out of the rest of us, you've probably got us in trouble with the law for wasting police time!'

'I promised Clare I wouldn't say anything,' he said. 'I thought she'd be back by now, I never dreamed she'd be gone this long. She said she'd be back before bedtime last night. She only wanted to meet him . . . just to see for herself what he's like.'

'There's no excuse for what you've done!' said his mother grimly.

'Lay off the boy,' intervened Chas. 'He was only being loyal to a friend.'

'Chas is right, Janice,' said Maddie. She turned to Barney. 'Why didn't Clare tell me where she was going?'

'Because she knew you wouldn't let her see her dad,' he said, looking at Maddie accusingly. 'Clare's wanted to see him for ages. She told me she isn't allowed.'

'How does she know where to find him?'

'She found the address of where you used to live on the envelope of an old letter that had been sent to you before you left him, Aunt Maddie.' Barney added in a fiercely defensive manner, 'Clare wasn't going through your things, she just came across it in an old handbag of yours – she was clearing out some cupboards while she was helping you with the spring cleaning. Ever since then she's talked of nothing else but going there to see him.'

'I see.'

The boy said boldly, 'If you'd let her see her dad this would never have happened.' His dark eyes were flashing angrily at Maddie. 'She's got a right to see her own father. I'd hate it if I couldn't see mine.'

There was a stunned silence, after which Janice roared, 'Don't you dare be rude to Maddie! Apologise this minute.'

Maddie put a hand on Janice's arm. 'Leave him, please.' She turned to Barney. 'I admire you for being so loyal to my daughter. Clare has a good friend in you and I'm sorry that your loyalty has got you into such trouble.'

'Don't matter,' he said. 'She'll kill me when she finds out I've told you, though. But when everyone started talking about murder, I thought I'd better say something.'

'Thank God you did!' said Maddie. 'You did the right thing.'

'I hope Clare sees it that way.'

'The reason I've kept her away from her father is because he isn't nice like yours,' Maddie said, thinking the boy deserved an explanation as he was so deeply involved. 'He's a very cruel man and I have to protect her until she's old enough to look after herself. When she's grown up, she can please herself.'

'Anyway, it's her own fault I had to break my promise,' said the boy. 'She should have come back when she said.'

Maddie froze. She'd been so relieved by the explanation for Clare's disappearance that the sinister implications of it hadn't fully registered. Knowing that Clare was with her father was almost as terrifying as not knowing where she was, especially as she hadn't come back as she'd intended. 'I have to go to Barking right away,' she said. 'Clare might be in trouble.'

'Hang on, Maddie,' said Sam. 'We'd better tell the police what's happened so they can call the search off here. They'll contact the Barking police who'll take up the search there. We need to give them Clare's father's address too.'

'I have to go there . . .'

'Yes, and I'll go with you,' Sam pronounced. 'But first we have to speak to the police. They can get to her quicker than we can.'

Clare Brown was sitting on a bench in Barking Park eating the second of two currant buns she'd just bought in a baker's shop. She was eating to satisfy her hunger but the food could have tasted of horse dung for all that she noticed. She was cold, dirty and tired, having spent the night in a draughty, derelict shed on some allotments.

She was also feeling desperate. She wanted to go home but her purpose in coming here hadn't yet been achieved. Anyway, she couldn't go home. Not after staying out all night. Her mother would go berserk and everyone at Fenner's would be angry with her for upsetting Maddie. It was all awful and she couldn't face any of them. Tears filled her eyes. If only Barney were here, nothing would be so bad.

Coming to Barking had been a pretty stupid idea, Clare had to admit. A dull pain throbbed inside her as she recalled the events of the previous evening . . .

She'd gone to the address on the envelope, a flat in a drab block of which she had no recollection though she knew she had lived

198

there until she was five. Trembling with excitement, she'd knocked at the front door and asked the woman who answered if Mr Dave Brown was at home.

'There's no one of that name here, love,' said the woman who was preoccupied with the demands of her children; she was holding a crying baby and had a toddler grizzling beside her.

'He used to live here,' Clare had said.

'Well, he ain't here now. We've been here a year and the people before us weren't called Brown. I do know that much 'cause letters kept coming here for 'em after they'd moved out.'

Her disappointment had been almost a physical pain. She had wanted to see her father for so long and believed she was going to, at last. 'Is there anyone around here who might know where he is?'

The baby began to scream louder and the woman became even less interested in what Clare had to say.

'The people at number fourteen have lived here a long time. They might know.' She nodded her head to the right. 'About four doors down.'

The woman at number fourteen certainly did remember Dave Brown.

'He moved out about three years ago – and good riddance too. We don't want the likes of *him* round here.' She looked at Clare shrewdly. 'I've no idea where he went.'

'Oh.'

'What do you want with him?'

'Just to see him – I'm his daughter.'

'Oh.' The woman looked puzzled. 'He never had any kids that I remember.'

'My mother split up with him years ago,' explained Clare, feeling obliged to offer some sort of explanation.

'Oh, well, I wouldn't have known your mum.' She gave Clare a hard look. 'Has she sent you out looking for him? Is she after him for maintenance or something?'

The girl shook her head. 'Is there anyone in the flats who might know where he is?'

'Shouldn't think so. I can't imagine anyone wanting to keep in touch with that spiteful bugger.'

'Oh.' The words felt like a body blow to Clare.

'I shouldn't go boasting about being his daughter either, love,' said the woman. 'Not everyone's as tolerant as I am. It's not your fault he's your dad, o' course. But if I was Dave Brown's daughter, I'd want to keep it very quiet. We take a dim view of blokes who batter women around here.'

Clare began to see the woman through a blur of tears. She turned to walk away but the woman called her back.

'You be careful, love,' she said. 'Make sure there's someone with you if you do find him or you could end up with a broken jaw. Men like him ought to be locked up!'

Unable to bear hearing any more, Clare had run along the landing and down the stone stairs, shaking and wanting to be sick. It was probably all just gossip, she told herself. But in the light of what her mother had already told her, that theory hadn't rung true. Deciding to resume her search the next day, she had kept walking until she had come across the shed on the allotments in which to shelter for the night. As despondent as she was, the idea of giving up and going home had not even occurred to her.

How to find him? that was the question she asked herself now. How was a twelve-year-old girl going to find a man she didn't know in a place where she felt like a total stranger? She'd felt so grown-up yesterday when she'd got on the train at Richmond station. Now she experienced the true powerlessness of childhood. She didn't have the means to find him. She couldn't ask around in the pubs as an adult could.

And did she really still want to find him now that she had been forced to accept the truth about him? When her mother had told her what he was like, Clare had refused to believe it. Now it had been confirmed by a complete stranger with no reason to lie.

It wasn't that she'd thought her mother was a liar, but Clare hadn't wanted it to be true so had blanked it out and conjured up rosy images of the sort of father her friends had, someone she could rely on. Someone like Uncle Sam.

Uncle Sam, Barney, Mum. She wanted them all, especially her mother, with such intense longing that tears gushed down her cheeks. But how could she go back and face them after what she'd done? You've really messed up this time, Clare Brown, she told herself.

She recalled how mean she'd been to her mother lately, and that made her cry even more. Everything had seemed different since she'd changed schools. She'd met new people, made new friends. Playground talk wasn't the same any more. The girls talked about boys, periods, and growing up most of the time. Clare was very much aware of being on the verge of something, and moods of melancholy had engulfed her for no reason at all. The longing she had always had to see her father had become almost unbearable, as though he was the missing link that would make everything all right. She'd blamed her mother because he wasn't around and punished her by freezing her out. She'd hated herself for hurting Maddie but hadn't been able to stop somehow.

Head bowed and sobbing into her handkerchief, she didn't notice anyone approaching her.

'Clare Brown?' she heard a deep voice say.

Looking up to see two policemen, she was so frightened she could hardly speak. 'Yes,' she said fearfully.

'You're a long way from home, aren't you, young lady?' said one of them. 'I think you'd better come with us.'

As she stood up to go with them Clare felt the final humiliation of wet knickers. Being confronted by two policemen who had known her name had been just too much of a fright.

'Don't you ever do anything like that to me again!' said Maddie on the way back to Richmond from Barking in Sam's car with Clare beside her in the back seat. The Richmond police had telephoned Fenner's to say that she had been found and they would keep her at Barking police station until someone collected her. Having discovered that Dave had moved away from the address Maddie had given them, they had mounted a general search of the area.

'I hope you realise that your poor mother has been out of her mind with worry?' said Sam from the driving seat.

'Sorry,' said Clare in a small voice.

'I should damned well think so too,' he said, with the sort of gruffness she wasn't used to from him. 'You can't possibly imagine what you've put us all through.'

'I didn't mean for you all to be worried,' she said meekly, having earlier told them what had happened last night.

'What did you expect when you just took off like that?'

'I thought I would be able to phone you from Dad's place to tell you where I was.'

'Did you think you were going to have a cosy chat with your father and he would tell you how much he'd been missing you all these years?'

That was more or less the gist of Clare's imaginings. 'Well, I . . .'

'Because you can forget those sort of dreams,' Sam cut in passionately.

'I realise that now,' she said humbly, remembering that heartbreaking encounter with her father's ex-neighbour last night.

'I hope you do because your mother is the one who'll give you all the cosy chats – *she's* the one who's looked after you all these years and worked hard to give you a decent life. And how do you show your appreciation? You bugger off looking for your waster of a father. That in itself isn't so bad, but the fact that you went without so much as a word . . . that's just plain cruel.'

'If I'd told Mum I was going, she would have stopped me.'

'Only because she knows what's best for you . . . as you must realise by now.'

'All right, Sam calm down.' Maddie had never seen him so angry.

'No, I won't calm down,' he said in a hard voice that was most unlike his. 'She needs to know the seriousness of what she's done.'

'I'm really sorry, Uncle Sam,' said Clare, close to tears. 'I . . . I suppose I just didn't think it through properly.'

'I'm glad to hear you admit it.' He paused, eyes on the road. 'But is this really going to be an end to this hankering for your father – or will it take a beating from him to cure you?'

'This is the end of it, I promise.' Clare was openly crying now. 'I'm very sorry for what I've done.'

'I hope you are, my girl,' he said sternly. 'Because you'll have me to answer to if you hurt your mother like that again.'

'Why are you so upset about it, anyway?' she said through her sobs. 'It isn't as though you're married to Mum.'

All Maddie could hear was the beating of her own heart as they waited for him to reply.

'That doesn't mean I don't care a very great deal about her,' said Sam in a hoarse voice.

A lump rose in Maddie's throat. He had been her strength and salvation this past twenty-four hours, which was why she hadn't stopped him taking a hard line with Clare. She knew his anger was born of affection for them both.

'And you too, Clare. You couldn't mean more to me if you were my own daughter,' he said in a voice that was ragged with emotion. 'That's why I'm so angry with you . . . I've been so worried.'

Fresh tears rushed into her eyes – and a warm feeling somewhere deep inside of her too. Adults were a funny lot. They always seemed to act the opposite way to how they were feeling, and they evoked the most surprising feelings in you just when you were least expecting them. But it felt so good to be back with Mum and Sam.

'Oh, Uncle Sam,' she said thickly, leaning forward so that her head was near the back of his. 'I care a lot about you, too.'

'I'm glad.'

'But I hope you're gonna stop being angry with me soon 'cause I don't like it one bit when you're like this. I promise I'll never go off again without letting you know.'

'She'll be too damned scared of the rollicking she'll get from you, I should imagine,' was Maddie's response to that.

'That's the general idea,' Sam said in satisfied tones.

Sitting back in her seat, Clare turned to her mother. 'I'm really sorry I've been so horrible to you lately, Mum. I've been feeling . . . well, it's hard to explain.'

'I'll forgive you,' said Maddie, slipping a reassuring arm around her daughter. 'And we'll talk about it later.'

Full of emotion, Clare gave a nervous giggle. Maddie and Sam were similarly affected, too, and the next minute they all howled with laughter in a glorious release of tension.

Maddie wasn't naive enough to believe that her relationship with her daughter would be all plain sailing from now on. But she was confident that Clare had come back to her – in more ways than one.

Chapter Seventeen

The relief that swept through Fenner's at Clare's safe return was so unanimous it created a mood almost of celebration. People seemed revitalised as they went about their work, formerly grim faces now wreathed in smiles – and everyone wanted to talk to Maddie. Even the cleaners and bar staff from the pavilion – with whom she only had a nodding acquaintance – made a point of seeking her out to tell her how pleased they were that her daughter was back home safe and sound.

'All this attention is making me feel like a celebrity,' she said jokingly to Sam the next day when she called at his wagon on her way to the office; she'd come to thank him for his help and support during the crisis. 'It's rather nice, actually, knowing that people care.'

'Just so long as Clare doesn't get any exaggerated notions,' he said, looking serious. 'She might begin to think it's worth doing again if it's gonna create this much attention.'

'There's no fear of that . . . not after being so horribly disillusioned about her father and spending a chilly night in a gardener's shed with all the spiders and things. Anyway, the attention she's getting is all disapproving. She's never had so many tellings off at one time in her life.'

'The more the better, if it'll get the message across to her.'

Maddie threw him a look. 'Her going missing really upset you, didn't it?'

'More than I'd have believed possible.' Sam's expression was grim. 'For the first time I had an idea what it must be like to be a parent.' He gave a slow shake of his head. 'I felt like a nervous wreck. What with being scared witless that she might be dead, and worrying about the effect the whole thing was having on you . . .'

'You seemed so calm.'

'It was all an act. It wouldn't have helped you to know what a hell of a state I was really in.'

'You were wonderful,' she said. 'Thanks again for everything.'

'No need to thank me.' He looked at her closely, his eyes warm. 'It seemed only natural for me to be with you at such an awful time.'

'Yes . . . yes, it did.' The closeness Maddie had felt with him during the ordeal was present again now. 'Well, it was much appreciated.'

She looked at her watch and hesitated for a moment before grinning wickedly. 'I'd better go to work now or I'll have the boss after me.'

'A tyrant, is he?'

'Not on your life . . . he's a pussy cat when you get to know him.' Sam was chuckling as he followed her to the door.

'Are you doing anything this evening?' he asked unexpectedly.

'No. Why?'

'I was wondering if you might fancy going out somewhere? For a meal, perhaps. Just the two of us. I think we could both do with a break after the stress of the past couple of days.'

'I'd love to,' said Maddie, beaming. 'I'll arrange for Clare to go in with Janice and Barney.'

'Good,' said Sam, looking pleased. 'It won't be quite so easy to get away in the evening once the season starts.'

She nodded. 'Might as well make the most of the time off while we can.'

'I'll book a table somewhere then,' he said, smiling at her. 'Shall we make a proper job of it and go up the West End?'

'Oh, that would be lovely.'

'And about time too,' said Janice at lunchtime when Maddie called on her to make arrangements for Clare. 'I thought that brother of mine was never gonna start the ball rolling.'

'He's only asked me out for a meal because we both need a break. So don't start making more of it.'

'As if I would.' Her incorrigible friend grinned. 'I won't start planning my wedding outfit for at least a fortnight.'

'You fool!' laughed Maddie. 'But seriously, will you have Clare for me?'

''Course I will.' She thought for a moment then giggled. 'She can stay overnight, if you like. So that you and Sam can have your place to yourselves.'

'You're doing it again . . .'

'Don't spoil my fun,' Janice cut in jokingly. 'Anyway, how many women has Sam been out with since Tania died?'

'I've no idea,' said Maddie. 'He doesn't account to me for his movements.'

'I'm willing to bet you're the first,' said Janice. 'And I think you know that too.'

'Be that as it may,' answered Maddie lightly, 'the important thing is – what am I going to wear? I've nothing special. All I have is stuff I wear for work here and some old things I used to wear when I worked at the pub.'

'You're welcome to borrow the dress I bought for the Showmen's Guild Christmas do,' suggested Janice promptly. 'It isn't too formal and it's quite a sexy little number.'

'I'm not planning to seduce him!'

'More's the pity. That's probably just what Sam needs.'

'Honestly . . .'

'Stop disapproving and come through to the bedroom and try it on.'

The dress in question was red satin with a low neck and gold trimming; it was very short.

'You'll knock him dead in that,' said Janice.

It did suit her, Maddie had to admit. Being blonde, red was a good colour for her. She thanked Janice, said she would like to borrow it, then changed hurriedly because she had to get back to work.

Seeing her to the door Janice was still in flippant mood. 'I hope you're gonna put your sexiest drawers on tonight?'

'Oh, really,' admonished Maddie, but she was laughing too. In fact she was still smiling when she got back to the office where one of her first jobs was to work out the rota for the new seasonal staff.

How quickly things changed. She'd thought she'd never smile again when Clare went missing. Now she felt positively jubilant.

Sam and Maddie went to a small, intimate restaurant in the back streets of the West End. It was classy and expensive with experienced waiters, soft lighting and candle-lit tables.

Maddie felt good in the red dress, and Sam was devastating in a sharp suit and crisp white shirt. He was very sure of himself when dealing with waiters, she noticed, which was surprising for such an unsophisticated man. Maddie was impressed with his style and guessed that his easy confidence came from years of marriage to a woman with expensive tastes.

'I'm really enjoying myself,' she said over coffee. 'It's wonderful to get away from it all for a few hours.'

'One of the occupational hazards of living on the job is that you don't get away from it often enough.'

'From what I've learned about fair people, that's the way they like it.'

He laughed, suddenly looking so boyish and sexy Maddie's desire for him was doubled. 'You're absolutely right,' he said. 'For a true showperson, their business is their life.'

'But tonight you've made an exception.'

He thought Maddie looked almost ethereal in the candlelight, her smooth skin so pale, thick blonde hair framing her face. 'Obviously I don't mean what I say literally. Everyone needs something besides work in their life. But there isn't such a definite divide between work and leisure in our business as there is in other jobs.'

'I know what you mean. I wasn't born into the business but I feel much the same way about it. Work is hardly anathema to me. I'm lucky to have found a way of earning a living that I enjoy.'

'I'm glad you feel like that,' he said, becoming suddenly intense.
'Are you?'

'Yes – you've come to mean a lot to me over the years, Maddie.'
He reached across the table and took her hand.

'Likewise.'

'I've only just realised how much you do mean to me.'

The touch of his hand was having the most extraordinary effect
on her. 'I was beginning to think you never would,' she said
breathlessly.

'The events of the last few days really brought it home to me.
How much I care for you – and for Clare.'

'You've always been very good to us both.'

'But you and me,' he continued, looking at her earnestly, 'we've
never really had a chance to get to know one another, have we?'

His remark surprised Maddie. 'I think we know each other pretty
well.'

'We know each other as friends and colleagues,' he said. 'We get
close when things are bad – after Tania died for instance, and when
we had that trouble with Alan King. And during Clare's
disappearance. We're good together in times of trouble but we've
never taken the time to have fun and find out how we get along
when there isn't a crisis.' He let go of her hand and raised both of
his in a gesture of mock surrender. 'My fault entirely. I've been
too busy clinging to the past to realise what I was missing in the
present.'

'I can't argue with that,' said Maddie. 'I was always here.'

'I know.' He took her hand again. 'Can you forgive me?'

'That shouldn't be too much of a problem,' she said softly.

'I was so obsessed with Tania, my mind was closed to the idea of
anyone else,' he said. 'I've been forcing myself to ignore my feelings
for you.'

'And now?'

'Now I want to put all that behind me. I'd like us to have more
times together like this – just you and me – to really get to know
each other,' he said. 'Away from work and family and responsibilities.'

'Sounds good to me.' Maddie felt compelled to inject a note of
reality into the romantic mood, though. 'Your timing's a bit off,
with the season about to start.'

'I was thinking about that while I was getting ready to come here
tonight,' said Sam. 'And I can see no reason why I shouldn't ask
Mum and Dad to stand in at the park for me while I have a regular
night off . . . say, once every couple of weeks?'

'They'd enjoy that, I think.'

'Yeah, I think so too. And you certainly deserve a regular evening
off, considering the amount of work you get through during the

day.' Sam paused, looking at her, his expression tender but serious. 'I want to make up for lost time. I want us to go out and have a good time together.'

'You certainly won't get any objections from me!'

'I've messed things up in the past because I've been so confused,' he said. 'Now I want to put that right.'

Maddie put his hand to her lips. 'I think it's a lovely idea,' she said huskily. 'I can't wait to get started.'

Having a love affair wasn't an easy thing when you worked and lived on a busy fairground surrounded by your lover's relatives, and had a twelve-year-old daughter to consider – since Maddie was determined that Clare shouldn't be made to feel excluded or threatened by Sam's new role in their lives.

But despite all the obstacles, Maddie and Sam managed it – ecstatically – during the spring and summer of 1967. When they finally became lovers properly in the privacy of Sam's bedroom, it was exactly how Maddie had wanted it to be the second time – not just an act to assuage the pain of grief but to celebrate the glorious fact that their friendship had turned into love for both of them.

True to his word, Sam arranged for them to go out together on a regular basis. Sometimes they went to the West End, other times they socialised more simply in a local pub or restaurant, or even just took a walk by the river. But they made a point of regularly having a few hours on their own together.

Sam spent more time with Maddie and Clare at home, too, having meals with them and setting the pattern for the family life Maddie hoped they would eventually have. He had been a father-figure to Clare ever since they'd been at Fenner's. Now that he was more closely involved with her, he became more like an actual father – the sort she had always wanted. Maddie thought he was brilliant – full of fun but stern when necessary. Clare knew she could only push him so far.

Although attitudes towards sex were generally more broad-minded these days, there was still a strong sense of morality in the fairground community which meant that Maddie and Sam had to exercise a great deal of discretion.

'Are you going to marry Uncle Sam, Mum?' Clare enquired one warm summer's day when Maddie and she were running the Helter-Skelter together.

Maddie didn't want to go into details at this stage about the fact that she was still legally married to Clare's father because Sam hadn't actually proposed to her.

'How would you feel about it if I did?' she asked.

'I wouldn't mind.' Clare was growing up very much in the mould of her mother with blue eyes and straight blonde hair. Although very slender, her figure was becoming curvier, with the beginnings of a bosom and more rounded hips.

'That's good, because I wouldn't do it if you weren't happy about it.'

'I think it would be fun,' said the girl. 'And it would be cool to have a dad, even if he would be a stepfather really.'

'We'll just have to wait and see what happens, then.'

Maddie was inwardly convinced that it was just a matter of time before Sam popped the question, though. They had become increasingly close this summer. Whilst savouring the thought of their future together, she was also enjoying every moment of the glorious present.

Eric was very much a creature of habit. An early riser, he would get up and make himself some toast or cereal then go for a walk with the dog. On his return he would take his mother tea in bed.

He enjoyed this morning routine, and his early riverside walk with Marlon was one of his greatest joys. He liked the freshness of everything first thing; mornings were a happy and hopeful time for Eric who didn't have a pessimistic bone in his body so never expected anything other than the best from the day ahead. His newly acquired reading skills had added to his pleasure in the riverside; he'd borrowed some children's nature books from the library and was now able to name some of the wild flowers and birds that he saw on his walks.

His mother said she was delighted that he was educating himself but he wasn't to bore everybody rigid with it, because there was only so much people wanted to know about wild poppies and riverfowl.

Just lately his morning walks had acquired a new dimension. He'd made a new friend, a plump, rosy-cheeked woman of about his own age called Vera Walters who was one of the early-morning cleaners at the pavilion. She was usually on her way out of the fairground as he was on his way back in, and they'd been brought together by Marlon. Vera had stopped to make a fuss of the dog, stroking his head and talking to him.

'You're ever so lucky, having a dog,' she had told Eric that first morning.

'Am I?' said Eric, who couldn't imagine life without Marlon.

'Oh, yeah.' Vera was emphatic. 'My mum won't have one in the house. She says they're dirty, smelly things and riddled with fleas.'

'I don't mind if he's a bit smelly at times,' said Eric, who wasn't in the least offended by her frankness. 'It's only natural for an animal. Anyway, Marlon's my friend and I like having him around.'

'Lucky thing.'

'Perhaps you could have a cat?' he suggested helpfully. 'They keep themselves clean.'

'Mum won't have one of those either,' Vera informed him regretfully.

'What about a budgie?'

She shook her head.

'Goldfish?'

'Afraid not. No animals, birds or fish allowed in the house,' she explained. 'Houses are for human beings, Mum says. The rest should be in fields and forests and rivers where they belong.'

'Marlon's a guard dog as well as a pet and he sleeps in a kennel,' said Eric. 'But Mum lets him come indoors too.'

'You're so lucky,' she said again.

Being told that he was lucky was a new experience for Eric and he liked it – it made him feel important.

After that first meeting, he saw Vera every morning and they had a chat. He began to look forward to it; it got so regular that she waited for him if he wasn't there when she finished work at the pavilion. Marlon always got excited when he saw her and jumped all over her. Unlike Eric's mum, Vera seemed to like it and didn't push him away, complaining about his muddy paws ruining her clothes.

Vera told Eric that her father was dead and she lived with her mother who was a pensioner.

'I'd rather work in a shop or a supermarket than do cleaning,' she told him. 'But I'm not clever enough to deal with money, and I'm too slow to deal with people like you have to in a supermarket.'

'Shame,' said Eric.

'I can do cleaning all right, though,' she said. 'And it pays for my keep. Mum says she can't afford to pay all the bills on her own. I have to pull my weight at home. Mum says I'm not too daft to do that.'

'Who says you're daft?'

'Everybody,' said Vera in a matter-of-fact manner. 'I'm what they call simple. That's what people call me, anyway. I've heard 'em.'

'They say that about me too.'

'Do they really?'

'Oh, yeah, all the time . . . I can read, though. Can you?'

She nodded. 'I'm not brilliant at it but I managed to pick up the basics at school.'

'Have you finished work now until tomorrow?' Eric asked.

'No. I'm going to work again tonight – cleaning some offices.' She paused, looking shy. 'Anyway, I'd better be going.'

'See you tomorrow, then.'

'Yeah. Are we friends, Eric?' she asked, turning back.

'Not half!'

'That's good,' she said. 'I haven't got any other friends.'

'I've got lots.'

'You're lucky,' said Vera again, and looked at him in a way that no one ever had before – as though she admired him.

The next morning Eric said, 'You could come for a walk with me and Marlon, if you like.'

'Haven't you just come back?'

'I don't mind going again . . . we needn't go very far.'

'Okay,' she said, and they walked towards the river together, the dog trotting by their side.

Josh woke up suddenly, drenched in sweat. He'd been dreaming about Tania again – had thought she was in bed beside him. The dream had been so piercingly vivid, he could still smell her scent, hear her voice, feel her body next to his. Even now, after all this time, she still dominated his life.

Now fully awake, loneliness engulfed him. He sat up and turned on the beside light. It was four a.m. Attracted by the light, a huge black moth flew in at the window and fluttered crazily around the room, hitting the walls and brushing Josh's cheek. He heard the ominous buzz of a hungry mosquito too. 'Bloody Spain!' he muttered under his breath, and got up and staggered into the kitchen to find some insect repellent.

Back in bed, having disposed of the Mediterranean wildlife, closed the window and turned off the light, he lay staring into the darkness, listening to the roar of a motor bike and the distant thump of an all-night disco. Night time was playtime to the holiday-makers. His own bar didn't close until two.

It was September but the nights were still as unbearably hot as they were in August. They should be getting more comfortable soon, he hoped. Another season almost at an end. Another rainy November in Spain to get through. Another Christmas alone. How was he to endure it?

As time had passed Josh had become even more homesick and tormented by thoughts of the past. Time was supposed to be a great healer. Well, it showed no sign of healing him. You could go to a foreign country where you were unknown – you could alter your way of life, change the way you looked and behaved – but you couldn't change who you were inside. You couldn't make what tortured you go away. Wherever you went, your conscience went with you. Josh knew that now.

Unable to lie still as regrets besieged him, he got up and sat on the edge of the bed, smoking a cigarette. Josh was in such turmoil, he didn't know what to do to make himself feel better.

It was Saturday afternoon, the last day of the season, and preparations

210

were in full swing for Fenner's special Fun Night and firework display. The fair was opening later today because of it. Maddie was busy in her kitchen, baking.

'Hey, stop that!' she said, slapping Sam's hand as he stole a piece of the gingerbread she was cutting into squares. 'It's for tonight.'

'Don't be so mean.'

'Yeah, don't be so rotten, Mum,' said Clare, sneaking a piece then erupting into giggles, which started Sam off too.

'Clear off, Sam,' said Maddie. 'And you, Clare, are supposed to be looking after the cheese scones.'

'They're not ready to come out of the oven yet.'

'Ooh . . . cheese scones!' said Sam. 'I fancy a couple o' those.'

Maddie turned to him, face flushed from the heat of the oven, eyes sparkling with fun despite her scolding.

'Haven't you got a fairground to run?' she asked him pointedly.

'Yeah.'

'Well, go and run it then and leave me to my work.'

'I love it when you get stroppy,' he said, laughing.

'Well, I don't love it when you hang around here trying to stop me getting on.'

'I think I'll go and see how Barney's getting on with the Lucky Dip,' said Clare.

'Oh, no, you don't,' said Maddie. 'You'll stay here and help me.'

'I just want to make sure he's doing a proper job of it.'

'I'm sure Barney can manage without your help,' said Maddie.

'Go on, you bully, let the girl have five minutes with her pal,' said Sam, deliberately provoking her.

Maddie raised her eyes in mock annoyance. 'Trust you to take her side. She's supposed to be in charge of the cheese scones.'

'I'll look after those,' offered Sam.

'No, thanks.'

'You mean, you really don't want me around?' he said, pretending to be hurt.

'That's right. So sling your hook and let me get this baking done.'

Clare slipped past them and out of the door. 'I'll be back in five minutes,' she said, grinning at Sam who burst out laughing. 'In time to see to the cheese scones.'

'That's your fault,' said Maddie, but she wasn't really angry. 'You encourage her to muck about.'

'She's only being young,' said Sam. 'If you can't muck about then, when can you?'

'Yeah, yeah, I know,' said Maddie, preoccupied with another tray of gingerbread to be squared.

He took a piece from the pile already cut and when she looked up indignantly, leaned forward and kissed her on the lips.

'Do you still want me to go?' he asked, teasing her.

'You know I don't. But if there's to be any food for the homemade stall tonight, I think you'd better.'

'Okay. See you later then,' he said, and left the caravan, smiling.

Sam couldn't remember ever being as happy as he'd been these past few months. He'd certainly never felt this way with Tania. Tormented with passion and unrequited love; briefly ecstatic on the rare occasions when she deigned to be nice to him. But never happy and fulfilled as he was with Maddie. He smiled at the thought of her elfin face, those smiling blue eyes. He was very fond of Clare too. The three of them got on famously together and had had a lot of fun these past few months.

Striding purposefully across the fairground on his way to the Scenic Railway to make sure everything was in order for tonight, he made a sudden detour to his wagon. From one of the drawers in his bedroom, he drew out a small red box and opened the lid to reveal a diamond cluster engagement ring nestling on a bed of dark red velvet.

Tonight he was going to ask Maddie to marry him and was cautiously optimistic about her reply. There was the complication of her husband to be resolved but if she agreed to be his wife, they could deal with that together.

He stared at the ring, heart bumping excitedly. It looked too small and fragile against his strong, roughened hands. The jeweller had agreed to alter it if it didn't fit her; he'd even offered to change it for another if it wasn't to Maddie's taste.

Of course, the sensible thing would have been to have gone out together to choose it but he'd thought it would be more romantic this way. Him – down-to-earth Sam Fenner – being romantic! He hadn't known he had it in him until recently.

But Maddie had brought out a side to his nature he hadn't known existed. Because she made him feel so secure in her feelings for him and sure of himself as a man, he wasn't afraid to be romantic. There was none of the fear of humiliation there always had been with Tania. Maddie's obvious respect for him gave Sam the confidence to be a good lover. And she had such faith in him, he knew he could also be a good father to Clare.

Taking the ring out of the box, he watched it sparkle in a beam of sunlight from the window. If things went as planned it would be sparkling on Maddie's finger a few hours from now. Then they could begin to take steps towards obtaining her freedom to marry him. All he wanted now was to make Maddie and Clare happy.

His spirits took a slight dive with the sudden thought that she might turn him down. But he didn't really think so. Not after what they'd been to each other these last few months. Sam was as eager as a teenager and couldn't wait for this evening. At some point during the festivities he would bring her here and propose in the old-fashioned way.

Barely able to contain his excitement, he put the ring back into the box and replaced it in the drawer. Then he went to work whistling the Beatles latest hit song 'All You Need Is Love'.

Chapter Eighteen

The rides had come to a halt; the last hoop had been hurled and the final ball of the season thrown at the coconut stands. Everyone had gathered at the edge of the fairground for the firework display which set the sky ablaze with colour, the air echoing with explosions.

Wearing a red anorak over a white polo-necked sweater and jeans, Maddie was standing beside Sam; Clare was in front of her next to Barney. The evening was cold with mist rising, the smoke from the fireworks adding to the haze.

Munching a hot buttered cheese scone and breathing in the savoury aroma of baked jacket potatoes and roasted chestnuts, Maddie was enjoying the special essence of the occasion. 'This is my favourite night of the year,' she remarked to Sam, who was working his way steadily through a bag of hot chestnuts. 'The last night of the season at Fenner's always sends shivers up my spine.'

'You should put your woolly drawers on then,' he said waggishly.

'Oh, very funny,' she said, slapping him playfully on the arm but smiling at him too. 'Shivers of excitement, I mean.'

'Only kidding,' he said, grabbing her hand and squeezing it.

He was looking exceptionally gorgeous tonight, she thought, running an approving eye over the tan leather jacket he wore with a roll-neck sweater and jeans. His thick hair was untidy from rushing about to oversee this huge operation but a touch of dishevelment suited him.

'Doesn't the last night of the season give you a special buzz?' she asked.

'Yeah, it does,' Sam admitted. 'It takes a lot of organising but once it's underway it's great. I always enjoy it.'

'Me too,' Janice cut in. 'Not least because the end of the season means we get the evenings to ourselves again.'

'That's a bit cynical,' said Maddie. 'There's much more to it than that.'

'Just teasing,' chuckled her friend.

'I'll never forget my first experience of it, seven years ago,' said Maddie. 'I was absolutely knocked out by it.'

'I remember that night, too.' Sam looked thoughtful. 'Clare was sitting on my shoulders if I remember rightly.'

'Me . . . on your shoulders?' She took a dim view of this. 'I must have been a real little twerp.'

'You were a sweet little thing.'

'Sweet?' she echoed disapprovingly. 'That is *so* uncool.'

'Barney was on his dad's shoulders,' said Sam in reflective mood.

'He'd crush me to death if we tried to do that now,' laughed Chas, who was standing next to Janice, a glass of beer in one hand and a cigarette in the other.

'He would too,' she agreed, looking fondly at her son. 'He's nearly as tall as his dad.'

'Yeah – he'll be standing his round at the bar before too long,' said Chas.

'Trust you to measure your son's development in those sort of terms,' said Janice good-humouredly.

'Just being honest.'

'Yeah, well, he's a long way to go before he'll be going up to the bar with you. He'll be my little boy for a while longer.' She leaned forward and hugged Barney. 'Won't you, son?'

'M-u-um,' he admonished, wriggling out of her clutches and squirming with youthful embarrassment.

The change in the children wasn't the only thing that had altered around here since Maddie first came, thought Sam. So much had happened in the last seven years. A stab of pain shot through him as old wounds resurfaced. Who could have predicted then that his wife would be dead and his brother disappeared into thin air?

He banished such morbid thoughts from his mind. Tonight was for fun and romance. When the fireworks had finished he was going to whisk Maddie away to his wagon, and when they returned to the party they would announce their engagement.

'Ooh, what a smasher!' she said as a shower of golden rain burst into the sky, causing a communal gasp of appreciation.

Someone tapped her on the shoulder and she turned to see Eric accompanied by a woman with smiling brown eyes and a mop of curly hair.

'This is my friend, Vera Walters,' he proudly announced.

'Hi, Vera,' said Maddie warmly. 'Welcome to the party.'

Eric introduced Vera to the others who were standing nearby and they greeted her in a friendly manner.

'I've heard such a lot about you,' said Maddie. Indeed, Eric had talked about little else but his new friend lately.

Vera beamed. 'Eric told me that you two are good friends,' she said.

'The best,' Maddie agreed.

'Lovely fireworks, ain't they?' said Vera with undisguised enthusiasm.

Maddie nodded.

'Vera doesn't usually go out at night time . . . well, only to work in the early evenings,' explained Eric.

'Too many dangerous people out on the streets at night,' she said. 'It isn't safe.'

'Oh, I wouldn't say that,' Maddie replied.

'Mum says I haven't the sense to take care of myself so I mustn't go out at night . . . not unless she's with me.'

'She let you come tonight, though?'

'Yeah – but only 'cause I've got Eric to look after me.'

'I see.'

Maddie realised then how difficult and isolating it must be for the parents of these exceptionally vulnerable people. For Sybil the burden was eased by the fact that they lived in a close-knit community where everyone looked out for Eric, and neither he nor his mother lacked for company.

'I go to the pictures with Mum sometimes,' Vera informed Maddie chattily.

'That's nice.'

'She goes to Bingo, too. But I don't go to that with her 'cause I'm too slow with the numbers and it gets on her nerves. Waste o' money taking me, she says.'

Vera's mother didn't sound like the most sensitive soul, but Maddie thought she was probably just an ordinary woman doing her best in difficult circumstances.

'I hope she plays Bingo at our pavilion?'

Vera nodded vigorously. 'She does. She was really pleased when it opened 'cause we live within walking distance from here.'

'That's handy,' said Maddie.

'It is,' agreed Eric happily. 'It's not too far for me to see Vera home later on.'

'Glad to hear you're such a gentleman,' Maddie commented.

He nodded vigorously. 'We have to go and see some more people now,' he announced, and led Vera away to meet more friends and relatives.

Sam said he had to go and see to a few bits of business. 'I'll try not to be too long,' he told Maddie. 'I have to pay the juggler and the high-wire act, then lock the takings in the safe for the night.'

'Can I do anything to help?'

'No. You stay and enjoy yourself.'

'Okay.'

He disappeared into the crowd while she watched the rest of the display, enjoying the warm friendly atmosphere. When the fireworks had finished Chas went to get some drinks, the children disappeared with a group of youngsters and Janice said she was going to find her mother.

Sybil appeared at Maddie's side. 'What do you think of our Eric

216

having a girlfriend then?' she asked, still in costume, red turban and flowing dress adding to the colourful occasion.

'I think it's lovely for him to have someone of his own,' Maddie replied. 'And Vera seems very nice.'

'She is nice. And about as soft in the head as he is!'

'That doesn't matter, does it?'

'It's inevitable, I suppose,' she said, sighing. 'He's hardly likely to get off with anyone very bright, is he?'

Maddie smiled at Sybil's frankness.

'He's not as dim as people seem to think.'

'So you've said before, dear, and I appreciate your faith in him. But we both know that no normal woman would go out with Eric because he'd drive her nuts – bless him – the way he rambles on about things in his slow way, not having the sense to see when people have heard enough.'

'I've never said he was a likely contender for Brain of Britain,' said Maddie. 'But neither is he a half wit.'

'You proved that by teaching him to read.'

'*He* proved it by learning.'

'Yeah, well . . . whatever,' Sybil said comfortably. 'But he'll never be the same as the rest of us, we have to accept that.'

'Maybe not,' Maddie agreed. 'But isn't it nice that he's found someone he likes to be with? A new friend – someone outside the family to talk to.'

'So long as that's all she is to him,' said Sybil darkly. 'Just a friend.'

Maddie gave her a sharp look, wondering what was on her mind. 'You wouldn't object to its developing into something more, though, would you?' she said, puzzled by Sybil's attitude because she was a devoted mother and her son's happiness of paramount importance to her.

'Don't get me wrong . . . nothing would give me more pleasure than to see my boy settled with someone to love him and look after him,' her friend explained. 'But it isn't quite so simple as that with those two, is it?'

Maddie pondered on the matter for a few moments. 'Well, I suppose they'll want to do what comes naturally – the same as everybody else – if that's what you mean.'

'It is, and it's the consequences that worry me. I mean – they can hardly look after themselves, let alone a baby.'

'Mmm.' Maddie could see the problem. 'I suppose you do have a point.'

'Anyway, would it be morally right for them to have kiddies? I mean, being the way they are?'

'Don't you think you're jumping the gun a bit?' said Maddie. 'All they do is go out walking together, from what I can make out.'

'At the moment that's all they do. But they're very friendly and the other side of it's bound to emerge eventually. After all, they're young and healthy and there's nothing wrong with either of 'em physically.'

'They'd have the nous to take precautions, wouldn't they?'

'I don't know, that's the problem,' said Sybil, looking worried. 'Eric's a grown man – he might be backward but he has his male pride. I don't want to embarrass him by spelling it out for him as though he was twelve years old.' She fiddled anxiously with one of her gold hooped earrings. 'It hasn't seemed necessary to mention it as he's never had a girlfriend before. Sex isn't the sort of thing you want to talk about to your grown-up son.'

'He must know the facts of life, though?'

'When he was lad I explained the basics, o' course.'

'Eric doesn't only know the things you tell him,' Maddie pointed out.

'No, but he's led a very sheltered life. Living here with me – in an enclosed community – protected from the outside world by the family.'

'Okay, so he's led a sheltered life. But he works on a fairground with men – down-to-earth men,' said Maddie. 'He couldn't have failed to pick up a few things from them since men are always talking about sex when women aren't around . . . or so I've heard.'

'That's true,' said Sybil brightening. 'But I still can't be sure if he knows enough to take care of things . . .'

'Why not ask Sam or Vic to have a chat with him, if you're really worried? It might be less embarrassing that way.'

'That's a good idea! I think I ought to do something, just to be on the safe side. I'd rather that than have Vera's mother chasing him with a paternity suit.'

'I think you're very wise.'

Sybil's expression softened. 'Despite all the problems, I'd be the happiest woman alive if the two of them could make a go of it.'

'Me too,' said Maddie. 'Everyone on the park would be happy to see Eric settled with a partner.'

The public were beginning to drift towards the exits, leaving just fairground staff, and family and friends.

Hetty wandered up to Maddie and Sybil. 'Nice to see your Eric fixed up with a woman, Syb.'

'Maddie and I were just talking about that, as a matter of fact.'

'Romance seems to be in the air around here lately,' said Hetty, giving Maddie a meaningful look.

She looked back innocently.

'Don't come the old innocent,' said Hetty, smiling at her.

'You know?'

''Course I do,' she said. 'Just because I don't live here all the time now doesn't mean I don't keep up to date with what's going on.'

Her eyes were tender. 'You're the best thing that's happened to Sam in a long time and I hope the two of you make a go of it.'

'Thanks, Hetty,' said Maddie, hugging her. 'I hope so too.'

Chas appeared with a tray of drinks and Janice in tow.

'I was just saying how pleased I am that Maddie and Sam are getting on so well,' said Hetty.

'Me too,' said Janice. 'I could do with a wedding in the family as an excuse to buy a new outfit. I fancy a good old knees up an' all.'

'Hey, don't get carried away,' said Maddie. 'Nobody's said anything about a wedding.'

'You'd better give him a nudge if he doesn't pop the question soon,' laughed Janice. 'My brother isn't exactly known for being a fast worker.'

They all laughed and Maddie knew she was in the presence of genuine affection.

'Since when did you need an excuse to buy new clothes, anyway?' asked Chas, looking at Janice.

Neither she nor Chas was in the least inhibited about airing their differences in public so everybody was used to it and took no notice. Janice gave Chas one of the lacerating looks she saved especially for him. 'I don't need an excuse,' she said. 'And as I pay for my own clothes, it's my business what I buy.'

'I'd willingly pay for your clothes and you know it,' he told her, laughing. 'Marry me and I'll buy you anything you want.'

'You already know the answer to that.'

'Just think how you could splash out on clothes if they were for your own wedding.'

'Don't start trying to twist my arm again! If a thing ain't broke, why fix it? We're fine as we are.'

'Why did I have to fall for someone as stubborn as you?'

'Because I'm so irresistible,' she suggested, laughing. 'And because you like a challenge?'

'I certainly got one in you.'

'You'll get more than a challenge if you don't leave off,' Janice threatened.

But Chas wasn't that easily deterred. 'You're keen enough to marry Maddie and Sam off, though, aren't you?'

'Sam's the marrying kind.'

'And I'm not?'

'No.'

'You can't be sure of that unless you give me a chance.'

'And what if it doesn't work out?' she said, without requiring an answer. 'We could end up hating each other and then we'd have to stay together as divorce isn't the done thing around here.'

'Oh, that's a good one,' he said with a roar of laughter. 'Since when have you worried about doing the done thing?'

'Well, I . . .'

'If you wanted a divorce, you'd get one and bugger what anyone thought,' he said. 'It's all just an excuse.'

'They're not even married yet and already they're talking about divorce!' said Sybil with a grin. 'Perhaps you'd better not take the plunge if that's the way it is.'

'Rubbish,' said Chas.

'Leave it, Chas,' said Janice.

The children appeared, eating hot dogs. Barney looked at his warring parents. 'They're at it again then,' he said, unconcerned.

'It's when they stop we have to worry,' said Hetty, and turning to Janice added, 'For goodness sake, marry the bloke and put him out of his misery.'

'All in good time, Mother – all in good time.'

'And you reckon your brother's a slow worker?' said Maddie.

'I'm thinking of entering you and Chas for the *Guinness Book of Records*,' said Hetty to her daughter. 'For the longest ever courtship.'

'She likes me chasing her, that's why she won't tie the knot,' he said.

'Yeah, well, I've gotta keep him on his toes,' said Janice, smiling at the company in general. 'Don't want him taking me for granted.'

'I can't imagine anyone ever doing that,' said Chas.

'Neither can I,' said Hetty.

Vic joined the gathering.

'You're just in time to protect me, Dad,' said Janice, slipping her arm around him.

'From who?'

'Chas and Mum are giving me a really hard time.'

'Leave her alone, you big bullies,' said her father with mock authority. He turned to Janice. 'Take no notice of 'em, love. You'll be all right now your dad's here.'

Maddie thought how different Vic was now from the overweight and rather overbearing man he'd been when she'd first come to Fenner's. He was still a big-built man but much less bloated, his eyes clearer and more alert.

Eric and Vera rejoined the gang followed by Sam who stood next to Maddie with his arm around her. People began to talk among themselves.

'Let's slip away,' he whispered into her ear.

'We can't go at the moment,' she replied. 'It would seem rude.'

'I want a few minutes alone with you – without Clare around.'

'You're eager tonight.'

'Not that.'

'What then?'

'Come to my wagon and I'll tell you.'

'Can't you tell me here?'

'No.'

'It sounds intriguing but your mother has just started making a speech,' said Maddie close to his ear. 'So we'll have to wait until she's finished speaking. It's only polite.'

'Damn!' he said because he was eager to show her the ring.

'Shush!'

Curbing his impatience, Sam turned to listen to what his mother had to say . . .

'Well, folks, we've come to the end of another season, and Vic and I would like to thank you all for your hard work.'

'Which keeps us in the lap of luxury,' added her husband.

'That'll be the day, when any of us lives like that,' said Hetty, smiling. 'But I must admit to having the best of both worlds – now that we are semi-retired.'

'She's right,' confirmed Vic. 'We're still closely involved with the business but not slaves to it any more.'

'You deserve some free time,' declared Sam.

'You've worked hard enough for it,' added Janice.

There was a hearty roar of agreement from the others.

'Anyway, thanks again for everything,' continued Hetty.

'That goes for me too,' said Vic.

'So let's raise our glasses to celebrate another successful season. And many more to come,' Hetty announced joyfully.

Maddie lifted her glass, intensely proud to be a part of this happy band at such a jovial occasion.

A moment later, however, the mood of the entire company changed dramatically when another guest appeared. A hush fell over the gathering. Numb with shock, Maddie watched Hetty's glass drop from her hand and smash to the ground.

'Hi, everybody,' said the newcomer. 'It's been a long time.'

'Josh!' gasped Hetty, and had to be supported by Vic as her legs buckled beneath her.

Chapter Nineteen

Feeling sick and powerless, Maddie watched Eric and Chas drag Sam away from his brother. The man so admired for his calm and gentle nature had gone berserk, leaping on Josh and grabbing him by the throat.

'Murderer!' he shouted, voice low and guttural with emotion as two men pulled him bodily away from Josh. 'You killed my wife . . . you killed her!'

Josh was visibly shaken by the assault. 'Calm down, mate,' he said, nervously straightening his jacket which had been almost ripped off in the attack.

'You expect him to be calm after what you've done to him?' intervened Hetty in a severe tone, though her voice was quivering.

'Perhaps if I could explain . . .'

Josh seemed more subdued and older, Maddie observed. Even in the warm glow of the fairground lights, she could see a gauntness in his face that hadn't been there before. He was still striking, though, deeply tanned and wearing smart continental clothes.

'You'd better explain why you've come back after all this time,' said his father coldly. 'Upsetting everybody like this.'

'I've come back to tell you what happened . . . and to make my peace.'

'You broke your mother's heart,' interrupted Vic bitterly.

'You could have given your father another heart attack,' said Hetty. 'Turning up out of the blue like that.'

'Heart attack – Dad?' Josh looked stricken. 'I didn't know . . .'

'"Course you didn't know . . . how could you?' said his mother in a strangled voice. 'Since you haven't bothered to get in touch for three years.'

'I'm sorry . . .'

'We could have been dead and buried for all you knew . . . or cared,' said Hetty.

'I *did* care.'

'You've got a damned funny way of showing it then,' she said.

Eric diplomatically removed Vera from the scene, muttering something about its being time for him to take her home and confirming Maddie's belief that he had more up top than he was

222

given credit for. She herself was worried about the effect all this was having on her daughter and drew her back from the crowd, telling her to go home to their living-wagon. Janice did the same with Barney and the two youngsters left, albeit reluctantly.

'I know it must have seemed as though I didn't care,' said Josh, with what seemed to Maddie to be genuine compunction. 'And I'm sorry for that.'

'Sorry is an easy word to say . . .' began Hetty, but was interrupted by Sam.

'You stole my wife,' he said, charging towards Josh again, only to be restrained by Chas. 'And not content with that, you murdered her and ran away like the miserable coward you are.'

'I didn't kill Tania, Sam – I swear it.'

But he was in no mood to listen. His rage was blinding. His voice was distorted and there were tears running down his face. 'You don't deserve to live,' he roared. 'You've taken a life so why should you have yours?'

'That's enough of that sort of talk, Sam,' cut in Janice, going over to him and taking his arm. 'You've every right to be upset but give Josh a chance to tell us his side of the story.'

'Why should I?'

'Because there are two sides to everything and we haven't heard him out.'

Sam was struggling with Chas and Janice, who were only keeping him away from Josh with great difficulty. Dreading to think what would happen if Sam did get his hands on his brother while in this state, Maddie went over to him.

'This is no way to carry on.' Her manner was kind but firm. 'You're letting yourself down and upsetting your parents. Don't let Josh do this to you – he isn't worth it.'

He looked at her as though she was a stranger, almost as though he wasn't aware of what had been happening these past few minutes. Then he shook his head, seeming to regain control of himself.

'Sorry, Maddie,' he said gruffly. 'But he's a murdering bastard.'

'You don't know that for certain. Anyway, violence never solved anything and you'd be telling us that if you weren't so upset,' she said. 'So, please, just listen to what Josh has to say.'

A stillness seemed to come over Sam then. 'Okay, I'll listen, but don't ask anything more of me than that.'

'All right.' She turned to Hetty and Vic. 'Why don't you all go off somewhere and talk things over in private?'

'Yeah, I think we'd better,' said Janice.

'I'll look after Barney while you sort things out.'

'Thanks.'

Although Maddie's feelings for Sam meant she was deeply involved, it seemed right to distance herself from such a serious family matter at this point. Josh's return had given her a sharp reminder of her position *outside* the Fenner family.

'I'm not having Hetty upset,' said Vic protectively.

'Stress isn't good for your dad,' she said with equal concern for him.

'Calm down, everybody, and let's go and sort it all out at my place,' said Janice, taking her mother's arm. She turned to Maddie. 'Thanks for having Barney. It isn't the sort of thing a boy his age should be hearing about.'

'No trouble. He can sleep over with us too.'

Sam looked around the fairground which was practically deserted by now. 'This is all very well,' he said, turning to his brother with an icy expression, 'but in case you've forgotten we are running a fair here and we still have a lot of clearing up to do.'

'We can do that tomorrow morning – as the season has ended,' Janice pointed out. 'This is more of a priority.'

There was a collective murmur of agreement and they all began to drift towards the living-wagons. The deep sense of belonging that had embraced Maddie earlier in the evening had disappeared, leaving her feeling wretchedly isolated. No matter how much a part of it she had felt ten minutes ago, she still wasn't a family member.

A shivering sense of foreboding crept over her. Josh's return spelt disaster, she could feel it.

'Yes, Tania and I were having an affair,' admitted Josh. He was standing by the unit dividing the living room from the kitchen. Everyone else was sitting down.

'I think we were all bright enough to work that out,' said Hetty acerbically.

'But it wasn't just some tacky affair . . .'

'What other sort is there?' she interrupted brusquely.

Josh ignored this and looked at Sam. 'I'm sorry, mate. I know how much this will hurt you. But it's important that you know the truth – that Tania was the only woman I ever really loved.'

'She was your brother's wife, for God's sake,' his mother blurted out. 'You had no business to love her. You should never have let the affair get started.'

'Do you think I don't know that?' said Josh, painfully meeting his mother's accusing eyes. 'But these things aren't always simple.'

'They are if you follow the rules,' she said, voice tight and breathless. 'Married women are out of bounds so you make absolutely sure that nothing of a romantic nature ever develops with one. You should have respected that. What you did was nothing short of mucky.'

'In a perfect world these things wouldn't happen,' agreed Josh. 'But we all know that this isn't a perfect world.'

'Grand words, but they don't cut any ice with me,' announced his mother. 'You're just making excuses.'

'Let him finish what he has to say,' said Janice who was sitting next to her. She put a comforting hand on Hetty's arm. 'Please, Mum.'

But Sam was interrupting now. 'And Tania loved you, I suppose?' he said to his brother in a broken voice.

There was a brief pause before Josh said in a solemn voice, 'Yeah . . . I believe she did.'

'She didn't know the meaning of the word,' pronounced Hetty.

'Shush, Mum,' admonished Janice again.

'No, I won't be shushed,' she said. 'All this talk of love . . . it's all just *lust*. Sex is what this is all about.'

'I know you're upset,' said Josh. 'But please let me have my say.'

'What about loyalty to your brother . . . to the family?' The words were pouring out of Hetty almost of their own volition.

Vic put a steadying hand on her arm. 'Let him finish, love.'

'Go on then, have your say.' She looked at Josh with tears in her eyes. 'But don't try to justify what you did with a lot of sloppy talk about love.'

'We were planning to go away together,' he continued at last, looking directly at Sam. 'We'd been talking about it for ages.'

'Bastard! You were going to take her away from me completely,' Sam accused darkly.

'You don't *take* a woman like Tania anywhere,' said Josh in a clipped voice. 'She called the shots, you must remember that.'

Sam shrugged his shoulders.

'Tania and I were two of a kind,' Josh went on. 'Not good-natured and decent like you are, Sam. We were both selfish – both wanted more from life than Fenner's Fun Park had to offer.'

'Are you trying to make out that she was to blame?' growled Sam.

'No, I'm not.' Josh was adamant about that. 'I'm just trying to tell you how it actually was – that I'm no angel and neither was she. What happened between us came about because we both wanted it.'

'Bigger than both of you, as they say in the films,' said Sam cynically.

'Yeah – that's exactly how it was,' said Josh. 'And until it happened to me, I was sceptical too.'

'Oh, give me strength!' protested Sam.

'Quiet, Sam,' said Janice. 'And let's hear the rest of the story.'

Josh continued. 'Tania was putting pressure on me about going away together – giving me a hard time because I kept putting it off. It had reached a point where I realised that I just couldn't go through with it. I just couldn't make that final break and take her away from you, Sam.'

'You'd already done that very effectively,' he protested.

'Yeah, I know.' Josh looked ashamed. 'I mean, I didn't feel able physically to remove her from your life. Too much of a coward, I suppose. And we couldn't go on as we were because it was tearing us both apart – and it was only a matter of time before you found out and got hurt.'

The silence was electric as they waited for him to continue.

'So I decided to call the whole thing off and go away *without her*.' He addressed his comments to them all. 'I thought she might settle down to life with Sam if I was out of the picture altogether, and none of you need ever know anything about it.'

'How thoughtful of you,' said Sam with withering sarcasm.

'Sam, please.' Janice looked from one brother to the other. 'Go on, Josh.'

'I waited until I'd booked a flight to Spain – so that I'd be less likely to back out – then arranged to meet her to tell her my decision.' He cleared his throat. 'We drove to Hanleigh Woods, parked the car and went for a walk near the quarry. It took me a while to pluck up the courage to tell Tania that it was over between us and I was going abroad on my own. My intention was to break it to her first then tell you I was going away just before I left. I never intended just to disappear without a word.'

'So what happened to change that?' asked Janice.

Josh paused and moistened his lips, dark eyes dull with pain.

'When I did finally get the words out, Tania went mad. She turned on me: kicking, punching, clawing at my face with her nails. It was terrible,' he explained. 'She begged me to change my mind – said she didn't want to live if she couldn't be with me. When she finally realised that I meant what I said, she stormed off in a fury.'

He mopped his brow, sweating from the ordeal of reliving the events of that traumatic day. 'I went after her but I couldn't find her . . . not for ages.' He stopped again as distress overwhelmed him, and swallowed hard.

'Eventually I looked down into the quarry and saw her lying there at the bottom. She must have slipped or something. I'm sure she didn't intend to kill herself. Suicide wasn't Tania's style, no matter how upset she was.'

The room was silent, the atmosphere charged with emotion. Sam's eyes were brimming with tears. 'So you saw her there and left her – just ran away, did you?' he said harshly.

'O' course I didn't. Give me some credit, man. I'm bad but I'm not that heartless,' protested Josh. 'I climbed down into the quarry.' He choked back the tears. 'I was in a terrible state.' He blew his nose and struggled for composure. 'I could see right away that she was dead – it was the worst moment of my life. I tried to bring her round but . . . but there was nothing I could do for her. Nothing anyone could do.'

'So then you left her?' Janice pressed.

'No. I stayed with her for a long time, just sat on this rock holding her in my arms.' Josh fell silent, thinking back. 'When I began to gather my wits, I knew I had to get away.'

'You could have come and told us what had happened,' said his mother.

'I knew people would think I'd killed her because of the circumstances of her death,' he went on. 'I knew that word of our affair was bound to get out too and . . . and I just couldn't face you, Sam.' He ran his gaze around the room. 'I couldn't face any of you. So I went back to my living-wagon to get my savings and scarpered. I stayed the night with a mate in Hammersmith. The next morning he drove me to the airport then took my car to a mate of his with a breaker's yard – a bloke who doesn't ask questions. I left instructions for them to take what parts they wanted from it then put it through the crushing machine so there would be no trace of it – and no comebacks for my mate.'

'Quite a story,' said Hetty, sounding slightly calmer.

Josh shook his head and blew his nose again. 'I'll never forget leaving her there all alone. I've had nightmares about it ever since.'

'She didn't know anything about it,' said his warm-hearted mother who was beginning to thaw towards him.

'That doesn't stop the nightmares,' he said. 'The regrets.'

'You don't deserve to sleep at all with what you've got on your conscience,' ground out Sam.

'I haven't been sleeping easy this past three years, if it's any consolation to you.'

'It isn't.'

'Well, anyway, that's what happened,' said Josh. 'I didn't kill Tania in the way that you all must have imagined, but I do feel responsible for her death. If I hadn't ended the affair she wouldn't have run off and had an accident.'

'And if you hadn't started the affair in the first place . . .' began Hetty.

'Exactly,' Josh finished for her.

'Well, it's taken you long enough to do it but at least you've come back to face the music now,' said his mother.

'The police were sniffing around here looking for you after her body was found,' Vic warned him.

'Don't worry,' said Josh. 'I've already been to the local nick and told them everything. I don't know if they believe me but I doubt they'll take any action against me because they don't have a case. I was in too much of a panic to realise that when I ran away.'

There was a general sigh of relief.

'So what are your plans now then, son?' asked his mother.

'I'm not sure. I've got a business in Spain . . . a bar.'

227

'You'll be going back then?' said Hetty, obviously disappointed.

'Probably,' Josh said non-committally. 'But I need some time to clear my mind. To decide what I'm going to do with the rest of my life. I found it hard to settle in Spain.' He paused. 'Actually, I was wondering . . . well, if you haven't rented my wagon out, I'd like to stay for a while.'

Hetty looked at Sam, knowing how hurt he'd been by his brother and not wanting to add to it. But, for all his faults, Josh was her son too.

'You're family, Josh, you can stay for as long as you like,' she said.

Looking furious, Sam stood up. 'Don't include me in the family welcome,' he said through gritted teeth, throwing an icy look in Josh's direction. 'I want nothing to do with you. You're no brother of mine.'

And with that he left.

Maddie spent a sleepless night wondering what had been happening next door. She'd expected Sam to come and give her an update. As this hadn't happened, she guessed he hadn't wanted to disturb her as it was very late when finally she'd heard the sound of people leaving next door.

She'd thought he would have a lie in after the late night, as the season had ended, and was surprised to see him out on the fairground with a broom quite early. Leaving Clare and Barney eating their breakfast, Maddie slipped into her anorak and hurried over to where Sam was sweeping, near the Ghost Train.

It was a dull morning with heavy clouds and a sharp breeze blowing spots of rain into her face.

'You're up early. Couldn't you sleep?' she asked lightly, meaning it as a joke.

'No, I couldn't,' he said in a grim tone. 'And is it any wonder?'

'What happened?'

'That bloody brother of mine is staying here.' He looked angrily in the direction of the living-wagons. 'He's moved back into his caravan, would you believe? Having been told by my mother that he can stay for as long as he likes.'

'Well, that's a turn up!'

Sam gave Maddie a hostile look, almost as though she was to blame. 'My feelings don't matter, apparently. Josh clears off and we don't hear a word from him for three years and then he comes back a hero . . . the golden boy of the family . . . just like that.'

'I'm sure it isn't like that, Sam.'

'I was there, Maddie – I heard what was said. I saw them all being taken in by him. But not me. Oh, no. I'm not such a soft touch. I walked out in disgust – and he only had the cheek to come to my wagon after he left Janice's! Said he was sorry for what he'd done

228

and we needed to talk . . . but I've nothing to say to Josh and I told him so. I didn't even let him in.'

While finding Sam's attitude towards his family perfectly understandable, Maddie found his change towards herself unwarranted and hurtful. Normally he would have greeted her warmly, whatever problems he had on his mind. This morning he was so preoccupied with his feelings for his brother, she barely seemed to exist for him.

'Did Josh tell you what happened to Tania?' she asked.

He winced at the mention of his late wife's name. 'Oh, yeah, he told us everything,' said Sam, staring into space, leaning on the broom.

'Sam, this is me, Maddie,' she said, waving her hand in front of his glazed eyes. 'Remember me? I'm the one who wasn't there last night and would very much like to know what Josh had to say.'

'Sorry,' he said absently, and gave her an account of Josh's revelations.

'At least he's not a murderer, that's something to be thankful for,' said Maddie when he'd completed the tale.

'Not legally. But it's because of him she's dead.' Sam's tawny eyes simmered with rage. 'He admitted it.'

'That's something in his favour, I suppose. That he actually admitted it.'

'It won't bring Tania back though, will it?'

It was as though they had stepped back three years in time and he was grieving for Tania all over again. Maddie could hardly bear it.

'It wouldn't do you any good if it could, though, would it?' she said, thinking it necessary to be brutally candid. 'As it was Josh Tania was in love with.'

'We only have his word for that,' said Sam miserably.

Maddie couldn't believe that this was happening. After going through years of hell, Sam had finally come to terms with the truth about his marriage and put the past behind him. And after waiting for so long, she had won his love at last. Now she was losing him – to an enemy she couldn't fight because it was inside his own head.

'I think you know in your heart that what he said was true, though, don't you?' Maddie pressed the man she loved.

'I don't know anything for sure,' he said. 'Seeing Josh again . . . hearing him talk about her . . . knowing how she died.' He looked bleak. 'It's really got to me, Maddie.'

He looked so distressed, she wanted to hold him in her arms. But she sensed that was the last thing Sam wanted. However, she wasn't prepared to stand by and let him go without a fight. 'Your life with Tania is over,' she said baldly. 'There's no point in waging a vendetta against Josh. It won't change anything.'

'You don't know what it feels like,' he said. 'No one can see into my mind . . . into my heart.'

'No, but you and I have got pretty close these last few months and I think that gives me the right to state my opinion.' She paused to calm herself. 'You have to let go, Sam, and move on.'

He looked desolate. 'I know I'm not being fair to you.'

'You wouldn't be human if you weren't upset by Josh's turning up and bringing it all back,' she said. 'I wouldn't expect anything else of you. But please don't let it come between us.'

He smiled awkwardly and reached for her hand. 'I'm sorry,' he said stiffly.

'That's all right,' said Maddie, but his words didn't remove the barrier between them.

'But if anyone is expecting me to be civil to my bastard of a brother, they're in for a big disappointment,' he growled.

'Stop it, Sam – please.'

'It's enough to make me think about leaving here altogether.'

'You wouldn't . . .'

'No, I won't let him drive me away,' he interrupted. 'But so far as I'm concerned, Josh is no relative of mine.'

'I don't think much of him as a person either, but I think you're wrong to take that attitude.'

'Why?'

'Because it will hurt you more than it will hurt him. It isn't in your nature to be vindictive.'

'We're all vindictive if the circumstances are bad enough.'

Maddie was silent for a few moments then she said sadly, 'It's up to you how you behave but I don't think you should let Josh ruin your life.'

He nodded but seemed miles away from her.

'I'll have to go now,' she said, wanting to get away from him because his distant attitude was so acutely hurtful. 'I left the kids having their breakfast.'

'Okay.' Sam thought for a moment. 'Can you tell Barney to come and give me a hand with the clearing up when he's finished eating?' Barney was now at an age where he was expected to help on the fairground to some extent. 'I'll go and shake Chas and Eric up if they're not out here soon, too. This place is like a tip after last night.'

'I'll tell him,' said Maddie forlornly, moving away.

'Thanks.'

She turned back. 'Oh, and Sam?'

'Yeah?' he said, looking at her.

'What was it you wanted to say to me last night that was so important?'

'Last night?' He looked blank.

'You said you wanted us to be on our own for a few minutes

because you had something to say to me . . . you wanted us to slip away, remember? Just before Josh appeared on the scene.'

He stared into space, picturing in his mind the small red jeweller's box in his bedroom drawer. That all seemed so long ago, when he'd felt like a different person – a man full of hope for the future. A fleeting moment of joy flashed through him at the memory of how happy he'd been then; to be immediately followed by anger and pain. His mind was in turmoil. He didn't feel able to cope with anything as emotionally demanding as a marriage proposal to Maddie when all he could think about was Tania.

'Oh, that was nothing,' he said, nevertheless experiencing a sharp pang of disappointment. His life was falling apart for the second time and he didn't seem able to do anything about it.

'It seemed quite urgent at the time,' Maddie pointed out.

'It was nothing – really.'

Maddie didn't believe him. But as he'd obviously changed his mind she didn't press him.

'I'll see you later, then,' she said, and walked back to her wagon, fighting down tears.

'I know you're angry with me for letting Josh stay on here,' said Hetty, looking at Sam across the table in his dining room, having made a point of calling on him that afternoon.

'What else do you expect?'

'I knew you wouldn't like it.'

'But you did it just the same.'

'I had to.'

'Why?'

'Josh is still my son, however badly he's behaved.'

'And I'm expected to be good mates with him, I suppose?'

'I don't see the point of hanging on to an old grudge.'

'*He slept with my wife.*'

'And I can't forgive him for that,' said Hetty. 'But it's over and done with.'

'Surely you don't expect *me* to forget it?'

'You could try.'

'God Almighty,' he said, shaking his head. 'I don't know how that bloke does it, I really don't. He goes away without a thought for any of us, and when he does show his face, he's treated like royalty.'

'Now you're exaggerating.'

'Well . . . maybe a little,' he admitted. 'But it didn't take him long to win you over.'

'Sam, Sam,' she said with feeling, reaching across the table and putting her hand on his. 'Do you think I don't know his faults? Do you think the fact that he walked out of our lives without a word doesn't still hurt?'

231

'Well – no, of course I don't think that,' he said, his heart breaking to see the pain in his mother's eyes. Which only made him angrier with Josh. 'But I just don't understand. I mean, he doesn't seem to give a damn about you and Dad but you still put out the welcome mat when he does come home. It just doesn't make sense to me.'

'Because you don't have children of your own, that's why you can't understand,' she explained. 'I can't desert Josh, whatever he's done. I thought I could when he first went away but I can't. The same as I could never desert you or Janice if either of you did something that really upset me. I feel your pain as my own, you see, son, and I love you all unconditionally. That doesn't mean I don't appreciate the fact that you and Janice are always there for your dad and me, and Josh isn't.'

Sam swallowed hard, almost choking on a lump in his throat; he was riddled with guilt for burdening his mother with his own problems when she'd been hurt by Josh too.

'I know I said he was no longer a son of mine when he first went missing. But that was because I was in such pain. I didn't mean it.'

'Oh.'

'Forget the past, son,' Hetty advised. 'It's time to think of the future. A future I hope will include Maddie.'

'Maddie?' She seemed so far removed from him now Josh had resurrected old memories and feelings.

'Yes, Maddie. The two of you have been an item just lately, haven't you?'

'We have been, yes,' said Sam, sounding doubtful about the future.

'There's no reason for that to change just because Josh has come back, is there?'

But Josh's return had reminded Sam of the strength of the feelings he used to have for Tania. He didn't think he could ever feel that passionately for Maddie, and the doubt scared him. 'I don't know,' he said slowly.

'Oh, Sam,' said his mother with deep concern. 'Don't lose the chance of happiness with Maddie just because your brother has come back.'

'I'm a bit mixed up at the moment, that's all,' he said. 'But I'll get it sorted – don't you worry about it.'

'I hope you do, for your sake.'

A surge of filial affection softened Sam's attitude. 'Look – about Josh,' he said. 'I can't pretend that I'm going to be mates with him because I'm not. But for your sake I won't let any rough stuff develop between us on the park, I promise you.'

'Thanks, son,' said Hetty, squeezing his hand. 'You're one of the best.'

* * *

232

Hetty went from Sam's wagon to Josh's and came straight to the point.

'I've said you can stay here for as long as you like and I meant it,' she said, walking into his living room which smelled damp and musty from being unused for so long.

'And I'm very grateful.'

'You don't have to be,' she said. 'You're family and there will always be a home for you at Fenner's . . .'

'I sense a "but" in there somewhere, though?'

'Yes, there is,' she told him gravely. 'And it's this. If you do anything else to upset Sam, you'll have me to answer to . . . and then I'll have to review the question of your staying here.'

'The very fact that I breathe upsets him,' said Josh.

'I know that, so keep out of his way until he's ready to talk to you,' she said. 'He'll come round, in time. It isn't in his nature to bear a grudge. But he's been very badly hurt.'

'I know.'

'Sam's been good to this family,' Hetty went on. 'He works hard – he's making a damned fine job of running the business.'

'I can imagine.'

'He's a good man.'

Josh nodded. 'Too good for Tania.'

'But you weren't?'

'As I said last night, she and I were two of a kind. It was our wickedness that drew us together.'

'That's no excuse for what you did! Being wicked is nothing to boast about.'

'I wasn't boasting – just stating facts,' Josh said seriously. 'It wouldn't have happened if Tania hadn't wanted it to. You knew her . . . can you honestly imagine her doing anything she didn't want to do?'

Hetty looked at her son; he'd lost weight and there were more lines on his face. But he was still a fine figure of a man. 'No. In all honesty, I can't. But that still doesn't excuse you.'

'I know that, and I'm not trying to excuse myself.'

'Good, 'cause it won't work.'

'You might find this hard to believe, Mum, but I really am very sorry.'

'I believe you – thousands wouldn't,' she said in a controlled voice but with a hint of her natural humour.

'I'm surprised myself by just how badly I feel about it,' Josh confessed. 'It isn't like me to suffer from conscience. Must be getting soft in my old age.'

'Perhaps you're growing up at last,' she said pointedly.

'That's my mum – always one to speak her mind,' said Josh affectionately.

'I'm a bit long in the tooth to change my ways now.'

'I thought about you a lot when I was in Spain, you know. You and Dad.'

'You surprise me. I thought it was a case of out of sight, out of mind.'

Hetty couldn't know how far that was from the truth, and no one was more amazed about it than Josh himself. 'No, it wasn't like that at all,' he said solemnly.

'That's something to be grateful for, I suppose,' she said in a casual tone to hide the strong emotion his words evoked in her. 'Anyway, do I have your solemn promise that you won't do anything to provoke your brother?'

'Yeah.'

'Good. Now that that's settled, you can make me a cup o' tea and tell me what you got up to in Spain.' She paused, grinning. 'Or, at least, the part of it that's fit for a mother's ears.'

Chapter Twenty

When Janice and Chas went away with the Gallopers a few weeks later – leaving Barney in Maddie's care as usual – Sam took the unusual step of going with them. His primary motive was to avoid contact with Josh, Maddie guessed, but it also made it easier for him to sidestep the situation with her.

His attitude towards her recently had been vague and distant, almost as though their relationship had never happened. He rarely sought her company, and when they were together he was withdrawn and avoided any sort of physical contact.

Realising that he was under a strain, she'd made allowances, given him space to work through the trauma of Josh's return. But this tacit denial of anything special ever having existed between them had a frightening air of finality about it. God, how it hurt!

And the worst thing of all was the fact that he wouldn't talk about it. If she broached the subject he apologised profusely for having upset her then conveniently came up with some pressing matter he had to deal with elsewhere. It wasn't like Sam to be so evasive. He'd turned into a virtual stranger.

Mulling over the problem while he was away, Maddie made the painful decision to leave Fenner's as soon as she had handed Barney back to his parents.

She didn't see what else she could do. She certainly couldn't stay on here as things were between them. The whole thing was destroying her. There was a limit to the amount of pain she was prepared to take. Leaving the area altogether wasn't an option because she didn't want Clare to have to change schools. But they could stay with Pat and Bob at the pub until she found something more suitable. There might be a job going there too. Autumn was always a busy time in the licensed trade. Maddie decided to get things organised before the others returned.

The disruption to her life was something she dreaded. She wasn't, therefore, feeling well disposed towards the cause of it when he engaged her in conversation one evening while she was working in the little garden she had made around her wagon; she was tidying it ready for winter, sad in the knowledge that it would fall back into its natural state when she wasn't around to look after it.

'All on your own?' said Josh, drawing on a cigarette.

Dressed in old jeans and a navy thick-knit sweater, Maddie was on her knees weeding the flower beds around the rose bushes; she was proud of her garden and wanted to leave it looking nice. 'That's right. The children are over at the bowling alley,' she said coolly, looking up and pushing a stray lock of hair from her forehead, her cheeks glowing from the chill in the air.

'It must be like Christmas every day for those two, having access to a bowling alley,' he remarked casually.

'One of the perks of having connections with the management.'

'The pavilion is really quite something,' Josh remarked. 'Mum has told me that it was all your idea.'

Maddie nodded.

'Seems you came up with a winner.'

'Yes, it does seem that way,' she said, in no mood for false modesty.

'It gave me quite a shock when I came back and saw it there, all lit up with neon signs,' said Josh. 'The old place didn't look the same.'

'There have been quite a few changes while you've been away.'

'So I've noticed.' He paused, drawing on his cigarette. 'Rumour has it that you and Sam are an item these days.'

'We were . . . that's all in the past tense now, though,' she said, pulling a weed out of the ground with unnecessary force.

'You've split up?'

'It seems that way.' Resentment towards him blasted through her and Maddie blurted out, 'And I have *you* to thank for that.'

'Me?'

'That's right. Sam's interest in me ended the instant he saw you again.'

Josh looked puzzled. 'My brother has cooled off towards you and *I'm* to blame?'

Put like that it did sound feeble, even Maddie could see that. 'You're deliberately misunderstanding me,' she protested.

'No, I'm not, honestly,' said Josh, seeming genuine. 'I'd really like to know how my coming back has come between you and Sam?'

'It's changed him. Presumably because you've brought back memories he'd managed to put behind him.' She threw the weed on to the pile in the bucket and stood up, looking at him. 'You do seem to have an uncanny knack for disrupting other people's lives.'

'Yeah,' he said, surprising her; she'd expected him to deny it.

'And that's something to be proud of, is it?'

'Not at all,' said Josh evenly. 'It's just a fact of life.' He glanced towards the bucket. 'As sure as weeds grow in flower beds, I upset other people's lives.'

Maddie was silent, taken aback by his capitulation. 'Why *did* you come back?' she asked after a while.

He considered the question, staring blankly ahead of him and exhaling smoke into the evening air. The light was fading and the pavilion lights looked even brighter in the dusk against the backdrop of trees, rich with autumn colours.

'I felt compelled to come back and make my peace with the family. I'm not sure why the need was so strong. Maybe because I have to end this chapter of my life before I can settle properly in Spain – or perhaps this place is in my blood after all and I should sell up in Spain and come back here. I don't know. I only knew that I couldn't go on as I was, being tormented by guilt and homesickness. I came on impulse – just left my manager running my bar and booked a flight home.'

'It never occurred to you to consider the effect your return would have on other people's lives, of course.'

'What are you saying?' he asked, giving her a hard look. 'That it would have been better if I'd never got in touch with the family again?'

She remembered how she'd felt when Clare went missing, and his mother's anguish when Josh had disappeared. There was a new bloom about Hetty since he'd been back – as though someone had physically lifted a weight from her shoulders. Maddie imagined how desperate she herself would feel if Clare walked out of her life one day and she never heard from her again. 'No, of course it wouldn't have been better,' she admitted.

'But you still wish I hadn't?'

'From a selfish point of view, yes. But for your parents' sake, I'm very glad you did.'

'You don't really think you've lost Sam because I've come back, though, surely?'

'It feels that way because everything was wonderful until the moment you turned up.'

'All I've done is stirred up his feelings for Tania again, and if he was really over her he wouldn't have had a problem with that. God knows I spelled out the truth clearly enough to him – that she was in love with *me*, not him. You'd have thought that would have cured him once and for all. Until Sam gets his head around that he'll never be able to move on and find happiness with someone else.'

'He *had* learned to accept that it was you she wanted,' said Maddie. 'But seeing you again has upset him to such an extent I don't think he knows what he feels any more.'

'Then it's high time he pulled himself together and got his feelings and his life sorted out,' said Josh briskly. 'Okay, I admit I'm a prize bastard. I had an affair with my brother's wife, I tried to let my cousin take the blame for my negligence on the fairground, and I went away and didn't even let my own mother know where I was or get in touch to see if she and Dad were all right. All unforgivable sins. But that doesn't make *every single thing* that's wrong with the world my fault.'

'Of course not,' said Maddie in a warmer tone because she could see that what he said made sense. If Sam had really loved her he wouldn't have let those echoes of the past split them up. 'I shouldn't have blamed you.' She sighed. 'I'm just so . . . so desperately unhappy. Things had been going really well. I thought we had a future together. Then Sam just shuts me out of his life completely, as though there was never anything between us.'

'What do you plan to do about it then?'

'There's nothing more I can do,' Maddie said. 'I've tried talking to him and he doesn't want to know. So I'm leaving Fenner's when they all get back and Barney is back with his parents.'

Josh looked shocked. 'That's a bit drastic, isn't it?'

'What Sam's done to me is drastic. One minute he's my lover – the next he's a stranger. It will be just too painful for me to carry on working with him and living on his doorstep.' Maddie gave a wry grin. 'And I can hardly expect him to leave, since I'm the outsider.'

'I wouldn't say that, Maddie, not after all this time,' said Josh. 'But I can see why you would want to leave.'

She studied his face, observing the lines around his eyes, the leaner contours. 'You've changed,' she commented.

'In what way?'

Grinning, she said, 'You seem slightly less hateful.'

He laughed. 'A double-edged compliment if ever I heard one.'

'Just being honest.'

'No more than I deserve, I suppose.' His expression became serious. 'I do feel different though.'

'A reformed character?'

'What, me? I wouldn't know how,' he said, adding thoughtfully, 'But I have noticed changes in myself. I worry much more than I used to.'

'Do you know why?'

'A number of things, I suppose. Getting older. Living abroad.' He drew in a sharp breath. 'And, of course, Tania's death had a profound effect on me. I was absolutely devastated by it. I don't think I'll ever get over it.'

'You really *did* love her, then?'

'Yeah, I *really* did.' His eyes glazed over. 'I wish now we'd gone away together as she wanted to. She'd be alive if we had.'

'No point in torturing yourself with those sort of thoughts.'

'I held back to save hurting Sam, and he was hurt even more in the end.'

'Yeah, well . . . it's all water under the bridge now, isn't it?' Maddie shivered and hugged herself as the evening dampness began to penetrate her clothes. 'I think it's time I went inside.'

'It is getting a bit chilly.'

'Fancy joining me for a cup of coffee?' she invited him.

'Well, well, do I detect a glimpse of an olive branch?'

'Life's too short to be at war with people,' she said, feeling at ease with Josh for the first time ever. 'Come on in.'

'Thanks, I'd love to join you,' he said, and followed her inside.

'*Leaving*?' said Sam incredulously. 'You're leaving Fenner's altogether?'

'That's right,' said Maddie. 'I'll work out my notice, though.'

He looked very distressed. 'But you can't leave, Maddie.'

'I can, you know.'

'But—'

'You'll soon find a replacement.'

'That isn't what I meant.'

'Isn't it?'

'No.'

They were alone in the office. He had come in to ask Maddie to chase up some maintenance materials they had on order and she had seized the opportunity to give in her notice.

'What *do* you mean, then?'

'Well . . . us,' he said. 'What about us?'

Maddie stood up purposefully and walked around the desk to face him. 'You've made it very obvious that there is no more us,' she said grimly.

'I didn't mean to . . . I didn't want us to finish altogether,' he said lamely.

She gave a dry laugh. 'Am I supposed to be made of stone or something?' she said, voice harsh with pain. 'Do you think there's no limit to my tolerance . . . to the amount of pain I can endure? Do you expect me always to be here waiting while you go through the next emotional crisis over your dead wife?'

'Well, no, of course not.'

'You do surprise me.'

'Maddie . . .'

'I tell you, Sam, there *is* a limit to what I can put up with and I have now reached that limit.'

'This isn't like you, Maddie,' he said in a conciliatory manner.

'I can't take any more punishment, that's why,' she said. 'I waited a long time for you. Ever since Tania died I've been there for you. You didn't want love then so I gave you friendship. Then – when you did want love – I was there for you with that too. And all I get in return is the door slammed in my face the minute your brother comes back to stir up all your damned memories. You're far too busy licking your old wounds to bother about how I feel.'

'I'm so sorry . . .'

'And so am I,' she said, angry and despairing. 'If you want to waste your life remembering how much you loved Tania, go ahead. But don't expect me to stay around to watch.'

Shifting from one foot to the other, he looked worried and bewildered, as though he was out of his depth in this situation. 'I've obviously hurt you very much.'

'*Hurt me?*You've nigh on pulverised me,' said Maddie, fury driving her on and keeping the tears at bay. 'But no more. Oh, no, I've had enough. As soon as I've worked my notice, I'm off to make a new start – to get on with the rest of my life.'

As he moved towards her, Maddie shrank back. 'Don't come near me,' she said, struggling against tears. 'Go away and leave me to get on with my work.'

Sam didn't move – just stood there looking pale and stricken.

'All right, if you won't go, I will,' said Maddie with a sob in her voice. 'I'll have my coffee break at home in my wagon this morning.'

She rushed from the office, leaving Sam standing where he was in a state of shock.

That evening Josh went to his brother's wagon and demanded to be let in.

'I've nothing to say to you,' Sam growled.

'Well, I've plenty to say to you, mate,' said Josh, who had met a heartbroken Maddie rushing out of the office that morning.

'Get lost!'

Pushing past him, Josh marched into Sam's living room and sat down on the settee.

'You've got a bloody cheek!' said Sam, following him. 'Barging in here . . .'

'Oh, stop moaning, for God's sake, man, and sit down and listen.'

Sam glared at him. 'Say what you have to say then, and get out,' he said, perching on the edge of an armchair.

'Just answer me this,' said Josh. 'Are you prepared to lose the chance of happiness with a woman who loves you because of memories of a dead woman who didn't give a damn about you?'

Sam leapt to his feet and lunged at his brother, dragging him to his feet.

'Go on, have a pop at me if it'll make you feel better,' said Josh, staring into his brother's face and making no attempt to fight back. 'But it won't make you happy in the long run.'

'You wife stealer!'

'Tania didn't need stealing, mate,' said Josh. 'She made all the running.'

'You *would* say that.'

'Yes, I would, because it happens to be true,' said Josh. 'Think back on your marriage and take an honest look at it. You had a

240

terrible life with Tania and you damned well know it.'

Sam let go of him and sat down slowly, looking bleak.

'I was the bloke she came to, to escape from her marriage, remember?' Josh continued, determined to make his brother see sense. 'I saw the two of you together. You were never right for each other and it's time you admitted it. Anyway, she's dead . . . it's over. Time for you to let go.'

'Shut up!'

'Not until I've had my say. Do you love Maddie?'

'Of course I do.'

'What are you waiting for then? Go and put things right.'

'Get out.'

Josh stood up. 'I'm on my way. But when you've lost her and you're missing her like hell, don't say I didn't warn you.'

'Why should you care?'

'Dunno, mate,' said Josh with a touch of his old nonchalance. 'It isn't normally in my nature to bother about other people.' He paused, his expression hardening. 'Perhaps it's because I think one lonely bloke in the family is enough.'

'You? Lonely!' said Sam cynically. 'You can have any woman you want.'

'But I don't want any woman. The only woman I ever wanted is dead,' Josh told him. 'Tania doesn't need the two of us grieving for her. I'm still doing enough for an army.' He walked to the door. 'Think about it.'

And without another word he left.

Sam did think about it – for a long time. Then he went into the bedroom and took the jeweller's box out of the drawer and opened it. He stared at the diamonds gleaming on their bed of velvet – just as he had the day he'd planned to give the ring to Maddie – and felt deeply ashamed.

Josh's return had unlocked repressed memories. All the wrong thoughts and feelings had risen up, crushing Sam's true emotions. What a fool he'd been! What a selfish, immature idiot. It would serve him right if Maddie didn't give him another chance.

A surge of love for her overwhelmed him, destroying all doubt and confusion. Tania's hold over him had been caused by the heightened intensity of the unattainable, the fact that she had always kept him at arm's length. The fear that he might have lost Maddie created a similar sensation.

He loved her – totally, helplessly. He loved her blue eyes and warm smile, her courage and sense of fun. He loved her slender body and great legs – everything about her. He couldn't bear to lose her now. He and Maddie were right together. The whole obsession with Tania now seemed pale in comparison.

Putting the ring into his pocket, he hurried over to her caravan and tapped on the front door.

Maddie was shocked to see him. 'Oh, it's you,' she said coolly, though her heart was racing. 'What do you want?'

'We need to talk.'

'There's nothing more to say.'

'Please, Maddie . . .'

Still hurting from what she'd been through because of his complicated emotions, and terrified of being let down again, she said, 'Leave me alone, Sam, please.'

'You've every right to be angry. I've been a selfish fool and I hate myself for hurting you,' he said, tears glistening in his eyes. 'But I love you, Maddie, more than anything in the world.'

Relief and pleasure surged through her but she was still afraid. 'Until tomorrow, when something happens to remind you of Tania again,' she said, forcefully.

'No, I'm over that, I promise you,' he said ardently. 'It's you I love. Only you!'

She wanted to believe him *so* much. But she had thought he loved her before and he'd turned back to Tania. 'How can I be sure of that?'

He spread his hands, appealing to her. 'I know it's asking a lot after what I've put you through but I'm begging you to find it in your heart to trust me.' He paused, looking at her. 'What I felt for Tania was an unhealthy obsession, like an illness. I realise that now. I can't explain exactly how I know this, but I do know it's over now.'

'Oh, Sam, if only that was true.'

'It is true.' He jumped back down the steps and went down on his knees on the ground, looking up at her. 'Will you marry me, Maddie?'

Seeing him so full of sincerity, her love for him was overwhelming.

'Please say you will,' he said. 'I really do love you.'

'Oh, Sam,' she said, laughing and crying simultaneously. 'I love you too. So get up off your knees and come inside.'

Maddie gazed at the ring which was now safely fitted on her finger. 'It's beautiful, Sam,' she said. 'I adore it.'

'They said at the shop that they'd change it if you prefer something else.'

'No, this one is perfect. I can't wait to show it to Clare.'

'Where is she?'

'Next door with Barney.'

'I hope she'll approve of me as a stepfather?'

'Don't worry, she will. I've already spoken to her about it.'

'You were that sure of me?'

'Before you went all moody on me, yes, I was,' she said candidly.

'And you can be again,' he said. 'I won't let you down.'

'I know.'

'You, me and Clare, together as a family. That's all I want.'

Maddie's brow puckered into a frown. 'There is the little matter of my getting a divorce from Dave, though,' she reminded him.

'Yes.' Sam looked thoughtful. 'Don't worry. We'll go and visit him together.'

'Visit him?' She had serious doubts about such a plan. 'I was thinking more in terms of a letter. I thought contact was usually made through a solicitor in divorce cases?'

'I was thinking that it might get things moving quicker if we faced him ourselves. He could just ignore a letter,' Sam told her.

'He isn't an easy man to get on with, Sam, I warn you.'

'I'm not worried about that,' he said cheerfully. 'Anyway, he might have mellowed a bit after all this time.'

'It's possible, I suppose,' said Maddie, but she wasn't convinced. 'He's probably got someone else himself by now.'

'I should think so.'

'But if you'd really rather not go to see him, we'll do it the other way.'

Thinking about it, Maddie knew she must face up to Dave before starting a new life with Sam. Cut the ties for ever. 'No, you're right, it'll be best if we actually see him.'

'You won't have to face him on your own,' he reminded her. 'I'll be with you every step of the way.' He paused, remembering what had happened when Clare had gone to see her father. 'He's moved house, though, hasn't he?'

'That isn't a problem,' said Maddie. 'He's got relatives in the Barking area. I can find out where he is from them.'

'We'll go over to Barking one day in the next couple of weeks then, yeah?'

Maddie nodded. 'And in the meantime, I intend to enjoy every single minute of our engagement.' She gave him a wicked grin. 'I've waited long enough for it.'

Sam smiled. 'I must have been mad. Can you forgive me?'

'Consider it done.'

'In that case I think we should start making up for lost time,' he said, taking her in his arms.

Chapter Twenty One

'What shall we do now?' Clare enquired of Barney on Saturday afternoon; they had just arrived back at the park with Marlon, having taken him for a walk.

'Dunno,' he said, unleashing the Alsation now that they were on home ground.

Approaching their teens and beyond childish games, they were at a loose end – Barney because Brentford was playing away this week, Clare because her girlfriends from school were all busy with their families today. The end of the season meant that they had lost their little fairground earners too.

The place was almost deserted on this cold, dismal afternoon, the sky an unrelenting grey, strong winds whistling through the closed rides and shuttered side-shows. All but a few of the maintenance workers had finished for the weekend and gone home, and the residents were inside their living-wagons keeping warm. Although the pavilion was open on a Saturday afternoon, its doors were firmly closed against the weather.

'Surely you can think of something?' said Clare, sighing with boredom.

'We could go bowling, if you like?' he suggested, his dark curly hair blowing in the wind.

'No, I don't fancy that today.'

'You choose then.'

'What about a mooch round the shops?' she suggested. 'We could stop by the record shop and listen to the new Monkees hit – "Daydream Believer". My friend's got it . . . it's really cool.'

'Okay,' Barney agreed amiably. 'At least it'll be somethin' to do.'

'If you take the dog back to Eric, I'll go and tell our mums where we're going.' Clare pulled the hood of her anorak more tightly around her face against the wind which had whipped high colour into her cheeks, making her eyes look even bluer.

'Come on, boy,' said Barney to the dog who was sniffing contentedly around nearby.

In the next instant, however, the sudden appearance of a cat streaking past completely undid the strict training of the normally obedient dog who shot off across the fairground in hot pursuit of the tabby.

Clare and Barney tore after him, afraid he'd find his way off the park and into the busy road while in this reckless mood. Following him around the back of the Ghost Train, they couldn't see him anywhere.

'He must have followed the cat in there,' said Clare, pointing towards the ride where maintenance work seemed to be in progress as the emergency door was open.

As Clare and Barney were strictly forbidden to go inside any of the ride buildings unless accompanied by an adult, he poked his head through the doorway and called to the workmen. There was no reply.

'The light's on and the door's open,' said Barney. 'So there should be someone in there.'

'The men have probably gone for their tea-break and not bothered to close the place up 'cause they know they won't be long,' suggested Clare, shivering against the wind.

They both shouted into the building but there was no response.

'I suppose I'd better go in there and get Marlon,' Barney suggested.

'You'll be in terrible trouble if anyone finds out.'

'We'll both be in even worse trouble if any harm comes to that dog or he wrecks anything in there.' Barney looked around. 'Anyway, they won't find out – there's no one about.'

'I'll come with you then.'

'Don't do that. There's no point in us both getting into trouble.'

But she went with him anyway. After a final look around they went furtively into the building, far too caught up in the daring of what they were doing to notice the door slamming shut behind them in the wind.

Josh was at a loose end this afternoon too. Bored and lethargic, he was sitting in front of the television set staring vacantly at a sports programme. The days seemed long and more aimless since he'd been back. He couldn't even kill time working on the fair as it was out of season. Sam had the maintenance work all sewn up, too, and had made it obvious that any offer of help from his brother would be resented. To be honest Josh was glad. Absence hadn't made the heart grow fonder so far as fairground work was concerned. He didn't belong here. But would he belong anywhere without Tania? He doubted it.

Still, at least his brother was looking a lot happier since getting engaged to Maddie a couple of days ago. He didn't appear to have had a change of heart towards Josh, though. He was still cool and distant whenever their paths crossed. Josh didn't blame him; he didn't like himself much either.

So – what was he going to do with himself for the rest of the day? Cinema, the pub later on, go up the West End for a wander round?

None of the options appealed to him. All he was doing was filling in time, wasting his life. He'd stayed on here because he hadn't felt able to face the loneliness of his life in Spain. But he was bored here so may as well go back. Yeah, why not? At least he had the business to occupy him there. Maybe now that he'd been home and faced the family, it would be easier to settle abroad, especially as he intended to keep in touch with the folks and come home to visit on a regular basis in future. He could even invite them to Spain for a holiday.

Having made the decision, he felt a whole lot better. His first move must be to tell his parents. He didn't think they would be too upset by his departure, not with the promise of regular contact and a holiday in the sun to look forward to.

Feeling more positive than he had in ages, Josh was fired with energy; he began to tidy the place – emptying ashtrays, collecting the build-up of dirty teacups and taking them to the kitchen.

The sink was under the window overlooking the fairground; from here he could see the back of various rides including the Ghost Train. 'The young buggers!' he muttered, filling the washing-up bowl with water and watching Clare and Barney look stealthily around them before going inside. He washed the cups, recalling the fun he'd had as a boy playing in the Ghost Train out of season with his brother and the other kids, which was all the more exciting because it was strictly out of bounds. 'Their mothers will skin 'em alive if they find out.'

Smiling to himself at happy childhood memories, he rinsed the cups and left them to drain on the draining board. Then he headed for the bathroom to get smartened up for the visit to his parents.

Although Clare and Barney could hear Marlon making a low growling noise somewhere inside the Ghost Train building, it took them a while actually to locate him because they had to follow the sharply curved rail track which was flanked on either side by plywood partitions painted black with garish images in brightly coloured luminous paint: ghosts, ghouls, skeletons. The idea of the partitioning was to increase the thrill for the punters by hiding other cars from view and creating a feeling of isolation in this 'terrifying' place.

Because maintenance work was in progress there were ladders and tools and piles of wood shavings scattered about on the concrete floor.

Marlon and the tabby were finally located in confrontation near a huge plaster skeleton which would light up horrifically and lift its arms when the ride was operating. Strategically placed along the track were levers which were tripped by the moving cars to activate the special effects.

It was difficult to tell which was more daunted by the other: the cat or Marlon. The former had its back arched and was hissing and spitting at the latter who was making a low rumbling sound in his throat but keeping his distance and trembling violently.

Clare talked soothingly to the dog to calm him, stroking and patting him, while Barney attached his lead. Seeing its chance, the cat escaped at high speed.

'Now that we've found Marlon, let's get out of here,' said Clare, finding it creepy even though the lights were on.

But having a mischievous streak in his nature, Barney couldn't resist the chance of some fun. He went over to the wooden lever and touched it whereupon the skeleton turned a ghastly shade of green with red flashing eyes, its great arms raised, a siren-like scream filling the building.

Clare shrieked, then giggled nervously.

'It's all right,' Barney reassured her. 'It's only special lighting, luminous paint and a simple wind siren.'

'It's still scary, though. Come on – let's go.'

But now that the dog was safely to hand, Barney was in the mood for devilment. He touched another lever which raised a hideous, hollow-eyed corpse from a coffin, accompanied by a loud creaking noise and a terrible moaning sound.

'Barney, stop it,' said Clare, hanging on to him as they continued along the winding track, treading through scattered newspaper and sweet wrappers.

'*Papier-mâché*, plaster and sound effects, that's all the ghosts and things are,' he said. 'We might as well have some fun as we're in here.'

'If they hear the noises outside, we won't half cop it.'

'They won't hear them 'cause they're all inside with the doors shut,' he said, throwing caution to the wind in his youthful exuberance.

Giggling and squealing, they progressed along the route, activating ghosts in white billowing shrouds, skeletons and ghouls of varying degrees of hideousness, a hairy giant spider that glowed red, and bats with green eyes and flapping wings. As if all that wasn't enough, there were cobwebs that swung down and brushed their faces and gravestones that became eerily shrouded in mist at the touch of a lever.

At the front of the building where the track ran through swing doors, several cars were lined up and various tools spread around as though the workmen had been in the middle of a job here just before they left.

'It doesn't half pong in here,' remarked Clare.

'Bound to smell a bit stale – being all closed up for winter.'

'It isn't only a stale smell,' she said, sniffing. 'I can smell burning too.'

'I can't smell anything.'

'Let's go.'

'Yeah, I suppose we'd better,' he agreed at last. 'We can't get out through the front way, though, 'cause the shutters are down outside.'

They made their way towards the rear of the building, avoiding horrible artifacts. The dog became overexcited suddenly, barking and straining at the lead.

'He must have got the scent of that cat again,' said Barney, bending over and stroking the animal's head. 'Hey, calm down, boy.'

'Can you smell burning now?' asked Clare, her nose wrinkling.

He sniffed. 'Oh, yeah. Somebody must be having a bonfire outside,' he said, leading the way to the exit.

'That must be what's upsetting Marlon. I'll be glad to get out of here.'

'Me too.'

As they turned the last corner where the partitioning parted for access to the emergency exit, they both stood rooted to the spot as the plywood panels burst into flames in front of them.

'Blimey!' gasped Barney. 'One of the workmen must have left a cigarette burning and it's set the rubbish alight.'

'There's a notice saying No Smoking,' said Clare in a small voice.

'That obviously didn't stop 'em,' he said. 'Come on, quick.'

He guided her and the dog past the flames, smoke already filling the airless building, the fire spitting and crackling as it swept along the wooden partitioning. They stumbled to the door, choking on the flames, the dog barking and howling.

Barney pushed the door.

'Hurry up!' said Clare.

'I can't open it,' he told her, coughing. 'It's stuck.'

'Oh, no!' She wanted to be sick; the building was already an inferno, the smoke so thick they could hardly see.

Struggling to keep hold of the dog who was tugging and straining to be free, Barney threw himself against the door.

'It just won't open.'

Coughing and retching as the smoke crept into her throat and lungs, Clare looked with dismay at the leaping flames. 'We're trapped,' she sobbed into the handkerchief she held clutched to her face.

Ready for the visit to his parents' house, Josh came out of his wagon.

'Christ!' he gasped, seeing flames light up the building opposite. 'The kids might still be in there.'

He tore towards the blaze, meeting Sam and Maddie on the way. Chas, Janice and Eric were also hurrying in that direction.

'Anyone phoned the fire brigade?' called Josh.

'Aunt Sibyl's doing it,' said Janice.

'The building's burning like a ruddy tinder box,' said Chas. 'It's all that wood in there.'

'Still, at least there's no one inside,' said Janice, sounding relieved. 'The workmen had gone for their tea.'

Josh's heart lurched. 'The kids might be in there.'

'What?' gasped Sam.

'I saw 'em go in the back door about ten minutes ago,' he explained. 'Dunno if they're still in there. . .'

'My God . . . I bet they are!' Maddie ran towards the fire.

Sam went after her. 'You can't go in there,' he said, grabbing her arm and pulling her back.

'My daughter might be inside,' she screamed, voice distorted with terror. 'So don't try and stop me.'

'You're *not* going in there.' He pushed her back and ran towards the blaze himself.

'Sam . . . Sam!' she shrieked.

But he had already disappeared into the smoke.

'God help him,' sobbed Maddie, biting back a feeling of rising hysteria.

Janice was also in a state of panic and tried to follow Sam but was quickly drawn back by Chas. The arrival of Sybil with the news that the fire brigade were on their way eased the situation slightly.

When Eric made a move towards the fire he was immediately restrained by his mother. 'Leave it to the professionals, son,' she said. 'The brigade will be here in a minute.'

'Where the hell are they?' said Maddie, distraught.

In all the chaos no one noticed Josh running towards the burning building – until he was about to go in.

'Josh is going in there, too,' cried Janice. 'Oh, God, the fool . . . the brave fool.'

'Isn't one hero in the family enough?' said Sybil anxiously.

Stupefied with fear and horror, Maddie watched Josh follow his brother into the conflagration.

Having forced the door open with a crowbar, Sam entered the building with a handkerchief held to his mouth. The heat inside was overpowering, scorching his skin and making his throat and chest ache. His eyes were streaming and he could hardly see an inch in front of him through the smoke.

Relief felt sweet when he spotted the children, huddled together on the floor with the barking dog between them. Because of the thickness of the smoke they hadn't realised the door had been opened. Thank God I've found them, thought Sam, stumbling towards them. He had almost reached them when something hit him across the shoulders and he realised that a burning rafter had fallen from the roof, knocking him over and falling across his leg with a sickening crunch.

Pinned to the floor, he shouted to the children to let them know that the door was open. But his voice couldn't be heard above the roar of the blaze. He wasn't sure if they were conscious; it looked from here as though they both had their eyes closed.

He had never felt more powerless in his life. Judging by the pain, his leg was broken. This, added to the effects of the fire, made him feel faint and he slumped back, drenched in sweat and drifting in and out of consciousness. In his feeble state he vaguely noticed a singed tabby cat shoot past him heading for the door.

Clare had her eyes closed because they hurt if she opened them. But hearing someone call, she opened them a fraction – just wide enough to see Uncle Sam coming towards them. But even as her heart leapt with hope he fell, and she held on to Barney's hand even tighter.

She tried to get up to help Sam but her legs buckled and she slipped back to the ground. She was past fear, and felt too ill to panic. Her throat and chest were hurting, she felt sick and faint and couldn't stop coughing. Barney was coughing a lot too, and he'd been sick several times. Neither of them was speaking because it was too difficult in the smoke. Nothing could save them now, she thought, but at least they were together.

Then suddenly she was being lifted; strong arms carried her until she could feel the shock of cold air on her face and was aware of the fact that she was shivering violently.

Back inside the burning building, having lifted the children and the dog to safety, Josh struggled to remove the rafter from Sam's leg. Hardly able to breathe, his skin smarting, he finally managed it with one hefty shove which took the skin off his own hands. In so much discomfort as to be almost beyond feeling, he dragged the barely conscious Sam to his feet and half carried him towards the door.

'Thank God for that,' he muttered as the doorway loomed through the smoke.

There was a loud crackling sound and Josh reeled with new pain as a falling timber struck his head. With a supreme effort he pushed Sam through the doorway before his own legs gave way and he himself fell to the floor just inside. Before he passed out he heard the clang of the fire engine's bell.

Although the children weren't seriously hurt they had to go to hospital for treatment for minor burns and smoke inhalation. They went in the first ambulance with Maddie and Janice. Chas followed in his car with Sybil and Eric, stopping off on the way to pick up Hetty and Vic.

Sam and Josh travelled together in another ambulance. Sam's leg

250

wasn't broken, after all, just very badly bruised, and he had some nasty burns. Josh's condition was much more serious. Sam could hardly bear to look at his blistered face – red raw and bleeding. Josh was in such agony, one of the ambulance team gave him a shot of something to calm him.

Sam sat up and looked at Josh who was lying down on the other stretcher. 'I owe you, mate, for saving my life,' he said emotionally, bitterness now replaced by gratitude and affection.

'You'd have done the same for me,' Josh managed to get out through scorched lips.

'You're a hero,' said Sam.

'You were first in there,' Josh reminded him.

'But you got me out – you saved the kids.'

'Leave off, you'll have me in tears in a minute.' Josh's words were barely audible, his lungs badly scorched and leaving him breathless.

'Me and the kids wouldn't be alive now if it hadn't been for you.'

'The little sods were doing what we used to do when we were boys,' said Josh, wincing. 'Remember, Sam?'

'I remember.'

'Childhood, eh. Great, wannit?'

'Yeah.'

'We were never close when it was over . . . not once we grew up.'

'No.'

'A pity, that.'

Sam was surprised by the remark. 'You never wanted it.'

'I know I didn't – always had too much to hide, I suppose.' Josh took an agonising breath. 'It's too late now.'

'Don't say that.'

'It's true.'

'No!'

Josh closed his eyes for a moment as though to gather his strength. 'I'm glad you and Maddie are back together.'

'Me too.'

'Tell Janice to stop mucking about and get herself spliced,' his brother said. 'She won't do better than Chas. Better late than never.'

'You can tell her yourself when we get to the hospital,' said Sam. 'Chas is taking her down there in the car.'

'I don't think I'm gonna make it, mate,' said Josh through his laboured breathing.

'"Course you're gonna make it,' said Sam, desperate for that to be true.

'Yeah . . . well, just in case I don't, you make sure you tell her not to end up lonely like me. Marry Chas and be sure of him. He's a good bloke.'

'I'll tell her,' said Sam, his heart like lead. 'But you're gonna come through this – don't worry.'

251

'I'm not worried,' said Josh in a tone of calm resignation that frightened Sam.

'I'd like to shake your hand like a mate but I don't think I'd better,' he said because Josh's hands were badly burned.

'No, don't. It might drop off if you do.'

'Thanks for saving our lives,' said Sam again, because it seemed vital that his brother knew how grateful he was.

'Don't go on about it,' said Josh painfully. 'Just don't make a habit of walking into fires, eh?'

'You have my word on that.'

'I should hope so, too.'

'Are we mates again?' asked Sam.

'That would make me a happy man.' Josh swallowed painfully. 'And sorry about everything.'

'Forget it.'

'I'll never do that, mate.'

'It's all in the past,' Sam was able to say truthfully at last. 'You just concentrate on getting better.'

'Yeah, I'll do that,' said Josh, his eyes closing. 'I just wanna sleep . . . get away from this bloody awful pain.'

By the time they got to the hospital his condition had deteriorated dramatically and the ambulance team were giving him oxygen. The doctor told his relatives that Josh had suffered very serious smoke damage to his lungs as well as burns. They were doing everything they could but there wasn't much hope.

When Sam was eventually settled in a ward, having had his wounds treated, he asked the doctor how his brother was and was told that he had died. The shock stunned him. To have felt so close to Josh for the first time since they were children, only to lose him again, was almost too much to bear.

Numbly he watched the family troop down the ward and gather around his bed in a sad little group. The women were crying; the men looked as if they wanted to.

'I know it isn't much consolation, Mum,' said Sam, taking his mother's hand in his bandaged ones. 'But Josh was a brave man – a hero.'

'I know he was. And so were you.' Hetty looked terrible, ashen-faced, her eyes raw from crying. 'I'm proud of you both.'

'He proved to us all what he was really made of at the end,' said Sam.

'He certainly did,' said his mother, her voice thick with emotion. 'God, it hurts, though. I mean, you don't expect to outlive your children.'

'I know, Mum,' Sam said gently. 'But I wouldn't be here if it wasn't for him. I'm proud to call Josh my brother.'

252

'Does this mean you made it up with him before he died?' she asked.

'Yeah, we were mates at the end.'

'Thank God for that!'

They lapsed into silence, everyone lost in their own thoughts.

'Where's Maddie?' asked Sam.

'With the children,' Janice informed him. 'They're keeping them in overnight, just to make sure they're all right.'

'Oh, I see . . . I think I'll hobble down to the ward to see them then.'

Maddie was sitting in a chair by Clare's bed which was empty, Clare having gone with Barney to watch television in the day room.

Although Maggie was enormously shocked and saddened by Josh's death, she wasn't as deeply affected as his family which was why she'd stayed away from them for the moment. She'd felt they needed time on their own together to cope with the first terrible impact of their grief. She would go and see Sam when she thought the moment was right.

At the sound of someone coming into the ward, she looked up to see him hobbling towards her on crutches.

'What are you doing here?' she asked, full of concern. 'You should be resting.'

'I missed you,' he said, sitting down painfully beside her. 'We were all there together – everybody except you.' He looked at the empty bed and she told him where the children were. 'Why didn't you join us when you weren't needed here?'

'Well, you know,' Maddie said hesitantly. 'I thought it was a family thing.'

'You *are* family . . . and soon you'll legally be a Fenner,' said Sam. 'I want you with me, Maddie. I need you.'

'I was just being diplomatic.'

'I know, but it isn't necessary.'

Seeing the sadness in his eyes, she said, 'You were both very brave – your mother should be proud of her sons.'

'I think she is.'

Maddie frowned. 'Josh died before I had a chance to thank him for saving my daughter . . . and the man I love.'

'He didn't seem to need any thanks,' said Sam, tears rolling down his cheeks. 'I think the fact that he'd done it was enough for him.'

'You and he . . .?'

'Yeah, he died knowing I'd forgiven him.'

'Good.'

'It's odd,' said Sam thickly. 'Josh never wanted to be mates with me up until he went away – not since we were kids. But in the end it really seemed to matter to him.'

253

'Perhaps he'd finally worked out what was important to him.'
'Yeah, I think he had.'

Chapter Twenty Two

While Sam and the rest of the family struggled to come to terms with Josh's death, Maddie put her own personal affairs to one side and did what she could to help them.

An official enquiry into the fire found the most likely cause to have been a cigarette but none of the maintenance workers admitted to breaking the No Smoking rule. The matter was eventually dropped and plans for a new Ghost Train put in hand.

Despite Hetty's gallant determination that life must go on, she was visibly withered by grief. She looked smaller, her face emaciated and now covered in wrinkles. She told Maddie that her one comfort was the fact that she could be proud of her son. Josh's last courageous act had wiped the slate clean so far as she was concerned.

Maddie guessed that Hetty – like any loving mother – would always mourn the loss of her first born, quietly inside herself. Maddie hoped that her restored pride in him would help to sustain her through these painful days.

The shelving of Maddie's own plans came as something of a reprieve. While eager to get divorce proceedings underway so that she could marry Sam, she dreaded the thought of seeing Dave again. Even knowing that Sam would be with her didn't stop her nerves jangling at the mere thought of being in the same room as her husband, so deep were the scars of his relentless cruelty.

So she bided her time, being there for Sam and the others, and waiting until he was ready to make their trip to Barking. She did take the necessary step of telephoning an uncle of Dave's to obtain his new address, though; he'd moved to a smaller flat in the same area, she learned.

Nobody felt much like celebrating Christmas that year but they made the effort for the sake of the children. It wasn't the Fenner way to be defeated by sorrow. Hetty invited everyone to the house for Christmas dinner and – because they knew she needed to keep busy – no one suggested that it might be too much for her.

The atmosphere was determinedly cheerful with everyone pulling crackers and wearing paper hats. But the merriment was punctuated with sombre silences when the effort became too much.

When they got to the Christmas pudding stage of the meal, the mood was suddenly lifted by a surprise announcement from Janice.

'I know we've not long had a funeral in the family and we're officially still in mourning,' she said. 'But Chas and I are going to cheer you all up with a wedding.'

'Well, stone me!' said Vic.

'I'd given up hope,' said Hetty, her sad eyes brightening.

'We've decided to tie the knot as soon as we can get it arranged.'

The approval was unanimous and everyone began to talk at once.

'So . . . what made you decide to do it, after all this time?' asked Sam.

His sister looked thoughtful. 'I suppose Josh's dying so suddenly made me think seriously . . . sort of clarified things,' she explained, looking around the table at them all. 'Josh told Sam just before he . . .' She swallowed hard. 'Just before he died to tell us to get on with it so I don't think he'd mind us getting married so soon after the funeral.'

'I'm damned sure he wouldn't,' said Vic, adding with a grin, 'One thing's for sure – no one can accuse you of rushing things.'

They all laughed.

'Your daughter is one stubborn woman,' said Chas jokingly to Hetty and Vic. 'It's taken a death in the family to get her to say yes.'

'Don't upset her or she might change her mind,' warned Hetty.

'She's only marrying me to cheer you all up,' said Chas, joshing. 'It isn't 'cause she's suddenly realised how much she loves me.'

He was wrong. Josh's death had brought Janice and Chas even closer and made her realise just how much she did love him. She couldn't get it out of her head that when Josh had woken up on that fateful Saturday he'd had his life ahead of him. By teatime he was dead. Life was too short and too precious to waste. Chas had been there for her through the good and bad times since they were in their teens. He'd proved his love to her a million times over. And that love had always been reciprocated even though she didn't make a great performance of showing it. She still didn't see marriage as the be all and end all of a relationship but she did think it was right for them now.

'It is, you know.' She turned to him beside her, eyes bright with tears, voice tender. 'You're everything to me.'

'Blimey,' said Barney with youthful disregard for tact. 'Mum's gone all soppy.'

'Don't knock it,' said Hetty. 'Your mum could do a lot worse than get a bit soppy over your dad now and again.'

The atmosphere was highly charged and Maddie felt a lump rise in her own throat. Despite the light-hearted banter, there was a great deal of sadness here today. She couldn't share their deep sense of loss but her empathy was total.

Hetty was also feeling emotional. She was grateful to everybody here for their wholehearted support since Josh's death. They were all doing everything they could to comfort her. But no one could – not really. Losing Josh was something that just had to be endured. There was no cure, no amount of kindness could ease the ache in her heart. All she could do was carry on.

'On the subject of weddings,' she said, turning her attention to Maddie and Sam, 'have you two done anything about getting Maddie's divorce underway so that you can start to think of a wedding date?'

'No . . . we haven't got around to it yet,' said Maddie. 'With everything that's happened.'

'The New Year is a good time for getting things done,' said Sybil.

'She's right,' said Sam, looking at Maddie. 'We ought to take that trip to Barking.'

'Yeah, I suppose we should,' she said, trying to hide her doubts.

Hetty turned her attention to Eric whose girlfriend hadn't been able to join them on this occasion. 'It's a pity Vera couldn't be here today.'

'She couldn't leave her mum on her own on Christmas Day.'

'She could have come too if I'd thought of it,' said Hetty.

'Never mind, he'll see her tomorrow, won't you, son?' said Sybil. 'She's coming to tea.'

'Home to Mum's for tea, eh?' said Chas, grinning at Eric. 'Things *are* getting serious. You'll be the next one to take the plunge.'

'Dunno about that,' he said in a serious tone because he didn't have much of a sense of humour.

'Take no notice of 'em, love,' said Sybil. 'They're pulling your leg.'

Hetty had serious doubts about the possibility of marriage for Eric and Vera. Could a couple as lacking in savvy as they were get married and manage on their own? She doubted it. 'Anyway we've enough weddings in the family to keep us occupied for the moment. What with our record-breaking courting couple finally making it legal . . . and, of course, Maddie and Sam.'

'Ours won't be for ages,' she said quickly. 'These things take time.'

'All the more reason to start the ball rolling – as soon as things get back to normal after the holiday,' said Sam, looking at her searchingly. 'What do you say?'

'Yes, of course,' she said, smiling to hide her inner trepidation.

Sam drove the car slowly around by the flats because there were so many children playing in the road, even though it was dark, and crowds of youths roaming the streets.

When they stopped outside the block where Dave lived, he turned to Maddie, taking her hand reassuringly.

'Don't worry,' he said. 'I'm here to see that no harm comes to you.'

257

Despite the bitterly cold weather on this January evening, she was soaked with perspiration; her heart was thumping so hard it was pounding in her head. 'I know, Sam,' she said, squeezing his hand gratefully.

The cowardly side of her nature was hoping that Dave wouldn't be at home. But this wasn't very likely because she had written to him to let him know that they were coming, explaining why they needed to see him and giving a definite time.

They made their way up the stone steps in the foul-smelling interior and past grafitti-covered walls until they came to a dingy brown door. Maddie rang the bell with a trembling hand.

The door was opened almost at once. 'Maddie.' Dave looked her over, smiling. 'How are you?'

'Fine.'

'You look well.'

'You too.'

'It's been a long time.' He paused, looking at Sam. 'Don't stand out there, mate – come on in, both of you.'

'This is Sam Fenner,' she said.

'Pleased to meet you,' said Dave, shaking Sam's hand.

Taken aback by the friendly welcome, she went inside, followed by Sam. The living room looked surprisingly clean but smelled stale. She wondered if it would have been so neat if they had turned up unexpectedly. Pieces of furniture that she recognised – the sideboard, the big black armchair that Dave had always used – brought back sickening memories of her life with him.

'You've moved house then?' she said.

'Yeah, I stayed on for a while at the other place after you left,' he said. 'Then I decided to get something smaller – with a lower rent.'

He hadn't lost his good looks, she noticed, those compelling eyes, the hard, sensuous mouth.

'So . . . how are things?' she asked by way of conversation.

'Mustn't grumble.'

'Still working at the same place?'

'Yeah, I'm foreman now.'

'Good for you.' Maddie cleared her throat nervously. 'You're still on your own then?'

'That's right.' His latest partner had moved out about a month ago; the silly cow had reckoned he was spiteful. Bloody cheek! 'But you're not, obviously.'

'No.'

Dave looked at Sam. 'You're planning on getting married then?'

'Yeah,' he said politely but in a tone that didn't invite argument. 'We thought it better to see you personally, rather than have you receive a solicitor's letter to let you know Maddie is filing for divorce.'

'I appreciate that, mate,' said Dave with astonishing cordiality.

'You've no objection to a divorce then?' said Sam, sounding relieved.

'No – not now. I would have . . . once upon a time. But not after all these years,' he said, looking at Maddie.

'I'm glad you feel like that,' she said rather lamely because he still had the power to make her feel guilty.

'I was very cut up about your leavin', naturally. In a hell of a state for ages,' he said to emphasise the point. 'But life goes on, dunnit? You learn to live with these things.'

'I had to go, Dave,' said Maddie, all the old terror flooding back, together with the need to justify herself to him.

'"Course you did, babe,' he said. 'I was right out of order.'

'Oh.' She could hardly believe she was hearing this.

'We've both moved on – you and me are past history,' he said. 'So the sooner we get it finalised legally, the better for us all. Let the solicitors sort it out, yeah? I'll get myself fixed up with one in the next few days.'

'Do you want to get married again then?' asked Maddie, unable to believe he would be this co-operative unless it was to his own advantage.

'No, not at the moment – but I might in the future,' he said casually. 'You never know your luck, do you?' He paused. 'Cuppa tea?'

Maddie shook her head.

'Not for me, thanks,' said Sam. 'We mustn't stay. It's frosty out and the roads will be getting a bit dodgy.'

It was almost as though Dave had reverted back to the good-looking charmer Maddie had fallen in love with all those years ago. Seeing him like this, it was hard to imagine that handsome face distorted with evil as he carried out acts of grotesque violence. He was being so nice she was almost beginning to feel sorry for him.

'Just as you like, mate,' said Dave easily.

'See you in court then – as they say,' Maddie dared to joke.

He nodded.

'I hope it doesn't get ugly,' she remarked chattily. 'I've heard that divorce cases sometimes do once the solicitors take over.'

'I don't see why ours should,' he said. 'Not as we both want it to go through. You certainly won't get any argument from me.'

'I'm so pleased we're able to be civilised about it.'

'No point in falling out, is there?' Dave said breezily. 'It's going to happen so we might as well stay friends.'

'Exactly.'

They made their way to the front door. As Maddie and Sam stepped outside, Dave said casually, 'Oh, there's just one thing . . . I might need to contact you if anything comes up about the divorce that I need to talk to you about. So can I have your phone number?'

Maddie felt a prickle of apprehension, the same feeling that had made her leave the address off her notepaper and go into central London to post the letter to him. 'I'm not sure . . .' she began.

'It doesn't matter if you'd rather not,' he said nonchalantly. 'I don't want to hold things up, that's all.'

Of course he needed a contact number. She was being paranoid. She rummaged in her bag for a scrap of paper and a biro, wrote the number down and handed it to him. After a little more stilted conversation, she and Sam left.

'Well, that wasn't so bad was it?' he said as they settled into their seats in the car.

'No . . . it wasn't,' said Maddie in a preoccupied manner; Dave's attitude still puzzled her.

'He was much more reasonable than I expected.'

'Yes – it was surprising.'

'From what you've said about him, I expected to come out of there with a couple of black eyes and a broken jaw at least.'

'He wouldn't have the bottle to hit another man,' she said, past experience giving her a clear-sighted view of her husband. 'Especially one who's stronger than he is.'

'There is that. It made it easier, though, him being so friendly.'

'I was amazed.'

'Still, it's nearly eight years since you left,' Sam pointed out. 'He's bound to have got used to being without you by now.'

'True.'

'If I didn't know different, I'd have thought he was a nice bloke.'

'Dave can be very charming when he chooses to be – which is how I came to be married to him.'

'Well, at least we've broken the ice,' said Sam. 'We can get the divorce underway now.'

'Mmm.'

'What's the matter?' he asked. 'You don't seem happy.'

'I don't trust him.'

'A bit too friendly, eh?'

'Definitely.'

'You think he won't be quite so co-operative when it actually comes to the crunch?'

'I'm not sure what I think, I just feel uneasy.'

'You'll have to try to put him out of your mind, love.'

'Yes, I know.' Maddie paused thoughtfully. 'Did you notice that he didn't ask after Clare?'

'I did notice that. He didn't even mention her name.'

'What kind of man isn't interested in his own daughter?'

'Forget him,' said Sam as they drove away through the dark streets with serried rows of houses lit by the electric glow of street lighting.

'We achieved our aim and told him of our intentions. He isn't worth another thought.'

'How can I tell my daughter that her own father didn't even ask after her?'

'She might not ask.'

'She will.'

'I thought she'd got him out of her system after learning the truth about him?'

'She has . . . more or less,' said Maddie. 'But I think she's still harbouring a grain of hope that there might be some good in him . . . that he cares a little for her. He is her father, it's only natural.'

'She has me now and I want to be a real father to her.'

'And you will be.'

'You both have me to care for you now,' Sam reminded her.

'And I thank God for that with all my heart,' said Maddie.

Dave Brown's expression changed the instant he closed the door behind his visitors. His mouth hardened and his eyes filled with malice. 'The cow!' he said out loud, kicking the wall to give vent to the blazing anger he'd managed to suppress while they were there. 'That hard-faced bitch has the nerve to walk in here with her new man and tell me she's filing for divorce. She walks out of my life nearly eight years ago without so much as a word, then strolls back in as though nothing's happened. What sort of a fool does she take me for?'

If she hadn't had her bloke with her she wouldn't have been so bold, he thought. Oh, no. He'd soon have had her begging for forgiveness when he'd let her know what he really thought of a woman who walked out on her own husband.

No sign of remorse for what she'd done to him – left him with no one to keep house for him or satisfy him in bed. Sometimes he'd even had to pay for sex, when it was his wife's duty to provide for him in that direction.

She'd obviously fallen on her feet, judging by the way Sam Fenner was dressed and the fact that he drove a decent car. Well, he'd see about that. He might not be so keen to have her on his arm when Dave had finished with her.

A vicious gleam came into his eyes when he thought of how they'd both been completely duped by him. He'd played the good guy up to the hilt to put them off their guard. He was rather proud of his performance.

He looked at the telephone number. He could tell from the code that it was an outer London number. All these years he'd imagined her in some far-off place, and the rotten bitch had been somewhere in the suburbs all the time.

It might take a while to find out exactly where, but he was in no hurry. He would savour the pleasure of anticipation. Maddie had seriously misjudged him if she thought she could get rid of him that easily. She was going to pay dearly for what she'd done!

Janice and Chas were married at the end of January. Because it was so soon after Josh's death, it was a small wedding with just family and close friends at the register office. But they had quite a large reception in a local riverside hotel afterwards.

Because of the woman Janice was, no one was surprised to see her looking more like a trendy model than a bride. She looked stunning, though, in a scarlet winter suit with a mini-skirt, long white boots and a white fur pill-box hat, the outfit finished off with a bouquet of white roses.

It seemed strange to see Chas's gypsyish looks against the formality of a dark suit with crisp white shirt and plain tie. But he looked terrific with his swarthy complexion and long rock-star hair.

'I thought scarlet was the most appropriate colour for me to get married in as I've been a scarlet woman all these years,' Janice said laughingly to Maddie when they went to freshen up in the powder room during the reception.

'That's all over now,' Maddie reminded her with a chuckle. 'You're a respectable married woman.'

'God, it sounds boring.'

'Sounds good to me,' said Maddie.

Janice was backcombing her long brown hair. 'The trouble with wearing a hat is that it's flattened my beehive.'

'The hat looked good, though,' said Maddie, running a brush through her own blonde hair which fell to her shoulders in a straight bob.

'At least that was white.'

'Would you have liked a white wedding then?'

'Most women want all the trimmings, don't they? But in our case it really wouldn't have felt right – not with Barney almost a teenager.'

Maddie freshened up her lipstick. 'How do you feel now that you've actually taken the plunge?'

'I feel good,' said Janice. 'I was happy with my relationship with Chas before, though, and we've been together for so long, I can't pretend to feel all that much different.'

'Oh,' said Maddie, sounding disappointed.

'I mean, I don't love him any the more just because we've got a piece of paper joining us together,' explained Janice. 'I was nuts about him anyway – always have been. This just sort of tidies things up.'

'True,' said Maddie, powdering her freckled nose in the mirror.

'We're gonna celebrate by having a new wagon.'

Maddie looked at her in the mirror. 'Wow! How exciting!'

'I think so too. We're gonna sell both our wagons and get something bigger,' Janice explained. 'Something really modern. There are some smashing luxury caravans on the market.'

'I can imagine,' said Maddie, adding, 'I suppose you've heard that Hetty and Vic want Sam and me to move into their wagon after we're married?'

'Yeah, I did hear about it and I'm glad. They don't need it now. It would have gone to Josh if he'd lived. It would never go out of the family.'

'I'm really honoured. And all that extra space!' said Maddie. 'I just can't wait.'

Janice met her eyes in the mirror. 'There's another piece of news, too,' she said. 'Chas is going to make an announcement at some point before the end of the reception but you might as well know now.'

'Go on . . .'

'Well, you know that for years we've all wanted him to join the firm?'

'Especially you.'

'Yeah – especially me.'

'And he wanted to keep his independence?' Maddie filled in for her.

'Well, he's finally decided to become a part of the firm. He's gonna hand his Gallopers over as an investment and he'll be a partner.'

'That *is* good news,' said Maddie, delighted. 'I know it's something you've always wanted.'

'I didn't twist his arm either.' Janice smoothed her backcombed hair then gave it added fullness with the tail of her comb. 'It was his decision. I think he got used to being around more and feeling part of the firm after Josh left and Dad retired. I suppose he found he didn't mind a more settled way of life after all. It makes sense for him to be part of the family firm now that he's one of us.'

'I wish my life with Sam would come together properly.'

'But your divorce is going ahead, isn't it?'

'It's in the hands of the solicitors. But it'll take ages to come through and I still can't trust that husband of mine not to have some trick up his sleeve to hold things up even more.'

'Even though he was co-operative when you went to see him?'

Maddie nodded.

'I can understand your not trusting him after the way he treated you,' said Janice. 'But he probably wants to be free every bit as much as you do, after all this time.'

'Maybe you're right,' said Maddie. 'Anyway, let's change the subject. This is your day.'

'We'd better get back to the party or they'll think we've left by the back door.'

Maddie laughed, feeling suddenly uplifted by the thought that Sam and Clare were out there enjoying the party together.

Vera's mother, Gladys Walters, was a shrewd old bird with soft white hair and darting blue eyes. She was especially pleased to have been invited to Janice's wedding because it indicated that the Fenners had accepted Vera as Eric's girlfriend. This meant that Gladys was one step nearer to her ambition of getting Vera settled, something she'd given up hope of until Eric had come on to the scene.

It wasn't that Gladys wanted her daughter off her hands so much as she wanted to know there would be someone to look after her when she herself was no longer around to do it. With the best will in the world she couldn't go on forever and she was in her mid-seventies now.

Bringing Vera up had not been easy, especially as Glady's husband had died when the girl was still quite young. As she'd grown up Vera had become more vulnerable rather than less. With her daughter possessing the body of a woman and the mind of a child, Gladys had had to be on her guard the whole time. At a time of life when she'd have preferred to take things easier, it was a strain having to be constantly watchful.

Eric didn't seem to be any brighter than Vera but he was young – well, youngish – and strong and healthy. Most important of all, he lived in a close-knit family community. If Vera married him, there would always be someone around to look out for her.

Gladys and Sybil had hit it off right away, both sharing similar problems and the same worries for the future of their offspring.

'Can I get you a drink?' offered Eric, appearing at Glady's side with a beaming Vera beside him.

'Yes, please,' she said. 'I'll have a small sherry.'

He went off to the bar and left Vera staring adoringly after him. 'You enjoyin' yourself, Mum?' she asked.

'Not half, dear.'

'I like parties,' said Vera. 'I haven't been to one before.'

'No, I don't believe you have,' said Gladys, reflecting sadly on how much that other people took for granted her daughter had missed. The one small comfort was the fact that people like Vera and Eric were not overly sensitive so didn't get as hurt by their exclusion as much as they might. But Gladys had felt it like a physical pain all Vera's life.

Maddie, who was mingling with the guests, came over for a chat.

'We're having a lovely time,' said Gladys, eyes shining and cheeks brightly suffused with an alcoholic glow. 'We don't usually go to parties.'

'I never want this to end,' confessed Vera dreamily.

Appearing at Maddie's side and catching the drift of the

264

conversation, Sam said, 'You won't have to wait too long for another party, we hope. Maddie and I are getting married soon and you're both invited to the wedding.'

The two women were thrilled to hear this and they all chatted generally until Eric came back with Gladys's drink. When Sybil joined them, Maddie and Sam managed a few minutes alone.

'This wedding of ours can't come quick enough for me,' he said.

'Nor me.'

Clare came over looking flushed and happy. 'The band's arrived,' she announced excitedly. 'And guess what?! It's a young modern group with a guitarist and a drummer and they're gonna be playing some of the latest hits. Barney's been talking to them.'

'That pleased you both, then,' said Maddie.

'I'll say – it's better than having a bunch of old fogeys playing stuff out of the ark.'

'We'll have to see what they're like,' said Maddie. 'And if they're any good we'll keep them in mind for our wedding reception.'

Clare beamed at her mother. 'Now that's one wedding I *really am* looking forward to.'

'So are we,' said Sam.

'Great. Well, I must go . . . Barney wants me,' she said as he beckoned to her from across the room. 'See you later.'

And she was gone, striding across the floor, a willowy girl of nearly thirteen in a bright blue mini-dress.

'My daughter is growing up,' said Maddie, watching her.

'Don't you mean *our* daughter?' Sam gently suggested.

'Yeah, of course I do,' she corrected herself, smiling at him.

Chapter Twenty Three

One morning a week or so after the wedding Vera came to Sybil's caravan looking for Eric. She was very distressed.

'Mum won't wake up,' she told him anxiously. 'I've prodded her and shaken her but nothing will shift her.'

'She's probably having a lie in,' he suggested.

'But she always gets up early,' said Vera. 'She wouldn't stay in bed this late – not unless she was ill.'

They explained the situation to Eric's mother who was outside pegging washing on the line. 'Don't worry, love – I'll come home with you to find out what's making your mum so lazy this morning,' said Sybil, her positive attitude concealing a horrible sense of foreboding. 'She'll probably be up and about by the time we get there.'

She wasn't. Gladys Walters had slipped away in her sleep.

'Dead!' cried Vera, white with shock. The doctor had just left, having confirmed the death, and Sybil, Eric and Vera were in the Walters's living room, a dismal, old-fashioned chamber in a tiny terraced house.

'I'm *so* sorry, love,' said Sybil.

'Me too,' said Eric, slipping his arm around Vera.

'It's not a bad way to go . . . in your sleep,' said Sybil, hoping to console her. 'Without any pain or suffering.'

'My mum can't be dead,' she said, staring vacantly ahead of her.

'I'm afraid she is, dear,' said Sybil kindly.

'But what will I do without her?' said Vera, looking so bewildered and forlorn Sybil could have wept for her.

'You'll be all right.' She managed to sound reassuring despite her own doubts.

'But Mum knows what to do about everything,' said Vera, tears filling her big brown eyes and streaming down her face. 'I can't manage without my mum.'

'You've got me,' said Eric gently, holding her closer.

'And me,' put in Sybil.

'I can't live here without Mum,' she faltered. 'Mum looks after me . . . she pays the rent and runs the house. I won't know what to do if she's not here to tell me.'

Sybil didn't hesitate for more than a moment before uttering her next words. 'When the undertakers have taken your mother to the chapel of rest and we've notified your relatives of what's happened, you can go and pack your things.'

'Why would I do that?'

'Because you're coming to live with Eric and me,' Sybil said, adding, 'if you want to, that is?'

God knows how it'll work out, she thought, but leaving Vera to manage here on her own would be like leaving a child to fend for itself. The only other alternative was Social Services who would probably put her in a loony bin for want of a better solution. Sybil couldn't let that happen. Having two of them under her roof was probably going to drive her round the bend. But she'd have to put up with it because she wasn't prepared to abandon Vera.

'Oh, thank you,' said Vera, and her obvious relief brought tears to Sybil's eyes. She knew she'd done the right thing.

Gladys's funeral was an unremarkable occasion, poorly attended because she had few relatives or friends. All the Fenners were there, though, mainly to give Sybil support; everything from the funeral arrangements to the clearing of the house had fallen on her shoulders. Gladys had made provision for the cost of her funeral but she had had nothing to leave Vera except the contents of the house, most of which were fit only for the rubbish tip.

'I think Sybil is tremendous to take Vera in,' Maddie said to Sam on Saturday morning, the day after the funeral, when they were in the office together. They had been discussing the posters they had just had printed to promote the opening of the fair at Easter, a pile of which were on Maddie's desk. 'It's a big responsibility.'

'Aunt Sybil's used to that kind of responsibility because of Eric,' he pointed out. 'But, yeah, it is good of her to do it.'

'At least Vera will be able to pay for her keep with the money she earns from her cleaning jobs.'

'There is that.'

'So the Fenners have come to the rescue again and taken in another stray?'

'What do you mean?'

'When I didn't have a place to go, you and your family took me in,' she reminded him.

'We offered you a job.'

'And a place to stay.'

'We didn't *give* you anything,' he said. 'You worked hard and quickly became an asset to us.'

'And now I get to marry the boss,' she said. 'Some people might think that makes me a conniving little schemer.'

'Ah, yes. I can see it all now,' he said, teasing her. 'Your hard work

267

and kindness was just a ploy to trap me into marriage. To get you into the Fenner family and business.'

'You must know that's the sort of woman I am,' Maddie riposted.

Sam gave her a tender look. 'The way I feel about you at this moment, I wouldn't care if you were.'

'You say the nicest things.'

They were in an embrace when Clare walked in.

'Oh, no, not snogging again. Shouldn't you be past that sort of thing at your age?' she said affectionately.

'Watch it, lady,' warned Sam. 'Or I might just change my mind about getting you that combined record and cassette player you want for your birthday.'

'Just kidding,' she said with one of her most melting smiles. 'You both look quite young actually.' She paused, looking wicked. 'Considering how ancient you really are.'

'If that's supposed to be a compliment, I should hate to be on the receiving end of one of your insults!'

Maddie was smiling. It warmed her heart to see Clare and Sam getting on so well.

The girl slipped her arm through his and grinned up at him. She was wearing a red coat over blue denim jeans and a black polo-necked sweater, her hair tied back in a pony tail. 'I'm only mucking about – I think you're both great.'

'So long as we get you that player?'

She burst out laughing. 'How could you think such a thing of me?'

'I was thirteen myself once, believe it or not,' Sam said.

'Did you get a wind-up gramophone for your birthday? I don't suppose electricity had been invented then.'

'You'll get nothing for yours if you don't stop being so cheeky.'

'Sorry, I just couldn't resist it,' she said, chuckling and looking from one of them to the other.

Sam looked at Maddie. 'Can't you do anything about your daughter?'

'Not when she's in this mood.'

He shook his head, glancing fondly at them. 'Well, I'll leave you to it.' He picked up one of the posters and rolled it up. 'I'm going over to the pavilion to show this to the manager and have a chat about business. See you later.'

They were both smiling as he closed the door behind him.

'He's great,' said Clare.

'I think so too.'

Turning to her mother, she said, 'Can I meet some of the girls from school in town this afternoon – for a look round the shops?'

'Sure, I've got nothing planned for you.'

'Thanks.' Clare took a poster from the pile and studied the

268

colourful artwork which had FENNER'S FUN PARK superimposed on a picture of a fairground. 'This is great.'

'Yes, it is rather good.'

'I can't wait for the season to start again,' she said. 'I like it when there's plenty of people around the place. There's always the chance to earn some extra dosh too.'

'Crafty.'

They both laughed, the atmosphere full of warmth and friendliness. Maddie was still smiling when she answered the telephone. 'Fenner's Fun Park,' she said.

'Maddie?'

'Yes . . .' Her smile faded, her voice dropped. 'Speaking.'

'This is Dave.'

'Yes, I recognised your voice,' she said in a tense tone. 'Is anything wrong?'

'No, nothing. I'm in Richmond and wondered if there was any chance of seeing you?'

'In Richmond? How did you know I was here?' Her heart was racing.

'I traced the area from the telephone code and made a few enquiries when I got here. Everyone around here has heard of the Fenner family. Anyway, can we have a chat?'

'About the divorce?'

Silence echoed down the line. 'Yeah, that's right,' he said eventually.

'Can't we discuss it on the phone?'

'Not really, I'm in a call box and the money will run out in a minute.'

'If I see you, I'd like Sam to be with me.'

'I'd rather see you on your own.'

'Why?'

'I don't know the bloke, do I?' he said. 'How can I relax in the company of a stranger?'

'I hope you're not gonna start being difficult about the divorce?'

'No, nothing like that,' he said. 'Quite the opposite, in fact. All I want is a chat to clear up a few little queries. It'll be quicker than doing it by post. Writing letters is a pain.'

'Mmm.' Maddie wasn't convinced.

'I want this thing finalised every bit as much as you do, you know.'

'You should have phoned me before coming all this way,' she said. 'We could have got a meeting properly organised.'

'Yeah, I suppose I should have,' Dave admitted, sounding contrite. 'But I came on the spur of the moment and as I'm here now we might as well get on with it. I don't want to have to come all the way back another day.'

'I can see your point.' Surely there could be no harm in seeing

269

him, especially if it would speed up the divorce proceedings? 'All right, you'd better come and see me here.'

'I'd rather meet you somewhere else.'

'Oh?'

'Like I said, I wouldn't feel comfortable with your bloke hanging around.'

Actually that suited her better; Dave's coming here spelled trouble, especially with Clare around.

'Okay,' she agreed. 'When and where?'

'There's a pub across the road from this call box called the Fiddler's Inn. Do you know it?'

'Yes, I know it.'

'Meet me outside there in . . . say . . . half an hour?'

'That soon? But I'm working at the moment.'

'Surely you can take an hour off?'

'I'll be there,' she said reluctantly.

Maddie was very pale and shaky when she replaced the receiver.

'That was Dad, wasn't it?' said Clare.

She nodded.

'You're going to meet him?'

'Yeah.'

'Can I come with you?'

'No, darling.'

'But why not?' persisted Clare. 'He is my father, after all.'

'This isn't the time, love.'

'There'll never be a right time, according to you,' said Clare sharply.

'As I've told you before – when you're old enough to look after yourself you can see your father whenever you like,' said Maddie, smarting at the thought of how little Dave cared for his daughter. 'Anyway, I thought you'd got over that thing you had about him – since you heard the truth about him from someone else?'

'I have, mostly,' said Clare. 'It's just that he's here in the area so there's a chance for me actually to see him in the flesh. I'm curious, that's all. It's only natural.'

'Yes, of course it is,' said Maddie in a more understanding manner. 'But he wants to discuss some aspects of the divorce with me. It just isn't the time for a father-daughter reunion.'

'I suppose not.'

'Look, love,' said Maddie, slipping into a fleecy-lined coat with a hood, 'after the divorce has gone through – if I can trust your father not to upset you – you can start seeing him. If that's what you both really want.'

'Oh . . . right.'

Maddie zipped her coat, wondering how she was going to rouse Dave's non-existent interest in his daughter. 'In the meantime, I'll go and hear what he has to say. I won't be long.'

'Are you gonna tell Sam where you're going?' asked Clare.

Maddie thought about this. If she went over to the pavilion and let him know, he would immediately drop what he was doing and insist on going with her. This would only upset Dave and possibly hinder the divorce proceedings.

'There's no need to bother him with it – he's got enough to do. I won't be gone long.'

'Where are you meeting Dad?' enquired Clare.

'Never you mind,' said Maddie as a precaution; she wouldn't put it past Clare to try and gate-crash the meeting.

'Charming!'

'If you're hungry and don't want to wait until I get back for your lunch, there's a macaroni cheese in the fridge. It only has to be heated up,' said Maddie, ignoring her mild sarcasm. 'There's plenty of fresh bread in the bread bin.'

'Okay,' said Clare co-operatively, but there was an artful gleam in her eye.

Maddie's stomach was churning nervously as she walked along the riverside towards the town. The weather was dry with a sharp breeze, pale wintry sunshine shimmering on the silently flowing waters of the Thames.

Dave was waiting for her outside the Fiddler's Inn, dressed in a sheepskin coat, face freshly shaved, hair combed neatly into place. He suggested that they have their discussion inside the pub as it had just opened.

'I had a hell of a job finding somewhere to park my car,' he said as they settled at a corner table with their drinks.

'It's always bad on a Saturday,' said Maddie, feeling the cool bitter taste of gin and tonic slip down soothingly. 'You found a place in the end, though?'

'Miles from here.'

'A few minutes' walk, you mean.'

'It seemed like miles,' said Dave with a wry grin. 'Near the river somewhere . . . though I don't know if I'll ever find it again. You know me, I'm lost outside of Barking and the East End.'

Maddie nodded, her expression becoming serious. 'So what is it you want to talk to me about?'

'I wanted to tell you that I've told my solicitor that I'll admit to cruelty,' he said. 'So your reputation can remain intact.'

'Oh. That's great!' She paused, looking at him closely. 'But is that all you have to tell me?'

'That's the main thing.'

'You could have told me that on the phone.'

'I know.'

'Dave, you are the limit . . .'

'Don't be mad with me,' he blurted out, looking almost humble. 'There are other things I want to say too.'

'Such as?'

'I wanted to tell you to your face that I'm sorry I gave you such a bad time when we were together,' he said. 'I shouldn't have done those things . . . I realise that now.'

'Do you *really* mean that?'

'I do.'

'Well, Dave, I'm very glad to hear it.'

'You didn't deserve any of what I dished out to you.'

'I always thought it was very unjust,' said Maddie, warming to him. 'I did my best to be a good wife, you know.'

'And you were. No man could have had a better wife than I had and I threw it all away,' he said, full of remorse. 'I don't know what it was with me. Something used to happen inside my head and I'd lose control.' He put up his hands as though in pain. 'I can hardly bear to think about the way I treated you.'

'I can't bear to think about it either.'

He looked hard at her, his eyes bright with tears. 'I'm sorry.'

'It's nice to hear you say it but it was all a long time ago.'

'How could I have been such a brute?' he said, a tremor in his voice.

Maddie reached out and put her hand on his arm to comfort him because she could see how upset he was. 'What you did to me was terrible, I won't deny that, but there's no point in dwelling on it. It's all over and done with. You just make sure you don't do the same thing to anyone else.'

'No chance of that.' He was emphatic. 'Losing you has brought me to my senses.'

'Thank God for that.'

'I wanted us to meet to put everything straight before we go our separate ways . . .'

'We did that eight years ago.'

'Officially.'

'Yes, I understand.'

They lapsed into silence. Maddie sipped her drink, realising that she was beginning to enjoy herself. The last thing she'd expected was to feel comfortable in Dave's company. But hearing him apologise for what he'd done and knowing it would never happen again was the sweetest feeling.

'Do you know,' he said in reminiscent mood, 'when I first saw you across the dance floor the night we met, I thought you were the most beautiful girl I'd ever seen.'

'You were pretty impressive yourself, Dave,' she said, voice tender at the memory of that first meeting.

'We had some fun, didn't we?'

'We did,' she said, casting her mind back to a time when he had seemed like a prince among men – a hero who had rescued her from a miserable home life. The happy times had been brief but wonderful. 'They were good days.'

'Do you remember that time when I took you home on the cross bar of my push bike . . .'

'. . . and we hit a brick in the road and ended up in a heap on the ground?' she finished for him.

'How we laughed!'

'We couldn't stop,' she said, chuckling at the memory. 'You were furious, though, when you saw you'd got bike oil all over your trousers.'

'So I did,' he said, laughing loudly. 'I'd forgotten that.' They chatted some more about old times and had a lot of laughs. Much to Maddie's astonishment she found she was in no hurry to leave, even though she knew she must.

'Well . . . it's been lovely but I have to go now,' she said eventually. 'Clare will be wondering where I've got to.'

'She must be getting quite grown up by now,' remarked Dave, pleasing Maddie even more by mentioning their daughter.

'She certainly is – nearly thirteen and quite the young lady,' said Maddie proudly. 'She's mad on all the latest teenage clothes.'

'Really?'

'Yeah. Her proudest possession is a pair of long boots that Sam and I gave her for Christmas.'

She was about to tell him how keen Clare was to meet him when she decided to wait, hoping he might broach the subject.

'Does she look like you?'

'So people tell me.'

'Maybe I could see her sometime?' he said. 'If she wants to see me.'

'She'd like that.' Dave was going up more in Maddie's estimation by the second. She pulled on her woolly gloves, picked up her handbag and stood up. 'We'll get something organised in due course. But right now I have to go.'

'Yeah,' he said, standing up. 'I must be on my way too.'

Outside the pub he looked around, seeming mystified. 'I'm blowed if I know where I left the car,' he said. 'I told you I didn't have a clue.'

'Didn't you make a mental note of the name of the road?'

'No . . . I was so busy thinking about seeing you, I parked without thinking much about it. Except that it was near the river . . . in a sort of lane.'

'You'll recognise the place once you get to the riverside.'

He looked at her pleadingly. 'You know the area, perhaps you could help me look for it? It shouldn't take long.'

'Okay,' she agreed. 'I'm going down towards the river myself. We'll go together.'

Across the street Clare was watching her parents from the doorway of a boutique, hidden from view by the Saturday shopping crowds. Having followed her mother with the idea of taking a look at Dave Brown, she'd watched them meet and go into the pub. Unable to resist the temptation, she'd waited to catch another glimpse of her father when they came out.

Now as they turned and walked along the main shopping street in the direction of the river, Clare followed. Her mother wouldn't allow her to meet her father but there was nothing to stop her from approaching him herself when he and Maddie had parted company.

Keeping at a safe distance, she darted through the hordes of people, keeping her parents in sight.

'I'm glad we're able to be friends after all that's happened,' remarked Maddie as she and Dave left the shopping crowds and joined the river walkway, almost deserted on this cold winter's day. The sun had gone behind a cloud and the wind had got stronger.

'Me too,' he said.

'It'll make things easier if you want to get to know Clare too.'

'Yeah.'

The riverside was bleak without the sunshine. The dark muddy waters lapping at the bank; moored boats empty and deserted at this time of year; leafless trees etched spikily against the leaden skies. The further they got from the town centre, the fewer people there were about. On a quiet stretch near the meadows beyond which Fenner's was situated, the towpath was deserted except for Maddie and Dave and a woman with some children feeding bread to the gulls and ducks along the river's edge.

'Did you leave your car along there, perhaps?' said Maddie, looking towards a narrow lane where cars were parked.

'No, that wasn't it. I think it was a bit further on.'

As they approached a cafe, closed and shuttered for the winter, Maddie remarked casually, 'You wouldn't recognise this place in summer . . . it's packed with people, especially at weekends.'

'I bet it is.'

'Fenner's is just round the next bend,' she said as the familiar sight of the Scenic Railway came into view in the distance above the skeletal trees. 'I'll have to leave you to it if you don't find your car soon.'

He looked towards the cafe beyond which lay a grassy area. 'I think there's a lane leading up to the main road behind there somewhere.'

'Is there?' said Maddie who knew this stretch of the river quite well. 'I've never noticed it.'

'It doesn't come right down to the towpath,' he explained. 'That's probably why you wouldn't have seen it from here.' He took her hand and guided her towards the cafe. 'Let's have a look.'

Lulled into a feeling of security by his friendly behaviour, she was happy to go with him. Once behind the building and out of sight of any riverside walkers, however, his attitude changed dramatically.

'Dave . . . what's the matter? said Maddie, as he grabbed her arms. 'Your car . . .'

'There is no car, you stupid bitch,' he snarled, holding her in an iron grip and staring at her intently.

'No car?' Her heart beat wildly; she could hardly believe she had been such a fool as to trust him.

'I came on the tube.'

'But you said . . .'

'I wanted to get you on your own, away from prying eyes,' he said. 'That's why I made up the story about the car. I sussed out the area beforehand – I knew you'd walk along here to get home.'

'Was all the rest lies too? Your telling your solicitor you'd co-operate?'

"Course it was,' he said. 'Do you think I'm thick or something?'

'But it was really nice between us back there . . .'

'That wasn't for real, you silly cow,' he said, pushing her against the brick wall of the cafe. She screamed and he hit her across the face. 'It was all an act so that I could lure you to this lonely spot and show you how I *really* feel about a woman who walks out on her husband.' He laughed harshly. 'I always knew you were dim but I didn't think you'd swallow it quite so easily.'

'But you seemed . . .'

'Like a nice sort of a bloke?' he interrupted. 'You thought I'd changed? It was all a performance, Maddie, every single word. I've been planning this for weeks – ever since I found out where you were living. I've been coming to Richmond at weekends to find exactly the right place.'

'I can't believe that even you would be this wicked.'

'The trick was getting you on your own, in a place where we could be private,' he said as though she hadn't spoken. 'If I'd asked you to meet me somewhere like this, you wouldn't have come. So I had to gain your confidence first. And it worked. You came, like a lamb to the slaughter.'

'But you were even talking about seeing Clare.' She winced from his bruising grip on her arms.

'All part of my nice guy act,' he said. 'Not a word of truth in it. I don't wanna see some kid I don't even know.'

'You're sick!'

'You must be pretty sick yourself if you thought I'd let you get away with what you did to me.' He pulled her towards him then slammed her against the wall of the cafe repeatedly until her head was throbbing and she felt faint.

'Please . . .'

'It'll take more than saying "please" to help you now,' he said. 'When you left me, you dug your own grave. I knew my chance would come one day if I waited long enough, and I was right.' He stared into her face, evil written in his. 'It's payback time, Maddie. And this time, I'm gonna make a proper job of it.'

Her head ached and she felt sick. But she was determined not to give up.

'What have you got to gain by this?' she asked, forcing herself to look at him.

'The sweet satisfaction of revenge,' he told her. 'No one makes a fool of me and gets away with it.'

'I'll have you done for assault,' she said, hardly able to breathe for the pain in her head and the pressure of his hands on her arms.

'You won't, they never do,' he said arrogantly. 'They wouldn't dare.'

'*They*?' she uttered. 'You mean, I'm not the only one?'

'Do I look like a monk?' he said. 'Surely you don't think I've been celibate all this time.'

'Well, no, of course not, but I thought it was only me who drove you to violence?'

'A bit of rough stuff is the only way to keep a woman in order.'

'You ought to be behind bars,' spat Maddie.

'And who's gonna put me there, eh?' he said in mocking tones.

'Me.'

'Don't make me laugh,' he said. 'You didn't have the bottle when we were together and you certainly haven't got it now.'

'I wouldn't be too sure of that.' She was racking her brains for a way out of this but he was so strong. Her arms were clamped to the wall, his body rammed against her own. With a shriek of terror she raised her foot and kicked his shin.

He yelled but didn't let go of her.

'You cow!' he growled. 'I'll teach you to kick me . . .'

Holding her by one arm, he brought his fist across her face so that she saw stars; while she was still unsteady, he hit her again and again until she fell to the ground, whereupon he dragged her to her feet so that he could do it again, enjoying her screams of pain and fear.

Clare had to stay well back when her parents reached the more deserted stretch of the river because there was a higher risk of being noticed there. Much to her annoyance she lost sight of them. They

276

seemed to have disappeared altogether. She broke into a run, scanning the path ahead of her, passing a closed and deserted cafe.

When there was no sign of them around the next bend of the river she thought they must have turned off into one of the narrow lanes she'd already passed. She turned and began to run back the way she had come. Having taken this much trouble to meet her father, she didn't want to fail now.

A sound caught her attention as she approached the deserted cafe; she halted her steps, listening. There was a scuffling sound . . . then something like an animal in pain, a kind of groaning then a piercing shriek. But no sign of life. The woman and children she'd seen earlier had now moved on. It was lunchtime. People were indoors.

Then she heard a human cry – a woman's strangled scream, ending abruptly. Strange! It seemed to be coming from the cafe but that was all closed up.

Hurrying past the shuttered hatch through which ice creams and soft drinks were served in the summer, she made her way round to the back – and stood rooted to the spot by the shock of what she saw . . .

He had her mother up against the wall and was aiming blows at her face and body. Clare's mind went blank with panic. Then with sudden inspiration she took a bottle of cheap grown-up perfume from her bag and ran over to her father, who was far too engrossed in the pleasure of inflicting pain to notice her approach. Too angry to be afraid, she pushed herself forward and sprayed the scent in his face. As his hands went up to protect himself, she snatched off her boot and hit him repeatedly with the heel. He staggered back from Maddie who limped painfully away.

'Get away from my mother!' Clare yelled, swinging the boot again as he recovered sufficiently to try to go after Maddie. 'Keep away from her!'

'Why, you little sod!' he said, lunging towards Clare and trying to grab her.

But she swung the boot hard towards him again, hitting him across the body until he finally cowered away.

'And to think I wanted to meet you, you piece of scum!' cried the girl, sobbing now. 'I'm ashamed to be associated with you at all – let alone call you my father.' She stared at him, still swinging the boot, tears running down her cheeks. 'If you come near me, you'll get the heel of this right in your face. And if you touch my mother again, you'll wish you never had!'

Dave moved back, looking bewildered. Then he uttered a string of expletives and hurried off along the towpath.

Mother and daughter fell into each other's arms, hugging each other and weeping.

'How come you're here?' asked Maddie.

Through her tears, Clare explained. 'Now I understand why you were so keen to keep me away from him.'

'I didn't want you to find out this way,' said Maddie through bruised lips, holding a handkerchief to a cut above her eye. 'I wish you hadn't seen him in action.'

'I'm glad I did,' said Clare, still crying. 'At least there are no illusions now that I've actually seen what he's like.'

'It's lucky for me you did follow us,' said Maddie. 'I don't think he'd have stopped until he'd killed me this time.'

Clare's tears abated slightly. 'Oh, Mum, your poor face.'

'I'll live.'

'All these years you've warned me about him and I still didn't want to believe it, even when I heard the truth from a stranger,' said Clare, blowing her nose. 'I thought he couldn't be all bad . . . as he was my father, and your husband.'

'I know how hard it must be for you, love,' said Maddie. 'I made excuses for him for years too. I used to tell myself he was sick and troubled and couldn't help the way he was. I even used to blame myself for upsetting him and making him violent. I never wanted you to think badly of him but I had to protect you.'

'Now I understand.' Clare was looking at her mother's battered face in concern. 'We need to get you to a doctor.'

'More importantly, I need to report this attack to the police while I've still got the evidence,' said Maddie. 'I'm not gonna let Dave get away with it this time. He thinks he's in the clear but I know his address.'

'Yeah, you must report it,' said Clare, her voice thick with emotion. Seeing her mother being beaten had been the most traumatic experience of her life. The strength of her protective feelings had surprised her almost as much as the depth of her hatred for her father. To see her mother so vulnerable had made Clare feel like an adult, strong and in charge.

'I shall hate doing it,' said Maddie. 'But I have to, for the sake of future victims as much as myself. He admitted doing the same thing to other women. If he's punished, it might make him think twice before he sets about a woman again.'

'Let's go home and tell Sam what's happened,' said Clare, feeling in need of his reassuring presence. 'He'll know what to do first.'

'Yes, let's do that,' said Maddie. With Sam beside her she knew she would have the courage to do what she should have done years ago.

Chapter Twenty Four

'It's ten years to the day – almost to the minute – since you and I first met, Janice.' Maddie had stopped by the Hoopla stall to chat to her friend; she was on her way from the office to the Helter-Skelter to see how Clare was coping with the Whitsun crowds who were here in their thousands.

'Is it really?' said Janice, handing some hoops to a punter.

'Yep – on the afternoon of Whit Monday 1960, I came wandering into your life.'

'We got off to a bad start, if I remember rightly?'

'We did. You offered me a free chance to win a goldfish for Clare.'

'And you wouldn't have any of it.'

'No . . . I was much too proud, daft bitch that I was.' Maddie gave a slow shake of her head, thinking back. 'God, I felt dreadful that day. There seemed only one way to go and that was down.'

'And now you're the boss's wife.'

'That's right.'

'A lot of things have changed at Fenner's in the last ten years.'

'I'll say.' Maddie decided to make a joke of it to avoid reminding Janice of the tragedy and drama that had occurred here over the years. 'For one thing, Clare wouldn't nag me for a goldfish these days so much as the latest pop record or something new to wear.'

She left Janice chuckling and went on her way in reflective mood. So far as the actual fair was concerned, everything was much the same as it had been when Maddie had first set eyes on it. Apart from the pavilion and a few new rides, nothing much had changed except, perhaps, the fashion of the punters' clothes, though mini-skirts were still as popular as ever.

Every year the Carousel keeps turning, no matter what, she thought. The crowds always come, pop music still blares out over the Tannoy and the family all work on the fair, including Hetty and Vic who come over to give a hand as always on a Bank Holiday.

Passing the Carousel, she stopped for a few words with Barney who was working with his father while on holiday from school. No one had been surprised when he'd expressed a wish to come into the business full-time when he left school at the end of the summer term.

'Wotcher, Maddie,' came Chas's cheerful voice from the paybox. 'Hi.'

'If you're looking for something to do you can give me a hand here,' he said, grinning and glancing at the queue.

'I'm on my way home for a tea-break but I'm going to see if Clare is coping on the Helter-Skelter first.'

'She will be,' said Chas. 'She's a natural.' He looked towards Barney. 'Like this one. You can have your tea with an easy mind.'

Maddie moved on feeling sentimental on this the tenth anniversary of her arrival. It was so good to feel she belonged at last. What a state she'd been in when she'd arrived here – desperate, battered and broke. Who would have thought then that she would become a part of all this? Who would have thought, too, that she would have the courage to bring charges against her husband after suffering in silence throughout her marriage?

Being responsible for someone she had once loved receiving a six month prison sentence had been a traumatic experience for Maddie. But her strength of character and Sam's unwavering support had carried her through.

Even though Dave was out of prison now she no longer feared him. He was legally barred from approaching either herself or Clare, and she doubted if he would break the law and risk another prison sentence. He'd been getting away with violence for so long he'd thought it would last for ever. Now he knew different! He must have had the shock of his life when Maddie had kept her word and taken him to court.

Two of his other victims had also found the courage to appear in court to corroborate Maddie's evidence of his violence after reading about his arrest in the Barking local paper. Maddie felt guilty for not reporting him before and possibly sparing those other women their ordeal. Still, justice had finally been done.

For a while after that last brutal attack two years ago, she had seemed to be surrounded on all sides by the legal system, with the assault charge and divorce proceedings both going ahead. But that was all behind them now. The proven attack on her had added credence to her claim of long-term violence within the marriage and helped the divorce to go through smoothly, so Maddie and Sam were able to get married at last.

'Hi, Mum,' said Clare now.

'Everything all right, love?'

'Fine. Vera and Eric are taking over from me so I can take a break in a minute.' She paused. 'Here they are now.'

'Come on then, let's go home and take a breather together.' Maddie looked at Eric and Vera. 'Will you two be all right here for half an hour?'

They nodded, happy to be able to work together on the fair, though

Vera still did a cleaning stint in the pavilion in the mornings, because she enjoyed doing so. They had also married recently and had moved into Maddie's old wagon. This was the perfect solution because there they had their privacy and a degree of independence but plenty of people on hand to look out for them. Sybil had them out from under her feet but near enough to keep a careful eye on them. That was the wonderful thing about living in a community like Fenner's. You were never really alone.

Maddie and Clare walked across the crowded fairground towards the large family living-wagon that had once been the home of Vic and Hetty, and where they now lived with Sam.

Passing the Scenic Railway, Maddie had a sudden mental image of Josh – so stunningly handsome and sexy. He would never be forgotten around here, though Tania was rarely mentioned. In fact, Josh had become something of a legend. Despite all the bad things he'd done, he had died a hero and that was what people remembered. Maddie certainly had a lot to thank him for, she thought, turning to her daughter and squeezing her arm.

'What was that for?' asked Clare.

'No particular reason,' said Maddie. 'Just glad to have you around.'

'Oh.' Clare grinned saucily. 'If you're in such a good mood, perhaps this is the right moment to talk about the salary I'll be getting when I start work in the office?' She had not been interested in working anywhere but Fenner's when she left school at the end of term so Maddie and Sam had suggested she get a thorough grounding in the business by starting as an office junior.

'We need to have a discussion with Sam about that,' said Maddie.

'We're in luck then,' said Clare, looking ahead to where Sam was striding towards them through the crowds. ''Cause here he is.'

'Ah, caught you skiving off, have I?' he said, jokingly.

'You have . . . we're going for a well-earned tea-break,' said Maddie. 'Fancy joining us for a cuppa tea and a bun?' She paused, smiling at him then looking at Clare. 'Though I warn you, this one wants to talk about her starting salary with the firm.'

'Oh, does she?' he said, looking at Clare with mock severity. 'I'm not so sure about that.'

'Come on, Dad,' she said. 'You can spare ten minutes to talk about my future prospects.'

'Oh, so I'm Dad when you want something, am I?' he said, laughing because she sometimes still called him Uncle Sam.

'You'll always be my dad inside here,' she said, pointing to her heart and looking serious suddenly. 'Even if I sometimes forget and the wrong words come out.'

'Just teasing,' he said lightly, but tears welled beneath his lids because being accepted as her father meant so much to him.

His eyes met Maddie's over the top of Clare's head and they both smiled. He took her hand and they followed their daughter up the steps into their home.